Beyond The Smiles

Minnie Lewis

ISBN: 979 8 88345 612 0

To four special people; one in Durham, one in Lincoln, one in Brooklyn and one in the room next door.

Also a big thank you to my brother Neil who inspired me to self-publish.

Part One

Laura's Story - An Unexpected Call

Chapter 1

Monday 17th August

Laura half opened her eyes and slowly peered at the clock on her bedside cabinet. It was just five forty-five am. She gradually stirred, bit by bit becoming conscious of the hum and aroma of Southwest London as it seeped through the open window.

She lay quietly for the next few minutes trying desperately to savour the remaining time before she'd have to rouse herself and get ready for her journey into the city.

As the bright rays of light pierced the small chinks in the curtains, Laura became mindful that Kieran was still beside her. His rhythmic breathing gave Laura a sense of comfort and seemed totally in tune with the other gratifying sounds and smells of that warm summer morning.

She raised herself up and leaned over her partner.

"You need to get up," she whispered gently, her lips just inches away from his. "You'll miss your flight."

Kieran slowly opened his eyes just as Laura's mouth tenderly met with his.

"Morning," he remarked, the smile on his face clearly indicating his appreciation.
They kissed again, this time for much longer and with greater passion.
"We have to get up," Laura announced as she eventually prised herself away from Kieran's arms. "If you don't shake yourself, you'll miss your flight."
"Shit!" he exclaimed as he saw the time. "The bloody taxi will be here in twenty minutes."
Laura sat upright in bed as she watched her boyfriend hurriedly make a dash for the small bathroom at the end of the corridor. Then, after a few seconds, and in complete contrast to Kieran, she leisurely put on her dressing gown and made her way downstairs.
To her astonishment, within the space of fifteen minutes, Kieran had managed to shower, shave, gel his hair, get dressed and join Laura in the kitchen.
"I've made you a coffee and there's a couple of croissants there, if you've time," Laura remarked, pointing to the table.
"Fabulous," replied Kieran, who gave Laura another loving lingering kiss.
"Are you going to call your folks?" he asked as he released her and grabbed the coffee mug.
"It might be better if I told them in person," replied Laura. "Let's do it together this weekend when you're back from Germany."
Kieran, looking a little perplexed, shrugged his shoulders. "But they'll still be in Spain," he said, his brow furrowed.
Laura shook her head. "No, they're flying in this Friday. So they'll be here when you get home."
Before Kieran could reply, he spied the taxi pulling up outside. "It's here," he remarked as he took a last gulp of

coffee and rushed into the hallway where his luggage bag was waiting.
"Have you got your passport?" enquired Laura.
"Yep," replied Kieran, who tapped his jacket to indicate it was in his pocket.
He pulled open the front door, but only a few inches.
"You're not going to change your mind, are you?" he asked as their two bodies became entwined again.
"No," replied Laura, "I won't change my mind, but Mum and Dad need to be told properly. I want to do it face to face."
Kieran kissed her once more. "Okay," he whispered, "but we tell them this weekend."
"Yes," Laura replied, "we will. Now please just bugger off and get your flight to Germany and leave me to get ready. I've got an early start, too, today."
With that, Laura kissed him once more before bundling him and his luggage out of the door.
As soon as Kieran's taxi was safely out of sight, Laura closed the front door, took a deep breath, and headed off to get ready for work.

Chapter 2

Laura had thought long and hard before she chose the house in Lavenham Road SW18. Although the list of attributes she'd been looking for in a property was reasonably short, she'd been ruthless in weeding out properties that didn't meet all her requirements.
Her number one necessity was the ability to get from her front door to her office, in Victoria, in no more than forty minutes and close behind this was the desire to avoid having to change tubes more than once during the journey.
For most women of her age, trying to find a property so close to their work in that part of London (without any savings to speak of) would have been a serious problem. Fortunately for Laura she had parents who were willing and able to pay £200,000 towards a deposit, which meant she was just about able to buy the pretty, well-appointed house, albeit her mortgage payments took a hefty proportion of her monthly pay.
Laura's forward planning gave her the luxury of being able to shut her front door and leave for work at seven twenty, knowing she would arrive in plenty of time to manage the meeting she'd arranged with the creative design and marketing team at eight thirty.

As she strode confidently down Lavenham Road and then right, into Elsenham Street, Laura was in a cheery mood, her thoughts predominantly on the meeting that morning, but also, occasionally, her mind drifting away to Kieran Hockley, the suave business executive who had captured her heart. However, by the time she'd arrived at Southfields Station and boarded the district line train, Laura had removed Kieran from her head and refocused herself completely on the morning's meeting. Laura took her work at Meridian Marketing seriously and would never allow herself to attend a meeting unless she was totally prepared.

*   *   *

"So that's settled," announced Laura confidently to the group of colleagues she'd assembled for her meeting. "We go with Jason's concept, but we need to make the strap line stronger, and we need to beef up the briefing document."
The six people gathered around the circular table all nodded.
"So when can we review this again?" Laura asked.
"I see no reason why we couldn't have something back for you by tomorrow lunchtime," replied Jason.
"I was thinking today," responded Laura. "I need to present this to the client on Thursday and I'd really like to get Vic's approval first. How about we get back together again this afternoon, say four thirty."
It was clear by the team's expressions they thought this was a tall order, but nobody seemed confident enough to challenge Laura. Her strong personality, the fact that she was, without question, the most successful Key Account Manager at Meridian, combined with her obviously

being Vic Chakraborty's current blue-eyed girl, meant dissention tended to be rare during Laura's meetings. One by one the team filed out of the room until Laura was left alone with Saskia Skinner, who had remained in her seat.

"So?" enquired Saskia.

"So what?" replied Laura pretending she had no idea what her colleague was talking about.

Saskia stood up, walked quickly to the door and shut it. "Did you hear back from McCauley and Bernsteins?"

Laura smiled. "Yep," she replied with a glint in her eyes. "They've offered me the job."

"Congratulations," replied Saskia, grabbing her friend's shoulders. "When are you going to tell Vic?"

"Hold on," said Laura, who was unable to hide her clear delight at being offered the position. "I've not said yes, yet. I need to think about it and maybe talk with Mum and Dad, too."

"And Kieran, of course," added Saskia. "But they'll all say go for it, surely?"

"Well Kieran already has," replied Laura, "but, of course, he's been keen for me to get over to the US for months now that his promotion and relocation have been approved. I'm ninety-nine per cent certain I'll take it, but I asked them to give me until the end of the week to give them an answer."

Saskia was beaming from ear to ear. "Vic and the team won't like it when they hear," she said.

"I've no doubt the team won't be too sad to see me go," countered Laura, "but I'm not looking forward to telling Vic. He's been great to me, and this does feel like I'm stabbing him in the back."

"Nonsense," said Saskia. "He'll certainly not want to lose you, but he'd not hold you back. This is a fantastic opportunity for you."

Laura looked back into her friend's eyes. "And for you, too," she remarked. "If I go, I reckon you'll get my accounts. So it may be good for both of us."
Saskia shrugged her shoulders. "Well maybe," she replied. "I'd love your job, don't get me wrong, but I'm not a shoo-in that's for sure."
"Of course you would be," insisted Laura. "You'd get it for sure. Vic really rates you; he's told me."
Before Saskia had an opportunity to answer, there was a loud knock on the door and Jason entered the room.
"Sorry to interrupt you both," he said almost apologetically. "There's a call come through for you, Laura. It's some guy called Father Mallory, he's insistent he talks with you. He says it's very important."
Laura's puzzled expression indicated that she'd no idea who Father Mallory was.
"Okay," she said. "Put him through in here."
Jason nodded and left the room.
"I'll leave you to it," added Saskia who quickly made for the door. "Are you going out at lunchtime?"
"Not sure," replied Laura as the phone started to ring. "I've loads to do. I might just grab a sandwich and eat it at my desk."
"Okay," replied Saskia as she reached the door.
Laura moved over to the phone, but before she picked it up, she shouted over to her friend who was just about to leave the room. "Remember keep this all to yourself, Saskia. I don't want anyone to know until I've thought it through and spoken with Vic."
As she exited the room Saskia smiled back and using her thumb and forefinger, made the mime of a zip being fastened across her mouth.
Laura picked up the phone at the same time as Saskia shut the door behind her.

"Laura Eastwood speaking," she said in a clear but businesslike fashion.
"Oh hello, my name's Father Mallory," came a nervous voice with a slight Irish accent. "We haven't spoken before, but I am calling with some bad news, I'm afraid."
"Yes," replied Laura, who was trying hard to work out in her head who this man was and what bad news he might be about to deliver.
"It's your father," he continued. "I'm so very sorry to tell you that he's passed away."
"What?" exclaimed Laura, who immediately on hearing the news had sat down on one of the many empty chairs. "He can't be. What about Mum, where's she?"
After a moment's silence Father Mallory replied and this time with even more nervousness in his voice. "With your father no longer being married," he said, "you're his next of kin and ..."
"You're talking about Billy McKenna aren't you," Laura interrupted as she realised what the clergyman was telling her.
"Yes," replied Father Mallory. "He passed away on Wednesday last week, but I'm afraid I only managed to track you down last evening and then I was only given details of where you work. I'm so sorry ..."
"It's fine," replied Laura with little emotion in her voice. "I'm of course very sorry to hear he's died but, to be honest with you Father, we were strangers to each other. In fact, I only ever saw him once in the last twenty-five years, so while I appreciate you telling me, I'm sure his death will be more significant to whoever he's been close to since he left my mother and I."
"I understand," replied Father Mallory. "I just wanted to just let you know and to also tell you that his funeral

service is planned for this Thursday, here at St Steven's church in Blythwold."
"Where's that?" enquired Laura.
"In Suffolk," replied Father Mallory. "It's scheduled for eleven. Will you be attending?"
Laura thought carefully. "As I said," she replied as firmly as she could, "I didn't have any dealings with him and, being very blunt with you, I didn't even consider him to be my dad."
"I see," replied Father Mallory with genuine understanding. "If you change your mind, please don't be afraid to come along. And do feel free to call me if I can help you at all. I know you weren't close, but you may find some solace in attending his funeral. It may give you some closure. Shall I give you my telephone number?"
"No, that won't be necessary," replied Laura resolutely. "Thank you for letting me know, but I won't be going to his funeral."
Laura replaced the receiver and sat silently, alone in the meeting room.

Chapter 3

"So Mike's not your real dad?" Saskia remarked, as she and Laura made themselves comfortable at a free table in Borini's, the small Italian Coffee House just off Vauxhall Bridge Road, which was a favourite place for them to have their lunch.
"No ... well not biologically," replied Laura. "But in every other respect he is. He's Mum's second husband and has been since I was about five or six; he's been the best father in the world, unlike my biological father."
"So what happened?" enquired Saskia, who didn't attempt to conceal her curiosity. "And why on earth did you not tell me before?"
Laura shrugged her shoulders. "I wish I'd never told you at all," she remarked with exasperation. "As far as I am concerned Mike Eastwood is my dad," she continued firmly. "He has been there for me for the last twenty-odd years. I
may have the misfortune to share Billy McKenna's DNA, but he's never been a part of my life and although he's now died, that changes nothing. Now, what are you going to order?"
Saskia could see that her friend was getting annoyed and was clearly not keen to talk about Billy McKenna, but that wasn't going to stop her questioning.

"I'll have my usual tuna mayo baguette and a large skinny latte," she replied without bothering to look at the menu. "So how come you've never mentioned this before?" Saskia asked for the second time. "We've been besties for six years."

"Because, my nosy friend," retorted Laura firmly, "it's not something I think about. I'm not a McKenna, I'm an Eastwood."

On that note Laura got up and walked over to the counter to place her order.

Saskia waited until her friend had returned with their food and drinks and had placed the small tray onto the table before she continued her interrogation.

"So how did he die?" she asked.

It suddenly occurred to Laura that she'd not thought to ask Father Mallory about the circumstances of his death. For the first time she felt a slight pang of guilt. "I don't know," she replied rather uncomfortably. "See, that just goes to prove how little that man means to me. Now, can we please talk about something else?"

"Okay, if you say so," said Saskia as she bit deep into the tuna mayo baguette.

Laura felt relieved that at long last Saskia appeared to have got the message.

"How was your weekend?" she asked, although she was not in the slightest bit interested. "How did your date go with the latest guy from the dating agency?"

Saskia's eyes widened. "Pretty damn well actually," she replied. "He didn't go home until this morning."

"What!" exclaimed Laura, her eyes bulging out of their sockets and her mouth open, aghast at this revelation. "But your date was on Friday evening. You hussy!"

Without a hint of shame, Saskia shrugged her shoulders and smiled brazenly.

"I'm twenty-seven next month," she reminded her friend. "I'm not yet at the point of desperation but I'm bloody close, and when I find a good man, I'll be buggered if he's going to get away. Not before he knows what he's missing."
Laura smiled broadly but shook her head in dismay. "You're terrible," she said, her astonishment etched across her furrowed, disapproving brow.

* * *

Laura's four thirty meeting lasted for three hours. As usual, she was meticulous in her attention to detail and although she was largely pleased with the campaign her team had created, she was not going to let any of them out of the room until she was one hundred percent happy with every facet and was ready to show her boss. She'd never had one of her campaigns rejected by Vic and even though she was almost certainly going to leave Meridian, she was not about to damage that statistic.
"I think we're there," she said as soon as Saskia had made the final tweaks to the costings. "I'll show it to Vic in the morning and unless he blows us out of the water, we should be good to present to Radcliffe's on Thursday."
The team started to clamber up out of their chairs and with their laptops and tablets in hand, the six worn out junior execs made their way towards the exit.
"Are you planning to present this alone on Thursday?" Saskia asked.
"Yes," replied Laura without any hesitation. "I think I'm up to the challenge."
Saskia smiled back. "I'm sure you are," she remarked. "I just thought it may be a good opportunity for one of us to get some experience at the sharp end."

Laura considered her suggestion for a few seconds. "I'll ask Vic what he thinks, but I think it may be better if I do this solo," she replied. "Radcliffe's are a quirky bunch; they may feel uncomfortable if we come mob handed."
"I hardly think one or two of us joining you would be mob handed," continued Saskia. "Having been intimately involved in this one I thought maybe it would be good for Jason and me to join you."
Laura could see Saskia already starting to position herself to take over, which she understood, but she wasn't about to let her get her way too easily.
"Like I said," she added firmly, "I'll speak with Vic about it."

*   *   *

The tube journey home that evening took longer than usual. Earlier in the day, some inconsiderate soul had decided to throw himself under a train at Earl's Court, creating massive delays on the District line, which resulted in it taking Laura nearly an hour and a half to get home.
As she walked slowly up Lavenham Road, she again started to think about the call she'd received earlier from Father Mallory.
In truth, she didn't know how she felt. She had rarely thought about her biological father, and when she had, it had been with indifference. But now she had been told of his death, she felt ill at ease. There was no grief, no sense of loss, just a slight emptiness. She did feel some guilt, but only because she wasn't particularly sad or miserable, emotions she assumed she should be experiencing given the news.

As soon as she had reached her house and had closed the door behind her, Laura kicked off her shoes, turned on her favourite band on the expensive sound system and poured herself a large glass of cold white Chardonnay. She was considering who she should call first, her mother or Kieran, when her mobile rang, and the decision was made for her.
"Hi, Mum," she said as cheerily as she could. "How are you both?"
"We're just fine, dear," replied her mother. "Your dad's just cooked one of his fabulous barbeques and we're laying back next to the pool taking in the sun."
"Sounds wonderful, Mum," replied Laura. "Are you still okay to fly back on Friday?"
"Yes, we get into Stansted airport at about four. So we'll be with you at about six thirty," she said with excitement. "It seems like ages since we last saw you."
Laura felt a little unsure how she was going to break the news to her mother, but the short pause that suddenly opened up in their conversation seemed the right time.
"I got a call from a priest in Suffolk today," she said trying hard to relay the news without any obvious sentiment.
"What did he want?" her mother replied, the tone of her voice suggesting she sensed bad news.
"He told me that Billy McKenna died last week," continued Laura, deliberately avoiding using the word dad, as she was keen not to give her mum the impression the news had any significance.
"How did he die?" her mum asked.
"I didn't ask," replied Laura. "All I know is that he died last Wednesday in a place called Blythwold in Suffolk and his funeral is on Thursday."
Laura fully expected her mother to make a disparaging remark, as she had done on almost every occasion Billy

McKenna had been mentioned in the last twenty-five years; not that his name came up that often. However, the line remained silent.
"Are you okay, Mum?" Laura asked.
"Yes," replied her mother, though her tone suggested otherwise. "Although he's been out of our lives for years and I will never forgive him for abandoning us, I am sad to hear he's dead. He would have only been fifty-two."
"Well," interjected Laura, trying hard to sound as matter of fact as she could, "I just thought I'd let you know. As you say, it's sad, but he was never a part of our lives. He's never been my dad, so I'm sorry, too, but it doesn't mean anything to me."
"Will you go to his funeral?" her mother asked.
"No," replied Laura emphatically and without hesitation. "And that's what I told Father Mallory."
"Well it's your choice, darling," remarked her mother. "If you feel you want to go that's fine with me and your dad. We'd understand."
"No, I've already decided I'm not going," confirmed Laura. "Anyway I've no idea where the hell Blythwold is?"
"It's between Lowestoft and Ipswich," her mother replied. "It's where Billy and I met and where he grew up. I didn't know that's where he settled. God I've not been back there in years."
"Anyway, it makes no difference," Laura remarked. "I've no intention of going to his funeral."
After a slight, awkward pause, Laura decided to shift the conversation on. "Anyway, how's Dad?" she asked. "How's his new fitness regime going?"
Her mother laughed. "In fairness to him he has lost some weight, but his daily visits to the gym have become more like weekly trips. And to be honest," she continued in a mischievous whisper, "he's hardly there long

enough to do himself any good. I'm convinced he only goes to check out the young women in their tight leotards."
Laura laughed. "Yeah, sounds like Dad!"
"Look I'm going to have to go, darling," her mother announced. "We're going to a drinks party in Alicante this evening, so I need to get ready."
"Okay Mum," replied Laura. "I'll see you on Friday."
"Love you," her mother said before she abruptly ended the call.
"Love you, too," replied Laura, although she knew full well her mother had gone.
She took a large sip of her Chardonnay, checked the time and decided to run a bath. She figured she'd call Kieran while she was enjoying a long, relaxing, bubbly soak.

* * *

Having laid in her bath for over half an hour and having drained her glass of Chardonnay dry, Laura leant over the side and pressed the quick dial number on her mobile. As soon as she heard the ring tone, she put the phone on speaker and placed it on the bathroom cabinet next to her bath.
"Hi, Laura," said Kieran. "What sort of a day have you had?"
Laura lay back down into the bubbles, smiled and sighed. Although they'd been a couple for almost a year, she'd never mentioned the fact that Mike Eastwood wasn't her biological father, and wasn't about to explain this to him over the phone. She decided she'd tell him when he got back.

"The usual," she replied. "We've got our pitch sorted for Radcliffe's on Thursday. I just need to bounce it off Vic tomorrow."
"Great," replied Kieran. "He'll be a breeze. He thinks you're Wonder Woman."
Although Kieran had met Vic on several occasions, he'd only seen the agency's
Managing Director at company socials when he'd been pleasant and ultra-friendly. Laura had seen him when he was in one of his pedantic moods and when Vic was unhappy he rarely held back.
"I hope you're right," she replied. "Anyway how was your flight and how did it go today?"
Kieran laughed. "The flight went fine. I had to wait for ages at Munich Airport for my bag, but other than that, it was fine."
"And your pitch," continued Laura. "Did they like your ideas?"
"Of course they did," replied Kieran in a tone that suggested to even ask was an insult. "They love the site, they've a few tiny tweaks, but it went great. If the other pitches go as well, my bonus for this year is in the bag."
"Fantastic," remarked Laura. "That's brilliant news."
"Look, I'm going to have to go," Kieran announced. "I'm meeting them for dinner in ten minutes, so I'll have to rush. I'll message you later and call you tomorrow night when I get to Stuttgart."
"Okay," replied Laura, who was disappointed her boyfriend couldn't spend more time talking but wasn't about to let him know. "I'll wait with eager anticipation."
"Love you," said Kieran.
"Love you, too," replied Laura, just a second before the phone line went dead.

Chapter 4

Tuesday 18th August

Laura was at her desk early. As she often did, she'd picked up a skinny latte and two chocolate croissants from Borini's on her way to work and was slowly working her way through her breakfast when the rest of Meridian's small staff began arriving.
"How come you stay so painfully thin?" enquired Saskia, as she plonked herself down at the desk next to Laura. "You can eat for England. I just have to think about food and my arse gets bigger or my belly swells up."
Laura looked up from her desk. "Morning, Saskia," she remarked. "How was your evening?"
"Promising," Saskia replied, in a manner which suggested to Laura that it would have inevitably involved a man.
Laura had known Saskia long enough to understand that whatever tactic she adopted, she wouldn't be able to get any peace until she allowed her old friend to unburden herself of the goings-on from the night before. She pushed her laptop to one side, sat up straight and looked Saskia directly in the eye.

"Anything you'd like to share?" she asked, in order to give Saskia the green light to recount the previous night's activities.
"Well," replied Saskia, pulling her chair nearer to Laura's and at the same time helping herself to a largish piece of Laura's chocolate croissant, which she started to munch as if she'd not seen food for some time. "His name is Martin. He's in banking and he's gorgeous. He's stinking rich, too."
Laura looked perplexed. "Is he the same guy you were with over the weekend?" she asked, although she was pretty certain what the answer was going to be.
"God no!" exclaimed Saskia. "He was Adam. With any luck he's still on the boil, but Martin's a new one."
"So how did you meet Martin?" Laura asked, desperately hoping she could get Saskia to relieve herself of all the details as quickly as possible.
"That's the weird thing," replied Saskia. "He was at the gym. We just started talking and well, one thing led to another."
Laura's brow started to wrinkle up. "Gym!" she exclaimed louder than she wanted. "When did you start going to the gym?"
Saskia grinned broadly. "It's a well-known fact that the easiest ways to find men are when you're walking your dog or at the gym. There's no way I'm getting a dog, so I thought I'd join a gym."
"And when did you join?" Laura enquired.
"Yesterday evening," replied Saskia, as if the question was the most ridiculous one she'd ever heard.
"So, when you say one thing led to another," Laura added tentatively.
"Nothing earth shattering," replied Saskia, a little disappointedly. "We just went for a drink afterwards at a bar Martin knew close to Sloane Square. But we've

arranged to meet again on Friday evening. He knows someone at the box office at the Theatre Royal, Haymarket. We're having dinner then going to a show."
"What show is that?" Laura asked.
Saskia looked back blankly and shrugged her shoulders. "He did say, but I can't remember," she replied. "Some musical, I think. It'll probably be crap like most of the shows in the West End, but I'm not going for cultural nourishment."
Laura grinned and shook her head. "You're unbelievable Saskia," she declared. "I don't know how you manage to find all these blokes. And how you manage to juggle them all at once is amazing."
Saskia was about to elaborate when the phone on Laura's desk started to ring.
"That's Vic," Laura said when she saw the extension number come up on the small screen. "I'll have to take it."
As Laura turned away from her friend to pick up the receiver, Saskia grabbed the last piece of Laura's remaining chocolate croissant, and guiltlessly started to bite it away in large chunks.
"Morning Vic," said Laura confidently. "When can you see me?"
After a brief pause, while she listened to his reply, Laura said, "That's fine I'll see you then."
Laura replaced the receiver and turned back to face her friend. "Did you enjoy my breakfast?" she enquired irately. "You do realise you'll now need to spend at least thirty minutes on the cross trainer this evening, working those calories off your bum!"

*   *   *

Vic Chakraborty was of Bangladeshi descent. His father had arrived in England with almost nothing, back in the eighties, but through hard graft had become a successful businessman. With the wealth that had come, hand-in-hand with success, he'd been able to pay for his children to go to private schools and obtain the sort of education he'd never had. Vic was the eldest son, dashingly handsome and sharp as a razor. Despite being still in his thirties, he'd already achieved much as a marketing consultant, and was building a strong reputation as a leading light in his field.

When she first arrived at Meridian, Laura was in awe of her boss, but now three years down the line Laura no longer saw him as her mentor. The respect was still there but tinged at times with frustration. Laura wasn't a rookie account manager anymore and although she always listened to Vic's advice, she didn't always follow everything he said, confident enough to follow her own instincts.

As always Laura felt completely prepared when she ran through her pitch to Vic. **"If you fail to prepare, prepare to fail!"** the mantra her lecturer had recounted time and time again back at Durham University, had become ingrained in her head. So much so that in the time she'd been at Meridian, she'd never once allowed herself to present to colleagues or clients without being completely convinced she was ready to field any difficult questions or overcome any potential objections. Today was no exception.

As was his way, Vic constantly interrupted Laura's presentation with questions and continuous requests for clarification, but this did not faze Laura. She had presented to her boss so often that she could almost predict when he'd interrupt. So much so that had he not

intervened as Laura had anticipated she'd have been disappointed.
By the time Laura had finished running through her presentation she was certain that any concerns Vic could have had would have already been covered,
but to ensure she did not give the impression of over confidence, she asked the questions she always asked at the conclusion of her pitches.
"Is there anything I haven't explained adequately?" she enquired with a confident smile. And then, when her boss had gently shaken his head to signify he was happy, she added her customary closing remark. "Then are you okay with me moving this forward with the client?"
To Laura's surprise, her boss remained silent.
"Is there anything wrong?" she asked as she started to sense her boss was about to make a negative remark.
"With the presentation, no!" Vic replied. "As usual Laura, you've done a great job."
"It was a team effort," remarked Laura. "For sure I'm the leader and the spokesperson, but, as always, it's been a team effort."
Vic nodded. "Talking of your team," he remarked, "I think it's time to develop some of the team members. Why don't we get one of them to make the pitch on Thursday?"
Laura's smile disappeared and her forehead wrinkled. "I'm not sure this is the right presentation to give someone else," she replied. "Radcliffe's are one of our biggest accounts. Don't you think it would make sense to try them out on one of the smaller clients?"
Vic opened his arms out wide and offered Laura a broad smile. "I don't want you to take this the wrong way, Laura," he remarked reassuringly. "You're clearly our number one account manager. I just want to give some

of the others a bit more experience. I'd still want you there in case things start to go pear shaped, but I do want to give someone else a chance to show what they are made of."

Laura could see Vic had already made up his mind. She knew full well that once he'd made a decision, it was almost unheard of for him to back-track.

"If that's what you want," she remarked with a forced smile. "So who do you want to lead on Thursday?"

Vic ran his hand over the short black stubble on his chin as if to suggest he was only now considering who that should be.

"What about Saskia?" he asked. "You went to college with her, didn't you. Do you think she's ready?"

Laura couldn't help thinking that there was more than an even chance her friend and her boss had already had some sort of discussion about this. Inside she was seething; however, the last thing she wanted was for her annoyance to show.

"If you're saying you want to try someone else then I'd agree, it has to be Saskia," Laura replied.

"Then we're agreed," remarked Vic, who rose from his chair and made his way to the door.

"Actually, Vic," announced Laura, just before her boss had managed to cross the threshold, "I wasn't going to ask, but as Saskia is going to lead on Thursday, would it be possible for you to go with her rather than me?"

Vic spun around to face Laura, his expression giving no doubt to his reaction to Laura's question. "Absolutely not," he remarked. "Just because I've decided to ask Saskia to present, it doesn't mean you're off the account. I want you to spend the next few days coaching Saskia and I want you there on Thursday to support your colleague."

Laura looked directly back at her boss. "I don't want you to take it the wrong way, Vic," she said as reassuringly as she could. "I learned yesterday that a close family member passed away, and that his funeral's on Thursday. Because of the importance of the pitch with Radcliffe's I wasn't going to attend the funeral, but to be honest I do feel I should be there. And if Saskia is to take the lead, I'd appreciate you allowing me the day off to pay my respects."
At first Vic wasn't sure what to think.
"In that case, Laura," he said slowly, "of course you must be there. Family is important. I'll sit in with Saskia, but I want you to work with her to make sure she's totally prepared."
Laura nodded. "Absolutely," she replied. "She'll be word perfect by the time I'm finished with her, you can count on that."
Vic's smile returned to his face. "I am sure she will," he remarked with a wry knowing smile. "I know you well enough to know you won't let me down."
Vic half turned away before turning back once more to face Laura. "Who in your family passed away?" he asked.
"My father," replied Laura, without hesitation.
Vic Chakraborty's expression was one of horror. "Your father!" he exclaimed.
Laura gave her boss a reassuring smile. "We weren't close," she explained. "He abandoned me and my mother when I was small and I've not clapped eyes on him in years, but he is my father."
"Nevertheless, my commiserations," remarked Vic with genuine sincerity. "You must be there on Thursday, family has to come first in these situations, whatever has transpired between you."

Laura smiled and nodded back at her boss. “Thank you, Vic,” she replied. “I’m just realising that too. I do need to be there.”

Chapter 5

Laura waited in the meeting room for a good ten minutes after Vic had left. She wanted to give herself time to think before she talked to Saskia.
Once she was sure she'd gathered her thoughts she picked up her mobile and called her friend.
"Hi, Saskia," said Laura calmly. "Has Vic talked with you about the pitch to Radcliff's on Thursday?"
"Well," replied Saskia rather nervously, "he did pop over to my desk earlier and ask if I'd like to play a bigger role on Thursday."
Laura didn't believe her friend was being totally honest with her but wasn't going to allow Saskia the satisfaction of seeing just how angry she was, so decided to play along.
"We just discussed your involvement on Thursday, and we decided that we'd like you to lead the presentation," Laura continued. "Isn't that good news?"
"Really," replied Saskia, who sounded surprised. "That's great news. So it will be me and you."
"Not quite," Laura responded. "I won't be there. It will be you and Vic on Thursday."
The silence that accompanied Laura's pronouncement spoke volumes.
"I take it you're okay with that Saskia?" Laura added, just to make sure her friend had to respond.
"I suppose so," replied Saskia unconvincingly. "Does Vic want me to have a run through with him?"

"He didn't mention it," replied Laura, who by now was starting to enjoy hearing her friend squirming on the other end of the phone. "Vic just asked me to make sure you were fully prepared, especially with Radcliffe's being one of our biggest clients."
"So can we start that right away?" Saskia enquired.
Laura looked up at the clock on the wall, which indicated the time was four twenty-five. Under normal circumstances, Laura would have been prepared to remain in the office for four or five more hours, if it meant her getting the presentation perfect, but on this occasion she decided that she'd leave the office at five pm on the dot, something she'd never done in the three years she'd worked at Meridian.
"Why don't you go over it on your own this evening," suggested Laura. "We can then get together in the morning and discuss it. I can also give you a heads up on some of the characters at Radcliffe's and give you some pointers on how Vic tends to like his presenters to operate."
Laura smiled smugly to herself. She could feel Saskia's anxiety oozing down the phone line, which gave her a sense of pleasure given that she still believed her friend had been more proactive with Vic than she'd so far admitted.
"Okay," replied Saskia. "But can we get together early tomorrow morning?"
"Absolutely, Saskia," replied Laura empathically. "I'll be at my desk at seven thirty and I'll keep the whole day free tomorrow to help you go through your presentation."

*   *   *

Laura spent the next twenty minutes surfing the internet to locate Blythwold and, more importantly, discover how easy it would be to get there from central London. Although it was probably no more than one hundred and twenty miles away from London, Blythwold was not the easiest place to get to by train, and not having a car, public transport was Laura's only means to get to the isolated Suffolk town. To her amazement, no matter how many different paths she traced, Laura could not find a route that would enable her to get to Blythwold without taking at least three trains and then a taxi. Furthermore, in order to be absolutely sure she'd arrive by 11am, Laura discovered that she'd have to leave home at 5:10am.
"Bugger that," she muttered to herself. "I'll travel over on Wednesday evening."
The clock on the wall reached five pm, so Laura decided to switch off her laptop and resume her search for a suitable hotel when she got home.
As she passed through the office, out of the corner of her eye, Laura caught a glimpse of Saskia locked away on her own in one of the small meeting rooms. She was staring intently at the costing slide from Radcliffe's power point presentation. Laura allowed herself a small self-satisfied grin as she imagined how Saskia would be struggling with the costings. Laura knew that her friend was no fool, and she was sure that Saskia had the confidence and personality to make a reasonably strong performance on Thursday. However, Saskia's attention to detail and her inexperience of the financial element of any pitch to customers were her two main deficiencies. Laura expected that her friend would be having a restless night, as she started to fully realise the enormity of the task that lay ahead of her on Thursday, especially

as Saskia now knew it would be Vic and not Laura who would be on hand to help her muddle her way through. "Be careful what you wish for," Laura mumbled to herself. A phrase her mum had often said to her when she was a child, but the significance of which up until that moment, she hadn't fully appreciated.

*   *   *

Laura's journey home was largely uneventful. There'd been an exhibition of some sort at Earl's Court and as a result, the tube carriage Laura was travelling in was packed with people carrying bags stuffed with catalogues and leaflets promoting what appeared to be large industrial heating and ventilation devices. However, this wasn't an issue for Laura, who was now well used to encountering people of all shapes, sizes, and nationalities on her journey to and from work.

As she strolled slowly down Elsenham Street, Laura's mind drifted back to the only time she'd seen her birth father since he walked out on her and her mum. She'd have been fifteen or sixteen and he was already at their house when she'd come home from school. Her Dad had not yet got back from work, so it would have been about four thirty in the afternoon.

She tried hard to bring to mind what was said but couldn't remember. She did, however, recall how tense the atmosphere was when she opened the front door and saw him sitting in the kitchen across the table from her mum. She knew at once who he was, quite handsome, as she thought of it, and it looked like her mum had been crying too.

Laura had not thought of that meeting for years: she'd neither wanted, nor felt the need to. But now Laura did feel the need. She did want to remember, and she felt

frustrated that try as she did, she couldn't recall much of that final meeting.
He'd tried to ask her how she was, she seemed to recollect, but Laura couldn't call to mind what was said or how they parted, which made her feel strangely guilty.
Having reached home, Laura decided to focus her mind on other matters, namely the practicality of where she'd stay over on the night before the funeral, and whether now would be a good time to call Kieran to tell him about her birth dad, and whether she should tell her mother she was going to the funeral.

Chapter 6

"Wow," Kieran remarked, his amazement evident in his voice. "I almost can't believe what you're telling me."
Laura had decided she had to tell her boyfriend about Billy McKenna, though she'd have preferred not to have to do it over the phone.
"To be honest," Laura replied. "I never think of him, so the thing that's the major shock to me is that I'm actually going to his funeral, if that makes sense?"
"No, you must go," insisted Kieran. "He is your father after all. If you don't go you may regret it later."
Laura wasn't so sure. She knew deep down that had Vic not annoyed her by suggesting Saskia lead the pitch to Radcliff's, she would never be going to the funeral.
"You may be right," she concurred, albeit without too much conviction. "My plan is to stay over tomorrow evening and then after the funeral service, get myself back home as quick as I can."
"I feel dreadful that I can't be there for you," Kieran remarked. "The timing is terrible!"
Laura chuckled. "Oh, that's okay, I won't be breaking down or anything. As I said before he meant nothing to me, he hadn't been part of my life since I was about five years old, Mike Eastwood's my real dad."
"I know," replied Kieran. "But all the same, I'd have preferred to be with you on Thursday if I could."
Laura smiled. She knew Kieran was sincere in his concern, which gave her a satisfying, warm feeling.

"Are you sure you don't want your mum and dad to know you're going on Thursday?" Kieran asked. "Don't you think they should know?"
"No," replied Laura steadfastly. "I'm not going to tell them; certainly not now. I may do at some time later, but not now."
It was clear from the pause coming from the other end of the line, Kieran didn't agree, but he wisely decided not to debate the point with Laura.
"And you mustn't say anything to either of them," continued Laura with firm resolve. "Do you promise?"
"I promise," replied Kieran reassuringly. "It's your choice, even if I don't agree."
"Thanks," replied Laura. "I'll call you tomorrow when I get to Blythwold," she added. "Love you!"
"I love you, too!" replied Kieran. "I hope your trip over is okay."
"Thanks," replied Laura as she placed her mobile on the coffee table and stared again at the photograph on her laptop of The Black Swan Inn, the hotel she'd booked for the following night.
Almost as soon as Laura had arrived home, she'd started to scour the net for suitable hotels in the town, but to her frustration, her choice was very limited. After almost an hour looking at pictures and reading reviews of tired, old-fashioned hotels and Airbnbs, Laura had decided to stay at what seemed like the premier hotel in town. Her overnight stay was going to set her back a little more than she ideally wanted to pay, but at least it looked clean and tidy; and judging from the reviews, the breakfasts sounded substantial, something that Laura felt she may need before attending the funeral.
Having spoken to Kieran, chosen a hotel and booked her train ticket online, Laura directed her attentions to what she'd wear on Thursday and what else she should pack

for the short trip to Suffolk; decisions that would take her the rest of the evening to resolve.

* * *

With her bags packed and ready. Laura lay in bed and again tried to summon up some recollection of that last meeting with her birth father. But no matter how hard she tried, she couldn't remember anything other than the frosty atmosphere, her mother looking uncomfortable and that she didn't feel anything at all for the man whose DNA she shared.

It was almost 1am by the time Laura eventually fell asleep, by which time her mind had returned once more to her friend, Saskia and how she would be feeling, given the task that confronted her on Thursday.

Chapter 7

Wednesday 19th August

Laura listened as intently as she could to Saskia's third run through of the Radcliffe presentation. It was four thirty and although she was not totally satisfied with the way her friend delivered the pitch, Laura was impressed by how well Saskia had risen to the challenge and was relatively confident her friend would perform reasonably well at the pitch the next day.

"I thought that was pretty damn good," Saskia announced as soon as she'd completed the run through. "I'm going to knock them dead tomorrow!"

Laura nodded encouragingly. "As long as you slow down and try not to go off script so much, I think you'll be fine," she remarked reassuringly. "But remember to expect some questions about the costings, particularly from Barry Horne. He's their finance manager so he'll try and get the price down. He's a tough nut, but fair, too. So, if you're confident about how the costs breakdown, you'll be okay."

Laura could see that Saskia wasn't fully listening, her thoughts seemed to be elsewhere; most likely on one of the various men friends she was juggling at the moment, Laura supposed. Under normal circumstances Saskia's lack of focus would have exasperated Laura and usually

it would have provoked some form of spiky comment. However, in truth, Laura's mind was also in another place, some one hundred and twenty miles east, to be precise.
Laura looked at her watch. "I'm going to love you and leave you," she said, borrowing another of her mother's overused phrases. "My train leaves Liverpool Street at five fifty, so I better make a move."
Her comment seemed to engage Saskia's full attention. "Good luck tomorrow," she said with sincerity. "I hope it goes well. Assuming it's possible for a funeral to go well."
Laura walked over to her friend and gave her a warm affectionate hug. "I think it's okay to say that," she replied. And as soon as she'd released Saskia from her tight embrace added, "message me when you're out of Radcliffe's."
Saskia laughed. "It's like you're my bloody mum," she replied. "I'll be fine. I'm a big girl now!"
Laura smiled back. Despite all Saskia's faults, and in Laura's eyes there were many, they'd been mates for ages and her heart was in the right place – well most of the time. "I'm off then," Laura announced before grabbing the handle of her case and heading off, her suitcase wheels gently squeaking as they turned on the office carpet.
Once Laura was out of the office, she took a deep breath and headed off towards Victoria tube station. She wasn't looking forward to the four-hour trip to Blythwold, however the uneasiness she felt about the journey was nothing compared to her apprehension about attending her birth father's funeral, the next day.

* * *

The warm summer's sun was already low in the sky as Laura clambered out of the ancient train carriage at Darsham railway station. Despite it still being only eight forty-five pm, Laura felt exhausted. She was the only passenger to get off at the station and as she made her way down the small platform, she couldn't help feeling a little lost and isolated.
This was a complete contrast to how she felt when she'd boarded her train at Liverpool Street. Then the train was so jam-packed, she'd only just managed to find a seat and the compartment had remained crowded until it reached Chelmsford, when almost all the passengers got off, leaving Laura and just a handful of people on board until arriving in Ipswich. At Ipswich station Laura had to make her only change, which was to a much older and smaller train which took her northeast towards Lowestoft, for the remainder of her journey. She'd had no problems finding herself a seat on that train, in fact her carriage was less than half full when it left the platform and by the time she got to the small Suffolk station, it was almost completely empty.
The desolation of the platform at Darsham extended into the ticketing hall, which she had to pass through to get out of the station. It was about then when Laura started to become concerned about the likelihood of getting a taxi to travel the remaining fifteen miles to Blythwold. Before that moment, it had never occurred to her that there wouldn't be taxis available, but having arrived in this sleepy backend of nowhere, this worrying thought started to ring clearly in her head.
Her fears, however, were misplaced as to her relief when Laura exited the station, she spied a bright yellow taxi parked up just a few yards down the road. Thankful that she'd found herself a means to get to her hotel, Laura

waved in the taxi's general direction, which prompted the car to quickly drive up to where Laura was standing. She peered through the open window of the cab. "I need to get to The Black Swan hotel in Blythwold," she announced.
The driver nodded back. "No problem," he replied in his thick Suffolk accent.
Laura climbed into the back of the car, which sped off before she'd had a chance to properly fasten her seat belt.
"Are you here on holiday, my dear?" enquired the driver, whose open friendly eyes looked back at Laura in his rear-view mirror.
"No," replied Laura. "I'm only going to be here a day. I've a funeral to go to in the morning."
"That would be Billy McKenna's," remarked the driver, much to Laura's surprise. "Are you a relative of his?"
Laura was shocked at the driver's revelation and had no desire to discuss her plans with a man she'd only met a matter of minutes earlier, so she decided to cut the conversation short.
"Do you mind if I make a call?" she said, holding up her mobile so the driver could see it in his mirror.
"Be my guest," he replied.
Laura, thankful of the opportunity to avoid further conversation, quickly dialled Kieran's number and placed the mobile up to her ear.
To her delight, her boyfriend picked it up in a matter of seconds.
"Hi, darling, it's me," she said loudly. "I'm in a taxi on my way to the hotel."
"How's sunny Suffolk?" enquired Kieran.
"Not so sunny now," replied Laura. "It's starting to get dark here."
"So how was the journey?" Kieran asked.

"Fine," replied Laura. "With no holdups, thank god."
As she spoke Laura could see the driver's eyes occasionally momentarily stare back at her through the rear-view mirror, which made Laura feel a little uncomfortable, but being in contact with Kieran made her less anxious than she would have been otherwise.
"Anyway, tell me about your day?" Laura said. "How was Stuttgart?"
"It went..." Kieran paused for a few seconds. "It was okay, but I don't think they were as interested as the clients we saw on Monday. I'm not sure we'll be doing too much business with these people."
"That's a shame," replied Laura. "But I guess not everyone's going to recognise your genius!"
Kieran laughed. "My thoughts exactly," he remarked. "Anyway, enough of me, what are your plans for this evening?"
"I'm just going to check into the hotel and chill out," Laura replied.
As she spoke, Laura was again conscious of her driver's eyes, which fixed their gaze in her direction for a few seconds before returning to the road ahead.
"What about you?" Laura enquired.
"We've already eaten," Kieran replied. "We're just having a quiet drink in the bar. Then I'm going to call it a day."
As he finished his sentence, the taxi stopped at a road junction, where Laura noticed a sign indicated that Blythwold was just two miles away.
"It looks like we're almost there," she told Kieran.
"We'll be there in a few minutes," replied the driver, who made no attempt to hide the fact he'd been eavesdropping.
Laura ensured that her conversation with her boyfriend continued until the taxi reached the imposing brick

building that was The Black Swan. Only then did she end her call, with a more pronounced than usual, "Love you."
"How much do I owe you?" she asked the taxi driver as soon as she'd clambered out and was safely on the pavement.
"That will be eighteen pounds exactly," replied the taxi driver.
Laura opted not to pay by card, as she'd normally do in London, and instead handed the driver a twenty-pound note. "Keep the change," she said, before quickly making her way into the hotel.
The taxi driver shook his head as he watched Laura disappear through the door, and once she was safely inside, he pushed the gear lever into first and sped off into the warm summer evening.

* * *

Laura was not surprised in the least when she walked into the foyer of the Black Swan. Having seen the photographs posted online at the time she'd made the booking, she'd expected the place to be dated, and was it ever!
The carpet, which looked as though it had been laid over fifty years before, was threadbare and pale. The oak panelled walls looked a throwback from the 1930s and although everywhere looked clean and tidy, Laura couldn't imagine the hotel attracting many people under the age of fifty – which to her was the entry age of the elderly.
However, the young eastern European receptionist was friendly, very welcoming and extremely helpful; and having established from her that St Steven's church was located no more than two hundred yards away from the

hotel, Laura clambered up the creaky wooden staircase to the first floor where her bedroom, room 15, was situated.
Once inside her room, Laura flung her case onto the deep springy mattress and opened the small glass doors which looked out over a small balcony at the front of the hotel.
As the warm summer air wafted into the room, Laura's nostrils filled with the scent of the sea, a pleasurable experience and one that reminded her of childhood holidays spend with her mum and dad on the south coast.
Laura peered out to her left, where in the distance she could see the flickering lights of ships dotted around in the vast expanse that was the North Sea. And every so often she could just about make out the sound of waves as they crashed relentlessly on what sounded to her like a pebbled beach.
Laura lingered at the window for several minutes taking in the sounds and smells. She had always considered herself to be a city girl at heart and was certainly not in Blythwold for a holiday, but as she remained motionless, she could not help feeling a sense of calm. If only Kieran was with her, she thought; and if only she was there for anything other than her birth father's funeral.

Chapter 8

Thursday 20th August

“Good morning, madam,” proclaimed the desk attendant with a welcoming smile. “I trust you had a good stay here at the Black Swan?”
“Very nice, thank you,” replied Laura. “Can I please check out.”
The receptionist looked at his screen and, after a few moments turned his eyes back towards Laura.
“The room and breakfast were already paid for with your booking,” he remarked with another broad smile. “So just the room service last night outstanding.”
Laura returned the smile. “How much will that be?”
“Fifteen pounds and fifty-three pence,” he replied.
Under normal circumstances Laura would have paid using her credit card, but for the second time since she arrived in Blythwold, she found herself handing over a twenty-pound note; but this time she waited for her change.
“May I leave my overnight bag with you?” she enquired. “I’m not sure what time I’ll be back to collect it, but it certainly won’t be later than two o’clock.”
“Of course,” replied the receptionist as he handed Laura eight coins and her receipt. “I will put it in the office.”
Having deposited the coins into her purse and with her bag now being wheeled into the office, Laura walked out of the hotel and turned right. Based upon the conversation she’d had with the hotel receptionist the

night before; she was aware that St Steven's church was only a short stroll from the hotel.
Laura had struggled to decide what she should wear to the funeral. She wanted to show due respect but did not want to feel too hypocritical by dressing as the daughter in full mourning, given that she still could not relate to this man as being her father and, if she was honest, she still felt no sense of loss at his departing. In the end Laura had elected to wear one of her business outfits, a navy two piece with a neat pencil skirt, a white plain cotton blouse and pair of reasonably flat navy shoes.
It was ten forty am when Laura left the Black Swan, and by ten forty-three she had arrived at the large and very imposing flint-covered church.
As she walked through the main entrance, she could already see about twenty people who had dotted themselves around the numerous pews, with no obvious sign of order.
Laura had very little experience of funerals. She had been too young to attend the funerals of her mother's parents, who had both died before she reached the age of ten. Her grandfather on her father's side was still alive, so the only memory she had was when she'd attended her granny's funeral, which was over ten years before, and was a quick and very low-key affair at the local crematorium.
Laura did know, however, that the next of kin traditionally occupied the pew nearest the front of the church on the right.
That particular pew remained empty, and although certainly her DNA would qualify her to take a seat in that row, her intention was to remain in the background, pay due respects to her absent birth father, then leave at the earliest possible opportunity. Laura, therefore, selected a seat in a pew three up from the back

of the church and at the end furthest away from the main aisle. Despite the obvious problem of being alone and being an outsider, Laura hoped her presence would be largely overlooked by everyone else at the service, but suspected her goal to remain anonymous would be hard to achieve.

As she waited, the church started to get busier until, by the time her watch told her it was eleven am, there must have been between fifty and sixty people sitting quietly, waiting for the service to begin.

At precisely that moment, the priest entered the church followed by a group of about six, mainly elderly people. Laura figured the priest had to be Father Mallory, who'd called her on Monday, and the procession of mourners walking slowly behind him had to be her birth father's loved ones, so, by association, almost certainly some would be blood relatives of hers.

Laura studied them all carefully as they made their way slowly down the aisle. She was intrigued to see whether she bore a likeness to any of them, but if she did she couldn't see it.

Laura was surprised not to see the coffin being brought in. Her experience of funerals was not extensive, but she was sure when she'd seen funerals on TV, the coffin, carried aloft by half a dozen pallbearers, normally followed the vicar or priest down the aisle at the start of the ceremony. But that certainly wasn't happening at this funeral.

It was only when the relatives had filed slowly along the pew that Laura noticed the coffin was already at the front of the church, presumably brought in earlier that morning or maybe even the night before.

Laura was not religious. She'd been to a C of E primary school and had good friends who were religious, but religion wasn't for her. As such the order of ceremony and the various rites and rituals that took place in the next hour were a total mystery to her. To avoid looking out of place, Laura watched and copied a couple in the pew in front of her, who seemed to know when to stand and when to kneel, and who kindly turned around and shook her hand vigorously when the priest gave the instruction to do so. A peculiar practice that seemed out of place at a funeral, she thought, but nevertheless one that did seem to bring the congregation a little closer, if only for a fleeting moment.

At one point, a tall elderly lady, one of the people who'd followed the priest into the church, stood up and made her way to the lectern. She proceeded to read a short passage from John 14, which Laura recognised as it included the words, 'I am the way, the truth and the life', a phrase she'd heard before, although Laura couldn't remember when or where.

The return of the old lady to the front row seemed to be the signal to Father Mallory that it was time for him to talk about her birth father.

Knowing practically nothing about his life, Laura was anxious not to miss anything that the priest was about to say. Totally focused on the priest at the front of the church, Laura listened intently.

"We are here today to celebrate the life of William Arthur McKenna," announced Father Mallory, his gentle Irish lilt adding an air of solemnity to the proceedings. "Billy, to those of us who knew him."

Father Mallory paused and glanced around the congregation before proceeding.

"I've thought long and hard about what I should say about Billy," he continued. "I only knew him for the last ten of his fifty-two years on this earth, but I can honestly say that the man I knew was the best of men. Of course, he was not without his faults, as none of us are. And

from all that I'm told he was quite a live wire when he was young. However, the person I knew was a good man, a kind man. He was a man who gave his time generously and willingly to help others less fortunate than he. He was instrumental in raising money for charities not only here in Blythwold but also in Uganda and Ukraine, where our links are strong, and their needs are many.
Billy was not always a practicing Catholic. In his youth, despite the efforts of his family, he lost his way. I often talked with Billy about those times, which included a few years at her majesty's pleasure, as Billy always described it. These discussions invariably would occur late into the evening in either the Admiral public house or the bar of the Black Swan. Billy never tried to hide his past. He wasn't like that. I recall one occasion, when I asked Billy why he came back to the church. His answer was quite simple. He said in his youth he'd blamed God when his elder brother was so tragically killed. He'd also blamed God when, at his trial, he was unjustly found guilty of fraud and given a custodial sentence and when his marriage so sadly broke up, he'd blamed God for deserting him once more. But he also said that in a strange way prison was the making of him. During his time inside, through the unwavering love of his mother, Mary and through the support of the chaplain, he realised that he had to change his ways and vowed that once he'd been released, he would change the way he lived his life. And change he did.
As I've said already, I never knew the angry young man who forsook the church, I never knew the person who became estranged from his wife and young daughter, and I never knew the man who was sent to prison. However, in Billy I did know the man who was

charitable, kind-hearted, friendly, approachable and such a loyal son to Mary.
Just a couple of weeks before he was so tragically killed, I'd spoken to Billy; as often was the case, it was late in the evening in the bar at the Black Swan. He told me it was time to make things right with his ex-wife, his daughter and those close to him. I'm not sure if he ever managed to achieve that reconciliation, but I sincerely hope he did." Father Mallory's eyes again scoured the congregation, before he concluded his short eulogy. "We are here today to celebrate the life of Billy McKenna, a good man, a Christian and a great friend."
For the remainder of the service Laura found it difficult to concentrate on anything that was being said. The words uttered by Father Mallory had taken her by surprise. She had no idea her birth father had been in prison and she knew nothing of him even having a brother, let alone the fact that he'd been killed in apparently tragic circumstances. And to learn that the man who had deserted her and her mother over twenty years before was a born-again Christian, who'd done so much for other people, was a real revelation and came as a huge shock to her. However, that news if anything, made Laura feel even more angry and bitter at being abandoned by Billy McKenna.
As the congregation filed slowly past the priest to take communion, Laura sat motionless in her pew. She had contemplated joining the rest of the mourners at the graveside, but now she just wanted to make as swift an exit as she could and get herself back to London.
Such intentions, however, were quickly thwarted when, without any warning, Laura noticed the tall old lady, who twenty minutes earlier had been reading the lesson, make her way down the aisle towards her.

"You must be Laura," remarked the old lady who then sat down next to her. "Yes," replied Laura, who was a little bemused as to how the old lady knew her name. The old lady's face remained stern and impassive. "You don't recognise me, do you?" she remarked.
Laura shook her head. "No," she replied. "Should I?"
"I suppose not," remarked the old lady. "After all, you were only a small child the last time I saw you. I'm your grandmother."
Laura had never considered that any of her birth father's parents would still be alive, so to be confronted by a grandmother she'd never known took her by surprise.
"I'm pleased to meet you," Laura heard herself saying. "I'm sorry for your loss."
The old lady looked back, emotionless. Then after a couple of seconds, she nodded gently as if to acknowledge Laura's words of condolence. "It's good you came," she remarked. "I wasn't sure you would."
Laura smiled back but wasn't sure what to say.
"I'd appreciate it if you'd stay for a short while after the service," she added. "I think we should take this opportunity to discuss certain matters."
Laura felt uncomfortable and was still in no mood to hang around.
"I'm afraid I can't linger too long after the funeral," she replied. "I need to be back in London this afternoon."
The old Lady stood up and started to make her way back down the aisle. "The funeral buffet is organised for twelve thirty at the Black Swan," she remarked. "I understand that's where you stayed last night. I'm sure we can conclude our discussions by one, so you'll have adequate time to get back to London, should you desire."

Then, without giving Laura any time to reply, she walked back down the aisle and resumed her seat on the front pew.

Chapter 9

Laura wasn't used to being told what to do. As her mother had said countless times, her daughter liked to plough her own furrow. In fact, with the exception of Vic Chakraborty and, very occasionally, her mother, Laura tended to disregard anything that sounded like an instruction, and, in most instances, she would deliberately do the complete opposite. It was therefore completely in character, after being asked so firmly by the old lady to attend the buffet, for Laura's initial thought to be to wait until the service was over and head back to the hotel, get a taxi and return to London as quickly as she could. However, something at the back of her head kept telling her she needed to stay. This had nothing to do with any sudden bonding with the man who had deserted her, more down to a desire to understand what sort of person he was, as her perception had always been a million miles away from the glowing, shiny image portrayed in Father Mallory's eulogy. Despite her change of plan, Laura had no intention of following the mourners as they trooped respectfully out of the church or to witness the coffin being slowly lowered into its grave.

She knew that the trains back to London from Darsham ran at eleven minutes to the hour every hour, so her new plan was to catch the two forty-nine train, which by her reckoning would have her back in London by around

five o'clock; and Laura calculated that as long as she was away from Blythwold by two she'd be okay.
To avoid being noticed, Laura made sure she was the last to leave the church. Instead of turning right, like everyone else, and walking the twenty metres to the newly dug grave, Laura carried on walking straight down thc path and out onto the main street. By the time the pallbearers had arrived at the graveside Laura was already almost half-way back to the hotel.

*   *   *

Laura sat quietly in the large foyer at the Black Swan. She checked her mobile to see if she'd missed any calls. She checked for emails, then she looked to see if she'd had any texts. Her search revealed two text messages: one from her dad, the other from Saskia. She opened Saskia's first.

Just having a break, seems to be going OK with Radcliff's, but that guy Barry Horne's a miserable arsehole! All he's done so far is gripe about the costs. I think Vic is getting quite pissed with him. Hope everything is going OK at the funeral. I'll call you later. Sas XX

Laura smiled and shook her head. She'd worried about how Saskia would cope with Barry but was a bit surprised to hear that Vic was getting annoyed with the customer. She'd never seen that happen.
Laura opened the second text.

Hi Superstar .... looking forward to seeing you tomorrow. Will call you when we land xxxx ☺

Her dad always called her superstar in his texts and always signed off with four kisses and a smiley face – well ever since Laura had shown him how to send a smiley face by text!
Laura fired off a quick text back to her dad.

Hi Dad – looking forward to seeing you both too!
Love you x ☺

As soon as she had pressed send, the old grandfather clock in the foyer struck the half hour and the mourners started to arrive. In clutches of twos and threes they entered the hotel foyer before making their way the short distance down the passage to the Dunwich Room, where the buffet had been laid out.
Laura remained seated at first, but as soon as she saw the willowy figure of her grandmother entering the hotel she stood up and followed the throng down the corridor. To Laura's surprise, the atmosphere inside the room was one of merriment. Copiously large quantities of alcohol were being drunk and the faces, which only a short while earlier had been long and sombre, were now quite cheery – almost party like.
Laura joined a line which had formed by the main table and waited her turn to gather a few sandwiches and a, much needed, cup of tea. As she waited, out of the corner of her eye, she noticed the aged and sinuous frame of her grandmother who was clearly making a beeline for her.

"Laura," she exclaimed with what appeared to be genuine pleasure. "I'm so pleased you decided to stay for a short while."
Laura smiled. "I can only stay an hour or so," she said, "but I thought it would be good to have a chat, given the circumstances."
"Get yourself something to eat and then join me over there," her grandmother said as she pointed to a small table at the side of the room.
"Aren't you eating?" enquired Laura.
"No," replied the old lady. "But you could get me a cup of tea, with just a drop of milk and no sugar."
Laura smiled again and as her grandmother walked away towards the appointed meeting place, Laura found herself able to shuffle a few feet forward, as the queue slowly edged its way to the buffet table.

* * *

It was another ten minutes before Laura finally managed to join the old lady at the prearranged table.
She carefully placed the cup and saucer in front of her grandmother and having rested her plate in front of her, she made herself comfortable.
"I'm sorry but this all seems very awkward," Laura remarked, although she forced a smile to try and project a sense of friendliness on her part.
The old lady stared back at her, at first impassively, but after a few moments she returned the smile. "Yes, it must be very difficult for you," she remarked understandingly. "You're probably the biggest loser out of all that went on, which is regrettable as you had nothing to do with any of it and were so young, too, when it happened."

"By it," Laura added, "I assume you mean the way your son abandoned my Mum and I?"
The old lady recoiled slightly in her seat on hearing Laura's words. "Is that how you see it?" she enquired. "Is that how your mother and Mike Eastwood sold it to you?"
The hard inflection given when she mentioned the name Mike Eastwood, left Laura in no doubt that her newly acquainted grandmother had scant regard for the man she called Dad.
"But that's how it was!" replied Laura angrily. "He left us!"
"Technically, yes," conceded the old lady. "But he had no choice. It was complicated, but you need to know that he always loved you, he did not want to leave you and he regretted not being part of your life."
Laura frowned. "I'm sorry, his funeral is probably not the best place to have this discussion, maybe I was wrong to come."
The old lady nodded. "You're right," she agreed "it's certainly not the time to go into the detail today. However, you need to know the full story before you judge your father. I think you owe it to him to at least try to understand what happened, from his side."
Laura looked at her watch, it was twelve fifty-five. Although she still had plenty of time to catch the two forty-nine from Darsham she was keen to make her escape and, in an instant, decided to aim for the one forty-nine instead.
"There's a train back to London in about fifty minutes," she said. "I really do need to get back."
As she finished her sentence, Laura stood up and, leaving the plate of untouched sandwiches, started to make for the exit. But before she had a chance to move

her feet, her grandmother rose quickly out of her chair and clasped her wrist tightly with her icy cold hand. Laura stared back into the old lady's eyes and was about to order her to let go, when her grandmother spoke.
"He's left you everything," she said in a calm but firm tone. "Ask yourself, why, if he didn't love you, he'd do that?"
As Laura pondered that question her grandmother spoke again. "Next time you see your mother and Eastwood, look them in the eye as you are looking into mine now and make them tell you the truth – all of it!"
The old lady released Laura's arm from her vice-like grip, nodded gently then returned to her seat.
Laura looked back at her grandmother for a split second before turning on her heels and making a speedy exit.

Chapter 10

Laura sat quietly in the train carriage as it sped through the pretty Suffolk countryside. The taxi driver had dropped her off at Darsham station in plenty of time to catch the one forty-nine, which arrived on time at platform one at Ipswich and, after a short wait, her connection bound for London Liverpool Street station had departed from platform two, once again, thankfully, on time.

As she travelled swiftly towards London, her eyes scoured the green fields and the small country cottages as they flashed past the window. And as little landmarks appeared then, as quickly, disappeared, the old lady's words echoed in Laura's head.

"Next time you see your mother and Eastwood, look them in the eye as you are looking into mine now and make them tell you the truth – all of it!"

Laura wanted desperately to believe that these words were merely spiteful utterings of a bitter old woman, but however hard she tried, she couldn't convince herself that her wish would turn out to be completely true.

Of course, she knew that Billy McKenna had walked out on her and her mother. There could also be no disputing the fact that he'd only managed to meet with her once since he'd abandoned them. And although Laura could not be totally sure her mum had told her every little

detail, she was certain her mum wouldn't have lied to her about her father.
So why, she asked herself, given all the weight of the evidence, did she still feel uncomfortable? Why on earth did Billy McKenna, a man who was in most respects a stranger to her, leave everything to her in his will?
And why did her heart keep telling her that there was some truth in what the old lady had implied?
Laura was still trying to work out a logical answer to all these questions when her mobile rang.
"Hi Saskia," she said, thankful that her agonising had been interrupted by her friend's call. "How did you get on with Radcliffe's?"
"Crap!" announced Saskia, with frankness that shocked Laura but also made her smile.
"Oh, no!" Laura replied. "What happened?"
"That bloody Barry Horne," continued Saskia. "He's basically told us that if we can't make significant cost reductions – and I mean by thirty-five per cent minimum - then he's not going to recommend the campaign to their board and, he's only giving us until Monday to make the necessary adjustments."
"Thirty-five per cent!" exclaimed Laura. "That's impossible to achieve without a major rethink and that's going to be almost impossible to do by Monday."
"Not according to Vic," replied Saskia. "He's committed to Radcliffe's that we'll present a new proposal to them on Monday morning which hits their budget."
"Really!" replied Laura. "Is he expecting the whole team to work over the weekend on it?"
"Oh yes," said Saskia. "And he's committed to Horne and the others that you'll be presenting it, as it appears I'm not up to the task."
Laura thought for a few moments. She hadn't expected Saskia to get through the presentation without a few

hiccups here and there, but she had thought it would be relatively successful. Given all the work that had gone into developing and preparing the pitch, Laura was astounded with what Saskia was telling her. It was certainly true that, on a bad day, Barry Horne could be an extremely awkward sod to present to, and even when he was on his best behaviour, he could be a difficult character, but in the past, he'd always eventually accepted any proposals she'd given, and to Laura's recollection he'd never even attempted to knock more than ten per cent off the proposed costs. So, for the proposal to be thrown out and a thirty-five per cent cost reduction be demanded, something must have gone disastrously wrong.

"What did Vic say after the presentation?" Laura enquired.

"He was clearly angry," replied Saskia. "But he didn't say too much to me after the meeting. However, he's calling a breakfast meeting for the full team that worked on the pitch for seven thirty tomorrow morning. I suspect he'll call you himself at some stage, once he's calmed down."

"So where are you now?" Laura asked.

"I'm back at the office," replied Saskia. "Vic drove us both back. He was in a foul mood and wasn't very talkative during the journey. To be honest I'm not totally sure I'll still have a job next week."

"I can't believe it's that bad," replied Laura, trying to sound as reassuring as she could. "Vic can't blame you. It was a team effort; I was the team leader and he vetted it himself. So, if it's gone tits-up we all have to shoulder the responsibility, including me and Vic, too."

"I'm not sure he sees it that way," replied Saskia; the anger that had been in her voice now having been

replaced by an air of despondency, which was uncharacteristic for her, normally robust, friend.
"Then I'll certainly be telling him when he calls," snapped Laura.
For a couple of seconds Saskia was quiet, which in itself was another rare occurrence.
"Anyway how did the funeral go?" Saskia asked.
"It was okay, I suppose," replied Laura, who wasn't yet ready to share all the details with Saskia. "I'm not sure I did the right thing going, but it's over with now."
"Were there many people there?" Saskia asked.
"Yes, a fair few," replied Laura. "I'd guess fifty or so."
"So, he must have had a lot of friends there," remarked Saskia.
"Oh, yes," replied Laura cynically. "It would appear he was very popular in Blythwold, a real local hero."
"How did he die?" Saskia asked. "Did you find out?"
A sudden feeling of guilt came over Laura as she realised that she'd not even asked her grandmother about the circumstances of her birth father's death. Rather than share the fact with Saskia, Laura decided to bring the call to an abrupt end.
"Look, it's difficult to talk now," Laura remarked. "I'll see you in the morning, we can talk then. I'll try and talk to Vic in the meantime to get his take on today's presentation but don't worry about it, we're a team and if we've messed up then we've messed up together."
"Cheers, Laura," replied Saskia, who sounded as if Laura's words had given her some welcome reassurance. "I'll see you tomorrow. Have a safe trip home."
Laura pressed the red button to end the call, placed her mobile on the table in front of her and once more stared out of the carriage window at the trees, fields, and houses as they hurtled by.

*   *   *

Laura's train was on the outskirts of London when she received the call from Vic. Having first asked how the funeral had gone, Vic calmly enquired whether Laura had spoken to Saskia.

"I have," replied Laura. "And it sounds as though it didn't go as we'd planned."

"That's putting it mildly," Vic remarked. "It was a total disaster, and you were right, Saskia's not ready to be a front-line presenter. She was dreadful!"

"Radcliffe's can be a difficult client," replied Laura. "It was probably unfair of us to give them to Saskia as her first pitch, but from what she's saying it was the costings that they objected to, so it sounds like whoever had presented, it would have gone badly."

"Your loyalty to your friend is admirable, Laura," he replied, "but you weren't there. Take my word for it, had you or I led the presentation it wouldn't have gone quite so badly. She wasn't close enough to the detail and when Horne started to ask questions about the costings, she just tried to wing it and got hammered. If she'd done her homework, we'd have closed the deal today, maybe with a small concession to the costs, but thanks to Saskia's cavalier attitude we now have to review the whole thing and present again on Monday."

By Vic's tone, Laura could tell he was angry, and knowing him as she did, she felt it would be smarter to talk to him face to face rather than argue Saskia's case on the phone on a crowded train.

"I believe you want everyone in at seven thirty tomorrow morning," Laura
said. "Why don't we meet at seven and talk this through together first?"

Vic sighed. “Seven it is,” he replied. “But don’t expect my position to soften one bit as far as Saskia is concerned. She’s responsible for the mess we’re in and, based on what I saw today, I don’t want her within ten miles of Radcliffe’s or any of our clients. I know you two are buddies, but you need to know how I feel.”
Laura took a deep breath. “You’re wrong, Vic,” she replied calmly. “I wasn’t there today, so I can’t comment on her performance, but she’s good at her job and she will make a first-rate account manager. I always thought this was just too big an account for her first presentation. I think we both need to take the blame for that.”
“Let’s talk in the morning,” Vic remarked. “I’m pleased all went okay today for you at the funeral, I’ll see you tomorrow.”
Vic ended the call, which was just as well as Laura’s train had started to slow down as it approached the grubby dark arches of Liverpool Street station.

Part Two

Saskia's Tale - A Friend Indeed!

Chapter 11

Monday 17th August

For the first time in weeks, Saskia Skinner had managed to arrive at the Meridian offices, on a Monday morning, on time, which gave her a great feeling of satisfaction. Having had to first eject her latest beau from her flat, then get herself presentable before negotiating the cramped, fifty-minute journey from one of the less sought-after areas of south London by bus to Victoria, Saskia had arrived at the office at eight fifteen am, a full fifteen minutes ahead of golden girl's team meeting.

It wasn't that Saskia disliked Laura; they'd known each other for six years and had been really close friends at Uni. However, it was fair to say the genuine delight she'd felt when they found out they'd both been offered a graduate trainee position by Meridian at the end of their degree courses, had long since been replaced by frustration tinged with a little envy.

At university the two young women had got on so well, probably because of their differing backgrounds and contrasting outlook on life. However, they were very different people, and the stark differences in their personalities had become far more noticeable once they both entered the corporate world.

To her frustration, Saskia realised quite early on that the company placed more importance on people like Laura

who were self-assured, reliable, confident and always well prepared.
In Saskia's eyes, Meridian, or to be more specific, Vic Chakraborty, looked down on people who were outspoken, undervalued individuals who were creative, and had no patience with anyone with an outgoing personality. So, for a free spirit like her it was always tough going having to constantly swim against the Meridian corporate tide.
And the bottom line, to use one of Vic's annoying phrases, was that it was Laura Eastwood, senior account manager and Vic's blue-eyed girl, who had the authority to summon Saskia and the rest of the team to a meeting at whatever time suited her. And Laura's latest whim dictated that everyone working on the latest pitch for Radcliffe's should meet at eight thirty that Monday morning.
However, Saskia had been quick to spot the small bright light on the horizon after Laura had confided in her, a few weeks before, about the possibly of taking up a role with a competitor in the US. Saskia had instantly recognised the chance, at last, to advance her career at Meridian, and she fully intended to grasp this opportunity with both hands.

*   *   *

As always, Laura's review meeting was long, drawn out and tedious to the point of nausea; and Laura was as picky as ever. How on earth she found the energy to go over every smallest detail was totally beyond Saskia. For sure it was important to cover all eventualities, but Laura's fixation with the minutiae of everything, in Saskia's view, bordered on the obsessive.

Nevertheless, throughout the meeting Saskia stoically maintained her facade of enthusiasm and at every opportunity attempted to supplement this smokescreen by demonstrating to her friend an air of passion and support, even if at times she felt she was about to lose the will to live.

Finally, after two and a half hours the meeting came to an end. And even though she was fed up and exhausted, Saskia continued to retain her outward show of positivity, even after Laura had commanded her troops to reconvene at four thirty that afternoon for yet another meeting.

As soon as Saskia and Laura were alone, Saskia asked the question that had been burning away inside her all morning. "Did you hear back from McCauley and Bernsteins?" she enquired with enthusiasm.

Annoyingly, Laura initially tried to appear as if she had no idea what Saskia was talking about, a poorly executed effort in Saskia's eyes.

When Laura did confirm they'd offered her the job, Saskia could not help herself from grabbing her friend's shoulders, her excitement at the thought of there soon being a vacancy almost impossible for her to contain. Saskia's delight, however, was quickly dampened when Laura irritatingly implied that she still needed to think about it and talk it through with Kieran and her mum and her dad.

Although Saskia had no idea what Laura's parents would say, she knew full well that Kieran was desperate to take Laura to the US with him. He'd made that perfectly clear the last time Laura had invited Saskia for dinner – after a few too many glasses of red wine, much to Laura's annoyance as Saskia gleefully recalled.

"But they'll all say go for it, surely," remarked Saskia, to try and glean something from Laura to confirm whether she was going to take the offer.
When Laura confirmed she was ninety-nine per cent certain about accepting the offer and was going to give McCauley and Bernstein's her answer at the end of the week, Saskia's hopes were raised once more and her heart started to beat hard again.
"Vic and the team won't like it when they hear," she said, although she was certain the team would probably throw a party to celebrate Laura's departure.
"I've no doubt the team won't be too sad to see me go," countered Laura, "but I'm not looking forward to telling Vic. He's been great to me and this does feel like I'm stabbing him in the back."
"Nonsense," Saskia lied, but with a perfect smile on her face. "He'll certainly not want to lose you, but he'd not hold you back. This is a fantastic opportunity for you."
"And for you, too," she remarked. "If I go, I reckon you'll get my accounts. So, it may be good for both of us."
Saskia had to try desperately hard to stop herself from agreeing and appearing so sure, but inside was thinking, "I bloody well intend to get it."
Saskia muttered a few words to imply it was no certainty, and as she expected, Laura replied by suggesting her appointment to fill her shoes was in no doubt.
The conversation was broken up by a loud knock on the door and the appearance of Jason Kennedy (who Saskia, to her utter embarrassment, had once spent the night with, after a very drunken office party).
"Sorry to interrupt you both," he said in his normal feeble voice. "There's a call come through for you,

Laura. It's some guy called Father Mallory, he's insistent he talks with you. He says it's very important." When Laura said, "Okay put him through in here," Saskia took that as being her signal to exit and get herself a well-earned cigarette.

"I'll leave you to it," she said. Then after enquiring whether Laura was going out at lunchtime, Saskia, who maintained her friendly smile, started to make her escape.

"Remember keep this all to yourself, Saskia. I don't want anyone to know until I've thought it through and spoken with Vic," Laura remarked.

Saskia turned to face Laura once more, smiled and using her thumb and forefinger made the mime of a zip being fastened across her mouth – but at the same time thinking, "too late, golden girl."

Chapter 12

As soon as Saskia came out of the meeting room, she made a beeline for the stairwell which led out the back of the office, to enjoy her first cigarette of the morning. Once outside, she spent the next few minutes pondering her next move, until she was joined by Brenda, Vic's new PA, and the only other person in the office who smoked.

"Hi, Saskia," said Brenda. "How's it going?"

Saskia smiled. "It's going fine," she replied. "How's the boss today?"

Brenda frowned. "Not happy," she replied. "I'm not sure why, but he's in a foul mood."

"His mood may get a lot worse in a few days' time," remarked Saskia with malicious joy.

Brenda lit her cigarette. "Tell me more?" she enquired.

* * *

Saskia was keen to probe Laura more about the job offer, so was overjoyed when Laura agreed to have lunch. However, her focus was diverted significantly when Laura dropped the bombshell about the nature of the mysterious call she'd taken that morning.

"So, Mike's not your real dad?" Saskia remarked in total shock.

"No ... well not biologically," replied Laura. "But in every other respect he is. He's Mum's second husband and has been since I was about five or six; he's been the best father in the world, unlike my biological father."
"So what happened?" enquired Saskia, who was keen to glean every bit of information she could. "And why on earth did you not tell me before?"
"I wish I'd never told you, now," replied Laura. "As far as I am concerned Mike Eastwood is my dad. He has been there for me for the last twenty-odd years. I may have the misfortune to share Billy McKenna's DNA, but he's never been a part of my life and although he's now died, that changes nothing. Now, what are you going to order?"
Saskia was loving it. Her prissy little friend with her neat and tidy, cosy family was actually more screwed up than her. She could hardly contain her excitement. "I'll have my usual tuna mayo baguette and a large skinny latte," she quickly replied to prevent Laura moving the conversation away. "So how come you've never mentioned this before? We've been besties for six years."
"Because, my nosy friend," Laura replied. "It's not something I think about. I'm not a McKenna, I'm an Eastwood."
Saskia waited patiently for Laura to return with their food and drinks.
"So how did he die?" she asked as soon as Laura sat down again.
By the look of confusion on her face, Saskia could see that Laura had no idea how her dad had died.
"I don't know," Laura replied to confirm Saskia's assumption. "See, that just goes to prove how little that man means to me. Now, can we please talk about something else?"

"Okay, if you say so," said Saskia who saw this as a great opportunity to return to the subject of Laura's job offer. But before she managed to go down that route, Laura started to ask her about her weekend, and by the time she'd finished reliving her carnal exploits with the latest no hoper she'd started to date, their lunch break was over, and it was time to return to the office.
"Bugger," Saskia thought. "I'll have to try again after the four thirty meeting."

*　　　*　　　*

Even by Laura's standards, a three-hour meeting to re-evaluate a presentation they'd already reviewed for two and a half hours that morning was excessive.
"Are you planning to present this alone on Thursday?" Saskia asked as soon as they were alone.
"Yes, I think I'm up to the challenge," replied Laura.
"I'm sure you are," replied Saskia who was not going to let this go without making her pitch to show what she could do. "I just thought it may be a good opportunity for one of us to get some experience at the sharp end."
Saskia knew Laura wouldn't be keen to include her, but she wasn't about to give in. So even when Laura suggested that she'd talk to Vic and expressed a concern about them being mob handed, Saskia continued to press for her way. "I hardly think one or two of us joining you would be mob handed," she said. "Having been intimately involved in this one I thought maybe it would be good for Jason and me to join you."
Saskia could see that Laura was uncomfortable, a position that was confirmed when she curtly closed the discussion by saying, "Like I said, I'll speak with Vic about it."

“I will too,” muttered Saskia under her breath, “when I see him tonight.”

Chapter 13

It was during one of her many discussions with Brenda as they smoked at the back of the offices, that Saskia had discovered Vic was obsessed with going to the gym after work. In a shameless attempt to try and endear herself to the boss, by hopefully fabricating an impromptu meeting with Vic in a more social setting, Saskia had decided to also enrol at the same gym, and she saw that evening as being as good a time as any to try to achieve her goal.

Her plan could not have worked better.

Having spied Vic, pumping iron in the gym, from her position in the gantry on a treadmill, Saskia was delighted to hear him tell one of the other good-looking, muscle-packed customers that he was going for a quick shower and then do a few lengths in the pool.

Saskia made her move. Although she had hardly ever done any kind sports activity and even though she could eat for England, Saskia had a shapely figure, and she knew she could turn most guys' heads when they saw her in her swimsuit. So, a meeting with Vic in the pool seemed perfect.

It took Vic three lengths of the small swimming pool before he spied Saskia seductively easing her way into the water. In truth he'd never given Saskia more than a second glance before then, but he recognised her face

immediately and was impressed by her curvaceous body, held snugly in the tight-fitting black swimsuit. Within a few minutes the pair had struck up a conversation, and within ten more minutes they were sat next to each other in the spa, chatting as if they were old friends.
"So where do you see your next move with Meridian?" Vic eventually enquired.
Saskia paused for a second or two, to try and give the impression she was considering the question.
"I'm not sure," she replied. "I'd really like to make a pitch to one of our clients, the only issue is that Laura's so good it's almost impossible to get a chance."
Vic nodded. "Yes, Laura's very strong in those scenarios," he agreed. "She's a real asset to the company. We're lucky to have her."
Saskia smiled sweetly back at the boss. "Absolutely," she added. "It would be awful if she ever left."
Vic nodded back and was about to change the subject when he noticed the look on Saskia's face, which suggested she had more to tell him. "Is there something I should know?" he asked.
Saskia shook her head. "No, not to my knowledge," she added. "But I guess it's true what they say that nobody is irreplaceable. So, if she were to go, I want you to know that I'd be more than willing to help out, if you felt I was up to it."
As Vic pondered what he'd just heard, Saskia smiled over at him and stood up.
"It's really hot in here," she remarked. "I'm going to have to do a few lengths to cool down."
Vic smiled back and looked up at the large white clock on the wall. "I'll be heading off soon," he remarked. "I'm just going to a have a few more minutes in here."

"I'll see you tomorrow," replied Saskia as she glided past Vic, making sure he got an eyeful of her shapely frame. "Don't boil yourself."
Vic smiled back and remained in the spa for a few more minutes before he clambered out and made his way to the changing rooms.
From the pool, Saskia watched as Vic disappeared. She felt extremely pleased with how her plan had been executed and was about to make for the changing rooms herself when she spotted a good-looking guy staring at her from the other side of the pool. "On second thoughts," she muttered to herself, "I might just hang on a few more minutes."

Chapter 14

Tuesday 18th & Wednesday 19th August

Saskia knew for sure that her discussion with Vic had been a success when, as soon as she'd sat herself down, he walked past her desk and gave her a broad smile; something he'd never done before. However, it was only after she'd taken the call from Laura that she fully realised how central her part would be at the presentation to Radcliffe's.
"We just discussed your involvement on Thursday, and we decided that we'd like you to lead the presentation," Laura had told her. "Isn't that good news?"
"Really," replied Saskia, who was amazed. "That's great news. So, it will be me and you."
"Not quite," Laura responded. "I won't be there. It will be you and Vic on Thursday."
Saskia hadn't expected that. She'd hoped that Laura would be with her and, for the first time, she started to feel nervous about the prospect of making the pitch. Her anxiety eased a little when Laura agreed to go through it with her before she presented, but never-the-less, Saskia suddenly felt worried that she may have thrust herself into a situation that was well outside her comfort zone.

*　　　*　　　*

Saskia spent three hours alone that evening, in one of the side rooms, going over the presentation; leaving the office at eight pm, the latest she'd ever left the building by choice since she'd started at the company.
Despite feeling she had the pitch word perfect, by the time she shut down her laptop, the butterflies in her stomach were still there and, no matter how hard she tried, she couldn't stop visualising the pitch being anything other than a disaster; a vision that remained with her all evening and one that meant she hardly got any sleep that night.
Her run through with Laura the following day was useful, but Saskia found it hard to concentrate and, although Laura did seem genuinely trying to help, Saskia found her brain fogging over whenever Laura talked about the cost breakdowns, which Laura did to the point of nausea.
By the time the clock reached four thirty Saskia felt she'd had enough coaching and critiquing from her friend and decided to wind things up.
"I thought that was pretty damn good," she announced, her way of saying to Laura that she'd had enough. "I'm going to knock them dead tomorrow!"
Saskia could see that Laura got the message, but annoyingly, and in Saskia's eyes unhelpfully, she'd then gone on to add some final comments that Saskia felt were uncalled for and a deliberate attempt by Laura to unnerve her.
"As long as you slow down and try not to go off script so much, I think you'll be fine," Laura had remarked, like some fussy teacher talking to a naïve adolescent.
"Remember to expect some questions about the costings, particularly from Barry Horne," Laura had then added, before telling her something that Saskia already knew; namely that Horne, Radcliffe's pernickety finance

manager, would almost certainly try and get the price down.
Saskia, not wanting to prolong the discussion any further, decided to say nothing, which seemed to have the desired result; namely that Laura then theatrically looked at her watch and declared she was leaving to catch her train to Suffolk.
Although she didn't really care, Saskia put on her interested face and cheeriest smile and wished Laura well.
"Good luck tomorrow," she heard herself saying, then, "I hope it goes well. Assuming it's possible for a funeral to go well."
Laura seemed not only to buy but also appreciate Saskia's phoney sincerity, as demonstrated by the huge affectionate hug she gave Saskia before sauntering away.
"Message me when you're out of Radcliffe's," had been Laura's final order before she grabbed her bag and headed off.
"It's like you're my bloody mum. I'll be fine. I'm a big girl now!" Saskia had replied, her template smile still visible, but at the same time thinking, for God's sake go, Laura.

Part Three

Laura’s Story – A Shift In The Balance

Chapter 15

Thursday 20th August

As soon as Laura got back to her house she switched on her laptop and *googled* Billy McKenna.
After sifting through and discounting several dozen people who were located in far flung destinations, such as Seattle, Springfield Illinois and the myriad of individuals located north of the border, Laura spotted an article which had been published in the previous week's East Suffolk Gazette.

Tributes paid to Blythwold charity fund-raiser who died in car crash

Billy McKenna, died from multiple injuries suffered in a crash on the Ipswich Road in the early hours of Wednesday morning.

Mr McKenna, aged 52, was well-known in the area for his fund-raising efforts – having raised tens of thousands of pounds for local charities in the last 10 years.

Alan Langham, of 5, Thorn Heights Blythwold, who was also in the car, suffered only minor cuts and bruises. He said of his childhood friend, "Billy had the biggest heart of anyone I have ever met"

And Father Mallory, the priest at St Steven's church where Mr McKenna regularly attended said, "He was a kind and generous man, always smiling and always putting others before himself."

Billy, who was born in Blythwold and went to school in Lowestoft, had a colourful life. Having worked at Barclays Bank in the town after leaving school, he had spent a short time in prison following a well-documented fraud case which had gained national prominence in the mid-nineties. Billy had been sentenced to five years for his crimes, but due to good behaviour had been released having served just over half his sentence. Upon leaving prison Billy returned to Blythwold, where he made a successful career for himself as an events organiser.

Billy McKenna never tried to hide his past and when interviewed by local television, last year had stated that prison had been a humbling but positive experience. He maintained that it had helped him reacquaint himself with God and realise how he needed to conduct his life. In that interview he'd revealed that when he was inside, he'd promised himself that upon his release he would do as much as he could to

help others; a vow he'd certainly appeared to have kept.

Of the many fund-raising activities undertaken by Billy, probably the most notable was his 120 mile charity walk, around East Anglia last year, which raised over £20,000 for local children's charities.

The crash happened when Mr McKenna was returning home from Ipswich, where he'd spent the evening discussing another ambitious charity event planned for spring next year. The red Vauxhall car driven by Mr McKenna collided head-on with a Land Rover at about 1.50pm. The female driver of the Land Rover suffered head, chest and leg injuries and was airlifted to Addenbrooke's Hospital in Cambridge. Another passenger in the Land Rover, believed to be her sister, escaped with only minor injuries.

Billy leaves a mother, Mary and a daughter, Laura. A funeral will be held on August 20th at St Steven's Church, Blythwold at 11.00am.

Laura read the article three times before clicking off and returning to the search for more details regarding her estranged birth father.
It didn't take her long to start finding several other articles, almost all related to his various fund-raising exploits. There was one in particular that caught her eye. It was a piece written four years earlier by the same East Anglian newspaper.

Mammoth 185 mile bike ride raises £10,000 for Blythwold Church restoration fund

48 year old Billy McKenna successfully completed a gruelling 185 mile cycle ride to the five main football stadiums in our region and has so far raised in excess of £10,000 towards the upkeep of St Steven's Church in Blythwold.

Starting out from Roots Hall Stadium, the home of Southend United, at 5:30am on Sunday morning, Billy then proceeded to cycle first to the Colchester Community Ground, then on to Portman Road, the home of Ipswich Town, before heading on to Carrow Road in Norwich and, finally, on to the London Road Stadium in Peterborough.

A weary but cheery Billy achieved this monumental challenge in 15 hours 25 minutes. "It was significantly harder than I imagined," remarked the exhausted cyclist. "I had planned to maintain a steady 15 miles per hour pace, and with three twenty-minute stops at each of the grounds along the way, I expected to arrive here at around 7pm. I was feeling great until we reached Norwich, but those final 80 miles from Norwich to Peterborough were very painful."

Despite arriving almost 2 hours behind schedule, Billy was greeted by over 50 friends and well-wishers, many of whom had followed his progress along the way.

When asked if he had any further fund-raising activities planned, the Blythwold businessman would only say, "Watch this space!"

Laura spent the next thirty minutes reading reports and looking at the smiling face of her absent father as the praise was heaped upon him for yet another well-publicised fund-raising activity. It was clear he enjoyed his fund-raising exploits, and, to her surprise, he was clearly a local hero on the coast of East Anglia.
"Just a shame he couldn't find the time or energy to spend with his daughter," Laura remarked out loud before switching off her laptop and heading off for a long soak in the bath.

*　　*　　*

With the relaxing hot water up to her chin and just her knees protruding out from the foam, Laura turned her thoughts to the two phone conversations she'd had with Saskia and Vic earlier in the day. She felt slightly guilty that part of her was pleased Saskia's presentation had not been a total success. However, her overwhelming emotion was one of sympathy with Saskia. Laura knew how keen her friend was to be an account manager with Meridian, and Radcliffe's were a really tough client for Saskia to be making her debut.
Up until that moment Laura had been unsure about the role in the US, however, after her conversation with Vic, she'd made up her mind that it was now time to move away from Meridian. With that decided, Laura wanted to do whatever she could to help Saskia achieve her ambition of becoming an account manager – not that this

seemed likely given what Vic had been saying about her friend.
Laura thought long and hard about how she would play her hand with Vic in the morning; for so long that by the time she'd formulated her plan, the water that surrounded her was stone cold.

.

Chapter 16

Friday 21st August

"Good morning, Vic," announced Laura in a self-assured and upbeat tone.
Vic raised his eyes from the small computer screen that had for the previous twenty minutes, kept him engrossed. "Glad to see you're on time," he observed, the implication being that if she hadn't been, she was in trouble.
Laura sat herself down a few places away from her boss and smiled back with a confident air.
"So, it didn't go too brilliantly yesterday," Laura remarked, keen to get the discussion onto the presentation at Radcliffe's, without any undue delay.
Vic glared back at his attractive young executive. "It was a total cock up!" he replied in his usual blunt, uncompromising manner.
Laura had fully anticipated Vic to pull no punches and was, as always, prepared.
"Well it can't have been so bad, or they'd have not given us the chance to re-pitch," she replied. "And I think it's only fair that we allow Saskia to lead again. If we replace her, we're as good as telling Radcliffe's and Saskia that she's not up to the job."
Vic glared back with a look of total incredulity.
"Laura!" he exclaimed. "She was a total disaster. If she'd been properly prepared, we would not be in this

mess. Did you not hear what I said to you on the phone last night? Saskia isn't ready to be a front-line presenter. Yesterday she was appalling!"
Laura took a deep breath and tried to project the impression of complete composure. "Vic, I have a few things to tell you," she remarked. "Firstly, I need you to be aware that I've been offered a position in New York, and I've decided to take it. I will fulfil my contract and work my three months' notice at Meridian, but I've decided to leave."
Vic remained silent and his expression did not change, which took Laura by surprise. "I'm of course sorry to be leaving, but it's a great opportunity for me, and Kieran's due to relocate to the US, too, so the timing's right."
Vic nodded slowly and looked away from Laura. "I see," he remarked coolly. Laura sensed inside he was quite angry and chose to say nothing while Vic digested what she'd just told him.
After a short, uncomfortable, silence Vic returned his gaze in Laura's direction. "You said there were a few things you wanted to tell me," he said calmly. "What other pronouncements do you have?"
Laura had rehearsed the next line in her head all morning and although she knew exactly how she was going to deliver the words, she was very unsure as to how Vic would receive them.
"Well," she started, trying hard to retain a self-assured air, "given that I'm going to be leaving, it's surely only sensible to allow my successor time to get to know my accounts while I'm still here to assist her. And although Saskia may have had a bad day yesterday, she's got what it takes to be a great account manager, so why don't we use the next three months to bed her in?"
Vic laughed. "Priceless," he remarked. "You must have a very high opinion of yourself, Laura," he added with a

hint of vitriol in his words. "You feel that you can appoint your own successor, do you?"
"No, of course not," spluttered Laura. "But she is the best candidate from the team."
Vic rested his head on the palm of his right hand. "Okay," he replied. "I'll do you a deal, Laura. I will allow your buddy to lead on Monday, but there are three conditions."
"Which are?" Laura enquired tentatively.
"Firstly, you work with Saskia today and, if need be, over the weekend to ensure that we retain the contract with Radcliffe's."
Based upon what Laura had already gleaned from her telephone conversation with Saskia the day before, she was anticipating an interrupted weekend anyway, so this condition was no real surprise to her.
"Secondly," continued Vic, who maintained laser-like eye contact with Laura, as if he was trying to work out her thoughts, "you tell me who is stealing you away from us and what sort of deal they're offering you, so I have the chance to consider whether it's appropriate for me to match it. How does that sound so far?"
Laura considered Vic's proposal for a few seconds. "It sounds reasonable so far" she replied. "But I've made my decision, and I won't be changing my mind, even if you were to beat their offer."
Vic's smirk suggested he didn't buy what Laura was saying.
"So what's the third condition?" Laura asked.
"That you don't tell anyone else here or any of our clients about your decision until at least after the Radcliffe's presentation has been concluded on Monday."
Laura nodded. "I have to give my new company my decision by the end of today, so it's my intention to call

them tonight," Laura remarked. "But I'll promise you I won't tell anyone else until after the Radcliffe's presentation, if you wish."
Vic smiled and nodded. "Then I'll agree to allow Saskia to lead on Monday," he said. "However, she's got to really step up if she stands a chance of becoming an account manager here. She may think that joining my gym is the key to promotion, but you can tell her that she's way off the mark."
The look of astonishment which Vic saw on Laura's face, only confirmed what he already expected. "Has your good friend not mentioned our chance meeting in the hot tub at my gym the other night?" he asked. "Maybe you should ask her about it!"
Laura could feel her cheeks start to redden. "We don't live in each other's pockets," she remarked. "I knew she'd joined a gym but didn't know it was yours. I suspect neither did she either."
Vic smiled again, this time a very confident, knowing smile. "Brenda tells me otherwise," he replied. "I think your friend is very calculating, Laura, especially now you're about to fly the coop."
Laura had no time to continue the discussion as, no sooner had Vic finished his sentence, the door opened, and Saskia and the rest of the team filed in.
"Give us a few more minutes," Vic told the team before any of them had a chance to become seated. "I need to talk with Laura privately for a while longer."
Jason and Saskia, who had been at the front of the group, nodded compliantly, turned on their heels and ushered the group out of the office.
As soon as they had departed and the door had been shut tight behind them, Vic fixed his gaze again into Laura's eyes. "So who is it that has poached my number one account manager?"

"It's McCauley and Bernstein's in New York," replied Laura.
Vic nodded sagely. "I see," he replied. "They're a reputable company for sure and they've some big accounts over there, so I can't argue against your choice, but what package are they offering?"
Laura smiled. "They're offering to pay relocation, the usual company benefits and," at that point she stopped and started to scribble down a six-digit figure with a dollar sign in front of it, in her notebook, "this is my new salary," she announced as she theatrically ripped the page from her book and passed it over the table to Vic.
Vic looked at the figure for a few moments before folding up the paper and putting it carefully into his pocket. "A very generous offer for someone with no experience in the US," he remarked rather spitefully. After a short pause, Vic then looked back at Laura and said, "You'd better bring Saskia and rest of the gang in, we've lots of work to be getting on with if we're to save the Radcliffe's contract."

* * *

Vic spent the first thirty minutes informing the team, in no uncertain terms, about how badly the presentation had gone the day before. Although he was liberal in his criticism, there was no doubt he laid the bulk of the blame for the failed pitch to Radcliffe's at Saskia's door. He concluded his rant with an ominous pronouncement. "We have to retain Radcliffe's account," he remarked as he slowly but deliberately turned his head and scanned the faces of the assembled team. "If we don't, there will have to be changes made, be under no illusions about that."

Vic, in a theatrical fashion, stood up and walked slowly towards the exit. “I will leave it to Saskia and Laura to take it from here, as they’re the people who will have to manage the presentation on Monday.”
“Do you want to hear the pitch again?” Saskia enquired. On hearing Saskia’s voice, Vic turned round and stared back at her; his brown pupils focused in her direction. “No,” he replied. “You need to resolve this between you. Just make sure there are no more mistakes.”

*   *   *

After six hours solid graft with only two short breaks, Laura sat back in her chair. “I think we’re as ready as we can be with the changes that need to be made, it’s just the delivery that now needs to be rehearsed. Does everyone agree?”
Whether they agreed or not, the entire team nodded. It was clear they had no appetite to prolong the meeting.
“It’s down to me, then, to make sure the delivery is perfect,” Saskia added. “I guess that’s the rest of my afternoon sorted.”
“And some of the weekend, too,” added Laura.
Wearily the team filed out of the room leaving Laura and Saskia alone.

“So what did Vic say to you about the pitch yesterday?” Saskia enquired as soon as they were on the own.
“He was unhappy, that’s for sure,” replied Laura. “And he does hold you responsible. However, he’s wrong and I told him so. He’s prepared to give us this last chance, but we can’t mess this up, Saskia.”
“You mean I can’t,” Saskia corrected her friend. “It’s my head on the block not yours.”

Laura didn't even attempt to argue otherwise. "Basically, yes," she said. "But you can do it, Saskia, and if you do, Vic will quickly change his mind. Believe me I know him, he's only interested in results. If you turn this one around, everything that went on yesterday will be forgotten."
Saskia's expression suggested she was fully aware of her task and the implications. "In that case I'm going to prepare like never before and on Monday, Radcliffe's are going to see the presentation of their lives."
Laura smiled. "Do you want me to help?" she asked, fully expecting her friend to grab this offer with both hands.
"No," replied Saskia firmly. "If it starts going tits up on Monday, I'd certainly appreciate you helping out," she remarked, "but this is my opportunity. You'll be off to the US soon and if I'm going to stand any chance of getting your job, I need to do this by myself."
Laura was amazed, but also impressed by Saskia's reply. "Okay, Sas," she replied. "I'll let you get on with it."
Laura stood up and made her way towards the door. "So have you told Vic you're leaving?" Saskia asked.
"No, not yet," Laura lied. "I'll do that on Monday after the pitch is over."

Chapter 17

Laura had left the Meridian offices at three thirty which was quite normal for her as officially they finished work at one on Fridays. By four fifteen Laura was walking down Lavenham Road and enjoying the warm summer afternoon, when her mobile rang.
"Hi, superstar, it's Dad," came the familiar-sounding voice down the line. "We're just at baggage at Stansted. If we're lucky with the trains, we'll be at the hotel by around six."
Whenever Laura's mum and dad came over they always stayed in a small hotel near Victoria Station, no more than a twenty-minute cab drive from her house, assuming the traffic was okay.
"Hi, Dad," replied Laura excitedly. "Did you have a good flight?"
"Yeah," replied her dad as he hauled Laura's mother's massive pink case off the carousel. "No problems."
"What do you want to do for dinner?" Laura enquired as she arrived at her door. "Kieran's flying back from Germany this afternoon; he should be getting back around seven."
"So, I'm going to have to share you with him, am I?" joked her father. "It doesn't seem that long ago when I was the only man in your life."
Laura smiled as she put her key in the lock. She idolised her dad and was always pleased to see him. "You'll

always be my number one man," she replied. "But I'm afraid you do have to share me now I'm a big girl."
"Why don't we come to yours for about seven thirty," her dad remarked as he spotted his case moving towards him down the carousel. "We can decide what to do then."
"Sounds perfect," replied Laura. "I'll see you then."
"Okay, my dear," he said as he lodged the phone between his shoulder and his ear, freeing both his hands to allow him to wrestle his case off the conveyor. "See you later." As he spoke, he grabbed the case and yanked it off the belt.
As soon as she was inside the house, Laura threw her mobile onto the sofa, kicked off her shoes and wandered over to the kitchen. As she did, she noticed the light flashing on the land line phone, which indicated she had a voice message.

*   *   *

It was six forty-five when Kieran arrived at Laura's house, and she was fuming.
"What's the matter?" he enquired as he caught sight of the pained expression on Laura's face.
"The job offer in New York's been retracted!"
"What?" exclaimed Kieran. "They can't do that."
Laura shrugged her shoulders. "They can and they have," she replied. "Their HR guy left me a message to call him and when I did, he just apologised and said they'd had an instruction from head office that there was an indefinite, company-wide head count freeze and that with immediate effect, all positions that had not been filled were to be put on hold. As I've not confirmed acceptance of my offer, they are now saying that it's

suspended with no indication of when it will be lifted, or even if it will be lifted."
"Well that doesn't mean the opportunity has gone," remarked Kieran, who was doing his best to keep Laura's spirits up. "It's just on ice for a while."
"Technically that's true," replied Laura. "But the HR guy said I shouldn't expect any news for months."
Kieran put his arms around Laura. "Well there's nothing you can do," he said.
Laura was determined not to cry. She clung on tight to Kieran and buried her head against his chest. "I just wish I'd said yes earlier and confirmed it in writing," she said. "If I'd done that they would have had to take me on."
Kieran had been urging Laura to accept the offer as soon as it had arrived but was not about to remind his girlfriend of the fact – not now anyway.
"It's a good job you've not told anyone at Meridian yet," he remarked in an attempt to cheer Laura up.
Laura raised her eyes so they met his. "That's the thing," she said with trepidation in her voice, "I told Vic this morning."

* * *

At seven thirty a black London cab drew up outside Laura's house and the heavily tanned figures of Mr and Mrs Mike Eastwood emerged and headed up the short drive.
Laura opened the door and gave her mum a huge loving hug. "Hi," she said. "It's great to see you."
Laura's mum loved living in Spain. She adored the relaxed way of life; she worshipped the sun and her villa was her dream home. However, the downside of living in Spain was that she missed her only daughter terribly,

and as such she made it a habit to come home at least three or four times a year.
"You look tired, Laura," she remarked as soon as their clinch had ended. "Are you eating properly?"
Laura laughed. "Mum," she scolded, "you always say that. I'm absolutely fine."
"You work too much, that's your trouble," continued her mother who then grabbed hold of Kieran and gave him a squeeze. As she did, Laura's dad took his turn to hug his precious daughter.
"Great to see you, superstar," he remarked with gusto. "Don't take any notice of what your mum says, you look a million dollars to me, as always. And we both know that at your age there's no such thing as working too hard. Work while you're young, make your fortune then retire, like your smart old man did."
Laura grinned broadly. "Thanks, Dad," she replied before depositing a massive kiss on his cheek. "That's the master plan. Well it's either that or winning the lottery."
Mike Eastman smiled. "As it happens it's a £122 million rollover tonight," he remarked. "I got a ticket at the airport, because you never know."
Laura ushered her parents through to the living room. "So, where do you want to eat tonight?" she enquired.
"How about that nice little Indian we went to last time," her father replied.
Laura's mother's eyebrows raised skyward. "He's been banging on about going back to that restaurant all bloody day," she announced as if she was talking about a naughty little boy.
"But, Bev, you can't deny how remarkably fresh and tender the food was last time," he replied. "My starter was out of this world, and that fish dish I had as a main course was outstanding."

"I think that was the Haryali Murg Tikka," Kieran interjected knowledgably. "We often get a takeaway from there, don't we, Laura, and I've got to say Mike's right, it's quite special, a bit pricy but well worth it."
"Don't worry about the bill," Mike enthused, "these meals are on me."
"In that case, an Indian it is then," said Laura with a shrug of her shoulders.

Chapter 18

The Indian restaurant on Merton Road was always busy on Friday evenings, but fortunately there were a few tables still free when they arrived.
"How's the new exercise regime going, Dad?" Laura asked, with a straight face.
"Fantastic," her father replied. "I've only lost a few pounds so far, but I feel tons better. I'm going at least four or five times a week, aren't I, Bev?" As he spoke, he glanced across at his wife who was nibbling on a poppadom while simultaneously rolling her eyes.
"Well I can vouch for the fact that you're going regularly, but I'm not sure it's doing you much good," she remarked heartlessly. "Since this new fad started, I doubt you've managed to chalk up more than one evening when you haven't flaked out, snoring in your chair by eight."
"Fad," exclaimed Mike, with mock indignation. "This is a major life-style change. It's no fad!"
The restaurant's friendly waiter, who had a broad smile and gleaming white teeth, brought over their starters and the conversation momentarily halted while they all enthusiastically tucked into the sumptuous food that had been placed in front of them.
"And how's your job going Kieran?" Mike asked. "I hear you went to Germany this week."
As the two men became engaged in a deep conversation about conducting business abroad and their various

experiences of dealing with the Germans, Laura turned sideways to face her mother.
“I went to the funeral,” she said carefully, looking to see what sort of reaction she was going to get.
“I see,” replied her mum. “I did think you might. How did it go?”
Laura was relieved to see that her mum didn’t appear to be at all perturbed by her confession. “It was fine,” she replied. “I didn’t hang around too long afterwards, but overall, it went okay.”
“Were there many people there?” her mum asked.
“Yes,” replied Laura. “There must have been around fifty or sixty people. I was a bit surprised.”
As she spoke, Laura could see that her dad had clearly caught some of what she was saying, and his expression indicated that he was not so happy.
“Did anyone realise who you were?” her mum asked, apparently oblivious to the look of derision on her husband’s face.
“Yes,” replied Laura. “I think I stood out a bit, being the only outsider.”
“Was Mary there?” enquired her mum.
“Yes,” replied Laura once more. “It hadn’t occurred to me that his mother would still be alive, but she was there, and she collared me after the service.”
“Witches live forever!” Laura’s dad announced, with unbridled hatred in his inflection.
“Mike!” exclaimed Laura’s mum, who was now starting to look uncomfortable.
“She was okay,” replied Laura. “She seemed to know lots about me, too, which took me by surprise.”
“She’s a witch, I’m telling you,” Mike remarked, although this time with a little humour in his tone of voice.

"Anyway," interjected Laura, who had no intention of allowing the conversation to go off course, "I did my duty and went to the funeral. I'm glad I went and am sorry that he's died, but the bottom line is that he wasn't ever a proper dad to me and I have no feelings for him at all, so let's change the subject."
"So, how did he die?" Laura's mum enquired, "After all, he was only fifty-two."
Laura shrugged her shoulders. "Actually, I didn't find out until I got home last night," she said a little guiltily. "They mentioned some sort of tragedy at the service, but it was only when I looked for some sort of announcement on the internet that I found out he'd been killed in a car accident."
"Oh, that is sad," remarked Laura's mum, with genuine sorrow. "That's such an awful way to die."
"I suppose that's the last we'll ever hear about him," remarked Mike as he bit into an onion bhaji. "And to be honest, I'm not sorry to say it," he continued with his mouth full of onion.
"Well, actually, no," replied Laura. "According to Mary, I'm his sole beneficiary."
"Really," exclaimed Kieran, rather too excitedly he realised just after he'd said it.
Laura's mum laughed. "It does surprise me that he's left everything to you, and to be honest it's good he's done that, but I wouldn't expect there to be that much in his estate, my dear. Billy was not what you'd call a highflyer."
It was now Mike Eastwood's turn to roll his eyes skyward. "Dive bomber more like it!"
Laura wanted desperately to ask what Mary had meant when she'd told her to ask for the truth, but she felt that this was neither the place nor the time. And, given the hostility that her dad had shown towards both Billy and

Mary, Laura also concluded that now was probably not the time to mention Billy's supposedly successful business and his notoriety in East Anglia as a fund raiser.
She decided to park these discussion items for another day.
"So, how long are you over for?" asked Kieran, who could see that Laura wanted to move the conversation on.
"It's just a fleeting visit," replied Mike. "We're flying back on Monday morning."
"What are your plans for the weekend?" Kieran added.
"Well, tomorrow, I promised we'd shoot over to Cambridge to see my brother and his wife, but we've nothing planned for Sunday."
"Why don't we just go down to Covent Garden or maybe go and see what useless exhibits they have at the Tate," Laura's mum suggested.
"We used to go there a lot when you were doing your O Levels, didn't we, Laura?"
Laura laughed, "Yes, remember the huge spider exhibition they had that time, and we couldn't work out whether that French person who'd made it was a man or a woman."
"It was a woman," her mum replied. "I can't remember her name, but it was definitely a woman."
"Have you been to the Tate?" Mike asked Kieran, his tone suggesting quite strongly that it wasn't his cup of tea.
"Actually, no," Kieran replied. "I don't think I have."
"You've had a lucky escape then," added Mike caustically. "It's ninety per cent rubbish and the other ten per cent is just weird."
"That settles it," Laura's mum announced. "On Sunday we're going to the Tate."

Mike Eastwood slowly shook his head. "You girls can go, and when you've finished, you'll find me in the nearest pub."
"I'm with you, Mike," added Kieran. "A few pints of beer sound much more enticing."

.

Chapter 19

Saturday 22nd August

The taxi from the restaurant had dropped Laura and Kieran outside the house in Lavenham Road, before it headed off to Laura's parents' hotel in Victoria. As soon as they'd closed the door behind them Kieran opened a bottle of red wine, which they demolished cuddled up together on the sofa.

Laura had no idea what time they had eventually gone to bed, but it was well into the early hours of Saturday morning and having not seen Kieran for five days, it was much later by the time she eventually went to sleep.

It was therefore no real surprise to Laura when, through one squinting blurry eye, she made out the time on her bedside cabinet clock as reading nine forty-seven. Tentatively she rolled over to check whether Kieran was still in bed – he was. Laura's head hurt a little, not a big thumping headache, but a dull dehydrated wooziness; a feeling she'd experienced many times when she'd been at university but not quite so much since she'd become a sensible high-flying executive.

With her head feeling as it did, the normally welcoming hubbub of Southwest London which seeped into the bedroom through the open window, seemed less appealing than usual and louder, too, she thought.

Laura lay silently for the next fifteen minutes in a desperate attempt to prevent her head from feeling any worse, but with no perceptible success. She knew what she really needed to help her was a drink of water, but getting up seemed such an effort. However, Laura's need for a cure outweighed her desire to remain in bed, so slowly and reluctantly she eased her naked frame from a horizontal to a sitting position, then with some considerable mental effort she stood up. Laura quietly made her way out of the bedroom, slowing down for just a few seconds while she quickly threw on the soft comfortable sweatshirt that Kieran had been wearing the evening before. As she exited the room she looked back over her shoulder at Kieran, who lay face upwards and dead to the world. Laura loved Kieran deeply. He wasn't perfect by any stretch of the imagination, but he was smart, he was kind, he was funny, he was great company and Laura thought he was incredibly good looking. Laura silently slipped out of the room and as quietly as she could, pulled the door closed behind her.
It took two tall glasses of cold water, the second of which had been infused with two paracetamol tablets which seemed to take an age to dissolve, before Laura's head started to feel any better.
She glanced up at the kitchen clock and, now being completely awake, decided to take a shower.
Fifteen minutes later, with the sweatshirt back on and her hair wrapped tightly in a towel, Laura returned to the bedroom to find her boyfriend in exactly the same position as she'd left him, but this time snoring quite loudly.
Laura sat on the bed with her back to Kieran and unfolded the towel, letting her damp hair fall down around her shoulders.

Suddenly a strong arm wrapped itself around her waist and pulled her backwards onto the bed.
"You smell nice," he remarked before planting a long lingering kiss on her warm lips.
Laura enjoyed the experience for a few seconds before pushing him away and sitting up. "You don't," she replied unromantically.
"Charming," replied Kieran who pretended to sniff close to his left armpit. "And there's me thinking we could spend the morning in bed."
"We can," replied Laura with a knowing grin. "But only after you've had a shower."
Kieran pretended to look shocked. "Yes ma'am," he replied before clambering out of bed and walking naked towards the door. "I guess there's no chance of a coffee?" he enquired as he walked onto the landing.
Laura chose not to answer. Having enjoyed the sight of his firm buttocks as they rose and fell with each of his steps, she then swiftly plugged her hairdryer into the power socket and started to blow the warm air through her hair. She wanted to make sure it was completely dry before Kieran came back to bed.

*　　*　　*

It was the afternoon before Laura's curtains were opened and the bright sunshine entered the small suburban bedroom. Having spent a pleasurable few hours in each other's arms, Laura finally brought Kieran the coffee he'd asked for when he'd stirred himself that morning.
"Have you thought any more about what you're going to do about your job?" he asked.
Laura shrugged her shoulders. "I'm not sure," she replied. "Technically I've not handed in my notice, so

I'm tempted to tell Vic that I've changed my mind, but I'm not sure what to do. To be honest, with the way he behaved towards Saskia, I'm actually not sure I want to stay working there anyway."
"Why don't you just quit and come over with me?" Kieran suggested. "You can look for a job when you're there?"
"Sounds tempting," replied Laura, "but I'm not sure it works like that. I think I'll need to get a work visa, otherwise you can't get a job over there."
"Surely that can't be such an issue?" Kieran remarked. "After all, I've got a work permit for my job."
"But that's the point," replied Laura a little tetchily. "You had your job offer already. I've not. Anyway, tempting as it is, I'm not keen to be a kept woman by you just yet. I need my independence."
Kieran sighed. "Talking of which," he said, "I'm going to shoot back home this afternoon. I need to sort out a few things. Do you want to meet up later?"
"What do you have in mind?" Laura asked.
"I'm easy," replied Kieran. "We could go down to the West End and try to see a show or just stay in and have a takeaway."
Laura thought for a few moments. "Why don't we try and catch the new Zac Efron film. I quite fancy looking at Zac Efron for a few hours."
"Zac Efron!" exclaimed Kieran. "Who needs Zac Efron when they've got me?"
Laura didn't reply, but her turned-down lips and wrinkled forehead gave Kieran the distinct impression that his question had been received with unadulterated incredulity and dismissed completely.

* * *

Laura was pleased to have the afternoon to herself. She enjoyed being with Kieran, but she also valued having time on her own.
With her headache having almost disappeared, she was able to turn her thoughts to Billy McKenna. From what she'd discovered in Suffolk and from the articles she'd read on the internet, Laura was curious to learn more about the life of her absent father. She fully intended to use the time she'd have alone with her mum the next day to find out more about their life together and if possible, understand a little bit more the reason why he'd left, but before then she figured she'd try and get some more details on Billy McKenna's life more recently. And to satisfy that interest, Laura once more would look to the web.
With a hot mug of coffee next to her, Laura typed Billy McKenna events organiser into the google search engine.
She hadn't thought too much about what sort of information she'd find, but Laura was amazed at how well established her birth father's business was and although his client list didn't have many names Laura recognised, the impression she got was that the business was certainly thriving.
Laura wondered who would be looking after the business now – nobody, she presumed.
For three hours Laura scoured the internet for information on her birth father. Whenever she came upon an article that she found interesting she'd print off a hard copy and also save it to her hard drive. By the time Laura called it a day on her sleuthing, she'd amassed a sizable pile of printouts, which she fully intended to show Kieran when he returned that evening. However, all was to change when at six, Kieran called her.

"Hi darling," he said in a tone that suggested immediately to Laura that all was not right. "I'm sorry, I'm not going to be able to get over to see you tonight. That pillock, Ryan, has got himself into bother again with the police and Mum's in a right state. I need to go over and calm her down."
Laura was slightly miffed that she'd have to delay sharing what she'd found about Billy McKenna for the time being, but she tried hard not to let it show in her voice.
"What's he done this time?" she enquired
"It's drugs again," replied Kieran, who sounded very frustrated.
Kieran's wayward little brother had a history of petty crime and antisocial behaviour, which was almost always fuelled by alcohol or drugs, so Laura wasn't totally shocked by what Kieran was saying.
"Don't worry, I understand," she replied. "I hope everything is okay. Give your mum a hug from me."
"I will," replied Kieran, "Look, I'm going to have to go, but I'll call you in the morning."
"Okay, darling," replied Laura. "I hope it's not too bad. Text me later if you get a chance." Despondently Laura ended the call and flopped herself down on the sofa ready for a lonely evening watching television.

Chapter 20

Sunday 23rd August

It took Laura and her mother less than twenty minutes before they surrendered to the urge for a coffee. They'd sat together in the same cafe on the first floor of the Tate Modern many times before, but not for at least ten years.
"You seem a bit on edge, dear," her mum remarked as she sipped her piping hot skinny latte with great care not to scold herself. "I assume it's to do with what happened on Thursday. Do want to talk about Billy?"
Laura was relieved her mum had brought up the subject. She knew her mum would be more comfortable talking about the funeral with her dad safely out of earshot but hadn't been quite sure how to raise the subject.
"Well, I do have some questions I want to ask," she replied, keen to get the conversation going, "but only if you're okay with it."
Laura's mum smiled. "I'm fine talking about him, my dear," she replied. "To be honest I'm a little angry with myself that we've never had this conversation before. All said and done he was your father, so I feel a little guilty I never told you more while he was alive."
"You don't need to be," Laura remarked reassuringly. "I can honestly say that I've hardly thought of him in the

last ten years. I don't consider Billy to be my dad, Dad's my dad."
"I know," replied her mother. "But you should have been told more before he died. That was my fault and I'm sorry."
Laura's mum looked genuinely remorseful, which Laura took to mean she did have much more she needed to tell her.
"What do you want to know?" continued Laura's mum.
Laura looked up from her coffee cup. "Did you know he'd been to prison?" she enquired.
"Yes, I did," replied her mother. "It was that which finally caused us to break up. He got five years for fraud. It was terrible."
"What did he do?" Laura asked.
Laura's mother paused, her head tilted to the side and her stare dropped away from Laura's face, giving the impression that she found the question, or rather the answer she was about to give, extremely awkward.
"I don't know all the details," she replied. "It was some sort of clever scam. Well, not so clever, really, as he got caught."
Laura's blank expression indicated she was stunned by what she'd just been told.
Laura's mum once more looked back into her daughter's eyes.
"Billy worked in the bank at Blythwold, it's where I met him. He'd done really well and was building a nice career for himself," recounted her mother. "When you came along, I left my work to look after you. There was no such thing as extended maternity leave in those days. Once you'd had a baby you had a few months to decide whether you wanted to come back, but if you didn't you just left, which is what I did."
"So, you were struggling for money?" said Laura.

"Yes, we were," replied her Mum. "But no more than others in our shoes, and Billy's income just about kept us ticking over."
"Then, what happened?" Laura asked.
"Well," her Mum continued, "what happened was that Billy, unbeknown to me, started to get into debt. He had always liked to gamble, you know, on the horses and a bit of poker with his mates. However, it got out of hand. I don't know how quickly it escalated or exactly how much he owed, but he found himself in deep trouble, owing huge sums of money to some unsavoury people and to dig his way out he started to steal from the bank."
Laura stared back at her mother, hardly able to believe what she was hearing.
"Anyway," continued her mum, who was clearly keen to make a clean breast of everything, "he committed fraud against the bank to extricate himself from the mess he was in."
"So, how much money are we talking about?" Laura asked.
Her mum shrugged her shoulders. "I'm not totally sure how much it came to in total, but when he was caught, they found about twelve instances of him committing fraud and I seem to recall the total debt was over twenty thousand pounds. And that was a lot of money twenty years ago."
"Bloody hell," she finally exclaimed, loud enough for the people at the adjacent tables to stop momentarily and give her disdainful looks. "That's awful," she added.
Laura's mum's face remained sombre and pained.
"When Billy went to prison, your Granddad initially had to help us out financially and if it hadn't been for Mike, I don't know what would have become of us."
Laura could see her mum was not enjoying having to recount the story, but she still needed to know more.

"So, how did you feel when this all came out?" Laura asked.
"I was worried and angry," her mum replied, "but to be honest, I could have got over that. It was the deceit I couldn't cope with. I had absolutely no idea he was gambling so heavily and for him to jeopardise our lives gambling, and then to make it worse by stealing from the bank, was crushing. When he eventually told me, I knew straight away that I could never forgive him. And I never have."
"Did you ever visit him in prison?" Laura asked.
Her mother shook her head. "Never," she replied firmly. "I got a divorce, which he thankfully didn't contest, and the only other time I saw him was when he came around that day when you were about fourteen or fifteen."
"What did he want, when he came that afternoon?" Laura asked.
"He told me he was sorry, that he had found God and he was a changed man," replied her mother.
"I told him it was too late," continued her mum. "Anyway, by then Mike and I were married."
"And that's the last time you saw him?" Laura asked.
"Yes," replied Laura's mum. "I've never seen or heard from him since."
Laura took a few seconds to absorb all she'd just been told.
"When I spoke to his mum at the funeral," Laura added. "She inferred that you and Dad had not told me everything. Is this what she meant?"
Laura's mum shrugged her shoulders. "I've no idea what she was talking about," she replied. "I probably should have told you about the fraud and about Billy going to prison, but as he was out of our lives, I thought it was all best forgotten."

Laura leant over and gave her mum a protracted hug. "That's okay," she remarked as if it was of no consequence. "I'm glad I know everything now, but it changes nothing. Dad's still my dad and all Billy McKenna and I share is genes."
Laura's mum smiled, "Your dad will be pleased to know that things haven't changed, he's not said anything, but I think he has felt a little bit uneasy since he found out about you going to Blythwold."
Laura shook her head. "He's no need to worry," she reassured her mum. "Nothing has changed as far as I'm concerned."
Laura's mum smiled; she was clearly relieved to hear her daughter's words. "Now, let's talk about something else," she remarked.
Laura didn't want to allow the conversation to move on just yet, as she was keen to learn more about Billy McKenna's brother and the circumstances of his death, however, she knew that she'd have her mother's undivided attention for at least two or three more hours, so decided to let it rest for the time being.
"What else?" she asked.
"We could start with Kieran and then your job," her mum replied as she grabbed hold of Laura's arm.

* * *

Kieran Hockley and Mike Eastwood had found themselves a quiet spot on a bench outside the Founders Arms. Having made themselves comfortable under a broad sunshade, they sat back, sipped their pints, and watched the crafts of various shapes and sizes as they chugged back and forth on the river Thames.
"Beats marching around that place looking at rubbish pretending to be art," Mike remarked.

"Absolutely," Kieran agreed. "And the beer's pretty damn good too."
As they spoke the two men made no attempt to make eye contact; they continued to gaze aimlessly at the activity on the busy waterway.
"Tell me, are you and Laura serious about each other?" Mike enquired in a tone that suggested he wasn't too bothered how his question was going to be answered.
"I think so," replied Kieran, who had been taken a little by surprise by Mike's question.
"Think so!" remarked Mike, as if that wasn't a suitable reply.
"What I mean is that I'm very serious about Laura," replied Kieran. "I'm sure she feels the same way, but you'd have to ask her."
Mike nodded as if to show he was satisfied with Kieran's answer.
"I'm amazed there aren't more accidents on the river," Mike announced rather randomly. "There doesn't seem to be any rules out there. They're all over the place."
Kieran thought for a few moments before replying. "I think the only rule is that big boats have the right of way over little boats," he remarked sagely.
Mike nodded. "Yeah, you could be right," he replied before emptying his glass of its contents. "Another pint, young man?"

*　　　*　　　*

Laura and her mother had spent almost three hours in the Tate before they decided to call it a day.
As they ambled down the path towards the Founders Arms, Laura decided to quiz her mum some more.

"At the funeral they mentioned that Billy had a brother," she remarked as casually as she could. "And that he'd died in some sort of accident."
Laura's mum stopped in her tracks and glared back at her daughter. "What did they say about him?" she asked, the inflection on him suggesting that he wasn't a favourite of hers.
"Nothing," replied Laura cautiously. "The Priest just mentioned him in his eulogy. He said he'd died tragically and I was just curious. I hadn't realised Billy McKenna had a brother."
For some reason Laura's words seemed to make her mum a little more relaxed.
"His name was Stephen," she replied. "He was quite a few years older than Billy so I didn't know him that well. Your dad knew him better than me, they played football together I think, when they were younger."
"How did he die?" Laura asked.
"He was drowned at sea just a few months before I had you," replied her mum.
"I see," remarked Laura. "I take it you didn't like him?"
Laura's mum shrugged her shoulders. "I hardly knew him," she replied, "but he wasn't a very nice man – no, I didn't take to him."
Her Mum then gave a faint smile and started once more to wander slowly towards the pub.
Laura took a few quick steps to ensure she caught up. "It's weird you never mentioned Stephen before," she remarked. "But I guess I'll need to talk with Dad about him, if he knew him better."
Laura's mum stopped suddenly and grasped Laura's wrist tightly. Her dark brown pupils, normally so caring and gentle, fixed firmly into Laura's eyes. "Leave it Laura," she commanded. "I can understand why you want to know more about Billy, especially as he died,

but don't start bothering your dad with questions. He's feeling a bit ..." Laura's mum paused for a moment while she tried to find the right word. "He's a bit concerned about the interest you're showing in Billy. I think he's just worried that you'll not see him as your dad anymore."

"That's ridiculous," replied Laura. "Nothing has changed, but I do feel it's time I knew more about Billy McKenna."

Laura's mother nodded. "I understand, I really do," she said, although her piercing stare suggested otherwise. "But please don't start asking your dad any questions about Billy or his family. If you need to know more about them, just ask me."

"Okay," snapped Laura, who was now getting irritated at her mum's reticence to talk about her birth father. "If you say so I'll not mention it again. But just so you know, I will have to go back to Blythwold to talk with his solicitor about the estate and, when I'm there, I'll almost certainly hear more about his life after he left us. I just would have preferred to hear more about the family from you and Dad first."

Laura's mum rolled her eyes to the heavens and gave out a cruel chuckle, "As I've told you already, don't expect him to have a big estate my dear," she remarked rather unkindly. "He wasn't a bad man, but to be honest he was always a bit of a waste of space. I'd be very surprised if Billy left much money, I'm afraid to say. And honestly other than what I told you earlier, there's nothing more either me or your dad can tell you."

Laura wasn't convinced her mum was being totally honest with her but was smart enough to realise she wasn't about to say much more.

"I expect you're right," she replied before giving her mum a reassuring smile. "Anyway, come on let's go and see what those two layabouts are doing," said her mum. As they walked leisurely towards the pub, Laura linked arms with her mum.
"Do you fancy a walk up to Covent Garden later?" remarked Laura.
"Yes, that would be nice," replied her mother. "It's been ages since we last went there."

*   *   *

After meeting Kieran and her dad at the Founders Arms, they all took a walk along the south bank of the Thames, crossed over at Westminster bridge, then back along the Embankment to Cleopatra's Needle, where they stopped to have lunch on one of the boats that was permanently moored up and reborn as a restaurant. They then made their leisurely way to the Strand and on to Covent Garden. With the afternoon punctuated with copious stops at coffee shops, they eventually found themselves at Old Compton Street in Leicester Square just half an hour before the evening performance of Jersey Boys was due to start.
"Here we go," remarked Laura's dad, as he pulled out his mobile and showed Laura the screen.
Laura gave her dad a hug, "You crafty old devil," she remarked. "When did you buy those?"
Looking pleased with himself her dad tapped the side of his nose with his finger. "Wouldn't you like to know," he replied with a broad grin.
"He bought the tickets online a few weeks ago," her mum announced. "He's so chuffed with himself. You know how backward he is with technology."
"I'm well impressed," replied Laura.

"It did take him about twenty minutes," added Laura's mum, "but credit where it's due, he managed it eventually."
As she spoke, they started to feel a few spots of rain, which within seconds, became quite heavy.
"Let's get inside before we get soaked," continued Laura's mum.
"That's good timing," remarked Kieran as he held open the door of the theatre and ushered everyone inside.

*　　　*　　　*

It was almost eleven by the time the taxi stopped outside Laura's house in SW 18.
"It's been great seeing you both," said Laura's dad, as he firmly shook Kieran's hand before giving his daughter a massive squeeze.
Laura kissed her dad's cheek, then hugged her mum.
"Have a safe journey home tomorrow," she told her, as they embraced.
Laura's mum kept tight hold of her only child. "Let me know how everything goes with Billy's estate," she whispered quietly. "I hope you're not too disappointed."
"I will," replied Laura, who kissed her mum before getting out of the taxi.
Even though it was still raining, Kieran and Laura remained on the pavement and waved away the taxi as it drove down Lavenham Road before turning left and disappearing down Merton Road.
"Let's get indoors before we get totally drenched," remarked Kieran.
Laura grabbed her boyfriend's hand tightly and headed off towards the front door.

Once inside, Kieran and Laura enjoyed a long lingering embrace.
"Did you mention America to your parents?" Kieran asked.
Laura shook her head. "No," she replied. "I talked to Mum about Billy McKenna, but I didn't see any point in bringing up anything about the job, now that it's not happening."
Kieran looked a little annoyed. "I've told you, just pack in your job at Meridian and join me. With your experience you'll find something over there in no time."
Laura shook her head. "No," she replied firmly. "I'm sure it's not that easy. I'll need a visa to work there and I'm not sure I'd get one without already having a job lined up before I go."
"So, what are you going to do?" Kieran asked. "You've quit your job at Meridian already, so if you stay here you'll be out of work anyway."
Laura wasn't impressed with the way Kieran was acting, but she didn't fancy arguing with him. "I'll just have to see how it goes tomorrow with Vic," she remarked. "I've not given him my notice in writing so technically I've not resigned. You never know, he may even offer me a raise to get me to stay, after all, he doesn't know the other job offer's been retracted – and I'm certainly not telling him."

Chapter 21

Monday 24th August

The Radcliffe's contingent remained impassive, as they had been for most of Saskia's hour-long pitch.
"Are there any questions?" Saskia enquired confidently.
The four middle-aged men in dark suits exchanged glances with one another but said nothing.
Laura sensed they were almost disappointed to have no obvious area to pick fault with, in content of the revised proposal or Saskia's well executed delivery.
"As you can see," Vic announced, with an assured glint in his eyes, "we took on board all that you said last Thursday, and we are now confident that our proposal will not only match your tight budget restrictions but also deliver the results you require."
Barry Horne, Radcliffe's finance manager nodded his acknowledgement. "Yes, the proposals look much more realistic from a financial perspective," he conceded with due candour. "I'm certainly more than comfortable with the plan and unless any of my colleagues have any questions I'm certainly happy to take this to our board."
Laura knew from her long experience with Radcliffe's that if Barry Horne was happy, they would all be happy. Horne had the ear of the board and was always the key

decision maker in the group, despite the others technically being at a similar level within Radcliffe's."
"In that case thank you for your time, gentlemen," Vic concluded. "We'll await your instructions once you've spoken to the board."
Within a matter of ten minutes, having completed the usual end of meeting niceties, Vic, Laura and Saskia were in the back of a black cab heading back to their office in Victoria.
"That was an amazing pitch," Laura remarked to her friend. "You nailed it that's for sure."
Saskia beamed, "I should bloody well hope so," she replied. "I spent all weekend rehearsing, there was no way I was going to give Barry the ammunition I gave him on Thursday."
Vic had said nothing since they'd got into the taxi, but his relaxed demeanour suggested he was delighted with the outcome.
"What do you think, Vic?" Laura enquired, with an expectant smile that she hoped would encourage him to lavish some sort of praise on Saskia.
"It was a much-improved pitch," he replied, "but that's the level you'll need to maintain as a minimum if you have any ambition to take a more active role with our customers."
Saskia's expression clearly indicated her disappointment at not getting a more generous tribute from the boss, but she tried not to look too disillusioned. "Thank you, Vic," she replied. "Be assured I've learnt from the experience of last Thursday."
Vic smiled and leant forward. "Driver," he said loudly. "Can you pull over at the next tube station."
"Right you are, Guv," replied the driver. "We'll be at Bank in a minute."

Vic turned back to face his two young executives. "As you clearly spent most of your weekend on the pitch, Saskia," he remarked, "why don't you take the afternoon off. You don't need to come back to the office with Laura and me. You can get out here and just head home. I'm sure you should be able to get home from here."
Laura glanced sideways at Saskia. She could see she was shocked at being given time off by Vic – so much so that once the taxi had come to a halt outside Bank tube station, all Saskia could say before she clambered out was, "Thanks Vic," and "I'll see you both tomorrow."
Laura glanced back through the rear window at her shocked friend as the taxicab pulled away towards Mansion House and the Victoria Embankment.
When she turned back to face Vic, Laura could see that he was engrossed in a text message on his mobile. She waited until he'd finished before starting up a conversation.
"I thought Saskia played a blinder today," she remarked.
Vic nodded. "Yes," he replied calmly. "If you do leave us I think she may well be able to step into your shoes. She may not have all your attributes when it comes to presenting but judging from today's performance she'll get there pretty soon."
Laura was eager to have a chance to carry on the discussions with Vic about the job in New York but had hoped he'd start it by making a counteroffer.
She decided to risk her arm. "Are you still considering matching their offer to try and keep me?" she asked, trying hard to sound as relaxed as she could.
Vic shook his head. "No, I've made a decision," he replied.

Laura gazed back at him to wait for his next words, but Vic simply put his head down and started to text on his mobile.
Laura felt uncomfortable. She did not want to appear to be too keen but was desperate to have the discussion before the taxi arrived at the office.
"As I said to you on Friday," she remarked, "I've pretty much made up my mind, so I guess it's just a cosmetic exercise, but I would be interested to know how much you do value me."
Vic let out a cocky snigger but maintained his focus on the screen on his mobile.
Laura waited for Vic to stop messaging. She was now feeling very uncomfortable but didn't want to give Vic any sort of hint that she wanted to stay at Meridian.
Vic, however, appeared to sense her anxiety. He put the mobile in his pocket and stared back at Laura.
"This is the one and only offer I'll be making, Laura," he said firmly. "If you don't feel it's enough then all I can say is good luck at McCauley and Bernstein's."
Laura could tell Vic meant it. "So what's your counteroffer?" she asked.
Vic smiled. "If you stay, I'll give you a five per cent salary increase immediately and a further ten percent at the next salary review."
"McCauley's offer was more," replied Laura.
"I know," remarked Vic with a smile. "But moving to the US will be a great risk for you. You're well set here, who knows one day you may even have my job."
Laura wanted to bite Vic's hand off but felt unable to do so without giving him reason to twig that something was amiss with the McCauley's offer. She was just about to say thank you I'll think about it, when Vic spoke again.
"As part of that offer I'd also like to make a few other minor changes," he continued.

"Which are?" enquired Laura who sensed her boss was about to add some additional responsibilities on her.
"I want you to hand over a few of your accounts, including Radcliffe's, to Saskia," Vic continued. "I think you're right; her performance today shows that she's ready for more responsibility."
"How many accounts?" enquired Laura.
Vic shrugged his shoulders. "I'm not totally sure at the moment," he remarked. "But I'd want you to work more closely with the creative team, so I'd say about half."
Laura's forehead wrinkled as she tried to make sense of what Vic was saying.
"Apart from the extra money, which is still less than McCauley's were offering," Laura remarked, her voice indicating that she was baffled by what Vic had outlined, "if I stay, my role looks like it would be almost a demotion."
Vic shook his head. "It's not how I see it," he replied. "It clearly allows me to become less dependent on just one account manager, I grant you that. However, you'll still be top dog, Laura. Anyway what do you mean were offering you, have McCauley's withdrawn their offer?"
Laura was annoyed with herself for making such a stupid slip of the tongue. "No, the offers still there," she lied.
Vic smiled confidently. "Well that's my offer," he remarked. "I want you to stay but I fully understand if you decide to seek your fortune in America."
As he spoke, the taxi arrived at the Meridian offices in Victoria.
"Why don't you take a couple days off to think about it," Vic added. "We will cope for a few days without you and I'm sure there are many things you still need to do regarding your father's estate. Why don't we get together on Thursday morning in my office? If you still

want to go I'll need your resignation in writing, if not then we can talk with Saskia and the rest of the team about the changes and move on. How does that sound?"
Laura was confused. She had not expected Vic to want to reshape her role as part of any counteroffer, and although she was delighted for Saskia, she could not help feeling that if she stayed her position at Meridian would be less interesting and carry less prestige within the team. However, circumstances meant she had little alternative other than go along with Vic's suggestion.
"I'm not sure what you're offering me will cut it, Vic," she remarked trying hard to appear to be totally disinterested. "However, you've always been straight with me so I will take a few days off to think it over."
"Excellent," replied Vic as he clambered out the taxi and opened his wallet to pay the driver. "You may as well stay in the cab," he added before Laura could also disembark. "Here's another forty quid, Driver. That should easily cover you taking my colleague on to Southfields."
The driver nodded, took the two twenty-pound notes and Laura, as instructed, sat down again in her seat.
"See you on Thursday," shouted Vic before shutting the taxi door and walking up the office steps.
For the next twenty minutes Laura sat silently in the taxi, trying to work out the implications of what Vic had just been saying. Her overall feeling was one of relief that her job was still available at Meridian and she was going to get a salary increase. However, she could not help sensing that her position at Meridian was going to be much weaker from now on, which made Laura feel extremely uneasy.

Part Four

The Role Model - Vic's Tale

Chapter 22

Monday 17th August

There were just two driving forces in Vic Chakraborty's life.
The first was a hunger to make his fortune. Although he was still in his thirties, Vic had already ticked that box, having all the material trappings he needed to demonstrate his achievements.
Vic's other driving force was an unquenchable thirst for women.
Of the two, his obsession for the latter was the stronger. Ever since the age of seventeen, when he and some of his fellow borders at Eton, had first managed to blag their way into the downmarket strip clubs in Slough, Vic's carnal fascination with women had become insatiable. Strip clubs, lap dancing bars and escort agencies featured large in Vic's life and the financial successes he'd had in business only served to fuel his passion and allow him even greater ability to indulge in his sexual fervour.
Even his marriage to Vivien, the pretty home counties girl from a well-connected family in the city and the delightful twin girls that she'd bore him, could only serve to temporarily postpone Vic's fixation with sex, or more specifically his involvement in paid sex. Within little more than three or four years of him making his wedding vows with Vivien, in the Catholic Church

which had been a non-negotiable condition of their union, Vic found himself becoming once more immersed, with evenings spent in lap dancing bars, where his desires could be satisfied at a price his wallet could easily withstand.

Vic was not stupid and had always been very careful to ensure that his unsavoury pastime remained tightly concealed from his business associates and work colleagues at Meridian, a deception which he'd managed for several years with consummate ease. Even outside of work there were very few people who knew what Vic mainly did in his spare time.

Vivien, however, was nobody's fool. She had found out quite early on in their marriage about Vic's antics. Her reaction at first was one of anger and disbelief, but once she'd realised there was little she could do to stop him, Vivien had resigned herself to the fact that this was how life would be for her and, as a result, had focussed all her energies on her children, her expensive hobbies and anything else she could think of to spend her unfaithful husband's vast salary.

After over ten years of marriage their routines were now almost set in stone, with Vic spending most of the week in a small flat he'd rented in London, then at the family's large Surrey home from Saturday afternoon to Monday morning. Vic did come home for the occasional night during the week if there was a dinner party, or a function at the children's school, but most weeks his nights were spent in London.

For her part, other than for family gatherings and important business dinners, Vivien tried as best she could to avoid any contact with her wayward husband, spending a great amount of her time at the tennis club, riding one of the several horses she'd bought over the years or shopping with her socialite girlfriends.

Despite several attempts by Vic to broach the subject of a divorce, Vivien remained consistently stubborn in her refusal to allow him to exit their marriage. This was partially on religious grounds, but mostly due to her desire to make her unfaithful husband as miserable as she could, and with Meridian having been largely funded by capital from Vivien and her family, Vic was in no position to demand too strongly.

On that particular Monday morning Vic was in a foul mood. On the evening before he'd once again tried to talk to Vivien about a divorce, but, again, she'd said no – and to make him even more angry she'd casually dropped into the conversation that she'd just booked flights to take her, the girls and Kasia, the girls' nanny, on a three week break to the west coast of America, and they were due to leave at the end of October.

When Vic arrived at the office that morning, he could hardly even bring himself to say hello to Brenda, his PA, and spent the morning ensconced in his office poring over the many emails that had been sent to him in the past few days.

"No interruptions this morning," Vic instructed Brenda when she did try to enter his sanctuary to see if he wanted a coffee. "And, unless it's my father, I'm not taking any calls, either."

"Right you are," replied Brenda who, despite only being in the job a matter of weeks, was already well acquainted with her boss's childlike mood swings.

* * *

As the morning progressed, Vic's mood improved.

By ten o'clock he'd got through most of his emails, and, to his delight, he'd received nothing other than good news – a very rare occurrence for a Monday morning.

By midday the company accountant had sent him the preliminary report of the last quarter's trading and from these interim figures they'd not had record sales in the quarter, but their margins were holding up well and the number of new clients they'd engaged had increased by fifteen percent over the corresponding period the year before.
Vic sat back in his chair and started to scribble down on his desk pad his best estimate of how these results would impact on his annual bonus. The results suggested that unless there was a disaster in the final quarter, he was well on the way to getting another six-figure bonus when the financial year ended at the end of October.
Vic sat back in the chair and placed his hands behind his head.
"Cause for a little celebration," he muttered to himself before he took out a mobile phone from his desk and dialled an all too familiar number.
The mobile rang for a few seconds before an equally familiar voice answered in a deep eastern European accent. "Hello, Svetlana speaking."
"Hi, babe, it's Rex," announced Vic. "Are you free tonight?"
Svetlana giggled seductively down the phone. "For you, Rex, you know I'm always available."
Vic smiled. "How about we meet at Antonio's at eight and then take it from there?"
"How about we skip Antonio's, and you get here for eight?" she replied suggestively. "I'll cook you something if you're hungry, although I suspect you don't want me for my cooking."
Vic laughed loudly. "I'll see you at eight, babe," he replied, "and don't worry, I'll eat before I come over."
"Don't eat too much," Svetlana teased. "I don't want you sleepy".

"Don't you worry, my dear," replied Vic eagerly. "I'll be as lively as ever."
Vic didn't wait for a response. He turned off the mobile and put it back into the desk drawer.
Vic, or rather Rex, as he called himself when with his beautiful, leggy, blonde Czech mistress, had been seeing Svetlana at least once a week for the last eighteen months. He knew that she had other male relationships, but the three thousand pounds a month he gave her to help pay her rent on her London apartment guaranteed that Svetlana was his property when he wanted – which was exactly how Vic liked it!
At two o'clock, buoyed by the good news he'd received that morning, Vic decided to vacate his office to find out if Brenda had any messages for him.
"Just the one," replied Brenda. "Laura Eastwood called to see if she could run through the Radcliffe's presentation with you."
"It will have to be in the next couple of hours," he replied. "I'm planning on leaving at five to go to the gym, then I have a dinner appointment."
"No," replied Brenda. "Laura suggested tomorrow morning. She's with the team again at three thirty to finalise things, so I can't see her finishing until at least five."
Vic laughed. "Knowing Laura, it will be more like seven thirty, she's very much into the detail is our Laura, that's why she's so damn good at her job."
Brenda smiled. "You're right," she conceded.
"Tell her I'll call her in the morning," Vic replied before disappearing back into his office.

*   *   *

With every expectation of an exhausting evening with Svetlana in front of him, Vic left the office at around four thirty. He'd skipped lunch, so decided to go first to Antonio's restaurant for a light meal before moving on to the gym for a light work-out and a swim - then on to Svetlana's.
It was Saskia's shapely legs that Vic spotted up on the mezzanine floor when he was pumping iron in the gym. He had no idea who they belonged to until she clambered down off the cross trainer.
Vic chose to ignore her. He'd an inclination that Saskia may have had a bit of a crush on him, if what Brenda had told him was true, but until then it meant little to him. He thought she was attractive, although not in the same way as Svetlana, but his golden rule was not to get involved with anyone at work – a philosophy that had worked well for him so far and one he was not about to break with Saskia. In any case, Vic knew Saskia smoked, which he hated.
If Vic was going to try his luck with one of the team, it would be Laura he'd choose as he knew she would prove to be a far greater challenge than her chum, Saskia.
After three or four lengths of the small swimming pool, Vic noticed Saskia as she slid into the pool in a tight-fitting swimsuit that left little to Vic's already fertile imagination.
"What the hell," he muttered to himself. "Let's have a bit of fun." Within a few minutes the pair had struck up a conversation, and within ten more minutes they were sat next to each other in the spa, chatting as if they were old friends.
"Where do you see your next move with Meridian?" Vic enquired, knowing full well what Saskia's game was.

"I'm not sure," Saskia replied. "I'd really like to make a pitch to one of our clients. The only issue is that Laura's so good it's almost impossible to get a chance."
Vic nodded. "Yes, Laura's very strong in those scenarios," he agreed. "She's a real asset to the company. We're lucky to have her."
Saskia smiled sweetly back at the boss. "Absolutely," she added. "It would be awful if she ever left."
Vic was a little taken aback by Saskia's reply. He knew the pair were close friends, so he assumed Saskia knew something. "Is there something I should know?" he asked.
Neither Saskia's theatrical shake of her head nor her denial did anything to pacify Vic. And when Saskia then continued by suggesting that nobody was irreplaceable, Vic knew for sure something was going on. Despite his concerns, he had no intention of letting Saskia know her words had made him uneasy, so just smiled back at her. As he pondered what he'd just heard, Saskia stood up and made her attempt at a seductive exit.
Vic remained in the spa for a few more minutes while he considered what Saskia had just intimated. He certainly did not want to lose Laura.
He spent the time it took him to get showered, changed and travel over to Svetlana's to hatch a plan to minimise the impact on the business if Laura was to leave.
However, once he arrived at the apartment and laid eyes on his Czech beauty, who, as always, looked amazing, Vic immediately forgot Laura Eastwood even existed.

Chapter 23

Tuesday 18th August

Vic arrived at the office early and headed straight for Saskia's desk.
"How do you fancy leading the Radcliffe's presentation on Thursday?" he enquired.
Saskia looked shocked but delighted.
"What about Laura?" she replied.
"Oh, she'll be with you, but I want you to lead. Is that okay?" said Vic, his teeth gleaming as he replied.
"Absolutely," remarked Saskia. "Thanks, Vic!"
Smug that his plan was starting to take shape, Vic wandered up to his office, where he waited for half an hour before summoning Laura to show him her proposed pitch – not that she was ever going to make it.
Vic had always had a thing for Laura. She was by far his best performer, but when they were together his thoughts invariably strayed from her abilities as an account executive. He was far more interested in her figure, her eyes and the reoccurring thought of what she would look like naked, than the quality of her work and the value she was to the business. However, he'd always maintained a professional relationship with Laura. There was no way he'd ever do anything so foolhardy as to try it on with her. Firstly, knowing Laura, he figured the chances of any approach by him failing were quite high and if he did fail, or if it got out, he knew the consequences for him would be significant.

During Laura's presentation he deliberately interrupted her continuously, hoping to get her flustered. This was a game he liked to play, but, as always, Laura was totally prepared and whatever question he threw at her she was able to answer with consummate ease – much to Vic's annoyance. As her pitch came to its conclusion, Vic realised, once more, that here he had an irreplaceable asset, and one which he wasn't prepared to lose without a fight.

"Is there anything, I haven't explained adequately?" Laura said as she always did at the end of her pitches. And her confident smile indicated quite clearly that she expected the answer to be no; which, of course, it was. Vic was fully expecting Laura to finish in this way – he'd heard enough of her pitches to know her style. As he'd planned, he decided to remain silent at this juncture which he expected would cause Laura to feel a little anxious. He was right.

When Laura had asked if there was anything wrong, Vic had given the reply he'd rehearsed in his head.

"With the presentation, no!" he'd told her. "As always, Laura, you've done a great job."

And when Laura had said, "It was a team effort. For sure, I'm the leader and the spokesperson, but, as always, it's been a team effort," her words played straight into Vic's hands.

"Talking of your team," he remarked. "I think it's time to develop some of the team members. Why don't we get one of them to make the pitch on Thursday?"

Vic took a great deal of pleasure in seeing Laura's smile disappear and her forehead crease as she wrestled with what he'd just said.

"I'm not sure this is the right presentation to give someone else," she argued, her voice showing clear signs of frustration. "Radcliffe's are one of our biggest

accounts. Don't you think it would make sense to try them out on one of the smaller clients?"
Vic was enjoying seeing Laura unusually stressed. He opened his arms out wide and offered Laura a broad smile. "I don't want you to take this the wrong way, Laura," he remarked reassuringly. "You're clearly our number one account manager. I just want to give some of the others a bit more experience. I'd still want you there in case things start to go pear shaped, but I do want to give someone else a chance to show what they are made of."
"If that's what you want," Laura remarked with a half-hearted smile, which just demonstrated to Vic that she was unhappy. "So, who do you want to lead on Thursday?"
Vic ran his hand over the short black stubble on his chin to try and give the impression that he was only now considering who that should be.
"What about Saskia?" he asked. "You went to college with her, didn't you. Do you think she's ready?"
"If you're saying you want to try someone else then I'd agree, it has to be Saskia," Laura replied begrudgingly.
"Then we're agreed," remarked Vic triumphantly, as he rose from his chair and made his way to the door.
What Vic was not prepared for was Laura asking for Thursday off to attend her father's funeral. This took Vic completely by surprise but given the circumstances he felt he had no alternative but to agree.
When Laura had assured him that Saskia would be word perfect, Vic was not convinced, but tried hard to ensure a positive smile remained on his face.
Vic left the room angry and frustrated that the plan he'd concocted on the previous evening had not worked out. And to make it worse, he'd now have to sit through the pitch to Radcliffe's.

He stormed into his office, slamming the door behind him which made Brenda, jump a few inches out of her seat.
"That will be no interruptions today, either," Brenda muttered to herself with a wry smile.

Chapter 24

Thursday 20th August

Vic had spent Wednesday evening at the Fez Club, one of his favourite lap dancing bars in London. By his standards it had been a fairly quiet evening, although it was still nearly two in the morning by the time he arrived back at his apartment having spent several hundred pounds on champagne and table dances.
Vic, fortunately, needed little sleep, so, by eight thirty when he arrived at the office, nobody would have ever known what he'd been doing less than eight hours earlier.
As they'd agreed, Vic met Saskia in reception and the pair drove in his bright red Audi TT across London for their eleven o'clock meeting at Radcliffe's.
At the start of the journey Vic attempted to make conversation with Saskia. Although she responded to a degree it was clear to him that Saskia's mind was elsewhere; probably nerves, he reasoned.
With an uncharacteristic sign of empathy, Vic decided to leave her to her thoughts and switched radio four on, which he listened to with occasional lapses in concentration as he studied Saskia's bare legs protruding from the inappropriately short skirt she'd selected for the meeting.

The traffic was, as always, slow, but they'd left early enough to allow themselves to arrive at Radcliffe's offices before the agreed time.

* * *

"Laura's not joining us today?" enquired each of the Radcliffe's team as they entered the meeting room.
"No," replied Vic each time. "She's had to attend her father's funeral at very short notice, so it's just me and Saskia today, I'm afraid."
Saskia's pitch started well. To Vic's surprise and delight she came across as a confident operator who delivered the presentation with a surety that even Laura would have found hard to match.
It was on the half-hour mark when things started to slide. A totally innocuous question from Barry Horne on the costing, seemed to totally floor Saskia, which was bad enough, but to compound matters, instead of saying I'm not one hundred per cent sure and agreeing to check and get back to him, Saskia concocted an answer which was so obviously inaccurate that it served to destroy all the good work she'd done before.
Sensing blood, the previously sedate line of grey suited Radcliffe's managers took this as their prompt to interrupt Saskia with alarming frequency, which she tried hard to handle but failed miserably, much to Vic's embarrassment and annoyance.
On more than one occasion Vic had to intervene to bring some calm to matters and by the time the presentation was over, Radcliffe's were so disillusioned that it took all Vic's skill to get them to agree to allow his team to regroup and present again, the following Monday.

* * *

During the drive back to the office, Saskia attempted to play down how bad the presentation had been, but Vic was having none of it.
"I've never experienced anything like that before," he told Saskia. "Quite honestly, I don't understand what you were playing at. Either Laura didn't brief you properly or you're just not up to the task."
Saskia didn't dare reply; she knew full well whatever she said was unlikely to improve matters.
For the rest of the journey, it was Vic's turn to switch on the silent treatment, which remained in force until he parked up outside the office.
"I want to have a breakfast meeting for the full team who worked on the pitch at seven thirty, tomorrow morning," he shouted. "Make sure everyone knows, including Laura. Actually, don't worry about Laura, I'll call her myself."

* * *

Vic remained in a stinking mood for the rest of the day. Talking with Laura didn't help matters either. Her pathetic attempts to defend her friend and suggest the failure was down to the whole team served only to rile Vic even more. Fortunately for Vic the usual antidote for a bad day was just a phone call away using his secret mobile phone and his alter ego, Rex.

Chapter 25

Friday 21st August

"Good morning, Vic," Laura announced, too cheerful by half for Vic's liking.
He slowly raised his eyes from the small computer screen that had, for the previous twenty minutes, kept him engrossed. "Glad to see you're on time," he replied.
"So, it didn't go too brilliantly yesterday," Laura continued.
Vic was still livid. "It was a total cock up!" he replied in his usual blunt, uncompromising manner.
"Well, it can't have been so bad, or they'd have not given us the chance to re-pitch," she replied. "And I think it's only fair that we allow Saskia to lead again. If we replace her, we're as good as telling Radcliffe's and Saskia that she's not up to the job."
Vic was finding it very difficult to control his temper. "Laura," he exclaimed, "she was a total disaster. If she'd been properly prepared, we would not be in this mess. Did you not hear what I said to you on the phone last night? Saskia isn't ready to be a front-line presenter. Yesterday she was appalling!"
When Laura told him that she'd been offered a position in New York, Vic's initial emotion was one of anger. Not so much with Laura, mostly with himself. In allowing her to become so entrenched in Meridian's best accounts he'd broken a fundamental rule of business;

he'd become too reliant on one person. Now, with the prospect of Laura leaving, he feared the worst. However, Vic was an accomplished negotiator and there was no way he was going to show Laura his true feelings. He kept calm and tried to conceal the distress he felt inside.
"You said there were a few things you wanted to tell me," he said, trying hard to sound as relaxed as he could. "What other pronouncements do you have?"
"Well, given that I'm going to be leaving," Laura said as if she were reciting a statement she'd obviously prepared earlier. "It's surely only sensible to allow my successor time to get to know my accounts while I'm still here to assist her. And although Saskia may have had a bad day yesterday, she's got what it takes to be a great account manager, so why don't we use the next three months to bed her in?"
Vic found himself laughing. He was keen not to lose his temper and maybe run the risk of saying something he'd later regret – after all, he did want to keep Laura. However, he was also determined to take control of the situation. He rested his head on the palm of his right hand. "Okay, I'll do you a deal, Laura," he remarked, thinking quickly on his feet. "I will allow your buddy to lead on Monday but there are three conditions."
"Which are?" Laura replied.
Upon hearing his first two terms, Vic got the impression that Laura was happy with the deal.
It was the third condition that was key to Vic. So, when Laura asked him what it was, Vic was keen to ensure she understood clearly.
"That you don't tell anyone else here or any of our clients about your decision until at least after the Radcliffe's presentation has been concluded on Monday," he told her.

To his delight, Laura agreed with no argument whatsoever.
Vic was pleased the delay would give him the weekend to work out what to do. "Then I'll agree to allow Saskia to lead on Monday," he conceded.
Before Laura made her exit, Vic wanted to tell Laura about his encounter with Saskia at the gym. He was fairly certain Saskia would not have mentioned it to Laura and the look of astonishment on her face only confirmed what he already expected.
Vic knew full well that this piece of news was likely to cause an issue between the pair, a situation he took great delight in knowing he'd created.
As soon as Laura told him it was McCauley and Bernstein's who'd made her the offer, Vic couldn't wait to get out of the room, and he departed at the earliest opportunity.
As he sat down in his chair and opened the piece of paper where Laura had scribbled down her new salary, Vic chuckled to himself. He gazed at his watch.
It would be about four more hours before he could speak with his old friend Ben McCauley, the son of one of the founders of McCauley and Bernstein's.
Vic and Ben had been at university together and although they were not close friends by any means, they did share one passion – for female escorts and lap dancing bars.
Ben was now on the board at McCauley and Bernstein's and Vic was confident that the entertainment he'd sorted out for Ben on the American's last visit to London earlier in the year, wouldn't be something the rest of the board of such a prestigious and ethically driven organisation would be keen to discover.
In Vic's mind a deal was almost inevitable!

Chapter 26

Monday 24th August

By normal standards Vic's weekend was relatively pleasant.
Vivien was civil almost to the point of being friendly and with the weather being warm and dry, Vic had taken the opportunity to take the twins to the local theme park, where he spoiled them with rides, ice creams and anything else that took their fancy.
Although his relationship with Vivien had cooled years before, he adored his girls, which they reciprocated in full, especially when dad was in one of his rare, good moods – as he certainly appeared to be over the weekend.
When Vic arrived at the office that Monday morning he was still in a happy frame of mind and keen to talk with Laura, knowing as he did that there was no longer an opening for her McCauley and Bernstein's.
But before he could take pleasure in seeing the potential defector squirm as she attempted to retain her position at Meridian, there was the not so small matter of the pitch to Radcliffe's, and Vic's confidence in the ability of the curvaceous Saskia to recover the account was low.

*　　*　　*

To Vic's surprise and delight, Saskia's performance was outstanding.
While Laura gushed with praise for Saskia in the taxi as they headed back to the office, Vic deliberately stayed silent. He was happy to let them congratulate each other but didn't want the two ladies to realise just how impressed he also was with Saskia's performance, well not Saskia anyway.
It was only when Laura asked him outright that he commented.
"It was a much-improved pitch," he reluctantly replied trying hard not to go too overboard, "but that's the level you'll need to maintain as a minimum if you have any ambition to take a more active role with our customers."
"Thank you, Vic," Saskia replied. "Be assured I've learnt from the experience of last Thursday."
Vic couldn't wait any longer. He was desperate to get Laura alone to discuss the McCauley's job.
With that in mind, he instructed the driver to pull over at Bank station and, as pleasantly as he could, made sure Saskia got out of the car.
By the look on their faces this seemingly snap decision to drop Saskia at the tube station and give her the afternoon off had come as a big shock to both ladies, neither realising his real motivation was to be alone with Laura.
Vic wanted to make Laura uneasy, so he pretended to be messaging on his mobile for a good three or four minutes, which he knew would seem a long time to Laura.
When Laura did break the silence and suggest that her chum had "played a blinder," he just nodded.

"If you do leave us, I think she may well be able to step into your shoes," he remarked mischievously. "She may not have all your attributes when it comes to presenting, but judging from today's performance, she'll get there pretty soon."
Vic was surprised at how calm Laura appeared and impressed when she tried to maintain that the offer still stood.
"Are you still considering a counteroffer to try and keep me?" Laura asked.
"No, I've made a decision," Vic replied coolly before again pretending to text on his mobile.
Out of the corner of his eye he could see Laura was looking very uncomfortable, and Vic was loving it.
"As I said to you on Friday," Laura continued, "I've pretty much made up my mind, so I guess it's just a cosmetic exercise, but I would be interested to know how much you do value me."
Vic had to admire her bare faced cheek but maintained his focus on the screen on his mobile.
Vic eventually put his mobile in his pocket, stared back at Laura and made his offer. As he outlined the proposal, he could see that Laura was initially relived. As well she should be, he thought. But once he started to share with her the conditions which Laura knew full well she'd have to accept if she wanted to stay with Meridian, he could see Laura's emotions change.
Vic knew Laura would hate the terms he was imposing, but he didn't care. In his eyes she had to be penalised for trying to leave, she had to know who the boss was. Laura's wrinkled forehead confirmed that his punishment had hit home hard, and he was not at all surprised when Laura tried to bluff her way out of the situation Vic was creating and reinstate the status quo.

Knowing he was firmly in the driving seat, Vic wasn't about to budge. "Well, that's my offer," he remarked with a smile. "I want you to stay but I fully understand if you decide to seek your fortune in America."
With perfect timing the taxi arrived at the Meridian offices in Victoria just as Vic finished his sentence. He couldn't have planned it better. "Why don't you take a few days off to think about it," he heard himself saying, a tactic he decided on the fly; but knowing the time would serve only to allow Laura to realise it was her only way out, a gesture he felt happy to make.
"We will cope for a few days without you and I'm sure there are many things you still need to do regarding your father's estate. Why don't we get together on Thursday morning, in my office? If you still want to go, I'll need your resignation in writing, if not then we can talk with Saskia and the rest of the team about the changes and move on. How does that sound?"
He could see that Laura wasn't happy, but that only heightened his sadistic pleasure.
"I'm not sure what you're offering me will cut it, Vic," she remarked trying hard to stick to the pretence that she still had options. "However, you've always been straight with me so I will take a few days off to think it over."
"Excellent," replied Vic who felt pleased with himself at how the conversation had gone and even more delighted when he thought of the anguish his terms would cause Laura over the next few days. "You may as well stay in the cab."
Vic paid the cab driver an extra forty pounds to take Laura home, before cheerily walking up the office steps, not even bothering to look back at the cab as it drove off in the direction of Southfields.

Part Five

Laura's Story

A Day At The Seaside

Chapter 27

Tuesday 25th August

Laura hadn't had the best of evenings, despite being told her job was still available at Meridian and being offered a five per cent salary increase, she felt troubled and uncomfortable with the conditions that Vic had stipulated.

Even though Kieran had tried hard to reassure her, Laura was still uptight and out of sorts when she was awoken by her boyfriend entering the bedroom with a hot cup of tea.

"Good morning," Kieran said softly as he sat down beside her on the bed and rested the cup on the bedside table. "Did you sleep well?"

The true answer was no, but Laura didn't want him to feel she was harping on about her job all the time, so she lied.

"I did," she replied as her arm pulled her boyfriend towards her. "You smell nice," she added as the fresh sharp smell of Kieran's shower gel reached her nostrils. "How long have you been up?"

Kieran bent down and kissed her warm mouth. "About an hour or so," he replied as soon as their lips parted. "It is nearly eight after all, you're usually at your desk by now."

Laura smiled and pulled Kieran even closer. "I guess that's one good thing that came out of yesterday's meeting with Vic. I get a few days off."
"That's more like it," remarked Kieran, who appeared relieved to see Laura taking a more positive slant on things. "And as you're going to be kicking your heels around for the next couple of days, I thought I'd take a few days off, too and we could do something together."
Laura's eyes widened and a broad smile burst across her face. "Why not start by staying in bed all morning," she suggested. "That's if you're up to it!"
"I imagine I can cope," replied Kieran as he swiftly clambered back into bed. "I can't have you feeling short-changed in the romance department."

*   *   *

It was ten thirty before Laura finally got out of bed, it would have been even later had her mobile not vibrated so loudly on the bedside cabinet.
"Hello," said Laura as she put the mobile to her ear and slumped back onto the bed.
"Oh, hi Sas," she said while at the same time raising her eyebrows to indicate to Kieran, she wasn't that keen to talk to her friend.
"Where are you?" her friend whispered down the phone.
"I've taken a few days off," Laura said. "I'll be back on Thursday."
"That was sudden," replied Saskia. "Is there anything wrong?"
"No, it's just I wanted to spend a bit of time with Kieran, and he's suddenly found himself free today and tomorrow, so I decided to take the days off, too," she lied.

"Oh," remarked Saskia, who by her tone was clearly not convinced. "Did you talk much with Vic after I got out of the car yesterday?"
Laura wasn't keen to have a long conversation and didn't want the subject drifting to the job at McCauley's, but she knew if she stayed on the phone, it might. "Sas, is it okay if we talk later today or tomorrow?" she remarked quite bluntly. "Kieran's chivvying me to get moving, so I'm going to have to go."
"Okay," replied Saskia, who sounded disappointed that Laura was cutting short their conversation. "I'm in the office all day, so call me when you can."
"If it is today, it will probably be this evening, at the earliest," Laura announced. "Are you planning to go to the gym again tonight?"
There was a brief pause from the end of the phone before Saskia replied.
"I may do," she remarked. "I'm not sure."
It was Laura's turn to pause. "Vic informs me that he and you share the same gym," she remarked. "You didn't tell me that."
"Oh, didn't I?" Saskia responded. "Isn't that a coincidence?"
From her reply, Laura could sense that Saskia was struggling to play down the association.
"It is," replied Laura knowingly. "As long as he's not your latest conquest, Saskia," she continued. "You know it's not wise to mix business and pleasure, so be careful not to get too intimate in the hot tub."
"No chance," replied Saskia, as convincingly as she could. "Vic's certainly not my type."
Laura smiled. From her experience she was coming to the conclusion that as far as Saskia was concerned, any male under forty with a pulse was her type.

"Look, I'm going to have to go," Laura said. "I'll call you when I can."
Saskia just had time to say bye before Laura ended the call.
"What was that all about?" Kieran asked.
Laura smiled. "My friend is trying to climb the greasy pole," she replied. "I only hope she knows what she's doing."
Kieran didn't fully understand what Laura was alluding to but wasn't inquisitive enough to push for the details.
"So, what shall we do for the next two days?" Kieran asked.
Laura paused for a moment. "Why don't we take a trip to the seaside," she remarked. "I think it'll do us both good."
Kieran smiled. "And do I take it that the specific seaside town you have in mind is in Suffolk?"
Laura smiled and shrugged her shoulders. "We may as well check out what vast sum of money I've inherited while we're taking in the sea air," she replied self-righteously.
Kieran shook his head. "Didn't I just hear you telling Saskia not to mix business with pleasure," he remarked.
"That was completely different," replied Laura.

Chapter 28

Within a couple of hours Laura and her boyfriend were heading east on the M25 in Kieran's open top BMW Z4 Roadster, his much-loved toy.
As they headed past the turn off for the M23, Laura slumped down in her seat to try and reduce the noise of the traffic as she dialled the number for the Black Swan hotel.
Kieran couldn't hear everything she was saying, but he worked out that Laura's confident assertion from earlier, regarding there being plenty of rooms available, was a little wide of the mark.
"Are we okay for this evening?" he asked as soon as she'd finished making the call.
"Yes," replied Laura. "But not in the Black Swan. Apparently, they are fully booked tonight, but they've a sea view room for us at the Admiral pub, which is just down the road and is part of the same group."
"That sounds good to me," replied Kieran with a grin. "I can't think of anything better than spending the evening with an heiress in a sea view room knowing there's an endless supply of beer downstairs."
Laura smiled knowingly. "Trust you," she replied with an air of admonishment in her voice. "I sometimes think beer is the main thing on your mind."
"I can think of worse things," replied Kieran as he put his foot down hard on the accelerator and quickly manoeuvred the car into the fast lane.

Laura closed her eyes and put her head back on the seat rest, she always felt happier when she was with Kieran and was really looking forward to spending a couple of days away with him.

*   *   *

Within three hours of leaving SW18, Kieran's dark blue BMW arrived in the sleepy seaside town of Blythwold. Laura, who had slept for most of the journey, opened her eyes as they passed the 'Welcome to Blythwold' sign, which also announced that the seaside town was twinned with a German town called Brunner and some unpronounceable town in France which also began with a B.

"That was quick," Laura announced as she blinked and yawned.

"Only if you were asleep for two thirds of the way," remarked Kieran with a wry smile. "Now where's this bloody pub?"

Laura tried to get her bearings. "I've only been here once," she replied, as if she was expecting the task to be difficult. "But it's a tiny town and the pub is right by the seafront, so it can't be that hard to find."

Kieran slowed the car down, to prevent them from missing an important turning.

"Shall I just stay on this road?" he asked.

Laura hadn't paid any attention at all when she had arrived in the town on the Thursday before, so try as she might, she couldn't remember any of the shops and houses they passed.

"Well?" Kieran remarked curtly when he received no response.

Laura was about to let fly with a less than polite response when, to her left, she spotted the tower of St

Steven's church peeking through between two of the houses.

"There's the church," she remarked, the relief audible in her voice. "Just carry on a bit. The hotel must be up here on the left, so the Admiral pub can't be that far away."
Within a matter of moments, they reached the Black Swan, which looked much more inviting than Laura had remembered.
"According to the man I spoke to earlier, the Admiral is at the end of a small road just after the Black Swan," Laura continued. "I think he said it was Stud Road."
Kieran eased the car into second gear and slowed right down.
"Stamp Lane?" he shouted as he read out the street sign on the first road they came across.
"Could be," replied Laura. "It was hard to hear everything he was saying on the phone, with the wind rushing passed us. Let's go down there."
Kieran indicated and turned down the narrow lane.
"I hope it is here," he remarked. "I don't fancy having to reverse back if you've got it wrong."
Laura slowly turned her head to face him and gave him a scornful look. "I see," she snapped. "If it's wrong then it's my fault, is it?"
There was no need to prolong the debate, as within a few moments they spotted a large colourful sign waving gently in the breeze above the road to indicate they had reached the Admiral public house.
"Here we are," said Kieran as the wonderful smell of hops and barley filled his nostrils. "I'm looking forward to staying there."

Laura shook her head, “Let’s get checked in before you start sampling the local ale,” she remarked in a tone more befitting to a grown up chastising an unruly child. Kieran laughed. “Whatever you say, my dear,” he replied with sham subservience.

Chapter 29

Their room at the Admiral was, at first glance, exactly as Laura expected. It had a small threadbare rug which covered just the centre of the room and was furnished with ancient drawers and a huge dark wooden wardrobe. However, it was large enough, it smelt fresh and clean and the plusses for Laura were the massive oak four-poster bed which dominated the room and a spectacular vista from the window out onto the North Sea.
"This is amazing!" Laura announced as they deposited their bags on the dark wooden floor. "What a view!"
Kieran was more preoccupied with the four-poster bed. "This will be interesting," he remarked as he bounced up and down on the lumpy mattress.
Laura opened the window and breathed in the warm salty sea air. "I really like it here," she announced. "It's so laid back compared to London."
Kieran frowned. "We've only been here ten minutes. Don't tell me, you're not thinking of moving out here, are you?" he asked.
"Good god no!" replied Laura. "But it would be great to have a bolt hole here wouldn't it!"
Kieran wasn't so convinced. "Maybe," he replied. "Although I suspect it may be a tad boring here at times, and I'd expect the property prices are quite high as a result of people like you from the smoke having the

same idea, but also having a bigger bank balance than us."
"You never know," Laura remarked, "if what Mary told me last week is correct, I may have just inherited a place here."
"Don't build your hopes up," Kieran replied. "Billy McKenna may have just been renting."
Laura chose to ignore his unhelpful contribution as she poked her head out of the window and gazed first to the right then to the left.
"They've got a small pier here," she announced with some glee. "Let's go down and have a look. We could even get an ice cream!"
Kieran's preference would have been a beer rather than an ice cream, but he refrained from any attempt to argue his case.
Within minutes the pair were walking arm in arm down the sea front towards the pier, which as they neared looked bigger and more impressive than it appeared from their bedroom window.
"It's quite unspoilt here," said Laura. "Almost like it's been frozen in time."
"You're really smitten with this place, aren't you?" Kieran remarked.
"Yes, I think it's lovely," she replied. "But you're right; I'm not sure it's somewhere I'd like to live permanently."
The Blythwold pier was a sturdy looking structure, with solid wooden planks which stretched out into the North Sea. Dotted down its length were several white painted buildings selling a variety of items from seaside knick-knacks, ice creams and sandwiches to pizzas and of course, fish and chips.
"How long do you reckon this pier is?" Laura enquired.

Kieran thought for few moments before replying.
"About six hundred and twenty-three feet would be my guess."
"Okay," said Laura, realising that his so accurate estimation had to be based upon some inside knowledge. "Where did you find that out?"
Kieran laughed and directed his eyes to a large noticeboard no more than ten feet away. "It says it there," he remarked with a cocky grin.
It took the couple almost fifteen minutes to travel the six hundred and twenty-three feet to the end of the pier, due to frequent stops to look at trinkets and the obligatory ice cream.
At the end of the pier was an elongated platform supported by seven thick, rust coloured metal stanchions, which protruded out from the waves some twenty feet; rugged and indefatigable against the powerful waves that ceaselessly crashed against them. Save for a few hardy fishermen attending to their lines, wrapped up in green, and a handful of tourists busily snapping photos of each other and the pretty view of the town, the pier's end was largely quiet. Laura and Kieran remained at this tranquil spot for a few minutes, mesmerised by the white-tipped waves as they rose and fell on their way to the pebbly shore.
"Will you marry me, Laura?" Kieran asked, his eyes fixed in her direction. "Sort out your inheritance here, pack up your job in London and come with me to America as my wife!"
Laura was stunned; she hadn't seen that coming at all. "Are you serious?" she remarked, partly to confirm she wasn't hearing things and partly to give her a few moments to think.

"Absolutely," replied Kieran who wrapped his strong right arm around Laura's shoulders. "I want you to marry me, Laura and come with me to the States."
Laura edged back a little. "Is this an all or nothing proposal?" she asked.
Kieran looked perplexed. "I don't get what you mean," he replied.
"Well, is the marriage proposal conditional on me dropping everything here and going with you to America?"
Kieran's face still looked as if he was struggling with the point Laura was making.
"I can take that as a yes then, can I?" Laura added, when there was a five second pause without a response. "If so then my answer has to be no!"
Kieran's jaw dropped and his eyes filled with a mixture of shock and irritation. "You love me, don't you?" he remarked, a little louder than he'd intended. "I've got a fantastic opportunity in America, with a really good salary, so what's the issue?"
Laura could see her boyfriend was hurt and angry. She put her hands gently to either side of his head and kissed him tenderly on the lips.
"I do love you, Kieran," she said with passion. "But you clearly don't know me that well if you think I'm just going to follow you wherever your career takes you, trying to find a suitable job as we go. I'm not like that and I wouldn't be happy if that was the deal."
"So, it's a no?" remarked Kieran who was now looking embarrassed and annoyed.
"If it's conditional, then yes, it's a no," replied Laura.
"So, what are your conditions?" Kieran remarked loudly with no attempt to hide his hurt.
"That's the point," replied Laura. "There should be no conditions."

"I'm sorry, Laura," said Kieran. "I don't get it. You either love me and want to be with me or you don't. And as I've got a fantastic opportunity in America it would be crazy for us to decide otherwise."
Laura turned away and looked out to sea. "I'll tell you what," she said, "I'll marry you tomorrow if you like, but only if you give up the job in America and we stay here."
Kieran shook his head and stared back. "That's just plain stupid," he remarked. "You're being pig-headed. I'd never forgive myself if I passed over this chance. These sorts of opportunities come round maybe just once or twice in a lifetime."
Laura turned back to face him. "Then my answer has to be no."
"Then I don't see any point in us continuing seeing each other," Kieran barked, which grabbed the attention of the fishermen and the holiday snappers. "We may as well call it a day."
The last thing Laura had expected when she woke up that morning was to receive a marriage proposal from Kieran. However, for him, within a matter of moments later, to suggest they split up was even more of a shock. For once in her life Laura couldn't think of anything to say and remained rooted to the spot.
Kieran waited a few seconds after delivering his bombshell, but as soon as he realised Laura wasn't about to try and argue that they should remain together, he turned away from her and marched off down the pier. Laura watched him push his way through the oncoming tourists who meandered up from the shore. She kept her eyes fixed on him as he continued to stride purposefully up the seafront to the Admiral pub. Only when he disappeared from sight did Laura turn back to face the

sea, the tears now streaming uncontrollably down her cheeks.
Laura remained at the pier's end for a further twenty minutes, which she knew would be enough time for Kieran to grab his possessions and make a getaway from Blythwold.
Laura knew Kieran well enough to know that there was now no chance of him hanging around to try and patch things up. After her crystal-clear rebuttal and his wild outburst, she knew full well that she was on her own and that would be the last she'd see of Kieran Hockley.

Chapter 30

Laura hadn't even crossed the threshold of the Admiral pub before she was accosted by the middle-aged landlady, who had checked them in no more than an hour earlier.
"Is everything okay?" the landlady enquired. "Your partner seemed to be in a hurry when he left earlier."
Laura put on her best reassuring smile. "Yes," she replied calmly. "He has had to rush back to London unexpectedly, so it will be just me this evening."
"Nothing too serious?" remarked the landlady, who seemed sincere enough, but was clearly keen for more details.
"Oh no," replied Laura, "just business."
"Well, if there's anything we can do," added the landlady, "just let us know."
Laura smiled politely and started to make her way upstairs. "Actually," she said, stopping abruptly in her tracks and turning back to face her hostess, "can you tell me how many solicitors there are in Blythwold?"
The landlady looked bemused by the request.
"Let me think," she remarked as she placed her right hand under her chin and rubbed her nose gently with her index finger. "There's just two, I think. "There's Diplock and Sturridge's on Main Street and then there's Bovis and Partners on North Street."

Laura smiled. "Thank you," she said courteously before carrying on up the stairs, leaving the landlady to ponder why her guest who had only just arrived that afternoon, would want to contact a solicitor.
As soon as she was in the room Laura checked out the two solicitors' websites on her mobile.
As she scribbled down the numbers, Laura noticed one of the free envelopes that were available to guests at the pub had been carefully placed on the mantelpiece with her name written on the front in Kieran's unmistakeable, almost illegible handwriting. She glanced at her wristwatch, which told her it was four forty-five. She guessed that the solicitors' practices would be closing any time soon, so she could have as little as only fifteen minutes to discover where her birth father had lodged his will. Laura decided to try Diplock and Sturridge first, for no other reason that it was such a wonderfully stupid-sounding name.
"Hello," she said after the receptionist had confirmed that she had indeed reached the solicitors' practice of Diplock and Sturridge. "I'm trying to locate the will of my late father," she continued. "I was wondering whether it had been lodged with your practice."
"And your name is?" enquired the lady at the end of the line.
"My name is Laura Eastwood," she replied, "but my deceased father was called Billy McKenna."
"Oh," replied the lady on the line with surprise in her voice. "Your father was one of our clients, I know for a fact. I was so sorry to hear about his death, my condolences to you, Ms Eastwood."
"Thank you," replied Laura. "I was wondering if I may meet with somebody tomorrow to discuss his will, as I'm led to believe that I am a beneficiary."

"You'll need to talk with Mr Nigel Diplock," replied the secretary. "He deals with wills and probate."
"Is it possible to see him tomorrow?" Laura reiterated.
"I'm just checking," she replied, the sound of computer keys being struck furiously at the other end of the line quite clearly audible to Laura. "Would ten thirty be suitable?"
"Perfect," replied Laura. "You've been most helpful, thank you very much."
"Not at all," replied the secretary. "We look forward to seeing you in the morning."
Surprised by the speed at which she'd managed to locate her father's will and highly impressed with the efficiency of the lady at the solicitors' practice, Laura felt a strong sense of smug satisfaction. She threw her mobile onto the ancient four-poster bed and proceeded to open the envelope Kieran had addressed to her. Inside was a tiny note and one hundred pounds in twenty-pound notes.

Dear Laura
Here's £100 to cover my share of the room for tonight and to pay for your train fare home tomorrow. My offer of marriage still stands and as I've still got three more weeks before I leave you can still change your mind and come with me.
I love you
Kieran xxx

"I love you, too, you pillock," Laura muttered, before she thrust the note back into the envelope and placed it in her handbag, "but there's no way I'm going to be your possession."

*　　　*　　　*

Laura's favourite place to do some serious thinking was in the bath. She was, therefore, delighted that her room had a deep bath, where she could almost totally immerse herself in bubbles.
The past week had been a whirlwind of change; her job prospects had diminished, albeit that her salary was now improved, her relationship with Kieran had all but evaporated unless she agreed to follow him aimlessly to the other side of the Atlantic, and she knew far more about Billy McKenna than she'd known or wanted to know before. She discovered she had a grandmother she hadn't met before; she was starting to have doubts about the strength of her friendship with her best friend Saskia, and tomorrow she was going to discover exactly what sort of legacy her birth father had left to her.
Even for a well organised mind like hers, this was a huge adjustment for it to manage.
Laura's tranquil repose was rudely interrupted by her mobile, which rang loudly.
She stretched out her arm and grabbed the mobile from the chair, where she'd left it on top of her clothes.
"Hi Sas," said Laura when she realised who was calling her. "I was going to ring you later."
"Before I forget I want you to know that there's nothing going on with me and Vic," Saskia announced. "It was a complete coincidence me enrolling at his gym."
Laura had little appetite to argue too much but wasn't about to let her friend off so lightly.
"Well Vic thinks otherwise," she replied. "He thinks you joined deliberately to curry favour with him."
"Does he now?" replied Saskia. "Well, that's just bollocks!"

Saskia was prone to lapse into profanity when she was cornered or incensed, so Laura took her use of bollocks as being a sure sign that Vic's theory was probably fairly accurate.
"Anyway," Laura continued, "it does seem to have worked. Seeing you in your swimwear and your performance yesterday at Radcliffe's have totally transformed his impression of you. He thinks you're wonderful now. In fact, I would be surprised if he doesn't ask you to have his babies soon!"
"Really!" replied Saskia. "Did he tell you that?"
"Well not the babies thing," replied Laura, "but he's talking about you taking on some big accounts, including Radcliffe's."
"You're kidding me," shrieked Saskia down the line. "Did he honestly say that?"
"Yep," replied Laura. "He wants to give you a much bigger role in the team."
"So, I'm assuming he knows about you leaving?" Saskia added. "How did he take that?"
Laura paused. "Well, that may now change," she said trying hard to sound as matter of fact as she could. "Vic's keen for me to stay and has made me a counteroffer. I'm thinking about it."
"So," replied Saskia, who sounded a little nervous, "is my bigger role not conditional on you leaving?"
"Cheers, Saskia," remarked Laura sarcastically. "I'm glad your overriding consideration is for me in all this."
"It is," Saskia replied emphatically, but not altogether convincingly. "I'm just confused. If you stay, will I still get some of your accounts?"
"That's Vic's suggestion," replied Laura. "I'd still manage some accounts, but I'd get a salary increase and be required to do more mentoring."

"Wow," shrieked Saskia. "That would be great. But what does Kieran say about this? He'll not want to go to America without you."
Laura wasn't quite ready to tell Saskia that she and Kieran had just split up, so attempted to play things down. "It's not definite yet about me staying," she lied. "I may still go to the US. I'm just thinking things over."
"Where are you now?" Saskia enquired.
"If you must know, I'm in the bath in my hotel room in Blythwold," she replied. "I'm seeing the solicitor here tomorrow morning to discuss Billy McKenna's will."
"You may be a millionaire!" Saskia suggested.
"More likely I'll inherit loads of debts," replied Laura.
"Can you do that?" Saskia asked.
Laura laughed. "I'm no lawyer, Sas, but I doubt if that's legal. At any rate I hope not."
"So, when are you coming home?" Saskia asked.
"Tomorrow evening," replied Laura.
"I'll see you on Thursday then," Saskia added.
"Yep," Laura replied, "bright and early, as usual!"
"Well, have fun tomorrow," Saskia remarked. "I hope you're pleased with your inheritance."
Laura forced out a small chuckle, "I'm not expecting it to amount to much," she replied. "But you never know!"
With the call now ended, Laura lay back in the bath and looked up at the ceiling, her thoughts again returning to the turmoil of the last week. A sense of total isolation washed over her; a feeling which was alien to Laura. She had always prided herself on being a stoically independent person in full control of her life, but in truth she'd always felt reassured that, if need be, her family, her friends and more recently, her boyfriend, Kieran, were there to support her.
However, in seven or eight days, her world had been turned upside down. The opportunity in America had

evaporated and her position at Meridian no longer seemed as important and prestigious as it had before. She was becoming uneasy with her relationships with Vic and her best friend, Saskia, neither of whom she felt entirely comfortable with anymore. She was wary about being open and honest with her mum and dad regarding her interest in her birth father, a feeling she'd never experienced before with her loving parents. However, the person that had hurt her the most was Kieran. With all that had been happening, Laura really needed him to be there for her, but in her eyes when she needed him most, he had let her down, preferring to see her vulnerable situation as merely his opportunity to get his way, to force her to abandon everything she held important as a cruel condition of his marriage proposal. Laura, for the first time in years, found herself sobbing uncontrollably, not so much from fear of what was happening, more through anger and a sense of disappointment in the people who until so recently she felt would always be there for her.

For several uninterrupted minutes, she allowed her tears to cascade unchecked down her cheeks and fall into the now lukewarm bathwater, before gritting her teeth and hauling herself out.

Laura wrapped herself tightly in one of the large bathroom towels and took a deep breath. There was no way she was going to allow herself to be defeated, she resolved. Whatever the next few days would bring, Laura was determined to ensure that she remained in full control of her destiny. Neither Saskia, Vic, Kieran, nor anyone else was about to tell her how to run her life – in that regard she intended to remain steadfast and indomitable.

*　　*　　*

Back in Victoria, Saskia couldn't help thinking about the conversation she'd just had with her friend. She was sure that Laura was telling her the truth about Vic's plans to enhance her role but was not convinced she was telling her everything. Saskia thought she knew Laura well; well enough to know when she was hiding something from her.
There was only one thing for it, she decided. She'd have to pay a visit to the gym that evening and try to have another chat with Vic in the hot tub. Irrespective of what Laura had told her on the call, she knew when men were attracted to her, and the way Vic had responded on their last encounter in the gym had told Saskia, without question, he was interested.

Part Six

Kieran's Story

Chapter 31

Friday 21st August

Kieran Hockley looked out of the small window at the glimmering blue water some fifteen thousand feet below him. The seventy-six-seater Embraer E170 had left Munich airport on time, which was a major relief to Kieran, who was desperate to get back home after a hectic week of business pitches to potential clients across Germany. He was particularly keen to see Laura, who, if everything went to plan, was going to tell her parents that weekend about their intention to move to America to take on new assignments, and hopefully a new and exciting adventure together.

Although Laura said she was going to take up her new role, Kieran couldn't help feeling that something would come up to thwart their plans, most likely Laura starting to have second thoughts if her mum and dad disapproved.

He so desperately wanted a new start, to be with Laura and to put some distance between himself and his brother, Ryan, who was now almost beyond redemption.

Kieran must have dozed off for a few moments, as when he next looked out of the window the plane was starting its descent into London City Airport. He had flown into London City many times before and, as always, the landing made him more than a little bit anxious. He knew full well that the plane would be almost touching the Thames before it suddenly bounced violently on the short runway and he was aware that as soon as rubber met concrete, the engines would be yanked into reverse to enable the screeching aircraft to shake and shudder itself to a standstill. However, this didn't prevent him from grasping the armrests firmly, his eyes tightly shut, until he was sure the landing was over.

Relieved and eager to get on his way, Kieran clambered out of the plane as quickly as he could, and once he'd made his way into the terminal building, he marched briskly down the long corridor until he reached passport control.

Having negotiated the ridiculously overly engineered zig zag cordon, which was largely empty, Kieran stopped for a few seconds while the bored immigration officer swiftly checked the details on his passport, then, having been given permission to enter the country, continued into the arrivals lounge and down to the London light railway to make his journey across London to see the lovely Laura.

It was six forty-five when Kieran arrived at the house in SW 18, and Laura was in a foul mood.

"What's the matter?" he enquired as he caught sight of the pained expression on Laura's face.

"The job offer in New York's been retracted!"

"What?" exclaimed Kieran, whose worst nightmare appeared to be coming true. "They can't do that."

Laura shrugged her shoulders. "They can and they have," she replied. "Their HR guy left me a message to call him and when I did, he just apologised and said they'd had an instruction from head office that there was an indefinite company-wide, headcount freeze and that with immediate effect, all positions that had not been

filled were to be put on hold. As I've not confirmed acceptance of my offer, they are now saying that it's suspended with no indication of when it will be lifted, or even if it will be lifted."
"Well, that doesn't mean the opportunity has gone," remarked Kieran, who was doing his best to keep Laura's spirits up but felt sick inside. "It's just on ice for a while."
"Technically that's true," replied Laura. "But the HR guy said I shouldn't expect any news for months."
Kieran put his arms around Laura. "Well, there's nothing you can do," he said despondently.
"I just wish I'd said yes earlier and confirmed it in writing," Laura said. "If I'd have done that, they would have had to take me on."
Kieran was angry with Laura. As soon as the offer had arrived, he'd told her to accept it, but, as always, Laura would not listen. He decided not to remind his girlfriend of the fact, but inside he was livid that she'd dragged her feet.
"It's a good job you've not told anyone at Meridian yet," he remarked.
Laura raised her eyes, so they met his. "That's the thing," she said with trepidation in her voice, "I told Vic this morning."
Kieran didn't say anything but inwardly felt his plans to be with Laura in America may not have been scuppered completely. As she'd effectively resigned, there may now be the possibility she'd agree to go with him.

Chapter 32

Kieran got on really well with Laura's mum, Bev. She always seemed genuinely pleased to see him and he never got the feeling she disapproved of her daughter's choice of boyfriend.
With Laura's dad it was different. Their conversations were always friendly, but Kieran wasn't as comfortable with Mike as he was with Bev, and their conversations often seemed more like interrogations than friendly chats.
Kieran was, therefore, slightly miffed when, that evening, he found himself sitting next to Mike in the Indian restaurant.
"How's your job going, Kieran?" Mike asked. "I hear you went to Germany this week."
Kieran took a deep breath, he knew full well that whatever he was about to say, Mike would be constantly interrupting him to trump anything he said with something from his own many years of travelling – a prediction which, for the next ten minutes, became a painful reality for poor Kieran.
Another thing about Mike that irritated Kieran was his unbelievably short attention span. On countless occasions Kieran had found himself effectively talking to himself, with Mike having seemingly drifted away to thoughts of other matters or, as it proved to be that

evening, eavesdropping on someone else's conversation; on this occasion it was Laura and Bev's.
"Witches live forever!" Mike had announced when Kieran was midway through telling him about the reckless way the German taxi drivers bombed down the autobahns, with scant concern about the safety of their paying passengers. He was not even sure that Mike had realised he'd stopped talking, mid-sentence, as his girlfriend's father didn't even try to return to their conversation.
As he'd done on more than one occasion in the past, Kieran elected to stop talking; and based upon the subject matter, he, too, now started to listen into Bev and Laura's conversation, but felt it wasn't his place to get involved.
It was only when Laura announced that she was Billy McKenna's sole beneficiary, that Kieran made any contribution to the debate.
"Really!" he heard himself exclaim and judging from the reaction he got from the others, possibly a bit more enthusiastically than he should have.
Laura's mum had tried to play down the sort of legacy Laura should expect when she had laughed and told her daughter that, in her opinion, there wouldn't be that much in his will as he wasn't a highflyer; a comment Kieran thought was uncharacteristically spiteful of Bev.
"Dive bomber more like it!" Mike had added; an uncharitable remark towards a dead man, Kieran had thought; but one which was typically Mike.
Kieran could see that Laura was looking more and more anxious and she clearly wanted to move the conversation on, so he tried to help by enquiring how long Laura's parents were planning to be in the UK and what their plans were for the weekend. And by the

relieved look on Laura's face, he could see she appreciated his intervention.
Having established that their trip was just a fleeting visit and that they were flying back on Monday, they then agreed to meet up on Sunday with the girls paying a nostalgic trip to the Tate Modern Gallery, while he and Mike would spend some time together at the nearest pub.
"I'm with you, Mike," Kieran had eagerly remarked when the proposition of a few pints rather than a few hours in the gallery had been put to him. If he'd felt he had a realistic choice, he would, almost certainly, have plumped for joining Bev and Laura in the Tate, as the prospect of spending time alone with Mike, listening to his opinions on the world, didn't fill Kieran with fervour. However, that was never really an option, so he resigned himself to more time being talked at by Mike, a prospect that even the compensation of a couple of pints couldn't make look in the slightest bit attractive.

Chapter 33

Saturday 22nd August

When Kieran woke up, the first thing he saw was Laura sat next to him on the bed. She'd had a shower and her damp hair hung loose around her tiny shoulders. Kieran decided that now was probably as good a time as ever to talk to Laura about America.
"Why don't you just quit and come over with me?" Kieran remarked, trying hard not to sound too desperate. "You can look for a job when you're there."
To his dismay, Laura's response wasn't great; emphasising the issues she'd have trying to work in the US without a work visa.
Sadly, and annoyingly, Kieran suspected she was right. And, when Laura started to sound more and more tetchy, reluctantly, Kieran decided to back off. He needed to get back home that afternoon, as he had to sort out a few things, but agreed to meet up with Laura later that evening.
As soon as Kieran was clear of Laura's house, he checked his mobile for messages; there were three missed calls, all from his mother's number.

"Shit!" he exclaimed out loud. He instinctively knew it would be bad news and he was ninety-nine percent certain it would involve Ryan.
"Hi, Mum," he said nervously as his returned call was picked up. "Are you okay?"
"It's Ryan," replied his mother. "The police came this morning and took him to the station. They say he's been dealing drugs again."
Ryan was Kieran's half-brother, the product of a brief dalliance his mother had enjoyed, eighteen years before, with a boyfriend who evaporated as soon as his mother had announced she was pregnant.
"Okay," Kieran replied as calmly as he could. "Which police station have they taken him to?"
"I don't know," she said rather vaguely. "I guess it's the main one in Harlow."
"Leave it with me," Kieran replied, as he had done so many times, whenever the idiot had blighted his life, over the last four or five years, "I'll find him and go and see what's going on."
"Thank you, son," his mother said, the relief palpable in her voice. "I don't know what I'd do without you."
The call ended abruptly, leaving Kieran frustrated and angry, with the, now silent, phone still held to his ear.
Kieran's first thought was to go back and let Laura know that their plans for that evening may need to be reviewed but stopped before he'd taken more than a few paces. He looked at his watch and decided that he might have time to get to Harlow Police Station, find out what was going on and still get back in time to take Laura out.
Kieran checked the numbers stored in his phone until he found the telephone number of Harlow Police Station, a number he'd had to dial more times than he cared to remember.

*   *   *

It took Kieran over an hour to get from SW18 to the main train station of the Essex new town, and then after a further five-minute taxi ride, he eventually entered Harlow Police Station.
The desk sergeant recognised him immediately. "Good afternoon, sir," he said in a jovial mood. "He's still in the cells. Until he's been questioned, I can't let you see him."
"Does he have a solicitor?" Kieran enquired.
"Yes," replied the sergeant. "It's Mr Pringle, as usual."
Gavin Pringle was Ryan's normal brief; he'd represented him countless times over the past few years.
"Is he still here?" Kieran asked.
"Actually, I think he's now in the canteen," said the desk sergeant. "He's been with your brother since about three, so probably needs a break."
"Can I go up and have a quick word with him?" Kieran asked.
The desk sergeant pulled a face that suggested he shouldn't, but then relaxed his facial muscles and nodded. "I can't let you do that," he said, "but I'll call up and ask him if he'd care to come down here to talk to you. You can go into the small interview room over there for some privacy."
As he spoke, the desk sergeant pointed to the door at the opposite end of the room.
"Thanks," Kieran replied.

*   *   *

Having spent only twenty minutes with Gavin Pringle, Kieran left the police station alone and with the bleak prospect of now having to tell his mother that the

chances of Ryan getting off, this time, without a significant custodial sentence, was as near zero as made no difference.
He looked at his watch. There was now little chance of being able to see Laura that evening. He texted his mum, to tell her he was on his way, but decided to hold fire on calling Laura until he was certain he couldn't get over to see her.
"The sooner I get to America the better," he muttered to himself as he wandered despondently to the nearest taxi rank.

Chapter 34

Sunday 23rd August

When he arrived at the Founders Arms, Kieran found Mike Eastwood outside under a large red sunshade.
"Do you want another pint, Mike?" he asked.
Mike had about half his drink in front of him, but without hesitation he accepted the younger man's offer.
"Beats marching around that place looking at rubbish pretending to be art," Mike remarked.
"Absolutely," Kieran agreed. "And the beer's pretty damn good, too."
As they spoke, the two men made no attempt to make eye contact; they continued to gaze aimlessly at the activity on the busy waterway.
The pair remained outside the pub for the best part of three hours before Laura and Bev joined them. Although their discussions had covered a range of subjects, from Kieran's intentions towards Laura to the navigational rules for boats on the Thames, their conversation, as always, appeared to Kieran like Mike was a High Court Barrister cross-examining a witness in the dock. So, Kieran was pleased when, eventually, Bev and Laura appeared, even though he didn't have an opportunity to talk privately to Laura until they arrived back at her house that evening.

Having waved off Laura's parents and with the rain now beating down hard, the pair rushed inside.
"Did you mention America to your parents?" was the first question Kieran asked.
Laura just shook her head. "No," she replied. "I talked to Mum about Billy McKenna, but I didn't see any point in bringing up anything about the job, now that it's not happening."
Kieran was frustrated. Given the situation with his brother, he was now even more desperate to get away. But however hard he tried, Kieran couldn't persuade Laura to join him.
"I've told you, just pack in your job at Meridian and join me. With your experience you'll find something over there in no time," he said irately.
Laura just shook her head again. "No," she replied firmly. "It's not that easy, I'll need a visa to do that and I'm not sure I'd get one without already having a job lined up."
"So, what are you going to do?" Kieran asked. "You've quit your job at Meridian already, so if you stay here, you'll be out of work anyway."
"I'll just have to see how it goes tomorrow with Vic," she replied in a tone that simply aggravated Kieran more. "I've not given him my notice in writing so, technically, I've not resigned. You never know, he may even offer me a raise to get me to stay, after all, he doesn't know the other job offer's been retracted – and I'm certainly not telling him."
It crossed Kieran's mind to bring up the subject of marriage, something he'd thought about quite a lot of late; however, on reflection he decided that this may not be the best time.

Chapter 35

Tuesday 25th August

With the opportunity for him and Laura to spend the next two days together, Kieran made a quick call to the office to advise them that he was also going to take the time off. He was now determined to ask Laura to marry him, and he felt sure that during the next couple of days he was bound to be able to find the right time to broach the subject.

Already showered, he greeted Laura with a piping hot cup of tea.

"Good morning," he said tenderly as he perched himself beside her on the bed and rested the cup on the bedside table. "Did you sleep well?"

"I did," Laura replied, much to Kieran's relief. Laura pulled him towards her. "You smell nice," she said. "How long have you been up?"

Kieran could see she was in a much better mood. He bent down and kissed her warmly. "About an hour or so," he replied. "It is nearly eight after all, you're usually at your desk by now."

Laura smiled and pulled Kieran even closer. "I guess that's one good thing that came out of yesterday's meeting with Vic. I get a few days off."

"That's more like it," remarked Kieran, who liked Laura much more when she was smiling. "And as you're going to be kicking your heels around for the next couple of

days, I thought I'd take time off, too, and we could do something together."
He could see from her expression that Laura whole heartedly approved, a fact that was reinforced when she suggested they started the day by staying in bed, something Kieran had no issues with whatsoever.

*   *   *

As they headed east towards Suffolk in his open-top BMW Z4 Roadster, Kieran felt relaxed. He stole countless sideways glances at Laura, who spent most of the journey with her head back and eyes closed. He loved her deeply and was eager to marry and for them to start a new life in America together.
Although there was no way he'd admit it, Kieran really liked the feel of Blythwold almost as soon as the car drove past the welcome to Blythwold sign, but he tried his best not to show it.
When Laura suggested they went to the pier, Kieran wasn't too keen, but he was eager for her to remain relaxed and happy, so he didn't argue.
As they walked arm in arm down the sea front towards the pier entrance, Kieran became more and more confident that the right moment was getting close.
As they reached the end of the pier, something in Kieran's head told him it was the right time.
"Will you marry me, Laura?" he asked, his eyes transfixed on hers, desperate to see them light up with joy. "Sort out your inheritance here, pack up your job in London and come with me to America as my wife!"
He had not intended to say more than will you marry me, but for some stupid reason, nerves most likely, he found himself saying more. And he knew as soon as

he'd finished his sentence that he may have made a massive error of judgement.
Laura's expression didn't look as cheerful as he'd hoped.
"Are you serious?" she remarked, as if the proposal had been made by a complete stranger rather than her long-term lover.
"Absolutely," replied Kieran who wrapped his strong right arm around Laura's shoulders. "I want you to marry me, Laura, and come with me to the States."
Kieran's hopes were dashed as soon as he saw Laura edge back away from him. "Is this an all or nothing proposal?" she said, which was not what Kieran had intended.
Stupidly he found himself just making matters worse. "I don't get what you mean," he replied, for some inexplicable reason.
"Well, is the marriage proposal conditional on me dropping everything here and going with you to America?"
Kieran's mouth became dry. The answer wasn't yes but he did want to go to America, and he did want Laura to come with him.
When Laura, who looked very angry, just added, "I can take that as a yes then, can I?" he knew her answer wasn't going to be yes.
And when the answer, no, eventually did come out of Laura's mouth, Kieran was distraught. "You love me, don't you?" he heard himself saying without any concern about who else could hear. "I've got a fantastic opportunity in America, with a really good salary, so what's the issue?"
Laura then put her hands gently to either side of his head and kissed him tenderly on the lips. At that moment

Kieran thought she'd change her mind and say yes. However, that wasn't what happened.
"I do love you, Kieran," she then said with meaning, "but you clearly don't know me that well if you think I'm just going to follow you wherever your career takes you, trying to find a suitable job as we go. I'm not like that and I wouldn't be happy if that was the deal."
"So, it's a no?" remarked Kieran, who was now angry and embarrassed.
"If it's conditional, then yes, it's a no," replied Laura.
"So, what are your conditions?" was the ridiculous response Kieran heard himself saying.
"That's the point," replied Laura. "There should be no conditions."
"I'm sorry, Laura," said Kieran, who was now so angry he could feel his eyes starting to water, "I don't get it. You either love me and want to be with me, or you don't. And as I've got a fantastic opportunity in America, it would be crazy for us to decide otherwise."
Laura turned away and looked out to sea. "I'll tell you what," she said, "I'll marry you tomorrow if you like, but only if you give up the job in America and we stay here."
Kieran was now so angry he could feel his fists clenching. "That's just plain stupid," he said. "You're being pig-headed. I'd never forgive myself if I passed over this chance. These sorts of opportunities come round maybe just once or twice in a lifetime."
"Then my answer has to be no," Laura said firmly.
"Then I don't see any point in us continuing seeing each other," Kieran shouted, although that was the very last thing he wanted to say. "We may as well call it a day."
As he turned on his heels and marched down the pier, Kieran couldn't believe how it had all gone so wrong. Although he wasn't in Laura's league when it came to

stubbornness, he could be pretty obstinate, too, and despite desperately wanting to sort things out, he wasn't about to go back and grovel. His overriding feeling was not merely to get out of that damn, back-of-nowhere, little town, but also to get away from his idiot brother and his pathetic, needy mum. He was going to America and nothing or nobody was going to stop him.

If Laura wanted to follow him then fine, but he wasn't going to beg her. She had three weeks to change her mind then he would be gone, and he was not coming back.

Part Seven

A Very Peculiar Inheritance.

Chapter 36

Wednesday 26th August

For the second consecutive night Laura got very little sleep.
Despite all her efforts to clear her head, all she could think about was Kieran. The way he'd tried to dupe her into following him blindly to America without a job, based upon a marriage proposal, still made her feel angry and let down. Especially as, in her eyes, he must have known full well how much he meant to her.
However, it was the cowardly way he'd just abandoned her at the end of Blythwold Pier, with little thought for her at all, that Laura found the most infuriating.
Laura wasn't prone to swearing, but with the events of the day, the sweltering sticky heat in the musty room and having to lie on the most uncomfortable mattress she'd ever experienced, she constantly found herself mumbling profanities that would have made even her so-called best friend, Saskia, blush.
By the time the sun finally rose at five fifty-four am, Laura decided to give up trying to sleep. She had no idea how much shuteye she'd actually managed to get but figured it couldn't have been much more than two or three hours in total, accumulated at most in twenty-minute snatches.

With her appointment at Diplock and Sturridge being at ten thirty, Laura wondered how on earth she was going to pass away the next four and a half hours.
She clambered slowly out of bed, ambled to the open window, pulled the thick curtains open a few inches and peered out towards the North Sea.
Although the day was only just starting, the sky was almost clear with only a few wispy clouds far off in the direction of the sunrise. A faint, cool breeze, travelling landward, caressed Laura's cheeks which felt refreshing after the muggy hours she'd spent in bed. Laura filled her nostrils with the salty, fresh air, and studied the breakers as they crashed against the pebbly shore before rolling back to meet the next mighty wave.
For the next twenty minutes Laura remained mesmerised at her window enjoying the sight, sounds and smell of the ocean. She loved the sea.
And had it not been for her desire for a hot cup of tea, she might have lingered even longer.

*　　　*　　　*

Nigel Diplock was nothing like the picture Laura had painted in her head as she'd waited outside his office door. The image she had of a middle aged, pompous, small-town provincial solicitor couldn't have been further from the mark. The tall, tanned, smart, young, and casually dressed vision that greeted her as she was ushered into the cosy-but-small meeting room, caught her totally off guard.
He was, as Saskia would have said, 'well hot'.
"I understand you're Billy McKenna's daughter," remarked the young solicitor as he put out a muscly right arm to shake her hand. "I'm Nigel Diplock. I am, or rather was, his solicitor."

"Laura Eastwood," she replied as she shook his hand. "Thank you for seeing me at such short notice."
To her utter dismay Laura found herself delivering her first words to the handsome solicitor in an embarrassing girlie voice; a nauseating trait that she so often criticised in others.
"For god's sake sort yourself out," Laura said to herself before taking a deep breath in an attempt to gain her composure and return to her normal business-like demeanour.
"No problem," added the solicitor with a warm smile. "Please accept my condolences on your loss. I knew your dad well; he was a great guy."
Laura gently extracted her hand from his firm grip and sat down. "I didn't know him, I'm afraid to say," she replied. "He didn't figure much in my life."
Nigel Diplock smiled again, before making himself comfortable on a chair next to Laura.
"I'm sorry to have to ask you," he said with a hint of humility in his voice, "but before I share with you the details of your father's will, I need to satisfy myself that you are who you say you are. I hope you don't mind."
Laura smiled to reassure the solicitor. "Of course," she replied. "Will my passport and driving licence do?"
Nigel Diplock nodded. "That will be perfect," he replied.
Laura delved deep into her handbag before extracting first her passport then her driving licence. "Here you go," she said genially as she passed over the documents to the solicitor.
Diplock studied the two documents for few seconds before getting up and walking to the door. "I'll just get a copy of these to show that we've proved your identity, then I'll gladly run through your father's will with you."

As he reached the door Diplock turned back to face Laura. “Would you like a drink?” he enquired.
“Tea with one sugar would be very nice,” replied Laura, who once again heard herself sounding more like a lovesick teenager than her usual everyday voice.
The solicitor smiled and exited the room.
As soon as he had left the room, Laura took another deep breath.
“For god’s sake pull yourself together, you idiot,” she said to herself. “He’s probably married anyway.”
Nigel Diplock was only out of the room for a matter of minutes before he returned with Laura’s documents and a buff folder under his arm.
“The drinks will be here shortly,” he remarked with a smile as he resumed his seat. “Here’s your passport and driving licence.”
He slid the papers across the desk towards Laura.
“Thanks,” replied Laura making sure she was once more speaking in her professional, young adult voice.
Diplock waited for Laura to place the documents back in her handbag before he opened the file marked Billy McKenna deceased and took out a cream-coloured document folder, which he placed in front of him.
“I’m more than happy to read it out to you,” Diplock began, “but it may make more sense for you to read it yourself. As wills go it’s very short, but in my view crystal clear and to the point. If you’d rather I read it, I’m more than happy to do so.”
Laura smiled back at the solicitor. “That’s absolutely fine by me,” she replied.
“I can read it.”
Diplock slid the document folder across the desk, so it rested in front of Laura.

"I'll give you a few minutes on your own to read it through," he remarked. "I'll just be next door if you need me to clarify anything."
Laura had never seen a will before and had assumed that it was a legal obligation for the solicitor to read the will to the client but was pleased and relieved to be able to have time in private to study it by herself.
She waited for the door to close behind Nigel Diplock before she started reading her birth father's final wishes.
Laura quickly scanned through the initial blurb, about this will revoking all previous wills, and got swiftly down to the meat of the document, which she studied closely. This did not take her too long as it was exactly as Nigel Diplock had indicated; short, direct, and crystal clear.
However, it was by no means as straight forward as Laura had expected.
Laura read the document twice more before Nigel Diplock re-entered the room.
"Do you have any questions?" he asked in a way that suggested to Laura he was fully expecting her to require further clarity.
Laura waited for the solicitor to resume his seat before replying.
"I certainly do," she replied. "But first, just so I'm totally clear, he appointed you as his executor and, after his funeral expenses, I inherit all his possessions, including his apartment here in Blythwold and his business. However, I cannot get my hands on his money for a year, this being conditional on me agreeing to take up permanent residence here in Blythwold and to manage his business for at least one year from the date of his death. And should I elect not to do so, I will inherit just one thousand pounds with the rest of his assets, including his apartment and business, being sold

by you and the proceeds being given to the various charities he supported."
"Those are exactly your father's wishes," replied Nigel Diplock, who seemed impressed with Laura's succinct summary. "A bit unusual I know, but those were his instructions."
Laura thought for a moment. "Am I able to appoint a manager for his business and continue to live in London?"
Diplock shook his head. "No," he replied firmly, "I discussed this at some length with Billy and he was very specific that you should relocate yourself here in Blythwold, on a permanent basis for one year, and that you should actively manage the business yourself. Of course, you can run the business as you see fit and employ who you deem fit, but to secure the full inheritance you need to live in Blythwold and actively run your father's business for at least a year. After that, of course, you can do what you wish with the apartment and the business."
Laura was stunned. "So, what sort of value is my father's estate," she asked.
The handsome solicitor smiled and extracted another sheet of A4 paper from the file. "It's quite a considerable sum," he replied. "Your father's savings and other monies on account total just over thirty-five thousand pounds. He had an endowment which has covered the balance of his mortgage on the flat and based upon an estimate I had done by Bennett's estate agency here last week, the property in its current condition is valued at five hundred and fifty thousand pounds. The events business is a little less easy to value. It's turning over around fifty thousand pounds a year, but for the last two or three years it's hardly made any money." At that juncture Nigel Diplock gave Laura a

broad smile. "To be honest, I'm not sure how Billy managed to get by. With all his outgoings, I suspect, knowing Billy, he was creative with his accounting – if you know what I mean."
Laura assumed by this that he was suggesting Billy had not declared all his income, which was something she would never dream of doing, but decided not to make that point.
"Bennett's best estimate of the value of the business is about one hundred and fifty thousand pounds which, after the various administration charges have been deducted and Billy's funeral costs have been paid, leaves you an estate worth approximately six hundred and fifty thousand pounds."
"Wow," replied Laura, who had no idea her inheritance would be that much. "I can't believe it. Are you sure the apartment is worth that much? It must be some place."
Nigel Diplock laughed, "Actually, it's a pokey, little two-bedroomed flat which needs a great deal doing to it. If you spent a little money on it the value could go up by about a hundred thousand pounds very easily. It has a sea view, you see, which is very sought after."
Laura was so shocked she could think of nothing to say.
"Are there any more questions?" Nigel Diplock enquired.
Laura thought for a couple of moments. "Actually, I do have a few," she replied.
Mr Diplock smiled in her direction. "Fire away," he said kindly.
"Do I have to pay tax on this?" Laura asked.
Diplock shook his head. "As it happens you won't," he remarked with some authority. "The estate is below the HMRC threshold, so you're not required to pay any inheritance tax."

Laura couldn't believe what she was hearing. "It's unbelievable," she giggled, her broad smile etched across her face.
"What's your other question?" Diplock asked.
"How will anyone know whether I fulfil the conditions of Billy McKenna's will?" she enquired.
The solicitor shrugged his shoulders. "That responsibility falls to me," he replied firmly. "And I'm duty bound to ensure that the conditions are observed."
"So, do I take it I can't gain access to the apartment yet or any of Billy's money?" Laura asked.
"Yes and no," replied Diplock. "You are appointed managing director of the business with immediate effect. You are also allowed to occupy the apartment, however, neither will legally fall into your ownership until one year has passed since Billy died. In short, they are both yours to do with as you see fit, apart from selling either of them. As for the money in Billy's account," Diplock continued, "that has to remain on deposit until the year has lapsed."
"I see," Laura replied, her elation now slightly dented.
Diplock smiled and passed over two sets of keys to Laura. "Would you like to see your business and your apartment?" he asked.
Laura took hold of both sets of keys and looked closely at them for a second before returning her gaze to Nigel Diplock's deep-blue eyes. "I suppose I should," she replied with a slight nod of her head, "especially if I'm going to have to decide whether it's worth abandoning my life and career in London."

Chapter 37

The Crow's Nest, Billy McKenna's cosy attic apartment, was at the top of a narrow, winding, wooden staircase. Nigel Diplock had walked Laura to the property but had left her outside the tall Victorian building as he had another appointment that he needed to keep, back at the office. However, before he departed, they'd agreed to meet for lunch back at the Admiral, and after lunch the solicitor was going to take Laura to the small office where Billy McKenna had run his events business.
Laura was pleased with the arrangement. She'd instantly warmed to Nigel Diplock, who seemed kind and helpful, but was pleased she was being allowed to see the apartment her birth father had lived in, on her own.
As the small wooden door opened, Laura was amazed by how tidy the place was. For sure, Diplock had been right when he said it was tired and in desperate need of redecorating, but it was very clean and not at all how she expected to find a flat owned by a single, late-middle-aged man.
The apartment consisted of just four rooms; a lounge diner with a small-but-adequate kitchen area in the corner, a reasonably sized bedroom with a window that looked out to the rear of the property, a tiny second bedroom just big enough to fit a bed and a small

wardrobe, and a compact bathroom which had a power shower, but to Laura's dismay, no bath.
In the lounge diner there were two old metal-framed windows which opened out to give a fantastic panorama of the seashore. Laura decided to let some air into the room and opened them wide.
As soon as she breathed in the salty sea air she was hooked.
In normal circumstances Laura was a sensible, level-headed, young woman who rarely made impulsive decisions, but on this occasion, she immediately decided she'd follow her heart. Even if Billy's business was a total nonstarter, she knew, there and then, that she was staying in Blythwold.
For almost an hour Laura stared out of the open window, absorbing the sounds and smells of the sea, delighting in watching the breakers hit the shore and seeing the joy on the faces and in the voices of the children having fun on the beach and playing dare with the waves. As she watched, Laura couldn't stop smiling. Blythwold and specifically this apartment was going to be her new home. Instinctively she constructed a plan of action in her head. She'd call Vic first and negotiate a leaving date from Meridian as soon as she could, then she'd rent out her house in SW18 to cover her mortgage and once the year was up in Blythwold, she'd sell the London house and start a new life in glorious Suffolk.
The only concern she had, and it was a big one, was the reaction of her mum and dad.
Laura knew she'd have to be careful how she told them as there was no doubt in her mind that they'd not be best pleased.

As she contemplated how to tackle that tricky dilemma, the door of the apartment opened and in strode the imposing figure of Mary McKenna.
"They told me you were back," remarked the old lady. "So, are you staying?"
The sudden appearance of Mary and her directness took Laura slightly by surprise.
"Of course, I am," replied Laura, without hesitation. "I suppose you're aware of the conditions of your son's will?"
Mary smiled. "Aware?" she replied as if it was a totally inappropriate word that Laura had chosen. "It was my idea!"
Laura could tell from the glint in Mary's eye and the smug look on her face that her grandmother wasn't lying.
"Why did you suggest I had to stay a year?" Laura enquired.
"Because if you are to inherit everything your father worked so hard for," replied the old lady sternly, "then you should show that you deserve it."
Laura felt a rush of fury, but unlike on their previous meeting, she no longer felt awkward in the old lady's presence, and she was not going to allow her to bully her. Her grandmother was certainly a force to be reckoned with, but that was not going to prevent Laura telling her exactly what she thought.
"What do you mean by that?" she replied angrily, her eyes glaring at the old woman. "Your son abandoned me! In over twenty years, your son only once came to see me, so I don't see how anyone can suggest I have to earn anything. If your son decided to leave everything to me in his will then quite frankly that is the least I deserve. So, don't you ever suggest I have to earn anything!"

Mary McKenna remained calm and impassive as Laura vented her spleen. She kept her dark eyes focused on her granddaughter and never once showed any sign of emotion.
"You're a prickly young thing," Mary said as soon as Laura had stopped. "I like that in a girl; you probably take after me in that respect."
"Was there any reason for your visit?" Laura asked, as if to imply that Mary should leave.
"What do your parents think of your decision to stay here?" Mary asked in a calm but mischievous manner.
Laura didn't reply, but she could see on the face of her grandmother that her expression had betrayed her.
Mary allowed herself a smug smile of satisfaction.
"You've not told them yet," she continued. "I'd pay a small fortune to be a fly on the wall when you have that conversation. They won't be brave enough to show their faces around here, I can tell you that for certain."
"Why do you hate us so much?" Laura enquired. "What have we done to you?"
Mary shook her head. "In fairness, Laura, you've done nothing," Mary conceded. "But your parents have much to be ashamed of. It's not my place to tell you, my dear; you need to talk with them."
"I don't believe you," Laura replied through gritted teeth. "My mum and dad have nothing to be ashamed of. You need to look closer to home, dear grandmother!"
Mary gently shook her head before turning to leave.
"Can I have your key, please?" Laura said, anger still raging inside her. "I assume that's how you got in. Well, you won't be needing a key anymore."
The old lady turned to face Laura once again.
For a few seconds she remained expressionless. Then, without warning, a genuine smile broke out across her face. Slowly she removed a key from her jacket pocket

and gently placed it on the cabinet next to where she was standing. “You are so very much like me,” she repeated. “I think we will have an interesting time, you, and me. That’s if you’re able to stick it out for a year here in sleepy Blythwold.”

The old lady turned round once more and made her way out of the room and down the winding staircase to the street below.

“Have no fears,” Laura shouted at her, “I’ll stick it out, my dear grandmother. There’s no way you or anyone else is going to deny me my inheritance.”

As soon as she’d finished her sentence Laura slammed the door shut.

“Dad was right, you are a witch,” she said out loud, “but you don’t scare me.”

Chapter 38

Laura sat in the only comfortable-looking chair in the apartment, fuming.
"How dare she treat me like that," she muttered angrily to herself as she imagined how Mary had schemed to make it so difficult for her to get access to the inheritance. "What sort of sick person thinks like that?"
Her irritation remained with her for the next twenty minutes, but her main concern wasn't Mary, it was how she was going to tell her mum and dad about moving to Blythwold. In that respect Mary was right, they weren't going to take too kindly to that piece of news.
Had it not been so close to twelve thirty, the time she'd agreed to meet Nigel Diplock in the Admiral, she would have called her mum there and then. However, Laura figured that call might be a lengthy one so elected to delay a little and make it some time that afternoon.

* * *

When Laura arrived at the Admiral, Nigel Diplock was already there, perched at the bar sipping on a glass of wine.
He saw Laura enter the room and, as she approached where he was sitting, he stood up and smiled at her, his perfect white teeth beaming out from the otherwise dark room.

Laura smiled back and joined him at the bar.
"What can I get you?" the handsome solicitor enquired. After her altercation with Mary what Laura really wanted was a large vodka, but she didn't want to give out the wrong impression, so decided on something less conspicuous. "I'll have a large diet Coke please," she replied.
"It's Pepsi," replied the barman, who like an obedient servant had been waiting for Laura to decide.
"Pepsi's fine," Laura confirmed before stretching her leg up to mount the barstool next to Nigel Diplock.
"So, what do you think of the apartment?" he enquired.
"I like it a lot," replied Laura with enthusiasm. "I can't wait to move in!"
Diplock smiled again, the same polished-white-teeth smile from earlier. "That's great news," he replied. "So, you will definitely be fulfilling the conditions of your father's ..." Diplock paused as he saw the frown appear on Laura's brow when he referred to Billy as her father. "I mean Billy McKenna's will?"
"Yes," remarked Laura as she sipped her cold Pepsi. "I'll have to work my three months' notice in London, but after that I'll be down here like a shot."
Nigel's gleaming smile rapidly deserted him. "No," he remarked rather nervously, "that will breach the terms of the will. You need to be here in situ and running the business within a month of Billy's death. It's now two weeks after he died, so you've only got until the ninth of September, which is just a fortnight from now."
Laura almost choked on her drink. "You've got to be kidding," she exclaimed. "That's totally unrealistic and anyway, the one-month deadline wasn't mentioned in the will."
Nigel looked back with a degree of sympathy but his slight shrug of his shoulders and embarrassed expression

left Laura in no doubt that he was going to be inflexible on this point. “I’m sorry, Laura,” he said calmly but firmly, “this was specified very clearly to me by Billy and is painstakingly spelt out in the written instructions he left me.”
“I’d certainly like to see those instructions,” replied Laura. “Surely, they can’t be legally binding as they are not part of his will?”
Nigel Diplock shook his head. “I’m sorry, Laura, they are I’m afraid.
But you are, of course, free to see the instructions if you wish.”
“I wish!” replied Laura firmly. “Actually, I’d like to do it now if we can, I’m not feeling very hungry anymore.”
Nigel Diplock looked shocked at Laura’s sudden change of mood but didn’t reply.
Laura downed a large gulp of her Pepsi, before thumping the half full glass onto the bar and propelling herself off the stool and onto the floor.
“Can you put these on my tab, George,” Diplock said in the direction of the barman.
George dutifully nodded and, without any further words being exchanged, Laura and the now chastened-looking solicitor made their way out of the pub and into the bright glare of the sunny street.

* * *

Laura sat quietly in Diplock’s office and carefully read the typed instructions which the now sheepish solicitor had produced from the buff folder.
“This is ridiculous,” Laura announced as soon as she’d finished. “I have to give three months’ notice at work, so how the hell can I satisfy these conditions without breaching that agreement?”

Nigel Diplock took the instructions back from Laura. "I'm sorry," he added with genuine feeling. "My hands are tied. As Billy's appointed executor I'm duty bound to follow his instructions to the letter."
Laura shook her head despondently. "Well, all I can do is see if my employers are sympathetic to this unreasonable condition, but I'm not confident."
A smile returned to Nigel Diplock's face, but not as generous as previously. "You do have two more weeks, Laura," he remarked, as if that was somehow a luxury.
Laura puffed out her cheeks to demonstrate once more her frustration, before slowly rising out of her seat. "I suppose I should get down and take a look at Billy's business," she remarked, although her words lacked any sign of enthusiasm.
"Of course," replied Diplock. "It's just a few hundred yards away so it won't take us long."
Diplock ushered Laura out of his office, gallantly holding open the door as they made their exit onto Blythwold High Street.
"It's down to the left," he indicated to Laura who dutifully followed his instruction.
As Diplock had suggested, it took little time to arrive at the front door of McKenna Events. A small brass plaque at head height indicated they'd arrived.
Laura had expected to find a pokey, messy office, empty of people but cluttered with papers. However, as she'd experienced with Billy's apartment, her initial impression was, pleasingly, much more favourable.
At first Laura didn't see the pretty young woman behind the computer screen at the far end of the office. It was only when she stood up and a shock of long, corkscrew, ginger hair caught Laura's eye that she realised they were not alone.

"This is Abigail," Diplock announced, his right arm stretching out in the young woman's direction.
Abigail looked nervous but smiled sweetly at Laura.
"This is Laura Eastwood," Diplock continued. "She's your new boss."
"Pleased to meet you," said Abigail, who walked over to them.
"So, what is your role here?" Laura asked.
Abigail smiled. "I was Mr McKenna's assistant," she replied. "So, I did just about anything he asked me to do."
Diplock smiled. "Abigail's being very modest," he remarked. "Billy relied very much on Abigail. She knows this business inside out and has been brilliant in keeping this place ticking over since Billy died."
"I don't remember seeing you at the funeral," Laura said.
Abigail's eyes dropped to the floor. "I wanted to go, but I was so upset. I just couldn't bring myself to go."
Laura smiled, "I'm sure he would have understood," she replied sympathetically.
"I hope so," Abigail replied. "Will you be keeping me on? Mrs McKenna indicated that my position here isn't guaranteed now that Billy's gone."
Laura's smile broadened. "Don't worry about her," she said. "Billy left the business to me, so Mrs McKenna won't be involved, and as I'll need your help to keep this business moving in the right direction, you shouldn't worry yourself about being made redundant."
Abigail lifted her head, the look of relief plain to see. "Thanks," she replied.
Nigel Diplock looked at his watch. "Can I leave you, ladies?" he said.
"I need to attend a meeting in a few minutes."

"That's fine," replied Laura, who was pleased to have an opportunity to talk with Abigail on her own. "I'll be heading back to London later this afternoon, but I'll be back as soon as I've spoken to my employer. I'll let you know the outcome."
Nigel Diplock smiled, nodded, and handed the office keys to Laura before turning on his heels and making a swift exit.
As soon as he'd gone and the door was firmly shut behind him, Abigail's demeanour seemed to change.
"He's a bit scary," Abigail said without any warning, "but fit!"
Laura instantly knew she'd get on well with Abigail.
"Yes, he is a handsome looking man, that's for sure," she agreed, "but I get the feeling he's a bit of a stuffed shirt."
Abigail smiled, "He's a reputation in the town as a bit of a ladies' man," she added, as if she was speaking to a long-standing mate rather than her boss who she'd only just met for the first time.
"So, he's not married, I take it?" Laura enquired.
Abigail shook her head. "No, he's very much the single man, if you know what I mean."
Laura didn't want to prolong the conversation any further as she wanted to start her way back to London within the next few hours and felt it more sensible to try and understand as much as she could about the business in the short time she had available. "Tell me, Abigail, what sort of projects are you working on at the moment?" Laura asked.
"I've not accepted any new engagements since Billy died," Abigail replied. "We've a few jobs I'm working on, but they'll all be completed in a month or so."

Laura had a good feeling about Abigail. Although she couldn't have been more than nineteen or twenty, she seemed really switched on.
Laura spent four hours with her trying to get a feeling for the business, which, whilst small, appeared to be relatively successfully run.
"Look I'm going to have to get on my way to London," Laura said as soon as the clock on the wall indicated it was five pm. "Here's my mobile number if you have any issues you need to discuss with me." As she spoke, Laura handed Abigail her business card from Meridian. "I'll call you tomorrow anyway and hopefully, all being well, I should be back in Blythwold within the next few weeks."
Abigail took the card from Laura and studied the details. "There is one thing," she said. "With Billy dying I've not been paid for the last two weeks."
Laura smiled back at her. "Well, that will have to be my first job," she replied. "I'll speak with Mr Diplock in the morning and ask him to make sure you get paid all that's due to you and I'll also make sure you get your wages paid into your account every week from now on."
Abigail looked blankly back at Laura. "Billy just paid me in cash every Friday," she replied. "I've never had my wages paid into my bank."
Laura was shocked at what she was hearing. "Really!" she exclaimed. "That's weird. What about national insurance and everything?"
Abigail shrugged her shoulders. "I don't know anything about that, Billy sorted all that out."
The last thing Laura wanted to do, was to frighten Abigail, who she was dependent upon to keep the business going, so she didn't push the conversation any further.

"Well let's just keep things going as they were," she said reassuringly, "certainly for the time being. I'll ask Mr Diplock to make sure you're paid in cash for now."
This seemed to set Abigail's mind at rest. "Thanks," she replied before walking back to her desk and disappearing behind the computer screen.
"I'll speak to you tomorrow then," remarked Laura before she made her way to the door.
"Have a safe journey," Abigail replied, her head peering round from the screen.
"Actually," remarked Laura suddenly. "I'd like to look at the order book and the latest accounts. Do you know where they are?"
"The accounts are all in that file over there," replied Abigail, pointing at large orange box file on what Laura assumed was Billy's old desk.
"I keep the order books on my hard drive," added Abigail. "Do you want me to print you off a copy?"
Laura picked up the orange box file. "It might be better if you just email it to me," she said. "My email address is on the card I gave you."
"I'll do it before I go home," Abigail replied.
Laura smiled before turning on her heels and heading out of the office.

Chapter 39

With there being only one train an hour, and with the entire journey from Darsham to her house in SW18 taking over three hours, Laura wanted to try and get the seventeen forty-nine, and was relieved when she managed to clamber into the dated and totally empty carriage just moments after her taxi had dropped her off. The fact that she had no ticket, due to the total absence of anyone from the operating company on the platform, did concern her, but she shrugged that off, figuring this was probably a frequent occurrence and she could buy her ticket on-line or at Ipswich during the ten minutes she had before her connection left for London.
She slumped back into the dusty, hard backrest and looked out over the flat-but-pretty countryside as it sped past the window.
Unlike the last time she was on the train heading for London, Laura wasn't pleased to be going home. She'd already made her mind up that she was leaving Meridian, she no longer had to consider Kieran's feelings and, had it not been for the trepidation of having to tell her mum and dad about her decision to move to Blythwold and the apprehension she felt about her conversation the next morning with Vic, Laura would have been reasonably relaxed and probably excited about the new path her life was taking. However, she was dreading both conversations, as she knew how ever

she tried to couch her words, neither was likely to be a total success.
As she was not going to be talking to Vic until the morning, Laura decided to put the thought of that delicate discussion to the back of her mind. It was the conversation with her mum that needed her immediate attention. Laura took a deep breath and dialled her mum's number.
"Oh, hi, darling!" came the delighted tone of her mother's voice. "I didn't expect to hear from you today. Are you okay?"
Laura had planned to try and start the conversation with anything other than the news she knew she had to tell her mum, but having been asked such a direct question, her best made plans deserted her.
"Yes, I'm fine," she replied, trying her best to sound as jovial as she could. "I'm on a train so it might be a bit noisy, but I wanted to let you know that I've been told the details of Billy's will."
Laura paused hoping her mum would reply with something upbeat – but she was sadly disappointed.
"Oh yes," was all she said, in a tone sounding as if she was now expecting to hear some bad news.
"It's true," Laura said as positively as she could, "he did leave me everything. And it's quite a tidy sum."
"Really?" replied her mum, who sounded genuinely surprised.
"Yes," Laura continued, "his flat and his business are apparently worth over six hundred thousand, so, it's a pretty big inheritance."
"Well, I am surprised," replied her mother. "I hadn't expected there to be anything much. Are you just going to put both on the market and sell them?"

It was almost as if her mum knew the details and was preventing her daughter from being able to sugar coat the news.
"Er, no," Laura responded rather sheepishly. "As part of the will I have to actively run the business for a year. Weird, I know, but unfortunately if I don't, I can't inherit."
"That's awful," replied her mum. "And to be honest, I'm surprised he would do that. Billy wasn't the most reliable person, but he was never malicious. It's almost like he knew you couldn't accept the terms and is taunting you."
"It wasn't his doing at all," Laura remarked. "It was his mother's idea to insert that condition."
"That figures," replied her mum caustically. "That is totally in character for her. So, what are you going to do?"
Laura took a deep breath. "I'm quitting my job at Meridian," she said as calmly as she could. "I'm going to rent out the house in London and I'm going to move to Blythwold. Then, after a year, it's all mine; I'll decide what I do from there."
Laura waited nervously to hear her mother's reaction. The few seconds' silence that elapsed seemed much longer to Laura, who was desperate for her mum to be understanding.
"Don't do it, Laura," remarked her mum. "You've a good job in London, please don't throw that away and move to Blythwold. I know losing the inheritance is unfair, but you won't be happy there. They are a weird bunch and I'd be worried about you being so close to Mary McKenna. Your dad is right, she's wicked."
"It will be fine," replied Laura, trying hard to make light of the situation. "Mary doesn't frighten me. She's got to

be in her eighties. Anyway, it will only be for a year, and then I can sell up and go, if I want."
"But what about your job?" Bev asked. "You're doing so well."
"To be honest, Mum, I was going to quit anyway," replied Laura. "I'm not upset about leaving Meridian."
"And what does Kieran say about all this?" her mum asked. "Surely, he won't like the idea of you moving to Suffolk?"
Laura took another deep breath. "Well," she said tentatively, "Kieran and I split up yesterday."
"I'm not surprised if you want to move out there," replied her mum with unusual insensitivity.
"Actually, we split up before I knew anything about the conditions of the inheritance," remarked Laura, who was quite annoyed at her mum's thoughtlessness. "If you want to know, he wanted me to pack up my job and move to the US with him."
"And you said no," interrupted her mum in a tone that was positively hostile. "Well, I think moving to the US with someone who cares for you is much more sensible than packing up everything you've worked for and moving to live with them ... them .... in-breeds!"
Laura had expected some strong resistance from her mum but was quite taken aback by her aggressiveness; it was so out of character.
She saw no value in continuing the conversation as she could sense her mum was in no mood to be talked round.
"I'm going to have to go," she remarked, "the trains coming into the station at Ipswich. I'm sorry you're angry with me, Mum, but I've made up my mind so I hope you can at least understand my reasoning, and I don't want to fall out with you over it".

"I don't know what your dad is going to say," replied her mum who appeared to be a little calmer. "We won't fall out, dear, but please reconsider. You don't know what those people are like in Blythwold. They aren't nice and they'll make your life a misery. I know you will lose out on your inheritance, but please don't move to Blythwold."
Laura could hear the despair in her mum's voice; something she'd never experienced before. She desperately didn't want to hurt her mum, but she'd made up her mind. And when Laura made up her mind, she rarely changed it!
"I'm going to have to go. The train's just pulling into the station," she lied. "I'll call you again in a few days."
Laura's mum remained silent on the other end. "Love you, Mum," said Laura as reassuringly as she could before she ended the call.
With tears streaming down her face, Laura sat quietly for the next thirty minutes as her train trundled across the level green terrain on its way to Ipswich.

* * *

Upon her arrival in London Laura discovered, to her misery, the district line in complete turmoil. After waiting for over half an hour on the crowded platform at Tower Hill, it eventually came to light that there had been a jumper on the line at Sloane Square. After a further forty minutes the trains started to get back to normal, but with the sheer number of people desperate to get on their way it took another fifteen minutes for Laura to board a train.
At ten o'clock Laura eventually arrived home in Lavenham Road, tired and totally cheesed off.

She jettisoned her bag in the hallway, kicked off her shoes and sauntered wearily into the kitchen. In the middle of the kitchen table Laura could see a neat pile of envelopes, the post from the last few days. And next to her post was a key, which she took to be the one she'd given Kieran. Laura had fully expected Kieran to have gone back to her house to collect his stuff, not that he had much there, so it was no surprise to find his key on the kitchen table.
Laura picked up the key and held it tightly in her hand for a few seconds. Then unceremoniously she threw it into the empty china fruit bowl which sat on the wooden table.
Laura picked up the letters and fanned them quickly to see if any looked interesting enough to open; none did. She opened her fridge, took out a carton of juice and poured herself a large glass of the orange liquid. It was then her mobile rang. It was Saskia's number that appeared on the tiny screen.
"Hi, Sas," Laura said with little fervour.
"So, how did it go today?" Saskia enquired, her voice full of enthusiasm. "What sort of inheritance have you got?"
For a split-second Laura considered fobbing her friend off, but she thought 'what the hell', Saskia would get to know sooner rather than later, so why not now?
"I get everything," replied Laura who had wondered into the lounge by that point and flopped herself down in her favourite comfy chair. "It's not a fortune but enough."
"Wow," replied Saskia. "Is it just money or is there a house, too?"
"He didn't have that much money," replied Laura, "but he had a really nice small flat and a small events business, too. And they are all mine."

Laura decided not to share the conditions of Billy McKenna's will with her friend but saw no reason to hide anything else.
"Wow," replied Saskia again. "So, are you going to sell them?"
Laura smiled. "Actually, no," she replied calmly, "I'm going to quit Meridian, I'm going to rent out this place here, and I'm moving to Blythwold to run my new business."
There was an audible gasp from the other end of the phone. "Seriously?" Saskia asked, her tone suggesting total incredulity.
"Seriously," replied Laura. "I'm going to tell Vic tomorrow that I'm quitting."
"But what about America?" Saskia asked. "And what does Kieran say about all this?"
"There's no job anymore in America, McCauley's have had a head count freeze, so that's no longer an option." Laura replied. "And Kieran and I have split up. We split up before I heard the details of Billy's will and he's not even aware of my decision."
There was a stunned silence from the end of the phone.
"So, you'll get my job for certain now," Laura added. "Congratulations!"
"Vic won't be pleased," replied Saskia.
"Vic will just have to manage without me," Laura remarked. "He may not like it but I'm leaving and, between you and me, I want to go as soon as possible. Now I expect he may not like that, but that's how it is."
"Wow," said Saskia for the third time. "I can't believe you're giving up Meridian and London just like that. I could understand if you were going to America, but Suffolk!"
Laura laughed. "You sound like my mum," she replied, "she doesn't get it either."

"So, when do you plan on leaving Meridian?" Saskia enquired.
"Friday," said Laura calmly.
"This Friday!" exclaimed Saskia.
Laura laughed. "Yep," she replied, "this Friday."
Saskia had been to the gym the previous evening but had been disappointed to find that Vic was not there, so she'd not had a chance to probe him for more information about her future. With Laura now having decided to leave Meridian, she could only see this as being good for her, but she wasn't going to take anything for granted.
"What time are you due to meet Vic tomorrow?" she asked.
Laura hadn't thought about when she'd speak to Vic, but decided she'd try and do it as early as possible.
"I'll let him get himself settled," Laura replied. "Then I'll try and see him at around nine thirty. He's usually more receptive after he's checked his emails and had a few cups of coffee."
Saskia laughed. "Good plan," she replied. "But don't expect him to be happy!"
Laura let out a deep breath. "I know," she agreed. "It's probably going to be a tricky conversation."
"Do you want to meet up beforehand?" Saskia asked.
"Er, no," replied Laura. "To be honest I'm probably only going to arrive at the office at about nine thirty myself. I just want to go straight in when I get there. But I'll find you afterwards and let you know how it goes."
"Well, good luck," said Saskia. "I'll keep my fingers crossed."
As soon as the call ended Laura ambled through to her bedroom to check whether Kieran had taken all his stuff

and see if he'd left a note – not that she expected him to have.

Chapter 40

Thursday 27th August

Laura left home just half an hour later than normal, but she had no intention of going straight into the office. Her plan was to spend an hour or so in Borini's, her favourite little coffee house just off Vauxhall Bridge, where she would have a leisurely croissant and large skinny latte while she rehearsed in her head exactly how she'd handle Vic. Laura also wanted to make the call to Nigel Diplock to ask him to make sure Abigail was paid the wages owing to her.
To reach the coffee house Laura had to pass the Meridian office and as she did, Laura glanced upwards at the top window, which was Vic's office. As she'd expected his light was on and Laura could see the back of Vic's head. What she also saw was the silhouette of a person standing in front of her boss, which she automatically assumed to be Brenda, his PA.
However, as Laura looked more closely, she noticed the woman was younger than Brenda and she had mousey curly hair, not the short dark crop that made Brenda so distinguishable. Laura stopped in her tracks as she realised who it was; and there was absolutely no doubt. It was Saskia.
Laura could feel her muscles stiffen and her hands start to clench tightly to form fists a prize fighter would have

been proud of. She could only think of one reason why Saskia would be in Vic's office at such an early hour and that notion made her furious.
"You cow," she said out loud, much to the surprise of the well-dressed businessman who passed by her at that precise moment; not that Laura noticed. She remained rooted to the spot as she observed the two figures in Vic's office. She could only see the back of Vic's head, so Laura had no way of judging his mood. However, Saskia's face was clear to see, and her expression was one Laura had seen countless times over the years; the cute little girlie look Saskia always reserved for when she was flirting.
Laura took a few steps backwards to move herself away from the pedestrians as they marched down the pavement, but never took her eyes off the goings-on in Vic's second floor office.
Laura took out her mobile and called Saskia's number. She only had to wait a few seconds before the phone rang and, as it did, she saw Saskia take her mobile from her bag, look at it – presumably see Laura's number appear, then show Vic.
"Answer, you cow," muttered Laura, this time so nobody else could hear.
Laura didn't have to wait long. To her surprise she saw Saskia put the phone to her ear, and a split second later she heard Saskia's familiar, sickly, smarmy voice.
"Hi Laura," Saskia said. "Can I call you back?"
Laura was seething but didn't want her friend to know.
"Yes," she replied as calmly as she could. "Are you at work yet?"
Without hesitation Saskia replied. "Yes, I've just this minute arrived. Where are you?"
Laura wanted to be certain her friend was lying to her.
"Have you seen Vic yet this morning?"

"No," replied Saskia, unfalteringly, "not yet. To be honest I'm not even sure he's in yet."
As she spoke, Laura could see Saskia pull a face at Vic quite clearly trying to give him the impression she was struggling with her lies.
"If you do," continued Laura, "please don't mention any of what we discussed last night. I want to tell Vic myself."
"Oh absolutely," replied Saskia. "That goes without saying."
"Thanks," Laura added. "I'll see you later."
"What time are you planning to arrive?" Saskia asked.
"I'll be there in a few minutes," replied Laura, although she had no intention of entering the office for at least another hour. "I'll come and find you after I've spoken to Vic."
With that Laura ended the call and watched with a mixture of irritation and amusement as Saskia relayed to Vic the details of their conversation before darting swiftly from his office, presumably to avoid being caught out by Laura.
"At least I know the score," Laura mumbled to herself before making off in the direction of Vauxhall Bridge and the coffee house.

*　　　*　　　*

It was two hours before Laura entered Vic's office. She had arrived fifty minutes earlier, but when Laura called him to find out whether he was free, Vic, in predictable fashion, had told her she'd have to wait until he'd made a few calls. Not that Laura minded. She was only too happy to have a few minutes at her desk, which she used initially to print off a copy of the order book Abigail had emailed her the day before, erasing that message and

then all other private messages that were stored on her computer. Laura also used the time to place the few small personal items she kept in her office into the larger than usual handbag which she'd brought with her that morning, for this specific purpose.
"Hi Laura," Vic remarked in a seemingly friendly manner. "I've asked Brenda to join us, I hope that's okay with you?"
Laura was shocked at this revelation but couldn't think of any reason to object. "It's fine with me," she replied with self-assurance before making herself comfortable on a chair a few feet away from her boss.
"Would you come in please, Brenda," Vic shouted through the open door.
Obediently the middle-aged lady entered the room clutching her note pad, which never seemed to be far from her side.
Laura smiled confidently at Vic's PA, who looked decidedly uneasy about joining them.
"Right," said Vic, with a smug grin on his face. "What's your decision going to be?"
Although Laura knew her boss was going to be fully aware of her decision, she didn't want him to know she'd seen him with Saskia, and for the benefit of ensuring that Brenda's notes were recorded in a manner that maintained this misconception, Laura elected to make her reply as if she knew nothing of Saskia's visit earlier.
"Your offer was really tempting, Vic," Laura opened, her false smile almost as good as Vic's had been earlier. "And to be honest, I was going to accept, however, yesterday I learned that I'd inherited a business from my late birth father, so with a heavy heart I've decided to leave Meridian, so I can take over the reins."

This news was obviously no great shock to Vic, but he attempted to pretend otherwise. "So, what sort of business is it?" he enquired.
"It's an events company," replied Laura. "It's very small and in the back of beyond, but to be honest, I'm looking forward to the new challenge."
Vic paused for a few seconds then looked towards Brenda. "Do you have Laura's contract?" he asked his PA.
Having clearly been asked to bring it in, Brenda extracted the contract from her notebook and passed it over to her boss.
Vic turned over the pages until he arrived at the page he was looking for. "So, you're on three months' notice," he remarked. "So that will take us up to the twenty-sixth of November. Do you have your letter of resignation?"
Laura handed over the letter she'd prepared the previous evening.
Vic unfolded the letter and read it carefully. "This says you want to leave immediately," he remarked as if the request was the most ridiculous thing he'd ever seen.
"Yes," replied Laura, a little uncomfortably. "I need to take up the position without delay. It's a very small business, so I do need to be in situ straight away."
Frown lines appeared on Vic's forehead, and he shook his head.
"No chance," he replied in a tone as uncompromising as was possible. "You can't expect us to let you go just like that. We'll need to replace you and there needs to be a proper professional handover of your accounts."
Out of the corner of her eye, Laura could see Brenda furiously scribbling notes.
Laura had fully expected Vic to be awkward, so her next line had been well rehearsed.

"Due to my circumstances I need to leave immediately," she announced with calm assurance. "I realise that it will take a short while to handover my responsibilities, but I was assuming that Saskia would be getting my job. Is that not the case?"
"I'll have to consider how I reorganise," replied Vic, "however, even if the job does go to Saskia, she'll need the three months of your notice period to get herself fully acclimatised. So, I'm afraid I can't allow you to go straight away."
Laura smiled. She had fully expected this would be his reply. "Well, to be fair, I did tell you I was leaving last Friday, which was the twenty-first of August. I also still have fifteen days holiday left, so if we were to stick to the contract, my finishing date would be the sixth of November."
Vic nodded, "Okay, I'll concede to that," he remarked.
"Well, what if I work two days a week until then," Laura suggested. "That will certainly allow whoever you chose to take over from me to get up to speed, but it will also allow me to start to manage my father's business right away."
Vic paused for a short while as if he was considering Laura's proposal. However, the shake of his head announced his decision before any words left his mouth. "I'm sorry, Laura," he said firmly, "you either serve your three months' notice or we'll have no other option than to take out an action against you for breach of contract."
Laura stood up and fixed her gaze straight into Vic's eyes. "Then I guess we'll have to sort this out via our legal people," she said. "It's such a shame it's come to this, but as I said before, I have to be in place in the new role straight away, so I have no option other than to tell you that I won't be in at all after tomorrow."

As Laura made her way to the door, she could hear Vic's voice booming out in her direction. "So, what about the job in the US?" he asked.
Laura turned around to face him, her annoyance evident in her face. "I'm sorry, Vic," she remarked caustically, "I thought Saskia would have already told you about that when you were together this morning. Did she not mention it?"
Vic ignored Laura's comment. "Brenda will send you a transcript of our conversation later today," he replied calmly. "But believe me, Laura, we will hold you to the terms of your contract. If you're not here on Monday, then we'll be taking legal action."
Laura gave Vic a contemptuous look and stormed out of the office.

Chapter 41

Having made her exit from the meeting room, Laura returned to her desk and started to look online at potential letting agencies to manage the renting out of her house in Lavenham Road.
She was so engrossed in the details that appeared on her screen that Laura failed to see the figure of Saskia as she surreptitiously crept up on her.
"So, how did it go?" Saskia asked, all smiles and with a sickening eagerness that instantly antagonised Laura.
Laura glared up at her. "I'm sure Vic will be more than happy to fill you in," she replied with no attempt to hide her anger, "just like you did this morning."
Saskia looked genuinely shocked. "I've no idea what you mean," she remarked.
"Cut the crap, Sas," Laura replied. "When I called you earlier you were already in his office. I saw you!"
This time the surprise on Saskia's face was real.
"Aren't you going to deny it, Sas?" Laura asked.
Saskia took a pace backwards. "No, why should I?" she replied as calmly as she could, although it was clear she was rattled. "So what?"
"And I thought you were my friend!" Laura shouted. "Well get this straight, Saskia, you're no friend of mine!"

Saskia smirked. “All’s fair in love and business, Laura,” she announced coldly. “It’s the survival of the fittest, and to be honest, I think our friendship ran its course a good while back.”
Laura felt her fists clenching once more. She wasn’t normally prone to thoughts of violence, but at that moment she would have happily punched that smug face – but she didn’t. There was no way she was going to compound her problems at Meridian by giving Vic and Saskia any easy ammunition to hurl back at her.
“Just get out of my face, Saskia,” Laura said, her eyes bulging out of their sockets with hate and anger. “I wish you every success in your new position but don’t expect any help from me. I’m out of here right now. And you can tell Vic that I’m not coming back whatever the consequences.”
Saskia theatrically turned on her heels, headed out of the door and down the corridor.
As soon as she knew she was alone Laura rested her head in her hands. In the space of two weeks her life had changed so much -almost too much for her to comprehend.
She would have probably remained in that pose for even longer had she not been interrupted by Brenda, who appeared almost mouse-like with two copies of the transcript of the conversation between her and Vic from earlier that morning.
“Vic has asked me to get you to check over this and sign both copies to say that it’s a true record of what you discussed earlier,” Brenda said almost apologetically.
Laura smiled at Brenda and took the documents from her. She read it thoroughly before nodding and putting her signature at the bottom of both, just under where Vic had signed.
“Do I get to keep a copy?” she asked.

Brenda nodded. "Oh yes, one's yours."
Brenda smiled kindly at Laura and took just one of the copies leaving Laura with the other.
"I thought you were very brave today," said Brenda quietly. "I do hope everything works out for you."
Laura looked into Brenda's eyes. She could see that she meant it, which she found surprisingly comforting.
"Thank you, Brenda," she replied with genuine warmth. "I certainly hope it's all going to be worth it, as I can't see Vic backing down about taking legal action."
Brenda smiled again. "You may be right," she said as she made her way to the door, "but don't lose heart, things often work out for the best, that's what I always say."
"If only that were true," muttered Laura once the PA was out of earshot. "If only that were true."

Part Eight

A New Start

Chapter 42

Monday 14th September

Once Laura put her mind to anything she was pretty much unstoppable. So, having decided to leave Meridian, rent out her house in Lavenham Road and move herself to Blythwold, it was really no surprise to see all three tasks almost completed in just under three weeks. In fairness Laura's new tenants still hadn't moved into Lavenham Road yet, but contracts had been signed and with any personal stuff she didn't want to take with her to Blythwold being put into storage, she had everything ready for her new occupants. The big plus for Laura was the amount of rent she was going to get. It was easily enough to cover her mortgage and the rest Laura knew would come in handy as, for the foreseeable future, the events business was certainly not going to afford her anything like the sort of income she had been used to.
On the subject of the events business, Laura was still trying to get her head around the finances. Based upon what she'd seen so far, she was struggling to understand just how Billy McKenna was able to post any sort of profit from the business. As far as Laura could see it was, at best, only breaking even.
The profitability of the events business, however, wasn't Laura's only issue. The threatening letter she'd received

from Meridian regarding her failure to honour her notice period was the thing that worried her most. Based upon how they'd couched it and the advice she'd received from Nigel Diplock, it looked like she could face a bill of over tens of thousands for breach of contract – a prospect which, in truth, had caused Laura numerous sleepless nights.

However, even with these concerns, she had no regrets about her new start in Blythwold. She still missed Kieran and would have liked her mum and dad to sound a little more supportive when they spoke on the phone, but all things considered Laura was confident she'd made the right decision – and if she hadn't, she knew that in twelve months she'd be free to sell the apartment and the business if she wished.

That Monday morning Laura rose early, she made herself a mug of coffee and sat serenely in her comfy armchair; one of the few items of furniture she'd brought with her from London. With the window wide open, the sun poured into the flat making every corner shine with a vibrancy no artificial light could ever match. In that natural brightness and with the sound of the waves as they crashed on the shore, with metronomic regularity, Laura felt a warm, safe feeling inside.

Although it was still technically summer, the feel of Blythwold had changed dramatically in the last few weeks. With most holidaymakers back at work and with their energised brood returned to school, the place seemed so much slower and calmer; the accent now on different senses, on the smells and sounds of wind and waves rather than the excited squeals of excited children.

Laura had not disliked the sound of the happy holidaymakers, it had reminded her of the bustle of

suburbia, but the soothing sounds of water on pebbles and the unmistakeable twang of the ropes as they rattled against the flag posts seemed somehow preferable.
Laura looked at the clock, it was seven forty-five am. She smiled to herself as she remembered what she'd have been doing at this time when she worked in London. If she hadn't already arrived at work, she'd be on the tube, no doubt squeezed into a corner as it rattled towards Victoria. Or even worse, she could be on the platform waiting after another poor jumper had halted the district line. Her journey to work these days was much simpler; a walk down three flights of stairs then five minutes on foot and she would be there.
However straightforward the journey, old habits die hard, and Laura made a point of arriving at her office by eight am, as she wanted to make sure she was always there before the dependable Abigail; the young woman Laura had quickly grown to like and admire.
Laura tipped the grouts from her mug into the sink and placed the vessel into the dishwasher. Grabbing her bag and a couple of bananas, she headed for the door and the start of a new week.

* * *

Laura had decided to spend the first part of the morning trying to look in more detail at the books to fathom out how it was that the business had managed to break even. She wanted to understand how Nigel had come to a figure of fifty thousand pounds as its annual turnover, as from what Laura could see, this was almost double what was recorded in the books. And with Abigail's wages and the rent on the office, Laura couldn't understand how Billy McKenna ever made ends meet.

She was certainly no accountant, but Laura figured she stood a reasonable chance of finding the discrepancies if she put her full attention to the minutiae of the order books.
She was already deeply engrossed in the details of incomings and outgoings when Abigail breezed in.
"Morning Laura, "Abigail announced cheerily as she closed the door behind her. "Did you have a good weekend?"
Laura looked up from her papers and returned a smile at the ginger- headed girl with the broad, sunny beam etched large across her face.
"I did, thanks," replied Laura. "How about you?"
"Mine was massive!" replied Abigail. "Me and the girls went up to Yarmouth on Saturday for a gig and met some army boys. It was really fun."
Although she was only just ending her twenties, Laura felt ancient when she listened to the exploits of Abigail and her pals. But in truth she had no desire to swap places, that's for sure.
"How was your meal at the Bull on Saturday?" Abigail asked.
Laura looked back at her with astonishment. "Good god!" she replied. "You can't do anything in this place without everyone knowing."
Abigail laughed. "You'll have to get used to that Laura," she replied with a wry smile, "especially when you're having dinner with one of Blythwold's most eligible bachelors."
Laura gave Abigail a knowing look. "Mr Diplock and I are just good friends. We were having a meal to discuss the business."
Abigail smiled from ear to ear. "Nigel Diplock fancies you rotten," she replied. "Believe me, if you looked like the back end of a cow, he'd never take you out for

dinner. And from what I hear this is at least the third time he's bought you dinner."
Laura laughed. "I can assure you and the rest of Blythwold that there's nothing going on between me and Nigel."
"Give it time!" Abigail replied. "He's considered quite a catch around here."
"Is he?" remarked Laura firmly, to ensure Abigail knew she no longer wanted to continue that particular conversation.
Abigail got the message and headed off towards the corner of the office where the kettle lived. "Coffee, Laura?" she shouted over.
"Yes, please," Laura replied with a friendly smile.

* * *

For the next two hours Laura poured over the business accounts. As hard as she tried, Laura couldn't work out how Nigel had come to put an annual turnover on the business of fifty thousand pounds. The invoices that Billy had recorded for the previous year only added up to just over twenty-eight thousand pounds and based upon current jobs they had on the books, hitting twenty-eight thousand pounds for the current year looked like it was going to be a major challenge.
Laura let out a deep sigh, stopped what she was doing and leant back in her chair, her hands clasped behind her head.
"Abigail," shouted Laura across the room. "I know you had little to do with the accounts here, but do you know of anything Billy didn't include in the books?"
Abigail looked up from under her wild, red corkscrewed hair. "Not really," she replied. "I didn't get involved."

Laura sighed again. "Did Billy keep any printed bank statements?" she enquired. "I can't see any anywhere."
Abigail shrugged her shoulders. "I never saw any," she replied. "I think he just checked them online."
"And I don't suppose you know the password he used?" Laura continued.
"Not a clue," replied Abigail with clarity. "But I can go and ask the bank for some copies if you want? They're just on the High Street."
"Will they give you them, if you just walk in?" Laura enquired.
"God, yes," replied Abigail. "My sister works on the counter, so she knows I work here."
Laura nodded. "Okay then," she said. "Can you ask them for statements for the last twelve months?"
Abigail stood up and walked over to the door. "I'll be back in ten."
True to her word, Abigail was gone no more than ten minutes.
"Here you go!" she remarked as she put down the handful of printed statements on Laura's desk.
As she did so, the phone rang.
Abigail immediately picked it up. "Blythwold Events," she said in her poshest sounding voice. After a few seconds pause, Abigail smiled and said, "She's right here, I'll pass you over."
As she handed over the phone to Laura she mouthed, "It's your friend, Mr Diplock," her grin as wide as her face.
Laura grabbed the receiver. "Hello, Laura speaking," she said
"Is it okay if I shoot off for lunch?" Abigail mouthed.
"Can you hang on a second, Nigel?" Laura remarked before putting her hand over the mouthpiece and looking

at her watch. "It's only just turned eleven!" she exclaimed.
"I know," replied Abigail, "but I'm starving. I didn't get much breakfast this morning."
Laura laughed. "I guess so," she replied. "I'll see you in an hour."
"Thanks, boss," replied Abigail, who picked up her bag and breezed out of the office.
As soon as Abigail was out of earshot Laura removed her hand from the mouthpiece. "I'm sorry, Nigel," she said. "I just had to talk to Abigail about something. I'm all ears."
"I was just wondering if you fancied some lunch today?" Nigel enquired.
Laura was tempted. There was no doubting the fact that she found Nigel attractive, and she had certainly enjoyed the meals they'd shared over the last few weeks. However, she was a little worried about jumping into another relationship so soon after breaking up with Kieran and although she'd shrugged it off when she'd been speaking with Abigail earlier, the thought of the entire town monitoring their every movement did unnerve Laura a little.
"I'd love to, Nigel," she replied, "but I've quite a lot on so I was just going to grab a sandwich and work through lunch today."
"A sandwich is fine for me, too," replied Diplock. "We could grab one from the cake shop then maybe go and sit on the seafront and eat them together."
Laura wanted to be firm but found her resolve crumbling. "Okay," she replied, "but I can only spare about thirty minutes. I've tons of things to do today."
"Shall I come over at say twelve thirty then?" Diplock suggested.
"It's a deal," replied Laura. "I'll see you then."

Despite her denials to Abigail, Laura knew full well that Nigel Diplock was interested in her. During their three dinners together, he'd never once made any sort of romantic advance towards her. However, she was sure that if she gave the handsome solicitor any sign of encouragement he would, and had it not been less than three weeks since she and Kieran had split up, she probably would have done so by now.
Laura allowed herself a tiny smile, before picking up the bank statements and starting to wade through them line by line.

.

Chapter 43

Laura and Nigel sat quietly together on the wooden bench facing the expanse of the North Sea.
"You're very thoughtful," Nigel remarked. "You haven't said more than a few words since we left the office."
Laura maintained her gaze frontwards towards the breakers. "I've been checking out the books all morning," Laura replied. "They only record about sixty per cent of the business that Billy was declaring. It doesn't make sense."
Nigel laughed. "It does to me," he replied flippantly. "Billy was no accountant. To be honest if you'd said they did tie up I'd have been amazed. Billy was a bit of a ducker and diver. I don't want to speak ill of the dead, but I'd not be surprised to hear he was hiding a few thousand here and there from the taxman."
Laura turned her head to face him. "If Billy was trying to pull a fast one, he'd have under-reported sales, but he was doing the opposite."
"What do you mean?" Nigel enquired.
"Well for last year the books only show about twenty-eight thousand pounds as recorded sales," said Laura. "However, he declared fifty-two thousand as the annual turnover. When I tried to reconcile the sums using past bank statements, I found that every month cash

payments of two thousand pounds were being made into the business account, but I've no idea what these were for."
Diplock shrugged his shoulders. "Beats me," he remarked. "Maybe he was doing a few cash in hand jobs and just forgot to record them."
Laura shook her head. "No, I don't buy that one," she replied. "These were very regular payments. They went in on the second Tuesday of every month. These don't look ad hoc to me."
Nigel shrugged his shoulders again. "Were they all cash payments?" he enquired.
Laura nodded, "Yes, that's what they look like."
Nigel seemed perplexed. "Do you want me to talk with the manager at the bank to see if he knows anything about it?" Nigel asked. "He's an old friend, I'm sure he'll tell me if he knows anything."
Laura nodded, "That would be good," she replied. "To be honest I'm not sure it's any of my business what went on before I took over, but I would like to know."
"Okay," remarked Nigel, "but it will come at a price."
Lines appeared on Laura's forehead to indicate her bewilderment. "What do you mean?"
As she ended her sentence Nigel leaned over and placed a warm gentle kiss on Laura's lips.
"That's my price," he replied as he pulled his mouth away a few inches from her.
Laura smiled. "Let me give you your change," she said as she planted an even longer lingering kiss on the solicitor's mouth.
When their lips eventually parted Laura looked up into Nigel's deep dark eyes, "I really have to go," she said. "I've a lot to get through today."
"How about dinner this evening?" Nigel asked.

Laura shook her head gently. "Actually, I was planning on a quiet night tonight, but how about you come round to my flat tomorrow evening, and I'll cook something?"
Nigel smiled. "It's a deal," he remarked. "What time do you want me?"
"How does seven thirty sound?" Laura replied.
"That's perfect," Nigel said, his face clearly pleased with the invitation.

*　　　*　　　*

"So, how was lunch?" Abigail enquired when Laura returned to the office, an impish glint in her eye.
"Back to work, young lady," replied Laura with a smile. "I'm not paying you to stand around making idle gossip. We've got a business to run here."
Abigail smiled broadly, before putting her head down and getting back to her work.
"Oh," she said as if she'd just remembered something important. "Your grandmother called earlier. She wants you to call in on her this afternoon."
"Mary McKenna?" Laura replied. When Abigail nodded Laura puffed out her cheeks. "I wonder what she wants," she said gloomily.
"Search me," replied Abigail.
Laura looked at her watch. "Well, she'll have to wait for an hour or so as I want to finish going through the books. Anyway, that woman needs to learn that I'm not about to drop everything at her beck and call."
Abigail frowned. "I'd not get on her bad side if I were you," she said. "She can be quite nasty when she wants to be."
Laura laughed. "She's just a bitter and twisted old woman. I'm not afraid of her."

Abigail didn't look convinced. "She has a lot of influence round here, Laura. She has a habit of making life really difficult for people she doesn't like. She stopped me going to Billy's funeral."
"Oh, it was her was it," Laura remarked. "I was going to ask you about that. So, what was it you did to cause her to stop you going?"
Abigail's expression changed, and she started to look uncomfortable. "I'd rather not say," she remarked coyly.
"You can tell me," continued Laura compassionately. "I promise I won't tell anybody if you don't want me to."
Abigail just shook her head. "No, it's nothing. It's private."
Laura could see Abigail had no desire to tell her anymore, so decided it was probably wise to drop the subject. "Okay," she said as kindly as she could. "That's fine. But remember I'm on your side, you can trust me."

*　　　*　　　*

Laura hadn't spoken to Mary McKenna since the day the old lady had visited her at the apartment, however she'd made it her business to find out where Mary lived, so she had no need to get directions to Dove Cottage, Mary McKenna's terraced house in the centre of Blythwold. Laura waited until almost four o'clock before she headed off to meet the person who had become her least favourite relative.
"I was starting to think you weren't coming," was the greeting Laura received when Mary opened her small, wooden front door.
"Good afternoon, Granny," replied Laura sarcastically, with a large smirk on her face. "Abigail told me you wanted to talk to me."

Mary took a step backwards and beckoned Laura in with a slight tilt of her head.
Laura entered the tiny front room and made herself comfortable on the two-seater sofa against the furthest wall.
"Make yourself at home won't you," remarked Mary to signify disapproval at what she took to be Laura's bad manners. "I won't offer you tea as I suspect you'll just refuse and at any rate you won't be staying long."
If Laura had ever met anyone quite as overbearing and rude as Mary McKenna, she couldn't recall, but in truth a short visit suited Laura perfectly. "So, what do you want?" she asked.
"A few things," replied Mary who eased herself down into the armchair as far away as possible from Laura, albeit that was only a few yards given the fact that the room was fairly pokey. "First of all, I wanted to find out how you're getting on with the business and that useless redheaded girl that works there."
Laura could feel her hackles rising, a feeling she seemed to get every time she met her paternal birth granny. "The business is doing fine, I'm enjoying it and if you are referring to Abigail, all I can say is that she and I are getting on really well. She's not at all useless, as you call her, in fact without her I'd have been really lost."
The old lady's face screwed up as she listened to what Laura was saying. "I'm saying no more," she added. "It's clear whatever I say or suggest you'll just do the opposite, so I'll let you find out about her yourself."
Laura took a deep breath. "And what do you mean by that?" she asked, her irritation evident in her voice.
"It's not for me to tell you," Mary replied curtly. "Ask her yourself."

Laura decided not to take the bait. "You said there were a few things?" she remarked, trying hard to move the conversation to another subject.
"Yes," replied Mary. "I want to talk to your mother. There are things we need to resolve. I suspect I'd be right in assuming she won't be setting foot again in Blythwold, even with you now living here, so I'd like her telephone number."
This was the last thing Laura expected her to say. "What sort of things?" she asked as soon as she'd composed herself.
"That's our business," Mary snapped as if she were addressing a cheeky child who'd answered back out of turn.
Laura shook her head. "Oh no," she said. "I'm not giving you her number unless I know what it is you want to discuss and only then if she agrees first."
Mary considered Laura's words. "I'll tell you what," she continued, "you call your mother and tell her I want to talk to her. Ask her to tell you what it's about. She'll know full well, but she won't have the courage to tell you. But I think it's only fair she has the opportunity to tell you first, after all she is your mother. However, once you've spoken with her if you still want to know why I want to talk to her I'll gladly tell you. But be prepared for some home truths that may not be the sort of things you want to hear."
Laura by now was getting really annoyed. She took several deep breaths to help retain some semblance of composure.
Once she was reasonably sure that she was in control, as calmly as she could, Laura ventured a question. "Do you have a good word to say about anyone?"

Mary's face remained expressionless. "I speak as I find," she replied as if that was enough to justify any amount of bile she spewed out of her mouth.
Laura stood up. "Well, you were correct," she remarked as she headed towards the door. "This was a very short meeting dear granny. Unless there's anything else you want to tell me or anyone else you want to slander then I'll get back to work."
Mary remained in her chair; her eyes fixed on Laura. "Sit down," she ordered. "I've not finished."
Despite wanting to stand up to the old lady, Laura found herself stopping in her tracks and even more surprisingly taking two steps backwards and placing her backside back down on the sofa.
Mary waited until she could see Laura was settled and paying attention.
"It's come to my attention that you've been seeing a good deal of Mr Diplock," the old lady announced, as if this were a mortal sin. "I want it to stop forthwith."
Even by her standards this latest pronouncement was outrageous.
Laura had neither the time nor the inclination to take deep breaths and compose herself. She shot to her feet and marched over to where Mary was sitting.
"You are the nastiest, most unpleasant, interfering old bag I've ever met," she shouted at her, their faces just inches away from each other. "How dare you tell me who I can and cannot see. For your information Nigel and I are just good friends, but if I chose to have sex with him on Blythwold Pier that's my affair and not yours. So, I'd kindly ask you to keep your big nose out of my business."
Laura didn't wait for a reply; she turned on her heels, stomped off to the front door and got out of the house as

quickly as she could, slamming the door shut behind her.

Chapter 44

Laura burst into the office, still fuming after her meeting with Mary McKenna.
"That bloody woman is unbelievable," she shouted.
"Who the hell does she think she is? Do you know what she said to me?"
Abigail had never seen Laura in such a foul mood.
"No," she replied sheepishly.
"She had the gall to try and tell me who I should date. Can you believe that?" Laura continued, her unbridled anger palpable in her voice. "She's also demanding that I give her my mum's telephone number. Well, she can bugger off!"
"Shall I make us both a coffee?" Abigail said in an attempt to calm down her new boss.
"Three sugars in mine," replied Laura, who only usually had one sugar in her coffee. "I need the energy boost."
Abigail smiled. "Coming up," she added as she scurried off towards the kettle.
"And what have you done to get under her skin?" Laura asked as soon as Abigail came over to her desk, coffee in hand.
"What do you mean?" replied Abigail who did a poor job of trying to fake her innocence.
"Abigail!" Laura remarked, her patience clearly now exhausted. "She called you useless and she also implied that you were hiding something, what did she mean?"

Abigail's gaze dropped to the floor. "I really don't want to talk about it," she said.
Laura could see Abigail was reluctant to tell her, but there was no way she was about to relent. "I told you earlier," she added, "I'm a friend, you can trust me." As she spoke Laura laid her hand on Abigail's wrist to try and reassure her.
Abigail lifted her gaze, "Billy and I were close," she said, a hint of fear in her eyes.
"I can understand that," replied Laura.
"No," continued Abigail, "we were really close." As she spoke her eyes widened and her head nodded as if to emphasise what she was saying.
"Lovers!" screeched Laura. "But you're just..."
"Just a young girl," Abigail remarked before Laura had time to finish her sentence. "And he was over thirty years older than me. I know what you're thinking, but it was real, at least to me."
Laura was stunned. "I had no idea," she replied. "Why didn't you say before?"
Abigail shrugged her shoulders. "Nobody knew when Billy was alive," she remarked. "It was only when he'd died that it came out. I mentioned it to Mr Diplock."
"Why?" Laura asked.
Abigail sighed deeply. "Billy had told me that he was going to make me a partner in the business, so I asked Mr Diplock if he'd ever made that known to him or put it in his will, but Mr Diplock said he hadn't."
Laura was still finding it hard to understand how such a pretty, young woman could fall for her father, who had abandoned her when she was small and was, as Abigail had said, at least thirty years older than her.
"So how did Mary McKenna know?" Laura asked,
Abigail shrugged her shoulders again. "I don't know," she replied despondently. "I did tell my mum and a few

of my friends about me and Billy, but that was only after I'd spoken to Mr Diplock. I can't believe any of them would have told Mary. All I know is that Mary knew by the time of the funeral. She came in here about two days before Billy was due to be buried and told me that I was nothing but a scheming little gold digger and that I wasn't welcome at the funeral and that I should ditch any thoughts of owning even a fragment of this business."

Without realising, Laura removed her hand from Abigail's wrist, which Abigail took as being a sign of her disapproval.

"I won't blame you if you don't believe me or even if you hate me," she remarked, her gaze once again diverted.

Laura put her hand back on Abigail's arm. "I don't hate you," she said reassuringly, "If I'm honest I can't understand why you'd want to date a man who's over twice your age, but I do believe you and I don't hate you!"

Abigail seemed relieved to hear Laura's words. "So, I can stay on here?" she asked.

Laura smiled. "Of course," she replied. "As I keep telling you, we're friends and you can trust me."

"And you me, Laura," replied Abigail with a broad grin.

*　　*　　*

Laura wasn't prone to drinking by herself in the evening, but after the afternoon she'd had she felt she needed one, so as soon as she got back to the flat that night, she opened a bottle of chardonnay and poured herself a large glass.

She sat in her chair gazing out of the window. She was still shocked by Abigail's revelation about her relationship with Billy.
She half hoped that Abigail was lying but, somehow, she couldn't bring herself to believe that she was capable of such deceit.
No, Laura found herself believing Abigail and, as a result, her overwhelming emotions were of guilt and pity rather than anger.
Guilt that it was she who Billy had left everything to and pity that Abigail had so cruelly been denied the chance of saying goodbye properly to Billy at his funeral.
Her thoughts then moved on to Nigel. Would he have told Mary? Having come to know him well, Laura couldn't see it, but she had to accept it may have been a possibility. Maybe the handsome, well-mannered young man who had been courting her affections for the last few weeks wasn't the man he made out to be. Laura struggled to accept that Nigel was deceitful but was certainly going to raise the issue with him when he came round for dinner on Tuesday evening.
"Bloody Mary!" Laura found herself saying out loud as she took a large gulp of chardonnay. "What other hornet's nest are you going to open for me?"
Her rhetorical question only served to worry Laura even more, as despite her intense dislike of Mary McKenna, she'd yet to be proven a liar – a fact that wasn't lost on Laura and one that was starting to trouble her deeply.
Laura didn't relish making the call to her mum, but she knew she had to, and she was fully aware that if she procrastinated on this one then her concerns would only linger and most likely multiply.
Laura topped-up her glass with more chardonnay, then picked up her mobile.

"Hi superstar," her dad shouted, having picked up the phone in their villa in Spain. "How are things going?"
Laura couldn't help grinning when she spoke with her dad; he was always so loud and almost always so cheery. "Different," she replied. "But I'm loving it."
"I'll give you six months," he replied in his normal no-nonsense manner. "I grew up in that back-of-beyond dump and I couldn't wait to get out. It's been left behind in the dark ages. Give me London or Spain any day."
"Yes, I know, Dad," Laura replied. "But I'm not you, am I?"
Her father laughed, "Let me get your mother."
Laura took a deep breath as she waited for her mum to appear on the other end of the line.
"Laura," yelled her mum. "It's nice to hear from you."
Laura decided to cut to the chase. "I need to tell you something," she said hesitantly. "I was summoned to see Mary McKenna today and she wants me to give her your telephone number."
"What!" exclaimed her mum. "I hope you didn't!"
"Of course, I didn't," replied Laura. "But she is keen to talk with you."
"What about?" Laura's mum enquired.
"She wouldn't tell me," replied Laura. "She maintains there are things you need to resolve, and she was sure you'd know what she was talking about. She told me to ask you, but then said if you didn't tell me, she would."
The few seconds' silence at the end of the phone suggested to Laura that Mary was indeed right and that her mum did know why she wanted to talk with her.
"Are you still there, Mum?" Laura asked.
"Yes, I'm still here," replied Bev, her voice now hushed and sombre. "Don't give her my number. Tell her I'll contact her."

"What's this all about, Mum?" Laura asked. "I'd really like to know."
"I wish you'd never gone back there, Laura," her mum said, her voice still cheerless and serious. "The truth is I'm not totally sure, but I have a feeling I know what it's about. But I don't want to discuss it over the phone."
"Does it affect me?" Laura asked in an attempt to get her mum to open up.
"No, not really," her mum replied, although not very convincingly. "Look, tell Mary I'll contact her, but don't give her my number. I'll talk with your dad to see how quickly we can get a flight over to the UK. I'll tell you when I'm over."
"You're coming to Blythwold!" Laura exclaimed, to make doubly sure she wasn't hearing things.
"I think I have to," replied her mum, "but god knows how I'm going to convince your dad to come, he's adamant he never wants to set foot back in the town."
"Okay," replied Laura, who was now worried that she'd upset her mum so much. "Will you call me to let me know when you're arriving?"
"Of course, dear," replied her mum.
After another awkward silence her mum spoke again. "Look I'm going to have to go, I'll call you tomorrow."
Laura was now very worried about the way her mum was sounding and anxious about what it was that could make her so crestfallen. "I love you, Mum," she said.
"I love you, too, darling," replied her mum before the phone went dead.
Laura placed the mobile on the table next to her and burst into tears.

Chapter 45

Tuesday 15th September

For the first time since arriving in Blythwold, Laura woke to the unmistakeable noise of heavy rain bouncing off the slate roof above her bed and the sound of water pouring down the old metal gutters which surrounded her attic apartment.
"Shit!" she muttered, remembering she'd left her bedroom skylight wide open as usual, a routine she'd adopted to prevent the room from becoming stuffy in the evening heat.
Laura leapt out of bed and rushed towards the window. However, as soon as she got within a few feet of the opening she could feel the cold water under her feet which, having poured through the open skylight, had soaked deep into the carpet making it saturated and spongy. "Bugger," she shrieked as she shut the window with a thud. "Bloody hell," she continued as she headed off to the bathroom to grab some towels to mop up the water on her bedroom floor.
Laura hardly ever swore, so three profanities being her first utterances of the day summed up how low she was feeling, a mood which had remained with her since speaking to her mum the evening before. Fortunately for Laura the puddle on the carpet didn't appear to be too

horrific, and three sodden bath towels later the carpet appeared to be largely free of water.
“I wonder what other revelations will emerge today,” Laura muttered as she wandered into the bathroom for an early morning shower to hopefully kick start her into action.

*   *   *

Fortunately for Laura her pessimism was unfounded, as her day in the office went by without experiencing anything of any real consequence. Abigail was as bright and breezy as ever and they secured a new contract to coordinate an event in the autumn for Patterson’s brewery, the main employer in the town. What was more surprising to Laura was the total absence of any new revelations from Mary McKenna when Laura made the quick telephone call to pass on her mother’s message. The day was so uneventful that by the time Laura arrived back at her flat she was, once again, back in an affable frame of mind.
That, however, changed when Laura opened her post. Laura read the letter from Meridian, the third or fourth she’d received since walking out on them three weeks earlier. Having absorbed its threatening contents, she unceremonially stuffed it into her drawer with the others. “Bastards!” she remarked. “They can take me to court. I’m not paying them a penny.”
Having made herself a cup of coffee, Laura looked up at the clock. She had just a little under an hour to get changed and prepare the dinner she’d promised Nigel Diplock, a task which was do-able, but only if she got a move on.
Thirty-five minutes later, with the salad prepared, homemade garlic bread ready to go in the oven, and her

shop bought pizzas modified with the addition of extra anchovies and a generous covering of mozzarella cheese sitting on the worktop, Laura headed in the direction of the bathroom for a quick shower and change of clothing before her guest arrived.
Before Laura had even entered the bathroom there was a loud knock on the door.
"You're too early!" Laura mumbled under her breath as she walked over to the door. "We said seven thirty, not ten past seven," she continued to mutter as she opened the door.
She hadn't considered her visitor would be anyone other than the handsome Nigel Diplock, so was totally flabbergasted when she saw in front of her the familiar frame of Kieran.
"Hello, Laura," he said with a faint, almost apologetic smile on his face. "Can I come in?"
Open-mouthed Laura opened the door wider, and her visitor entered her apartment.
"What are you doing here?" Laura enquired. "I thought you'd be in America by now."
"I fly out on Saturday," Kieran replied rather sheepishly. "But I couldn't go without seeing you again. I didn't want to go without… without…" Kieran struggled to find the right words.
"Without trying to blackmail me into marriage," Laura interrupted with a directness that shocked even her.
"No," Kieran replied forcefully. "No, that was never my intention Laura, I think you know that. My proposal was genuine and unconditional; it just came out all wrong."
Laura wasn't in the mood to make Kieran's attempt to explain any easier for him. "Well, that's how it sounded to me," she replied again, her tone rather more forceful than she'd actually intended.

Kieran gently took hold of Laura's wrists. "It wasn't how it was supposed to be," he said calmly with genuine feeling. "I wanted you to marry me, that's all, with no strings."
Deep down Laura knew that Kieran was telling the truth. If she'd been honest with herself earlier, she'd have realised that all along, but, for whatever reason, she'd convinced herself that Kieran's intentions were conditional.
Laura pulled her arms free. "I'm not sure we're right for each other," she said. "And as I've no intention of following you to America, I don't see it working, do you?"
"Then I won't go," Kieran replied, the sincerity clear in his eyes.
"Really?" Laura said with astonishment. "You'd give it all up for me?"
Kieran took hold of her again. "Yes," he replied sincerely, his eyes staring deep into hers. "If that's what it takes."
Laura's shocked expression said it all.
"I'm serious, Laura," Kieran continued. "If I have to choose between America and you, I'll pick you every time."
To her surprise Laura's initial instinct wasn't to fling her arms around Kieran's shoulders and tell him she loved him. She somehow just couldn't do it. Had he made the same proposal in the same way, weeks earlier when they'd been together on the pier, Laura was sure she'd have said yes instantly, but for a reason she found hard to explain, the proposal still didn't feel right.
"What do you say, Laura?" Kieran asked, his voice trembling as if he knew he was about to be turned down.

"I do still have feelings for you, Kieran," Laura replied trying to be as sensitive as she could. "But I'm not sure we should marry, not now anyway."
Kieran's face portrayed his disappointment.
"Why not?" he urged her. "What's stopping you?"
Before she had a chance to answer, the sound of footsteps coming from the communal stairwell reached Laura's ears and she suddenly remembered Nigel Diplock and their dinner date.
"Look," Laura said in a hushed voice, "we need to talk about this, but I can't now. I've invited the solicitor who's been handling Billy McKenna's estate to have dinner. I think he's on his way up."
Kieran shrugged his shoulders. "Can't you just tell him something's come up?" he said.
"It's not that easy," replied Laura who was feeling very uncomfortable about the situation and the impending meeting of Kieran and Nigel.
"I see," Kieran replied. "Are you saying you want me to bugger off?"
Laura pulled a face which portrayed her embarrassment and clearly indicated she wasn't happy with Kieran remaining.
"Would you mind?" she replied. "We'll probably be no more than two or three hours. You could go to the pub, and I'll see you later. We can talk then."
Kieran, not for the first time since he'd been dating Laura, found himself being outmanoeuvred. "Okay," he remarked compliantly. "Why don't you text me when the coast is clear. I'm assuming you haven't deleted my number."
Laura smiled. "No, I haven't," she replied firmly just as the sound of footsteps stopped indicating that Nigel Diplock had reached the top of the stairs. "I'll text you when he's gone."

Laura gave Kieran a warm but less than passionate peck on the cheek, which after she'd done it seemed totally inappropriate. As she did there was a loud knock on the door.
Laura opened the door to reveal the familiar figure of Nigel Diplock who stood before her smiling, with a huge bunch of flowers in one hand and an even bigger box of chocolates in the other.
As soon as the handsome solicitor saw Kieran his broad grin evaporated, but true to form he remained as polite as ever.
"Good evening," Diplock announced to the pair. "Am I too early?"
Laura put on a forced smile. "No," she replied. "Although I'm not quite ready yet"
"Nigel, can I introduce you to Kieran," Laura announced with no attempt to explain who he was.
Diplock smiled graciously. "Pleased to meet you, Kieran," he said warmly.
"Are those for me?" Laura remarked pointing to the flowers and chocolates.
"Well, I'm certain they're not for me," quipped Kieran sarcastically, and clearly a little shocked and perturbed at seeing such a generous gift from a mere dinner guest.
Laura ignored Kieran's dig and took the flowers and chocolates from Nigel. "These are lovely," she said warmly. "Why don't you come in?"
As soon as his hands were free, Nigel Diplock put out his right arm in Kieran's direction.
Kieran, rather less generously, shook the solicitor's hand. "Enjoy your dinner," he said although the tone of his voice didn't match the words.
Kieran eyed the handsome solicitor up and down for a few seconds before turning to face Laura. "I'll see you later then," he remarked, a comment that was

deliberately designed to alert Laura's guest that his departure was only temporary.
"Yes, we'll talk later," Laura replied with a forced grin behind angry eyes.
Kieran turned his head to face Nigel Diplock. "It was nice to meet you," he said in as friendly a tone as he could. Without waiting for a reply, Kieran made his way through the still-open door and quickly descended the stairs.
As soon as Kieran was halfway down the stairwell, Laura closed her door.
"Sorry about that," she said trying hard to mask her embarrassment, "I hadn't expected to see Kieran this evening. He arrived out of the blue."
"I take it he's an ex-boyfriend," remarked Nigel, who was trying hard to understand where Kieran fitted in.
"Sort of," replied Laura, who was still feeling very uncomfortable about the whole situation.
After a short but uneasy pause, Laura pointed at the sofa. "Please take a seat," she urged her guest. "I'll put these in some water and quickly get changed."
Nigel Diplock smiled and did as he was told.
"Do you want a drink?" Laura asked as she headed towards the kitchen area.
"Yes, please," replied Nigel. "What do you have?"
Laura placed the flowers on the draining board. "I've got some beers and a bottle of chardonnay in the fridge."
Nigel smiled. "A beer would be good," he replied. "But I'll sort it out, you go and get yourself ready."
Laura smiled back at the handsome, well-mannered solicitor. "Thanks," she remarked before heading off towards her bedroom. "There are glasses in the cabinet above the sink."
As soon as Laura was alone behind the door in her bedroom, she let out a huge sigh of relief. This certainly

wasn't going to be anything like the evening Laura had anticipated.

.

Chapter 46

When Laura emerged from the bedroom Nigel Diplock had poured himself a beer and was standing by the window watching the goings on down below.
As soon as he realised Laura had returned, Nigel turned to face her.
"You look stunning," he remarked.
Laura could not help but smile as she heard those words. In fairness to Kieran he'd often made similar comments, and she'd always been flattered, but when Nigel told her she looked stunning, for some unfathomable reason, it seemed more important to her. It certainly gave her a greater thrill.
"Why thank you," she replied with a smile. "I only hope you like the dinner, too."
As she spoke, Laura realised that she'd not yet put the pizza and garlic bread in the oven.
She quickly made her way over to the kitchen area to remedy her error, only to be confronted by the sight of an empty worktop and the smell of cheese coming from the oven.
"Oh, I hope you don't mind," remarked Nigel, "but I put the dinner in the oven. I thought it would cook better."
Laura smiled back at her handsome guest. "I don't mind at all," she replied.

Had the telephone not rung at that precise moment who knows what would have happened, but the phone did ring and as soon as Laura picked it up, the moment disappeared.
"Hi, Mum," Laura said when she realised who was calling. "Can I call you back a bit later?"
"It won't take long," remarked her mum. "I'm just calling to tell you that we'll be arriving at Stansted tomorrow. We'll hire a car and get over to you as soon as we can."
"Tomorrow!" exclaimed Laura. "That's quick. What time do you expect to get here?"
"The plane lands at around three," replied Laura's mum. "I guess by the time we get through immigration, get our bags, pick up the car and get on our way, it will be about four. So, we'll be in Blythwold at around sixish."
"Right," replied Laura. "I'll see you tomorrow then."
"I'll call you when we arrive," added her mum before the phone went dead.
"Good news?" enquired Nigel, who couldn't help but hear Laura's conversation.
"Yes," replied Laura who could not help thinking that the conversation her mum and she would be having the next day must be serious for her to arrange a flight over so quickly. "My mum and dad are coming over tomorrow."
"That's nice," replied Nigel. "Are they staying long?"
Laura shook her head. "To be honest, Nigel, I'm not sure how long they'll be here for."

*   *   *

As soon as Kieran left Laura's apartment, he headed straight for the Admiral public house and a pint of Patterson's best bitter.

He plonked himself on a stool at the bar and within a few minutes was gulping down the dark amber liquid. An hour later and three pints already consumed, Kieran was starting to feel the effects of the strong local brew.
"You look like you could do with some company," remarked a voice behind him.
Kieran half turned and was taken by surprise to see the person who made the remark was a priest, his off-white dog collar giving his occupation away.
"Feel free to join me," replied Kieran with an affability he always acquired after a few pints.
"You're not from the area," observed the cleric as he slipped onto the bar stool next to Kieran.
"No," replied Kieran. "I'm just up to see someone who lives here."
"And do I take it from the fact that you're on your own that this person's late?" enquired the priest.
Kieran laughed. "No," he replied, "she's at a business dinner with her solicitor at the moment. I'm just killing time before I see her later."
"Then I can't think of any better way of doing that than sipping Patterson's beer in this welcoming pub," replied the cleric. "My name's Father Mallory, I'm the priest at St Steven's."
As the two men shook hands, Kieran introduced himself and offered to buy the priest a pint.
"I'll have a Head Banger," the priest replied. "It's got an unfortunate name but it's a terrific pint.
The barman, hearing Father Mallory's request, took a clean glass from the shelf above the bar and started to gently pull a pint of the dark brown creamy beer.
"So, if you don't mind me asking," continued Father Mallory in his soft Irish lilt, "who is your lady friend? Is she a local girl?"

Kieran stared down at his pint. "Her name's Laura Eastwood," he replied. "She's recently moved down here."
"Oh, Laura," replied Mallory. "I don't know her well, but I knew her father."
"You know Mike!" remarked Kieran, who was surprised at what he'd been told.
"No," replied the priest. "Billy McKenna."
Realising that Mallory was talking about Laura's birth father, Kieran nodded. "I thought you were talking about her stepdad," he remarked.
"I still consider Mike Eastwood to be her father. Until he died, I had no idea who Billy McKenna was."
At that point the barman placed Father Mallory's pint on the bar.
"Cheers," remarked the priest as he lifted the glass to his lips.
Kieran gently raised his glass a few inches off the bar and as he returned the toast, was impressed to see Mallory demolish about a third of the contents of his glass in a few deep gulps.
Kieran had very limited experience of the clergy, but he'd never thought of priests as being beer drinkers.
"And I'd imagine the solicitor your friend Laura is dining with is young Nigel Diplock?" the priest enquired as soon as he'd placed his glass back on the bar.
"That's right," Kieran replied. "Do you know him?"
"I do," replied the priest. "He's a charming and popular young man in the town."
"He certainly seems to be a hit with Laura," muttered Kieran.
"So, I've heard," replied the priest, much to Kieran's surprise and consternation.

*   *   *

After her conversation with her mum and with the prospect of meeting Kieran again later, Laura's mind was largely elsewhere all evening, a fact that was not lost on Nigel Diplock.
"That was a great meal, Laura," Nigel said as he finished the last morsel of garlic bread. "It's been a great evening."
Laura was pleased to hear Nigel's compliments, but she knew she'd not been the best company that evening.
"It was nothing special, as you know and let's face it, had you not put everything in the oven then we'd still be waiting to eat now."
Nigel laughed and took hold of Laura's wrist. "The food was excellent, but to be honest it's not the food I'm here for."
As he spoke, he looked directly into Laura's eyes. "But you know that don't you?"
Had Kieran not arrived earlier and had she not spoken to her mum, it's likely that Laura would have welcomed Nigel's advances with open arms. However, both events had naturally unsettled her, and she felt very uneasy. All she could hear her head saying was to hold back as the last thing she needed at that time was to complicate matters even more by launching herself headlong into a new romance – no matter how much her heart desired it.
Laura gently extracted her wrist from Nigel's grasp.
"I'm not sure I'm ready to get too involved, Nigel," she said as firmly as she could but without hurting his feelings. "I need more time."
"You've not got over Kieran yet, have you?" Nigel said.
Laura fidgeted in her seat. She found the directness of Nigel's simple question quite unnerving.
"I thought I had," she replied. "But I'm not sure."

Nigel smiled. "I understand," he said sympathetically. "You know I have feelings for you, but I'll not push you."
Laura felt pleased and more than a little relieved that Nigel appeared to appreciate the situation.
"Thank you, Nigel," she replied with relief in her voice. "I'm glad you're so understanding."
Nigel leant across and kissed Laura on her cheek, a gesture that Laura welcomed. "I'll be getting on my way," he said. "I know you've things to do."
Laura smiled and ushered him towards the door.
"Actually," Laura said as she remembered the conversation she'd had with Abigail earlier in the day, "did you tell Mary McKenna about Abigail's relationship with Billy McKenna?"
Nigel looked surprised by the question but was quick to reply.
"Yes," he replied. "It was a big mistake; I was just trying to establish whether she knew of the affair. Billy never mentioned it to me, so legally Abigail had no claim at all on his estate. However, to be fair to Abigail, I just wanted to know if Mary had any inkling about the two of them. She didn't and I'm afraid all I did was to turn Mary against poor Abigail. I bitterly regret what I did, but it was done with the best of intentions."
In a weird way Laura was pleased to hear Nigel's explanation, although what he'd done had backfired badly for Abigail, at least it vindicated her initial belief in Nigel's honest and upright character.
"I thought there would be a good reason," she replied with a broad smile.
"I also talked to the bank manager about the cash payments made into Billy's business account every month," Nigel continued.
"What did he tell you?" Laura asked.

"Well, they were paid in by Billy himself," Nigel replied, "as regular as clockwork, but according to the manager, he had no idea where the money came from."
Laura shrugged her shoulders. "I suppose we'll never know where the money came from in that case," she replied, "but I guess it doesn't really matter."
Nigel smiled. "I think you're right," he remarked. "It's all water under the bridge."
As they reached the door Laura opened it and grinned broadly. "Thank you for coming, Nigel," she said. "And thanks again for being so understanding."
The handsome solicitor bent down and kissed her again, this time full on her lips. "It was my pleasure," he replied, before heading down the stairwell.
Laura waited at the entrance of her apartment until she heard the large wooden door at the bottom of the staircase slam shut, which indicated that Nigel had left. Once she knew he'd gone, Laura went back inside her apartment, closed her front door, picked up her mobile phone and started to text Kieran.

* * *

Despite sending her text message to Kieran at nine forty-five, it was almost ten thirty before Kieran arrived at Laura's apartment. After three pints of Patterson's best and a further three pints of Head Banger, Kieran needed a little help from Father Mallory to navigate his way from the Admiral to Laura's front door.
"You look awful," Laura announced as he fell into her flat. "How much have you had?"
"Enough," replied Kieran with an infantile giggle. "So, what's it to be my darling, are you going to marry me or take up with that flash git lawyer?"

Laura wasn't impressed in the slightest. "I'm not going to waste my time trying to talk to you tonight," she told him. "You can sleep here on the sofa, and we'll have our chat in the morning when you're more capable."
"Suit yourself," replied Kieran who slumped down on the sofa. "Have you got any beer?"

.

Chapter 47

Wednesday 16th September

Laura spent a restless night tossing and turning in her bed. Her mind was a blur of thoughts; confusion about her relationship with Kieran and whether she should choose him over Nigel, anxiety about the potential costs she'd have to pay Meridian, nervousness about what revelations her mother would be delivering the next day and for the first time since she'd moved to Blythwold, she was having serious doubts about whether her new life was really what she wanted.

With all these issues bouncing around her head and the sound of Kieran's drunken snoring echoing around the flat, Laura couldn't have had more than two or three hours sleep before her alarm clock rang to signify it was seven am.

After a welcome warm shower and a steaming hot mug of coffee, Laura decided it was time to wake up the dishevelled lump that only a few weeks ago she had loved with all her heart.

It took a few sharp nudges before Kieran stirred, and immediately it was clear he was still in a pretty awful state.

"My head," he muttered almost inaudibly. "That's the last time I go drinking with a priest."

Father Mallory had not accompanied Kieran up the three flights of stairs on the previous evening and this was the

first time Laura knew about the priest's involvement in Kieran's predicament.
"Priest!" repeated Laura. "You were drinking with a priest?"
"Yes," replied Kieran almost apologetically. "He said his name was Mallory and he knew you and your dad."
Laura perched herself next to Kieran and looked down into his bleary eyes. "He was the priest at Billy McKenna's funeral," she confirmed. "He seems very nice, but I don't know him well."
"Well, he can drink for Ireland," replied Kieran. "He downs them as if he's drinking water."
Laura couldn't help feeling sorry for Kieran, but she was still angry with him and was resolute in her desire to mask any sign of sympathy for him or the self-induced mess he now found himself in.
"Do you want a coffee?" she asked curtly.
Kieran nodded and attempted to sit up. "And a couple of paracetamols would be good, too," he added. "Soluble ones if you've got them."
Laura wasn't impressed but sauntered to fetch her dishevelled and decidedly rough ex-boyfriend the remedy he'd requested.
"I guess I'm not helping my chances of persuading you to marry me," he announced when she returned.
"Hardly," replied Laura, who in truth did feel for him as he sat there, looking pathetic and totally sorry for himself. "You're not exactly the best catch."
Kieran was in no position to argue. "How did it go with the lawyer?" he asked, as he watched the tablets slowly dissolve in the glass.
"We had a pleasant evening, if you must know," replied Laura. "Unlike you, he's a proper gentleman."

Kieran could wait no longer; he downed the contents of the glass even though the paracetamol tablets were only partially dissolved.
"So, what's the situation with him and you?" Kieran asked.
Laura took a deep breath. "There's no situation between Nigel and I," she replied, her irritation palpable in her voice. "We are good friends, that's all."
Kieran shook his head slowly. "But he would like it to be more," he replied. "You don't buy chocolates and flowers unless you're after something."
Laura laughed. "What would you know about buying chocolates and flowers; I don't recall getting that many when we were together."
Kieran could sense he was getting nowhere, so elected to change the subject.
"Okay," he said, his blurred gaze now focused as best he could on Laura. "I realise that I made a cock up of the proposal the other week, and yes, it wasn't the smartest move getting pissed with that bloody priest last night, but you know I love you and you know we are good together, so what's to stop us getting married. If I turn down the job in America I can just as easily work from Blythwold as I could London, so what's the issue?"
Laura sat down next to Kieran once more, but this time without any anger. "Well, two things," she replied candidly. "Firstly, I don't want to be responsible for you turning down the job in America. I know how much that means to you."
"And secondly?" enquired Kieran.
"And secondly," replied Laura. "I'm not sure I want to be with anyone at the moment, you, or Nigel Diplock. I've got loads on my plate and to be honest, I'm enjoying my freedom."

Kieran looked dejected. "I see," he remarked, the sadness etched across his face. "So, are you saying that's definitely it then?"
Laura nodded. "I think I am," she replied.
Kieran's eyes remained fixed on Laura, as he took in what she'd just told him. "In that case I better be on my way."
Laura shook her head. "You're not fit to drive, Kieran," she replied. "I need to get to the office, but I suggest you stay here for a while until you feel a bit better. You shouldn't be driving for at least a few more hours."
Kieran knew she was right. "Okay," he said as he slumped back on the sofa. "I'll hang around and get off at lunchtime."
Laura bent over and kissed his brow. "Take care, Kieran," she said with sincerity. "I'm sorry things haven't worked out between us."
Kieran forced a faint smile. "Be careful of that lawyer, Laura," he remarked. "He seems far too smarmy for his own good."
Laura smiled and stood up. "Don't worry about me, Kieran," she remarked, "I'm quite capable of looking after myself."

* * *

Abigail thought something was not right when for the first time in weeks, she had to open the office that morning. Her suspicions were confirmed when she caught sight of Laura's miserable expression.
"Christ what's the matter with you?" she remarked, with a lack of tact extreme even by her own standards.
Laura puffed out her cheeks. "Nothing I'm in the mood to share this morning," she replied abruptly. "If it's alright with you I'd like to have a quiet start to my day,

so for once can we dispense with the normal mindless chatter."
Abigail's eyes widened and for a moment Laura thought her young assistant may even do as she was told. However, Abigail was not one for following orders.
"Do you think a coffee would help?" she enquired, as if she was proposing to supply her boss with a drug to cure all her ills.
"No thanks," replied Laura, who plonked herself at her desk and switched on her computer.
Five minutes later Abigail arrived at Laura's desk with a mug of steaming coffee and a chocolate biscuit. "I figured you actually meant yes," she said with her sympathetic smile shining out from her mass of red curly hair.
Laura smiled back and took the mug from her young assistant. "Do you ever do as you're told?" she enquired.
Abigail thought for a few seconds then shook her head. "Occasionally," she replied, "but only when it's what I want to do, too!"
The two women worked in almost silence for the rest of the morning, with breaks only for more coffee.
Just before eleven Abigail suddenly shouted over to Laura. "Oh, I've just remembered," she said with more than a little excitement in her voice. "I spoke to Becca last night."
"Whose Becca?" Laura asked.
"My sister," Abigail replied, as if Laura was an idiot not to know. "She's the one that works in the bank."
"Oh, I see," replied Laura, who was wondering where all this was going.
"Well Becca told me that the two grand that was paid into the business account each month came from Mary McKenna," Abigail announced, her voice animated with excitement.

"But that can't be true," replied Laura. "Mr Diplock told me it was Billy who paid it in."
Abigail shook her head. "That's not what Becca said," she continued.
"She said that each month there was a transfer made from Mary McKenna's account to Mr Diplock and when that arrived, he'd draw it all out in cash and pay it into Billy's business account. She was one hundred per cent certain."
Laura's forehead creased as she tried to absorb what she'd just been told. "Well, that's not what Mr Diplock told me," she repeated.
Abigail shook her head. "Becca told me that she'd get the sack if it came out that she'd told me, so please don't say anything that may get her into trouble. But if she said it was Mr Diplock who paid the money in each month, it will be. Becca isn't scatty like me, she wouldn't have got it wrong. I'd wager my life on it!"
"But if that's true," Laura said, "why would Mr Diplock want to hide what he was doing? And why didn't Mary not just pay the money straight into her son's account?"
Abigail shrugged her shoulders. "It looks like they were trying to conceal something," she replied, "but I've no idea what."
Laura stared into space. Maybe Kieran's intuition was right, and the charming Nigel Diplock wasn't all that he seemed, she thought.

Part Nine

Abigail's Story

Chapter 48

Abigail Adams was the youngest of four girls. Her father was the caretaker at the local primary school and her mother worked as a nurse at Lowestoft hospital.
At school Abigail had always been one of the brightest pupils, but her carefree nature and a tendency to get too involved in chattering rather than working had never endeared her to her teachers, so with her behaviour and her flaming ginger hair it's fair to say that Abigail was never able to just fade into the background.
When she left school, despite putting in little in the way of revision, Abigail achieved a creditable six GCSE grade Cs and to her parents utter surprise, an A in Maths.
There was no question of her going on to take her A levels as Abigail had made it abundantly clear for almost two years that, as soon as she could, she'd be leaving school and getting herself a job.
Ironically it was the very traits that made her so exasperating for her teachers that seemed to help her when she applied for jobs, and Abigail had no problems in securing employment.
In her teens it was keeping those jobs that proved the challenge for Abigail. With her proclivity for calling in sick, her poor timekeeping and her general penchant for arguing the toss with her seniors, in the first three years

after leaving school Abigail secured then lost around a dozen or so jobs, ranging from shop assistant to accounts clerk.
It was only when she saw the small advert for the job with Billy McKenna that Abigail seemed to find a job that suited her, that challenged her intellect and that was with a boss who seemed happy to tolerate her less than perfect timekeeping. And in fairness to Abigail, after she'd been in the job for about three months, her attitude improved, her timekeeping issues seemed to disappear and she became totally immersed in her work; and, consequently, became an invaluable support to Billy McKenna.
Initially Abigail found Billy to be just an interesting off-the-wall, older man. There was nothing in particular that attracted her physically or romantically to him, but over the months they grew closer, and she realised he had a fondness for her. At first this was no more than just a fatherly sort of relationship, but after about a year Abigail noticed a change in how she felt about Billy and to her surprise, she discovered that she wanted to be with him more and more. When he asked her to join him for a drink one evening after work she didn't think twice before accepting.
To keep anything quiet in Blythwold was almost impossible, but Billy and Abigail maintained their association without anyone seeming to know. They knew full well that their relationship would not be well received in the town, so they figured that at least initially they should keep it their secret.
Abigail was more than happy about the whole clandestine nature of their affair, as in many ways it seemed to add to the excitement.
It was after they'd been together for almost a year that Billy first talked about making Abigail a partner in the

business. When he initially mentioned it, Abigail was thrilled, but when they started to discuss the practicality of how they should go about it, Billy seemed to struggle. However, true to his word, Billy eventually told Abigail that he was going to sort it out with his solicitor. That was over the weekend when they cuddled up together in Billy's flat watching TV and eating a takeaway.
Sadly, it was just four days later when Abigail was told about the accident and that Billy had died.
For anyone, the news of losing a partner is traumatic, but for Abigail, who worked with Billy and whose relationship with him was such a secret, the news was devastating.
At first, she thought that she'd continue to keep her grief to herself, but after a few days she decided she needed to tell people, as she needed it to be known.
Abigail told her Mum first, who confided that she'd suspected all along. Her Mum liked Billy and despite the age difference, saw no issue in them having had a relationship. It was her Mum who suggested that Abigail speak with Nigel Diplock to see if Billy had made any mention of her regarding the business, as she figured that if he'd have confided in anybody it would have been his friend and solicitor.
Abigail went to see Nigel Diplock a few days before Billy was due to be buried. Although the solicitor seemed very genuine in his expressions of sympathy and never questioned her honesty, he assured Abigail that Billy had not mentioned their relationship at all, and that there were no references to her in his will.
Abigail was heartbroken at the news, but she was pragmatic enough to realise that her chances of getting anything would be small, after all, in law she was just Billy's girlfriend and his assistant at work. She had no right to expect anything, even though she had secretly

hoped he'd have made some sort of gift to her as a sign that his love for her was real.
It was the bombshell that she received the next day that really threw Abigail. To be told quite coldly and heartlessly by Mary McKenna that she was not welcome at Billy's funeral was by far the cruellest blow of all.
On the morning of Billy's funeral Abigail got up early and went to Billy's apartment. As eleven am arrived, Abigail stood alone in Billy's flat, gazing out to sea, clutching one of the pillows from his bed, their bed, and sobbed uncontrollably.

Chapter 49

When Abigail heard that Billy had left everything to his estranged daughter, Laura, she felt strangely relieved. She didn't know Laura, Billy had never mentioned her, and although she was still feeling aggrieved that she'd been left nothing, the thought of Mary McKenna getting nothing, too, was a great comfort. It was almost like Billy was at last sticking two fingers up to the woman who so clearly had dominated his life from the second he was propelled from her womb.

And despite everything, Abigail took an instant liking to Laura as soon as she was introduced to her. There was no denying that Laura was Billy's daughter; she was the image of him. She didn't have his carefree attitude to life, but she did seem to share his quirky sense of humour, and, on the positive side, it was clear she was smart when it came to business matters, something her poor departed dad couldn't have put with any honesty on his CV.

As time passed, Abigail felt more and more comfortable with Laura, so much so that she decided to let her know about the relationship she'd shared with Billy. As she'd hoped, Laura seemed very sympathetic, even to the point of seeming genuinely sorry that she had been so

badly treated by the family and so overlooked in Billy's will.
One thing, however, did concern Abigail, and that was the close bond her new boss appeared to be creating with Nigel Diplock. Although Abigail could not be sure, she was convinced that Diplock, whether directly or indirectly, had been the cause of her being so cruelly excluded from the funeral. Abigail was as certain as she could be that Nigel Diplock wouldn't have pretended to know nothing about her relationship with Billy, had Billy actually told him, but her instinct told her to be very wary about Nigel Diplock; and as Laura appeared to be very much under the spell of the handsome and charming solicitor, Abigail decided to also remain a little detached from her new boss, despite the numerous and, on the face of it, genuine pleas from Laura that she was on her side and could be trusted.

Part Ten

A Time For Transparency!

Chapter 50

Wednesday 16th September

Laura's mobile rang at four forty-five pm.
"We're just going over the Orford Bridge," her mum shouted down the phone. "According to your dad, we'll be arriving at about five forty."
"Okay," replied Laura. "Have you booked a room anywhere yet?"
"Yes," replied her mum. "We're in the Black Swan, it was the only decent place we could find with any rooms at such short notice. I hope they've modernised it since I was last there, for the prices they're charging I'd bloody well hope so."
"I wouldn't set your hopes too high, Mum," Laura remarked. "I stayed there the night before the funeral and it's nice, but a little bit tired."
"Did you talk with Mary?" Laura's mum shouted down the phone.
"Yes," replied Laura, who found herself shouting, too. "I did that yesterday. She's aware that you're going to contact her, but I haven't told her you're coming over today."
"Good," her mum retorted. "She's going to get a big surprise later in that case."

"You're not planning to go and see her tonight, are you?" Laura exclaimed.
"No," her mum replied. "I'll go over in the morning but, of course, I want to talk with you first. Can you meet us at the hotel at about six? We should have checked in by then."
"Yes, of course," replied Laura, who was quite taken aback by how decisive her mum was being; she'd never heard her so forthright. "I'll just get home and change, and I'll be with you at six."
"Good," replied her mum firmly. "But don't tell that bloody witch I'm in Blythwold. In fact, don't tell a soul. That town's full of busybodies and tittle-tattlers, it would only get back to her; so, don't tell anybody."
"Okay," replied Laura again. "I'll see you both at six."
The phone went dead, which indicated that either her mum had hung up or, more likely, she'd gone into a poor reception area.
Laura turned to Abigail. "Can you lock up tonight?" she asked. "I need to rush off."
"Is your mum arriving tonight then?" Abigail asked, having pieced that much together from what she'd heard Laura saying – or rather, shouting.
"Yes," replied Laura, "but please don't mention it to anyone. I don't want the town to know she's here."
Abigail moved her thumb and forefinger across her mouth to indicate it being shut like a zip. A gesture Laura had last seen Saskia do, which had meant absolutely nothing.
Laura couldn't be sure whether she could trust Abigail to remain quiet about the news of her mum's arrival, but she had no alternative other than to have faith in her young assistant.
"Thanks, Abigail," she said as she headed for the door. "I'll see you in the morning."

*   *   *

Laura rushed back to her apartment and hurried up the three flights of stairs to her attic room. The last thing Laura expected to see when she opened the front door, was Kieran still in the room.
"What are you still doing here?" she enquired, her voice shrill and scolding.
Kieran had almost completely recovered and had been safe to drive for several hours, however, he'd no pressing need to get back to London and, as soon as he'd shaken off his hangover, had decided to stay and try and get Laura to change her mind.
Having encountered the threat that was Nigel Diplock, he'd figured that his only chance to persuade Laura to marry him was to remain in Blythwold.
"I thought I'd hang around until I got a positive answer," he remarked with a mischievous smile.
"Sorry," replied Laura dismissively, before shaking her head, "I thought we'd talked it through this morning. I'm not marrying you, Kieran."
By the look on his face it was clear that Kieran wasn't going to give up.
"Look, I've no time to talk about this again now," Laura added. "Mum and Dad will be arriving in an hour or so and I've agreed to meet them at the Black Swan at six."
"I'll come with you if you like," Kieran suggested.
Laura considered the offer. "Okay," she replied as she kicked off her shoes and headed towards her bedroom. "You can keep my dad occupied somewhere while Mum and I talk."
"That's cool," Kieran said with another grin. "I'll take him to the Admiral!"

"No!" Laura exclaimed as she entered her bedroom.
"I'm not having you coming back here in the same state tonight as you were last night."
"Anyone would think we were already married," replied Kieran wittily.
Laura turned back to face him, her expression one of unadulterated admonishment. "Please, Kieran," she said firmly, "don't come home half cut tonight."
As the door shut behind her, Kieran was left feeling reasonably positive. In his eyes he'd certainly made a little progress with Laura. Things clearly weren't as they'd been before, but at least she hadn't thrown him out, so maybe there was some chance of winning her round.

Chapter 51

Their meeting in the foyer of the Black Swan was as loving as always, but Laura could tell by her mother's uneasiness and the expression on her face that she was not herself. Even her dad seemed uncharacteristically awkward.

As soon as her bear-like embrace had ended, Laura's mum forced a smile. "We need to talk," she said, her watery eyes fixed on those of her daughter. "Alone."

Laura was now feeling apprehensive. She wanted to know the truth, but by the look on the faces of her parents, she was starting to fear the worst.

"Why don't you and dad go for a beer?" Laura remarked to Kieran, as if it was news to him that the two men were not required.

"Yes," replied Kieran with enthusiastic compliance. "Do you fancy a beer, Mike?"

Laura's father would normally leap at an offer of an evening in the pub. However, on this occasion, he showed no signs of his normal zeal as he nodded his consent. "I'll see you later, Bev," he told Laura's mum before giving her a tender peck on the cheek.

"Come on then, Kieran," he said in the young man's direction. "It must be your turn to buy the first one."

The two men trundled off into the evening air leaving Laura and her mum alone in the foyer.
"I thought you and Kieran had split up?" her mum remarked.
Laura rolled her eyes and shrugged her shoulders. "We have," she replied. "I'll explain later."
It was clear that Laura's mum had more pressing things on her mind, so she didn't even try to probe her daughter for more details.
"Let's go up to the room," she suggested. "We won't be disturbed there."
Laura nodded. "Okay," she replied, her throat dry and her hands starting to feel clammy as her nerves took hold.

* * *

In keeping with type, Laura's mum and dad had opted for the Black Swan's most expensive suite, with a balcony looking out onto the small market square. Laura sat herself comfortably on the small floral two-seater sofa, her mother sat opposite on a large easy chair, covered tastefully in a matching fabric.
"So, what is it you need to tell me?" Laura asked, her patience now completely exhausted.
Her mother looked uneasy, and Laura now fully expected that her next utterance would deliver a monumental bombshell.
"I wish you'd never come back here," she remarked with a weary tone in her voice. "You didn't need to know."
"Know what!" retorted Laura, who was trying hard to remain calm, but was finding it increasingly difficult.

Laura's mum took a massive intake of breath. "Let me tell you everything," she remarked, her moist eyes now fixed directly into Laura's.
Laura remained silent.
"When I first met Billy, I thought he was really handsome," her mother started in a deliberate and measured manner. "We were both quite young. He was a cashier in the bank. He was eighteen and I was a year or so younger than him. I was working at Perry's, which was a large department store. It's gone now of course, but back then it was the biggest shop in town."
As her mother spoke Laura could see quite clearly that her mind was drifting back to a time over thirty years before.
"At around two thirty every day I used to pay in the cheques from the store," continued her mother. "We had to do that to ensure they were all processed before the bank shut. Well, it was clear Billy liked me and after a few weeks he asked me out and that was that."
"Mum," Laura remarked frustratedly. "I know all that. You've told me how you met before."
Laura's spiky comments seemed to shake her mum out of her daydream. "Of course, you do," she replied. "I guess all I wanted to say was that at first everything was just fine between us, in fact it was more than fine, it was near perfect."
"So, what's Mary on about," Laura enquired, her exasperation obvious in her voice.
"Well," her Mum continued, seemingly oblivious to the agony her daughter was experiencing, "it all started going wrong a few years later, shortly after you were born. Although Billy had got a promotion at the bank to their securities and lending desk, we were struggling financially and we, I guess like many young people, started to argue. Billy was going out more and more in

the evenings with his pals, which meant we had less money, and in turn we'd argue even more. This went on for a few months until, one evening, he came home and threw five thousand pounds on the kitchen table, which he told me he'd won at cards."

"And did you believe him?" Laura enquired.

Her mum shook her head. "No," she replied, "not in the slightest. The group he hung around with wouldn't have had that sort of money, so I knew he was lying. But we were really struggling, so I foolishly didn't question him."

"And what happened then?" Laura asked.

Her mum rolled her eyes. "Do you know what tomb stoning is?"

Laura shook her head.

"Well tomb stoning is what Billy was doing," she continued. "It's a clever fraud that Billy was doing at the bank."

"Is this how he ended up in prison?" Laura enquired.

Her mum nodded. "Yes, he eventually got caught and was sent to prison. Apparently, he'd taken tens of thousands of pounds from the bank and in those days, that was a load of money."

Laura's brow started to wrinkle. "So, what is tomb stoning?" she asked.

"Tomb stoning is a scam," replied her mum. "What Billy was doing was inventing fictitious people, opening accounts for them, and then agreeing to lend them money. He'd then transfer the funds into his own account and pocket the cash. He'd keep up the repayments on the loans for a few months but then stop."

"I don't get it," replied Laura. "I can sort of understand how he'd be able to get the money out, but once the

lender, well him I suppose, stopped paying, wouldn't that be when the bank would catch him?"
Laura's mum smiled and shook her head. "That's the clever bit," she replied. "Billy knew the bank would always write off small debts under a certain value, so all he did was make sure that each debt was below that threshold. As long as he did that, he knew he'd stand a good chance of getting away with it."
Laura couldn't help feeling a little impressed with her birth father's ingenuity and his nerve but was not about to articulate that to her mum. "But he did get caught?" she said instead.
"Yes," replied her mum. "He did, and he was made an example of by the bank. They decided they wanted to demonstrate that they'd not tolerate fraud and pressed charges. He had no choice but to admit it and was convicted and sent to prison."
Laura shook her head. "So that was why he left us so suddenly when I was small," she remarked.
"Yes," replied her mum. "That was why he disappeared from our lives."
"And when he came out, you were with Dad," Laura added.
Her mum nodded. "That's correct," she replied. "Billy and I got divorced while he was in prison, and your dad and I married shortly afterwards. Mike, in every sense, from then on became your father."
"I see," Laura said. "But why is Mary so desperate to tell me all this?"
"She's not," continued her mum. "What she is keen for you to know is that up to Billy going to prison, he and Mike were great friends. Your dad worked in the bank, too, and when Billy was sent to prison, he asked your dad to make sure I was alright. What none of us knew at that time was that over the coming months, your dad and

I would grow close and would eventually fall in love. What Mary is angry about is that fact that I divorced Billy, then married Mike, and he took on the role of your father while Billy was in prison. Mike, in her eyes, betrayed her son."
Laura, for the first time, felt some sympathy for Mary McKenna. "So, when Billy came to see me when I was a teenager, had he just come out of prison?"
"No," replied her mother. "Billy knew Mike and I had married, he knew you were happy, and he knew you saw Mike as your father, so for a few years after he was released, he kept away. So yes, that day was the first time we'd seen him in years, but he'd been out for a good few years by then."
"When he came out, didn't he want to see more of me?" Laura asked.
Her mum nodded. "Yes," she replied candidly but with some remorse in her voice. "He did, but I told him I didn't want him to see you again as by then you'd forgotten him, and Mike Eastwood was your dad."
"Mum!" exclaimed Laura angrily. "I love Dad and he'll always be my dad, but what you did was wrong. You should have let me choose whether I saw Billy McKenna or not. It wasn't your decision to make."
"I know," replied her mum timidly, "but what I did was what I thought was the best for all of us."
"Except Billy and his mother," retorted Laura angrily. "And what about me? I should have had the opportunity to decide for myself."
"You were still too young to decide," replied her mum, her voice starting to rise, too. "You were just a teenager."
"But I've not been a teenager for nearly ten years!" Laura shouted at her mother. "You had bloody years to

tell me. Instead you let me think that he didn't care. That's such an awful thing for you to do."
"I know," replied her mother, "but what I did, I did for the best."
Laura got up from the comfort of the sofa. "The best for you and Dad, maybe," she shouted, "but not for anyone else."

* * *

The church bells were chiming to indicate the time was eleven o'clock when Kieran arrived at Laura's flat. As he reached the top of the stairs, he could see the door had been left slightly ajar.
Kieran slowly pushed the door open to discover Laura standing in the dark with her back to him looking out to sea.
"Why didn't you reply to my texts?" Kieran enquired. "I've been sending you them almost every ten minutes since nine o'clock."
Laura didn't turn round and didn't answer.
Kieran closed the door behind him and walked over to where Laura was standing. "Laura," he enquired, the concern clear in his voice, "what's up?"
As he reached where she was standing, he could see she'd been crying, and although her tears had long since dried away, in the half- light of the streetlights which shone up through the window, he could see her eyes were red and her cheeks were stained with traces of mascara.
"What happened?" he enquired with genuine feeling, his arms suddenly engulfing her.
Laura half turned to face him. "She lied to me, Kieran," she replied, her disbelief at the disappointment evident in her words. "I always believed that Billy McKenna

didn't want anything to do with me, but that wasn't true. It was her that stopped him seeing me."

Kieran hugged her tightly but said nothing. In truth he didn't know what to say.

Laura wrapped her arms around him too and held on tightly. "Everything's changed," she said. "I don't know who I can trust anymore."

"You've got me, Laura," replied Kieran. "I'll always be here for you."

Chapter 52

Thursday 17th September

When Laura's alarm went off at seven neither she nor the naked man who lay next to her were awake. "Surely it can't be seven already," she muttered to herself in disbelief.
Kieran remained motionless, seemingly oblivious to the ear-splitting screech, but Laura, now rudely disturbed by the painful noise, could only think of one thing; to stop it as quickly as possible. She leaned over and through slitty eyes, aimed a single blow with her clenched right fist to hush the shrieking imposter. It did the trick.
It was a bright morning, and the sun was already streaming through the open window. Outside the seagulls' screams seemed even louder than usual.
Laura sat up for a few seconds before falling onto her side and engulfing Kieran within a mixture of her arms and the white duvet which she pulled up under her chin to shield herself against the morning chill.
"You're freezing," Kieran pronounced. "Stop sucking the heat out of me."
Laura giggled. "If you intend to marry me, you'll have to get used to this."
Kieran rolled over to face her. "Is that a yes, then?" he asked, his sleep-filled eyes inches from hers.

Laura smiled and kissed his lips. "It's a yes," she replied. "But with one condition."
"Oh, here we go," remarked Kieran, his voice a mixture of elation at her acceptance but tinged with an element of anticipated frustration. "What's the condition?"
"I want you to go to America," replied Laura. "I know it's what you want to do, so you have to go."
"And what about you?" Kieran enquired.
"For now, I'm staying here," Laura replied.
"Doesn't sound the best way to start married life," Kieran replied. "Being three thousand miles apart may prove to be a bit of a problem, don't you think?"
Laura kissed him again, but this time a long, lingering kiss, to demonstrate her devotion. "We don't have to get married straight away," she announced. "We can be engaged for a year or so before we get married. That's okay, isn't it?"
"You're determined to see out your year here, aren't you?" Kieran remarked.
Laura kissed him again, another passionate kiss, a kiss to match any kiss she'd given him before.
"Yes," she said as soon as their lips separated. "After a year we can decide what we want to do, whether it's a life in the US or here in Blythwold. But I want to make sure the inheritance comes to me and I want you to have your chance in America."
Kieran thought for a moment. "Okay," he replied. "It's a deal. But I have one condition, too."
"Which is?" replied Laura.
"That I buy you a ring today and you promise to wear it always," he replied. "I'm not having that stuck-up lawyer thinking he's got a chance with you once I'm out of the way."
Laura laughed. "My relationship with Nigel Diplock is purely platonic," she replied. "He's just a friend."

"Right!" replied Kieran with a look of incredulity. "Are you telling me he's never tried it on?"
Laura didn't want to have this conversation, but she also didn't want to lie to Kieran.
"I know he fancies me," she replied. "And before you came back and I realised it was you I wanted, I have to say that I was tempted, but that's as far as it went. Anyway, I'm not sure my mum's the only person that's been lying to me. When I next see Nigel Diplock I have a few questions I want to ask him."
Kieran seemed reassured and, to Laura's relief, changed the subject.
"So, are you going with your mum to see Mary McKenna?" he enquired.
"No chance," replied Laura with a firm bluntness that suggested there was no way she would be talked round. "They have things to discuss and it's up to them to sort it out. I'm not about to get involved or take sides."
"That's a bit harsh," replied Kieran. "I agree she should have told you, but Bev's a good person, she loves you and I'm sure she did it with the best of intentions."
Laura starred straight into Kieran's eyes. "I don't want to discuss it, Kieran," she replied firmly. "Now get your arse out of bed, have a shower and then let's go and get the most expensive engagement ring we can find in this sleepy little town."
Kieran smiled and dragged himself out of bed. As he did, he wrapped the duvet around his shoulders and headed for the bathroom leaving Laura naked on the bed. As he reached the door, he glanced back and smiled broadly when he saw her face shocked and outraged at being left so exposed and vulnerable.
Throwing the duvet back at her, Kieran went into the bathroom, closed the door, and shouted, "I'd like a bacon sandwich, wife to be. And be sure it's ready for

me once I'm sufficiently preened and looking my ravishing best."
"Could take a lifetime," Laura muttered, before wrapping herself up in the duvet and pinching a few more minutes in bed.

*　　　*　　　*

Kieran was still in the shower when there was a loud knock on the door.
Laura glanced at the clock; it was not yet seven thirty.
"Who the hell can that be?" Laura muttered as she quickly threw on a pair of jeans and the nearest jumper she could find.
There was a second knock, this time even louder, before Laura had time to get to the door. "I'm coming," she yelled before opening the door wide.
"Oh, it's you," she remarked rather disparagingly when she saw her dad standing on the doorstep. "What do you want?"
"Can I come in?" her father asked quietly but in a way that suggested there was only one appropriate answer.
Laura stood aside to allow her dad to enter the living room.
"I'm not going to forgive her," Laura remarked before her dad had a chance to say anything. "She should have told me the truth years ago, actually you both should have."
Her dad nodded. "We should have," he replied, "but we didn't, and we can't change that."
"So why are you here?" Laura enquired, her tone still one showing no signs of forgiveness.
"Can I sit down?" her dad asked.
Laura moved her head to one side to signify he could sit on the sofa.

"I've got to get to work soon," she added to emphasise the fact she didn't want their conversation to last too long.
Her dad half smiled before sitting down on the sofa as Laura had indicated. "I'll not linger too long, my dear," he replied. "Your mum is going to see that old cow this morning, then we'll be on our way back to Spain," he said calmly but firmly. "I just wanted you to know two things."
Laura remained standing with her arms folded in front of her.
"Go on," she said.
"Firstly, you need to know that we realise we were wrong. We should have told you that it was us who insisted Billy stayed away, but we did it to protect you from him and that family."
"And the second thing?" Laura asked, totally ignoring her dad's words.
Her father laughed. "Sweetie, you really don't know what Billy was like. He was bad news, Laura. He'd become a really unpleasant person and his family are even worse."
"What family?" Laura shouted. "Apart from Mary, I'm the only family he had, and you both denied us the opportunity to know each other."
Her father stood up and walked towards Laura but stopped in his tracks when Laura held her palms up to show her unwillingness for him to touch her. "Mary's not the only McKenna," he remarked. "Billy has an older brother called Stephen."
"He died," Laura shouted back at her father as if he was an imbecile. "How do you know he's dead?" replied her father. "They never found a body."

"What are you talking about?" Laura said, shaking her head as she spoke. "Why on earth do you think he's still alive?"
Ignoring Laura's earlier signal to keep his distance, her father moved within inches of his daughter and looked her straight in the eyes. "I've no way of proving it, Laura," he remarked as he took tight hold of her arms in his strong hands. "But I've always thought he was alive. I believe they fabricated his death to get him away."
"Away from what?" Laura asked.
"Away from the mess that he had created," replied her dad, his eyes staring directly into hers.
"You're talking in riddles," Laura remarked with anger and frustration. "If you know something you have to tell me and do it now!"
At that precise moment the naked figure of Kieran burst out of the bathroom, rubbing his hair vigorously with a small hand towel.
"So, where's the bacon sandwich, wench?" he said jokingly before noticing Mike Eastwood standing in the middle of the room.
"You two back together then," Laura's dad remarked.
"Sorry, Mike," said Kieran, his embarrassment clear and highlighted by his attempt to cover his private parts with the towel.
"Actually, we're not only back together," remarked Laura, "we're going to get married. Kieran asked me again last night and I've said yes."
Mike Eastwood smiled broadly. "That's great," he said. "Congratulations, your mum will be pleased."
Kieran, still trying to cover his embarrassment, smiled, and pointed towards the bedroom. "I'll put some clothes on," he said before quickly making his exit.
Laura waited for Kieran to go before again asking her father, "What do you know about Billy's brother?"

"He's evil," replied her dad. "Always was and always will be. In fairness to Billy, he wasn't always a wrong-un, but by the time you were born, he'd changed. But Stephen was pure evil, and Mary knew what they were like and did all she could to protect them, especially Stephen."
"Why should I believe you?" Laura asked.
"Because there's no reason for me to lie to you," replied her dad.
Laura didn't know what to think. A few days earlier she would have believed her dad without question, but things had changed between them and now, except for Kieran, she no longer trusted anyone.
"He's dead, Dad," Laura said, her voice low and her words spoken slowly. "He died years ago. And now that Billy has died, too, there's just Mary. In fact, other than Mary, I'm the only one with the McKenna genes."
Laura wanted her comment to hurt her dad, and, by the look on his face, she certainly appeared to have achieved her goal.
"Be careful, Laura," he said. "They are an evil family, and you may have their blood in your veins, but I pray to God your upbringing and your mother's genes keep you as honest and loving as her."
Laura took a deep breath. "Is that everything?" she enquired, meaning the conversation was, in her eyes, over.
Her dad nodded. "I'm really pleased you and Kieran are getting married," he remarked as he walked over to the door. "At least it's good to know that he'll be here with you."
Laura decided against telling her dad about the arrangement she and Kieran had made.
As he reached the door, he turned to face Laura. "We love you dearly, Laura," he said with genuine warmth.

"I hope one day you'll understand what we did and forgive us, but I want you to know that we'll always be there for you and we'll always love you."
Laura desperately wanted to rush over and hug her father, but she didn't. Her pride wouldn't allow her to forgive, not yet anyway.
By the time Kieran emerged from the bedroom, this time fully clothed, Laura's dad had departed.
"That was a quick visit," he remarked. "What did your Dad want?"
Laura shrugged her shoulders and threw her arms around her new fiancé. "He was just trying to make up."
"You are going to forgive them, aren't you," Kieran said, as a statement of fact rather than a question.
"I guess I will, eventually," Laura replied as she planted another passionate kiss on Kieran's open mouth. "But not just yet!" she added as soon as their lips parted.

Chapter 53

“Morning Abigail,” said Laura cheerily as she entered the office. “I want you to meet someone.”
Abigail peered around her computer screen.
“This is Kieran,” Laura announced, her left hand stretched in his direction.
“Hi,” replied Abigail. “Nice to meet you.”
Kieran smiled. “Hi, Abigail,” he said before offering her his hand. “I’ve heard lots about you.”
“Really,” replied Abigail, who seemed confused. “I’ve never heard anything about you.”
Laura smiled nervously and shot Abigail an admonishing stare. “Kieran and I are engaged,” she proclaimed. “In fact, we’re just about to go to that jeweller on the High Street to buy an engagement ring.”
“Van Boom’s!” exclaimed Abigail. “They’re really pricey. I’d take a deep breath before you go in there.”
“But they have some lovely things in there,” Abigail quickly added, when she saw the stern expression on Laura’s face.
“Is there anything we need to discuss, Abigail, before we go?” Laura enquired.
“Actually, there is,” Abigail replied.
“What is it?” Laura asked.
“It’s the charity coastal trek in May,” Abigail remarked.
“What charity trek?” enquired Laura, her brow furrowed, demonstrating her bewilderment.

Abigail sighed, as if she were astounded that Laura didn't know what she was talking about. "The coastal run!" she exclaimed.
"Abigail!" Laura replied. "I have absolutely no idea what you're on about."
"Have we never discussed it?" said Abigail, her tone suggesting a slight realisation that maybe this was indeed the first her new boss had heard of it.
"No!" Laura exclaimed. "Believe me, if we had I'd have remembered."
"It's the main fund-raising event of the year. Billy did it last year and raised over twenty thousand pounds. He'd promised to do it again next year," Abigail replied. "We've already secured several sponsors and yesterday evening one of the major charities called to make sure everything was still going ahead."
"Well I hope you told them that Billy McKenna has died, so there won't be any coastal trek," said Laura, her voice raised a little more than normal.
Abigail's cheeks blushed and she made an expression that suggested she'd said no such thing.
"Abigail!" exclaimed Laura. "I'm not a runner. There is absolutely no way I'm standing in for Billy McKenna."
"How far is the trek?" Kieran asked.
"About one hundred and twenty miles," replied Abigail. "It took Billy four days last year. The target for next year is to do it in the opposite direction but taking just three days. It's due to start in May."
Kieran roared with laughter. "My God, you'd never last three hours," he remarked. "Three days would kill you!"
Laura bristled at the rebuke and, in typical style, decided to prove Kieran wrong. "Oh really," she said, her eyes narrowing, and her lips pursed. "Call them back, Abigail," she continued. "Tell them that everything will be going ahead as planned, but this time there will be

two people doing the trek – Laura Eastwood and Kieran Hockley."

Kieran's expression changed. "Oh no," he said, "I'm not doing it. Anyway, I'll be in America, so I can't do it."

"Oh yes, Kieran," Laura added. "You'll just have to take some time out to come over."

Abigail smiled. "I'll call them straight back."

"Good," replied Laura. "And when you do you can tell them that you're going to personally take charge of all the arrangements and all the fund-raising activities. If I'm going to have to spend the winter getting fit enough to do this mammoth trek, I'll be damned if you're getting away with this."

Abigail shrugged her shoulders. "That's fair, I guess," she conceded.

Laura looked at her watch. "What time does Van Boom's open?" she asked.

"About nine, I think," Abigail replied.

"That gives us half an hour to understand a bit more about what this trek will entail," Laura remarked.

"You two can chat all you like," Kieran muttered. "I'll make us all a coffee, cos I'm not going to be part of it in any shape or form."

As he wandered over to the kitchen area, Laura mouthed "he is" in Abigail's direction. Abigail waited a few seconds before whispering to Laura, "Does Mr Diplock know about Kieran?"

Laura shook her head. "He knows about Kieran but not that we're engaged."

Abigail's mouth turned down at the sides. "He won't be happy," she muttered.

"It's none of his business," replied Laura. "I've told you before, there's nothing going on between Mr Diplock and me."

Abigail raised her eyebrows. “Laura,” she remarked still in a whisper, “you were seen cuddling up together the other lunchtime. You should know by now that there are no secrets in Blythwold.”
“How do you take your coffee, Abigail?” Kieran shouted from the other side of the office.
“White with one sugar, please,” Abigail replied, before turning back to Laura. “I think he may be a bit put out,” she said in a hushed voice.
“From what I hear, he doesn’t like losing, so you may find that he’ll take it badly.”
“I really don’t think he will,” replied Laura. “But, if he does, that’s his problem.”

*   *   *

Van Boom’s jewellery shop was as expensive as Abigail had suggested and, true to her word, Laura wasn’t about to settle for the cheapest ring in the shop.
Within an hour the happy couple had successfully purchased a ring, which Laura proudly sported as they made their way down Blythwold High Street.
“I feel we should be celebrating!” Kieran announced.
Laura laughed. “We could go in here for a coffee, I suppose,” she replied as they passed one of many small tea shops designed to cater for the town’s summer tourists.
As they sat sipping their drinks, Laura realised that she’d never once asked Kieran about how his mum was doing or Ryan, his wayward younger brother. “What do you think your mum will say when you tell her we’re engaged?” she asked.
Kieran smiled. “She’ll be delighted,” he replied. “She needs some good news. Ryan was sentenced a few weeks ago; he got twelve months. What with that and

me about to head off to America, our engagement will hopefully lift her spirits."
"How is Ryan coping?" Laura asked.
"Not that well as far as I can gather," replied Kieran. "I've not had a chance to visit him yet, but Mum went last week, and she says he's finding it hard."
"That's a shame," Laura remarked with genuine compassion in her voice.
"I don't agree," Kieran replied firmly. "I'm hoping the next twelve months are the worst in his life. It's the only chance I can see of making him see sense."
"Sounds a bit harsh," remarked Laura. "But I guess you're right."
"I bloody know I'm right," Kieran said with conviction. "Anyway, I'm not going to lose any sleep over Ryan from now on, he's a big lad now, so he must make his own way. If prison doesn't cure him, I have no idea what will. Certainly, there's bugger all Mum, or I can do for him now, not that Mum will ever give up on him."
"Well I can understand that," Laura remarked.
Kieran raised his eyebrows and nodded towards the window, which looked out onto the high street. "Talking of mums," he remarked, "there's yours."
Laura looked out and could see her mum walking back towards the Black Swan, her meeting with Mary clearly now over.
"I think you should talk with her again, Laura, before she leaves for Spain."
Laura looked for a few seconds before turning to face Kieran. "No, I'm not ready yet," she replied. "I'd just get angry with her and I don't want to make things any worse than they are. I'll call her in a
few weeks and try to talk to her, but I need some time to get my head around what she did. Anyway, she deserves to suffer a little."

Kieran shook his head. “I think you’re wrong, Laura,” he remarked. “I think you need to get it all out of your system today before she jets off home. I think it won’t just be your mum who suffers if you let all this fester.” Laura knew deep down that Kieran was right, but she was far too angry and far too stubborn to admit it.

Chapter 54

Abigail's whispered comments earlier that morning, about being spotted with Nigel Diplock on the bench, had stuck in Laura's head. In her eyes, she and Nigel had never been an item, but, in fairness, she had accepted several meals with the handsome solicitor, she'd allowed him to kiss her and, when they'd last met, she'd cooked him a meal and had played down any romantic involvement with Kieran.

So, although she didn't believe he'd be too upset when he found out that she had become engaged to Kieran, Laura did feel a little anxious about how he'd take the news and decided she needed to give him the news herself, before the unbelievably efficient, Blythwold bush telegraph sprang into action.

Her dilemma, however, was how to get Kieran out of the way, so she could deliver her message without him being around.

After they'd finished their coffees, Laura took hold of Kieran's hand. "I need to get back to the office," she told him. "Do you think you can occupy yourself for a few hours?"

Kieran kissed her tenderly. "I'm sure I can," he replied. "In fact, I need to make a few calls to America this afternoon to sort out some final details regarding the new job and I also want to make sure the apartment I'm renting is all ready for me when I arrive on Saturday. If

you give me your apartment keys, I can do it from there."
Laura, pleasantly surprised by how easy it was to divert her fiancé so effortlessly, smiled, removed the keys from her handbag and placed them in Kieran's hand. "I'll try not to be too late," she promised.
Kieran returned her smile. "That's fine," he replied. "Maybe we could find a cosy little restaurant and have dinner tonight. I'm going to have to be away early tomorrow, so it would be a nice way to celebrate our engagement and say goodbye for the next few months."
"Or maybe I could cook us something," Laura suggested, thinking it may be better to stay in, given that it would be a while before they saw each other again.
Kieran frowned and shook his head. "I love you for many, many reasons, Laura," he replied calmly, "but your cooking isn't one of them. I'm not sure a shop-bought pizza with a few added toppings and some garlic bread is what I had in mind this evening."
Realising that Kieran was having a dig at the meal she'd thrown together for Nigel Diplock on Tuesday evening, Laura slapped Kieran hard on the shoulder.
"That hurt," Kieran yelled, although he was beaming from ear to ear.
"You'll never learn," Laura remarked with a smile. "Your big mouth has already cost you one of the most expensive engagement rings you're ever likely to find in Suffolk, and now your cruel tongue looks like it's going to cost you an expensive meal at 'le Rayon de Miel,' Blythwold's most expensive restaurant. When I get back to the office, I'll book us a table for seven."
Kieran smile widened. "You're worth every penny," he pronounced before giving her another passionate kiss.
"You may be singing a different tune when you see the bill," Laura replied.

*   *   *

The church clock was striking eleven when Laura and Kieran left the Tea Shop and made their way in opposite directions down Blythwold High Street. Laura walked slowly and kept looking back to see when Kieran was out of sight. It took him several minutes to disappear around the slight bend near the Black Swan, which was en route to Laura's flat.
"Good," Laura muttered to herself as she turned around and started walking the opposite way towards the practice of Diplock and Sturridge.

*   *   *

Laura had to wait no more than two or three minutes before Nigel Diplock appeared in the reception area.
"I wasn't expecting to see you this morning, Laura," he said as he saw her standing there, her right hand clasped firmly over her left hand, obscuring the ring that Kieran had placed in her finger less than two hours earlier. "Come through."
Laura tried to appear her normal self. "I just need a few minutes of your time if that's okay, Mr Diplock," she said, mainly for the benefit of the practice receptionist, who had been exhibiting a nauseating forced smile ever since Laura had stepped over the threshold.
"Of course," replied Nigel. "Go through, you know where the office is."
Laura did as she was asked but felt as apprehensive as a small child who'd been summoned to see the teacher after doing something wrong.

"I really enjoyed Tuesday evening, Laura," Nigel remarked even before Laura had a chance to sit down. "We must arrange to do it again, but maybe ..."
Before he could finish his sentence, Laura had sat down and, removing the protective cover of her right hand exposed her engagement ring, in all it's glory. Just in case her actions hadn't been observed, Laura then placed both of her hands on the desk.
"I wanted you to be one of the first to know," Laura interrupted. "Kieran and I have decided to marry."
The normally calm and controlled solicitor for once looked lost for words. Open-mouthed he sat down in his large leather chair behind his expensive-looking oak desk.
"But the other night you said you needed time," Nigel remarked firmly and with a touch of anger in his voice. "It's been less than two days since we had that conversation. What changed?"
Laura could feel herself starting to tremble, and for the first time, the polite, affable, and chivalrous Mr Diplock was starting to sound a little less civil, a little less friendly and, to her surprise, a little threatening.
Laura had no intention of arguing with Nigel, but equally she wanted to ensure that he knew she wasn't about to be chastised or insulted by him.
"Nigel," she said calmly, "we were never a couple. We had a few meals together and we have become good friends, but that is all it was ever going to be. I've known Kieran for a long time, and I've realised that I love him."
"So, the kisses we shared meant nothing to you?" Nigel retorted, his face now becoming quite flushed.
Laura now did feel threatened. "Nigel," she replied firmly, "I'm marrying Kieran. If you can't accept that or be civil about it, then that's your problem."

As she spoke, Laura rose from the chair and made her way to the door.
"And given your behaviour, Nigel," she added as she opened the door, "it may be wise if I appoint another solicitor to manage the legal affairs from now on."
Nigel smiled back at Laura; a smug, knowing and intimidating smile. "I'm afraid that wouldn't be allowed, Ms Eastwood," he replied, the emphasis being on the Ms. "You appear to be forgetting your father's will," he continued. "Until one year has passed you don't legally inherit anything, so whether you like it or not, you're stuck with me until August next year. That's if you stick it out that long."
Laura was shocked at the sudden change in Nigel Diplock's behaviour, but her overriding emotion was one of anger and a desire to make doubly sure she met the terms of the will and secured her inheritance.
"I was warned about you, Nigel," Laura shouted back at the solicitor, whose appeal had evaporated completely in Laura's eyes, "but I ignored that as being just a spiteful person trying to stick their nose in where it wasn't welcome. However, she was right."
"I take it the advice came from that gold-digging little tart who works for you," Nigel shouted back. "I wouldn't put my trust in her if I were you. Let's face it, she's only after Billy McKenna's business. Why else would she have been sleeping with a sad old man like him?"
"So, she wasn't lying when she told me she was in a relationship with Billy," Laura replied calmly. "I thought you said you had no knowledge of any relationship, just like you told me Billy was paying the two thousand pounds into the business accounts every month, when we both know, Nigel, that it was you."

Nigel's face became ashen when he realised, he'd spoken out of turn.
"For once, Mr Diplock, you appear to be lost for words," Laura added before turning on her heels and making her exit.

*   *   *

"That bloody man," exclaimed Laura as she burst into the office.
"Are you talking about Mr Diplock or Kieran?" Abigail enquired, her voice calm and cheery.
"Bloody Nigel Diplock," Laura replied, ignoring her assistant's attempt to lighten her mood.
"So, he didn't take the engagement well?" Abigail asked again with a joyful edge to her voice.
Laura stopped in her tracks and smiled. "Okay, smart-arse," she replied with a wry smile, "you were right. Nigel, god's gift to women, wasn't best pleased when I broke the news to him."
"What did he say?" Abigail enquired.
"At first he suggested I'd led him on, I think," Laura replied, "but very soon he made it quite clear that I'm lumbered with him until every aspect of Billy's will has been satisfied, and I sense he's now going to do all he can to derail me."
"Bastard!" Abigail remarked in her thick Suffolk accent.
"I couldn't have put it better myself," Laura agreed. "At least I now know what sort of man he is."
"Yeah," Abigail added. "Good job you chose Kieran."
Laura shook her head. "As I've told you several times already," Laura continued, "Nigel Diplock and I were only ever just friends."
Abigail raised her eyes skyward. "Well I'm not sure how friends do things in London, but here in sleepy old

Suffolk they don't tend to kiss and cuddle on a bench at lunchtime."
Laura could feel her cheeks reddening. "Anyway," she said, trying hard to change the subject, "in the heat of the moment Nigel Diplock said something that makes me think he may have been lying about not knowing about you and Billy."
"Really," replied Abigail. "What did he say?"
"It wasn't very flattering, I'm afraid," Laura confessed. "And I can't remember the exact words he used, but I'm now starting to think he did know about you and Billy well before you mentioned the will."
"I knew he would have," Abigail remarked. "Not that it really makes any difference. Anyway, enough of him, let me see that ring!"
Laura smiled and held out her hand so her assistant could see her shiny engagement ring."
"Wow," Abigail enthused. "That's a rock and a half!"

* * *

Laura arrived back at the flat at five thirty. After three loud knocks Kieran opened the door. "Did you book a table?" he asked as soon as Laura walked inside.
"Yes," replied Laura before planting a kiss on his lips. "It's all sorted for seven."
"Great," said Kieran. "How was your day?"
Laura exhaled heavily to signify that it hadn't been brilliant. "Pour me a glass of chardonnay and I'll tell you."
"That bad," replied Kieran.
With her glass in hand, Laura spent the next ten minutes relating to Kieran the gist of her conversation with Nigel Diplock and then with Abigail, which she did in some detail although she deliberately excluded any reference

to her and the solicitor being anything other than just friends.
"I told you he was a smarmy bugger," Kieran remarked as soon as Laura stopped for air. "To be honest, if you hadn't said he'd shown you Billy's will, I'd be inclined to say that he'd made it all up."
Laura smiled. "Unfortunately, that's one thing I can't accuse him of," she conceded. "I saw the will and I'm certain it was genuine."

Chapter 55

Le Rayon de Miel was a charming jewel of a restaurant, located high on the cliff top, looking out over the North Sea. It had two Michelin stars and was promoted by its owners as being the best French restaurant in East Anglia.

Laura had been there once before as a guest of Nigel Diplock and she'd instantly fallen in love with not just the cuisine but also the rustic, Gallic charm of the eatery and its small yet cosy, romantic setting. In short, she knew it would be the perfect place for her and Kieran to celebrate their engagement and to have their last meal together before he headed off to America.

"Looks very fancy," Kieran remarked as he ducked his head on entering the candlelit dining room.

"We have a reservation," Laura told the grinning waiter who met them at the door. "It's in the name Eastwood, a table for two."

The waiter scoured the booking list, before looking back in the direction of his two guests. "I have a table," he said in a bemused French accent. "But it is for four persons."

"That's correct," interjected Kieran without hesitation. "That will be ours."

The waiter smiled and, picking up four menus, marched over to an empty table by the window."

"Four," Laura whispered. "I ordered a table for two."

"I'll explain later," Kieran replied, while at the same time holding out his arm to signify to Laura that she should follow the waiter.
Laura did as she was told, but her facial expression indicated she was far from happy.
"May I get you some drinks?" the waiter asked once they had settled themselves down on the dark wooden chairs.
"Can we have a couple of glasses of champagne?" Kieran asked. "We've a special celebration."
"Of course," replied the waiter. "May I ask what the celebration is for?"
"We got engaged today," replied Kieran.
"Congratulations," replied the waiter, who then scurried off to fetch their drinks.
"Why have we got a table for four?" Laura asked, fully expecting an answer which she may not like.
Kieran looked anxious as he started to reply. "I know you said you didn't want to talk to her," he started, "but this afternoon I went to see your mum and dad at the Black Swan. They want to talk to you and are keen to join us in celebrating our engagement."
"So, you've invited them here!" Laura interrupted, her eyes showing her annoyance.
"Not quite," Kieran replied.
"So why a table for four?" Laura retorted with an angry look in her eyes.
"They want to join us," continued Kieran, "and, yes, I did call the restaurant and change the table booking to four, but they both said they'd only come if you were happy for them to join us. If you still don't want to see them then they will stay away and leave us alone."
"Well that's easy," replied Laura uncompromisingly. "I still don't want to see them."

As Laura finished her sentence, the waiter suddenly appeared and placed two glasses of champagne next to Laura and Kieran. "These are on the house," he remarked in his distinct French accent.
Laura looked up at the waiter and gave him her best forced smile. "Thank you," she remarked before taking a small sip.
"And will the others be joining you soon?" the waiter asked.
Kieran looked at Laura, hoping she'd change her mind. Laura put down her glass on the table and shook her head gently indicating some displeasure, but also that her resolve was starting to thaw. "You need to ask my fiancé," she replied coolly. "The surprises seem to be all his, this evening."
It was now Kieran's turn to give a forced smile. "I'll message them to see how long they'll be," he replied. The waiter nodded and departed to leave the newly engaged couple alone.
"So, the plan was to get my approval and then message them to give them the all clear," Laura remarked.
Kieran nodded. "That's what we agreed," he replied sheepishly.
"Well you better message them quickly," Laura continued. "I'm starving and I don't think our genial host will remain so genial if we sit here without ordering for too much longer."
Laura's mum and dad arrived within ten minutes of receiving Kieran's message. As they approached the table, Kieran stood up to greet them and having shook Mike Eastwood's hand, warmly embraced Laura's mum. Laura, however, remained in her seat. In fairness she did give them both a smile but was still not ready to allow her parents to feel they were forgiven.

"Oh, this is a nice place," Laura's mum remarked as she sat herself down opposite her daughter.
"Bloody expensive I suspect," remarked her husband as he eased his hefty frame down onto the small wooden chair.
"This is our treat, by the way," added Laura's mum. "It's the least we could do."
"To make up for deceiving me for all these years," Laura announced caustically.
"No," Laura's mum replied firmly. "To celebrate your engagement. I know it will take me forever to get your forgiveness for the other matter, but I don't want it to spoil this evening."
"So, you're looking for a truce," Laura remarked.
"If you want to put it that way, then yes," replied her mum. "If only for this evening."
"That sounds a brilliant idea," Kieran remarked, trying hard to prevent Laura saying or doing anything that might cause a scene and that she may regret later.
"On one condition," Laura added, her body language still suggesting she wasn't comfortable breaking bread with her parents.
Kieran, sensing the condition was almost certainly going to aggravate the situation tried hard to divert the way the conversation was going. "Why don't we just try and have a nice evening without any conditions?" he suggested feebly.
"What's your condition?" her dad asked, knowing that when she was in one of her stubborn moods, Laura was unlikely to snap out of it that readily.
"I want you both to tell me everything," Laura replied. "No more surprises."
Her parents glanced at each other before Mike Eastwood nodded. "Okay," he said, "but before we do, I need a drink."

Kieran signalled to the waiter, who arrived at the table within seconds.
"We appear to have missed out on the champagne," Mike remarked with a smile. "Can we have another bottle, and we'll also have a bottle of house white and a bottle of house red, too."
The waiter smiled and rushed away.
"It is a nice place." Laura's mum remarked for a second time, her attempt to avoid an embarrassing pause. "It's such an intimate little restaurant with an air of timeless charm."
"You should write their promotional bumf," Kieran remarked, trying to jolly the conversation along.
Laura's mum laughed. "Yes, I'd be good at that," she replied with a warm and welcoming smile.
Kieran opened the menu and, in another effort to circumvent any silences, started to read out loud. "Try our renowned homemade Gallic specialities in our laidback yet romantic ambience," he said in his best attempt at a French accent. "Our menu features reliable favourites like classic, succulent steak frites or juicy chicken breast stuffed with wild mushroom duxelle and Dijon sauce. Other popular creations include classic moules mariniere steamed with white wine."
"I thought this was a French restaurant?" Mike remarked. "Not German."
Fortunately for Kieran, at that point the waiter returned with a bottle of white wine in one hand and a large wine cooler in the other.
Following close behind him came a short, dumpy waitress in a tight-fitting white blouse and tiny black pencil skirt, carrying their champagne and red wine.
"Would you like me to open the champagne now?" the waiter remarked, his accent highlighting the paltry impression made by Kieran a few seconds earlier.

"I think so," replied Mike Eastwood.
With a loud pop, the bottle was opened and after a few moments, their four glasses were full, and Mike Eastwood made a toast.
"To Laura and Kieran," he said, raising his glass high.
The smiling waiter stood attentively as they made their toast. "Do you want to taste the wine?" he enquired, his words directed at Mike Eastwood, who he appeared to have identified as the person in charge.
Laura lifted her empty wine glass and moved it slowly towards the waiter. "Just pour, please," she remarked, in an effort to move proceedings along and demonstrate to the waiter that her dad wasn't the one calling the shots.
The waiter smiled and, with consummate ease, opened the bottle of white wine, poured some into Laura's glass then placed the remainder, wrapped in a white napkin, into the wine cooler. He then with equal efficiency and effortlessness, opened the red and placed that bottle in the centre of their table.
"Are you ready to order?" he then enquired, "Or shall I give you a few more minutes?"
"If you can give us a few more minutes, please," Kieran replied.
The waiter smiled again, and in a movement, Uriah Heep would have been proud of, bowed gently before making a silent but speedy retreat.
"Who's having red and who's having white?" Laura's mother enquired.
Laura was getting very agitated by the amount of time it was taking for her parents to start telling her what she needed to know, her impatience evident in her stern expression. However, she managed to keep a lid on her feelings, stay calm and avoid articulating her frustration.
Having established that Mike and Kieran wanted red, and Laura and her mum were on white, and having

ensured that all four glasses were filled, Mike then cleared his throat. "Let me kick this off," he said, his eyes fixed on Laura and his hands clasped around his wine glass as he spoke. "Hopefully after you know everything, Laura, you'll maybe understand better why we never told you before, but I'll leave that to you."
Laura looked directly back into her dad's eyes but elected to remain silent to avoid any further delay in attaining the truth.
"To give you a full background to everything, we need to go back forty or fifty years." Mike Eastwood announced. "In those days, the McKenna clan were big fish in these parts. James McKenna, who was Billy's grandfather, was a councillor here and ran many of the local shops. When he died, Robert, his only son, took over the shops and he, too, was on the town council. As I recall, Robert was even mayor for a while." As he spoke, he glanced over to his wife who nodded in agreement. "Well, Robert was a bit of a womaniser by all accounts and had several relationships, one of which was with Mary Doverman, the daughter of a local farmer. The result of that relationship was that she got pregnant and her father, who was also very influential in the area, insisted that they married. They had a son who they called Stephen and, about five years later, she had another son, your birth father."
At that point Mike stopped and took a large swig from his wine glass.
"Anyway," he continued, "as far as I'm told the marriage was never that strong and eventually Robert got caught with his pants down with some other woman and the result was that Mary filed for a divorce. I'm not totally sure of all the details, but the upshot was that he had to sell everything, and, after the split, he just upped and left, I think to make a new life for himself in New

Zealand or Australia. In any case, as far as I'm aware, neither Stephen, Billy nor their mum ever saw him again."
"When was that?" Laura asked.
"It would have been when Billy and I were about six or seven," her dad replied.
"Mary brought the two boys up on her own?" Laura added in an attempt to clarify the story.
"Yes," replied Laura's mum. "I know Billy never had any contact with his dad, in fact I can't recall him ever mentioning his father".
"That's all very interesting," Laura remarked, "but what relevance does that have on you both hiding the truth from me?"
"I'm coming to that," her dad replied, his curt response suggesting he was starting to become annoyed at his daughter's rude and aggressive attitude. "The boys were Mary's life and she spoilt them rotten. They always had the best toys and if there was ever any trouble in the town, she would always stand up for them even when everyone knew they were involved."
"Were they bad children?" Kieran asked.
Mike Eastwood pondered the question for a few moments. "Initially I'd say no more than any other kids," he replied. "However, as they got older, they did start to get worse, especially Stephen."
As he spoke, Laura's mum nodded to again reinforce his words.
"In fairness to Billy," continued Mike, "he was just a bit of a tearaway, but with Stephen it was much more. By the time he was in his late teens he was totally out of control and, to make matters worse, his mum seemed to just turn a blind eye to everything he did."
"What sort of things are we talking about?" Laura asked.

"You name it," replied her dad offhandedly. "Criminal damage, theft, even a case of arson at the local scout hut. Stephen, of course was always too clever to get caught and when he was suspected, his mum would always stick up for him, but take it from me, he was completely off the rails."
"So, what happened to him?" Laura asked.
"Well, it all came to a head one summer when he was about twenty," Mike replied. "Billy and I were still at school, but there was talk locally about him attacking a young woman who worked in a travelling circus."
Laura frowned. "Are you saying he raped her?"
Mike Eastwood glanced at his wife before answering. "It was never proven," he replied, trying hard to choose his words carefully, "but the story was that one evening, after one of their performances, Stephen followed the young woman to her caravan and tried it on, but when she turned him down, he raped her. The word is, that to avoid any prosecution, Mary paid the girl a huge sum of money to keep her mouth shut, but as I say, this never came out."
Laura shook her head slowly. "And how long after this did Stephen die?" she enquired.
Before Mike Eastwood had a chance to reply, the waiter returned to the table once more. "Can I take your orders?" he enquired.
"Yes, I think I'm ready," Laura's mum replied, although neither she nor anyone else had taken much notice of the menu so far.
As she gave the waiter her order, the other three hurriedly opened the menu to select a starter and a main course.
With three classic moules mariniere and one minestrone soup in his notebook, followed by two succulent steak frites and two juicy stuffed chicken breasts as the table's

main courses, the waiter departed to allow Mike to finish his story.
"Stephen was a keen sea fisherman and often went out in a small motor-powered boat to fish," Mike Eastwood continued as soon as the waiter was out of earshot. "It was about three or four months after the rumours of the woman at the circus came to light that he went missing."
"Was he drowned?" Laura asked.
Mike Eastwood shrugged his shoulders. "That was the verdict of the coroner he replied. "However, no body was ever found, so he may have made it look like he drowned, when in fact he just did a bunk."
"Like his dad did," Laura observed.
"Like father like son," Kieran added.
"Why not," suggested Mike. "I wouldn't put it past Mary to help him and it would have given him an opportunity for a fresh start somewhere else."
"What about the woman at the circus?" Laura asked. "What happened to her?"
Laura's mum and dad exchanged a glance.
"I've no idea," Mike replied. "The circus came back every summer for three or four weeks, but she was never with them."
"Maybe the money she got from Mary was enough to help her find a new life, too," Kieran suggested.
"That's what I always thought," replied Mike. "Mind you, given what probably happened to the poor girl, who'd blame her for not coming back here."
As Laura pondered what her dad had just told her, the attentive waiter and his tubby colleague returned to their table carrying their starters.
"Those moules mariniere smell wonderful," Laura's mum announced, even though she had chosen the soup.
The waiter smiled, grateful for the compliment, before once more retreating from the table.

"So, Stephen was a bad boy," remarked Laura, "and clearly, Mary is quite capable of losing her moral compass to protect her boys, but so far, you've hardly mentioned Billy McKenna. What's his dark secret?"
"As I said before," Mike continued, "Billy was nowhere near as wild as Stephen, in fact when we were young, his antics were quite endearing. Billy and I were in the same class at school from when we were about four right up until we were sixteen and I guess you could say Billy and I were childhood chums. Not that we were together all the time. In those days we did fall out now and then and there were several lads who hung around together. It was only after we finished school when we were sixteen that we became close friends. That's because we both joined the bank as clerks at the same time."
"But something did go wrong, and Billy ended up in prison," Laura added. "So, what happened?"
Mike Eastwood gazed over towards his wife as if to signify that it was probably her turn to pick up the story. Laura's mum finished a spoonful of soup before turning sideways to face her daughter.
"As I told you yesterday, Billy and I became a couple, we got married and not too long after, we found that I was expecting you," said Laura's mum. "It was then that Billy started defrauding the bank."
"The tomb stoning scam," Laura remarked to confirm she knew what her mum was talking about.
"Well, what I didn't tell you yesterday was how I discovered what he was doing," her mum continued.
"So how was that?" Laura asked.
"I told her," her dad interjected. "I stumbled upon what he was doing by sheer coincidence. He'd made a silly error in setting up two fictitious borrowers at the same address. When we'd written off the first one, I'd

remembered how strange the address was and it stuck in my head. So, when a few months later, we were writing off another bad debt at the same address, it started to ring alarm bells in my head."
"What did you do?" Kieran asked.
"I didn't want him to get caught, so, foolishly, I confronted him and told him that as long as he stopped, I'd not report him," Mike replied.
"But I suppose you're going to tell us that he didn't" Laura suggested.
"It was worse than that," Laura's mum added. "He not only continued, but he also set up future loans with Mike's name as the bank employee who made the loans, so that if Billy was detected, it would implicate your dad, too."
"Did you know this, dad?" Laura asked.
"He told me after he'd done three or four," replied her father. "He even offered me some of the money to keep me sweet."
"So, you reported him," Laura suggested.
Her father shook his head. "I didn't know what to do," he replied. "So, I decided to speak with Mary. I figured that if anyone could stop him it would be her."
"And what did she say?" Laura asked.
"She offered me ten thousand pounds to quit the bank and to keep my mouth shut," Mike replied.
"What did you do?" Kieran asked.
Mike Eastwood lowered his eyes. "Like a fool, I took the money and did what she said," he replied. "And I've regretted it ever since."
"So, how did he get caught," Laura asked, her brow furrowed as she posed the question.
"I reported him," her mother announced. "I begged him to stop and he promised me he would, but he just

couldn't help himself. It was such easy money for him. So, one day I rang the bank's head office anonymously and I told them what he'd been doing. They sent some inspectors into the branch within days. He was suspended, then prosecuted and finally sentenced."
"I can't believe it," Laura exclaimed, her shock clear in her voice. "You shopped him!"
"How did you avoid getting implicated?" Kieran asked Mike Eastwood.
"Because, despite initially trying to make out I was also involved, Billy did, in the end, admit it was just him," replied Mike. "And the police decided not to press charges against me."
"From everything you've told me that seems out of character," Laura observed. "Why did he do that?"
Mike Eastwood looked awkward, but was saved from replying when once again, the attentive waiter appeared at the table.
"How is your food?" he enquired with a look of surprise to see that most of their starters remained on their plates.
"Really good," replied Kieran. "We've been talking too much that's all."
The waiter smiled again and once more made his exit.
"We should finish our starters," Laura's mother added. "Otherwise they'll get cold."
For the next few minutes, the four diners ate in virtual silence, although it was clear to all of them there was more that needed to be said.
Once their plates had been removed by the chubby waitress, Mike topped up first Kieran's, then his wine glass.
"You're of course right, Laura," Mike continued. "It was out of character. I did a deal with Billy, a deal that was communicated via Mary."

"And what was that deal?" Laura enquired.
"That I'd take care of your mum and you, Laura, until Billy was released from prison."
Laura nodded. "Well, you certainly did that," she remarked sarcastically, before filling up her own glass with more white wine. "You went over and above the call of duty on that one."
The temporary pause in the conversation was an uneasy one but was broken by Mike Eastwood smiling broadly. "Yes, sweetie," he replied, "I did and of course, when Billy found out we'd married, and I wanted to adopt you, he was none too happy."
"Your main courses," announced the waiter, who had arrived at the table unseen.
Once again, the diners waited in silence as their main courses were set down in front of them.
For the next half hour, they ate their meals and the conversation moved to other subjects, like Kieran's job in America and the outstanding food that they'd been served. It was only when they had finished the last morsels from their plates and were studying the dessert menu that the conversation returned to Billy McKenna.
"What I don't understand," Laura remarked, "is why Billy didn't fight harder for custody of me or to see me when he came out of prison. After all, it's not like he was a million miles away."
Mike Eastwood took a deep intake of breath. "Well, you've asked for the truth, so I'll give it you," he replied, his eyes again fixed on his daughter. "Do you remember that ten thousand pounds I told you Mary gave me?"
Laura nodded.
"Well, I never spent a penny of it," her father replied. "I was so ashamed of what I'd done that I put it in an account, and it languished there for the best part of ten

years. In those heady days you could get a good return on your money and by the time Billy came out, it was worth more than double what Mary had given me. The deal was simple, I gave him the money and he promised to stay away from us all for good."
"So, let me get this straight," Laura exclaimed. "He agreed to give me up for twenty grand. Was that all I was worth to him?"
Laura's mum, seeing how hurt Laura was, put her hand on her daughter's arm. "It all sounds awful," she conceded, "but, given the circumstances, it just seemed the right thing to do. Billy needed the money, and we were desperate to keep you happy."
"Why couldn't Mary give him some money?" Laura suggested. "She's evidently loaded."
Mike Eastwood shook his head. "To be honest I don't know," he replied. "Maybe he was too embarrassed to ask."
"Or maybe, selling me to you was just easier," Laura replied angrily.
Again, silence descended on the table leaving Laura to take in everything she'd been told.
"Would you care for desserts and coffees," remarked the waiter, who appeared by Kieran's side. "I can recommend the honeycomb ice cream sundae; it's the chef's speciality."
"Let's go for four of those then," Kieran replied, seeing the others had not been paying attention.
"And four strong coffees, too," added Laura who was still stunned and angry.
When, once again, the four of them were alone, Laura turned to her mother. "I still can't totally forgive what you did, but I do think I'm beginning to understand why."

"And I guess, by leaving you everything, it was Billy's way of making things up to you," Kieran added, trying hard to help his fiancé come to terms with the fact that he'd taken Mike's money all those years ago.
"I suppose so," Laura replied, despondently. "It does appear my inheritance is not so much an act of love, but more one of remorse."
Her mum, relieved that at last the ice was starting to thaw, embraced her daughter and gave her a large hug.
"I'm sorry I didn't tell you sooner," she remarked with a tear trickling down her cheek. "I should have been more open. It's just that after time, I hoped it would all go away."
"I know," Laura replied with a forced smile. "Now tell me what happened when you met Mary earlier?"
"Well, turning up on her doorstep did seem to throw her," her mum replied, "but she's a robust old bird and it didn't take her long to regain her poise."
"What was it she wanted to talk to you about?" Laura asked.
"Well," replied her mum, pausing for a few seconds, choosing her words carefully so as not to upset Laura any more than necessary, "she actually tried to strike a deal with me to help get you to leave Blythwold and go back to London."
"What sort of deal?" Laura enquired, frowning once again as she expected another painful bombshell.
"She offered me fifty thousand pounds to help persuade you to leave," her mum replied.
"What!" Laura exclaimed. "She tried to bribe you!"
"Mary clearly doesn't know Laura very well," Kieran whispered in Mike's direction, much to Mike's amusement. "Nobody, not even Bev could persuade Laura to leave."

"I hope you told her to get lost!" Laura remarked firmly and in a louder voice than she'd anticipated.
"Of course, I did, dear," replied her mum, "but now that you and Kieran are engaged and he's off to America," she added with a faint smile, "I was wondering whether I should have cashed in, as I'm assuming you'll be following him quite shortly."
Laura scowled. "No way," she replied. "I'm staying put until every penny of my inheritance is in the bank. That old witch isn't going to be driving me out, not that easily."
"Your bill," announced the waiter as he set a small silver tray on the table which supported a folded piece of paper and four thin mints.
Mike Eastwood picked it up and with his eyes enlarging, read the amount that was due.
"That's beans on toast for us for the next six months," he remarked before returning the tray to the table with his credit card resting on top of the bill.

.

Chapter 56

It was just after eleven o'clock when Laura and Kieran arrived back at the apartment. They'd said their goodbyes to Mike and Bev, who were keen to return to their hotel room, given that they would have to leave the Black Swan at five thirty the next morning in order to get to Stansted in time to catch the nine twenty flight to Alicante.

"So, are you angry with me for inviting your mum and dad along?" Kieran asked once they were safely inside Laura's apartment.

"No," Laura confessed as she planted a huge kiss on his lips. "I'm pleased. You were right, it would have been wrong to let them go without knowing why they hid the truth from me. It's better that it's all out in the open now. But I won't lie; I'm still annoyed about what they did."

Kieran nodded and smiled. "It was interesting what your dad said about the McKenna family. Even though he went to prison, it sounds like Billy was an angel compared to the others."

Laura playfully pushed Kieran away. "That's my family you're talking about," she remarked. "Remember, I've got the same blood flowing through my veins."

"I know," he replied. "I'm going to need eyes in the back of my head because your DNA is scary."

Laura flopped herself down on the sofa. "What time are you leaving tomorrow?" she asked.

Kieran smiled. “Well I was going to tell you earlier,” he remarked, “but with everything else you were hearing from Bev and Mike, I decided to wait to tell you until we were alone.”
“I’m getting the feeling I’ve a few more surprises coming,” Laura replied, her eyes narrowing as she spoke.
“Well,” continued Kieran, “I spoke with the Americans earlier and they’ve agreed to allow me to delay my arrival for two more weeks.”
“Really!” replied Laura. “How did you manage that?”
“I told them I’d got a family issue,” replied Kieran.
“I’m a family issue am I,” replied Laura playfully.
“No,” Kieran replied. “Ryan’s my family issue. Not that I’ll be going to see him. However, now that there’s so much for us to start looking into, I think it’s good I’ll be around for a couple more weeks – don’t you agree?” As he finished his sentence Kieran plonked himself down next to Laura on the sofa and pulled her close to him.
“What needs looking into?” Laura enquired.
Kieran looked at her as if she was barmy. “There’s loads to be investigated,” he replied.
“Like what?” Laura asked, her facial expression indicating total bemusement.”
“Well, there’s Stephen McKenna for starters,” remarked Kieran. “Is he dead or did he just do a bunk? Then there’s the question of why Mary was prepared to pay your mum, a woman she doesn’t like at all, fifty thousand to get you to give up your inheritance. Do none of these things puzzle you?”
“You certainly are full of surprises,” Laura replied with a smile. “I never had you down as a budding Hercule Poirot.”
“But there are weird things going on here,” Kieran continued, “don’t you think?”

Laura pondered the question for a few seconds. “Yes,” she conceded. “I can’t deny that things are a bit odd, but I think it’s just Blythwold. I’m starting to think that odd is actually quite normal here.”
Kieran smirked. “I can’t argue with that,” he replied.
“Well, you’ve got two weeks to get your little grey cells working,” Laura remarked in her best French accent. “I’ve got more practical things to concern me, like how I can make a loss-making business profitable, and how I can get Meridian off my back regarding the money they want me to pay for breach of contract.”
“Oh, that reminds me!” Kieran said. “I forgot to tell you. When you were in the shower before we went to the restaurant, you got a call on your mobile from Saskia."
“Really, what did she want?” Laura asked.
“She just asked if you could call her back,” Kieran replied.
“No chance,” Laura announced. “There’s no way I’m talking to that cow!”

* * *

Laura spent an uneasy night tossing and turning in bed as she digested the disclosures from earlier that evening. She was relieved that Kieran was able to stay a couple more weeks, and was certainly intrigued as to what, if anything, they’d find out about Stephen McKenna’s disappearance.
However, Laura was more interested in what the two-thousand-pound monthly payments into Billy’s business account were for, why Nigel Diplock lied about the payments, and why he concealed any knowledge about Abigail’s relationship with Billy. Laura was also curious to find out what her treacherous friend Saskia wanted.

She decided she'd start her investigations into all of these mysteries in the morning; with the help of her own Hercule Poirot.

Chapter 57

Friday 18thth September

Kieran was still asleep when Laura left for work. Having written him a simple note saying she'd be back at lunchtime, Laura slipped out the front door and gently closed it behind her, making sure it wouldn't make a noise and wake him.
As Laura stepped out into the fresh morning air, the smell of salt filled her nostrils and, although from the pavement she couldn't see the waves crashing upon the shore, their soothing repetitious sound made her feel good inside; and brought a smile to her face.
She looked at her watch, it was seven fifty. Unless there had been heavy traffic, her mum and dad should, by now, already be at Stansted Airport. Laura remained stationary as she composed a short text message.

Hope you have a nice flight. Thanks for dinner see you soon xxx

Laura figured that with this short text her mum would know that she'd forgiven her.
She'd walked no more than twenty or thirty paces before she heard the unmistakeable ping of her mobile, telling her she'd received a reply.

Just going through departures now. Dad unhappy he has to take his shoes and belt off. I think he needs

some breakfast. Take care darling see you soon Mum xxx

Laura chuckled to herself as she imaged her grumpy dad cursing as he went through the x-ray machine in his socks, holding onto his trousers to stop them falling down.
When she neared the office, she met Abigail walking towards her.
"How was dinner last night?" Abigail enquired.
"Different," Laura replied.
"Different good or different bad?" Abigail asked.
"Different different," was Laura's reply, which left poor Abigail none the wiser.
"You're going to have to tell me more than that!" Abigail protested as they arrived outside the agency.
Laura smiled as she opened the door. "Okay," she replied, "but it will cost you a coffee."
"You were getting one of those anyway," Abigail remarked. "So that's fine with me."
Laura felt comfortable with Abigail, but their relationship was still not yet at a point where she felt totally happy sharing everything she'd heard the evening before. However, Laura did want to see if Abigail knew anything more about Stephen McKenna. So, when the redhead returned with two steaming cups of coffee, Laura started to probe her young assistant.
"Did Billy ever mention anything about his brother, Stephen?" Laura asked. "My dad told me he was drowned at sea when they were teenagers."
Abigail shook her head. "Billy never mentioned him," she replied. "But I have heard some stories about him, and they aren't that complimentary."
"What sort of stories?" Laura enquired; her appetite whetted by Abigail's response.

"Well, I've heard that he was a right one," Abigail continued. "Always in trouble and the joke is that he could well be the father of quite a few of the thirty somethings in Blythwold, if you know what I mean."
"A bit of a ladies' man, then," Laura said, in an attempt to get Abigail to say more.
"I think he did alright for himself," replied Abigail.
"My dad mentioned a story about a woman at the circus?" Laura enquired. "Do you know anything about that?"
Abigail shook her head. "No," she replied. "I've not heard that one. Do you mean the Donnelly's Circus that comes around every summer?"
Laura shrugged her shoulders. "I don't know what it was called," she replied.
"What was the story your dad told you?" Abigail asked.
"Just that Stephen was involved with one of the women that worked at the circus," replied Laura, who was keen not to say too much in case what her dad said wasn't correct.
"You could ask Miriam I suppose," Abigail replied.
"Who's Miriam?" Laura asked.
"She owns the tearoom on the high street," Abigail replied. "She used to work at the circus years ago, but she gave it up and settled here. She might know."
Laura smiled. "It's not that important," she replied before taking a sip of her coffee. "So, what are the rumours about Stephen's accident?"
Abigail held out her arms with her palms upwards to indicate she didn't know. "People don't talk about it that often," she replied. "But my grandfather used to work on the lifeboat, and he reckons it was all very iffy."
"What do you mean?" Laura asked.
"He always told us that when Stephen was last seen, the weather was quite calm," Abigail replied. "He knew

Stephen well and reckoned he was a good swimmer. He always believed that Stephen didn't drown at all. He thinks he faked it and did a runner."
"Really," Laura replied. "That's what my dad thinks, too."
"To be honest, though," Abigail added. "It happened so long ago, and this place is so full of rumours, I'd not be surprised if most of what is said about Stephen McKenna is completely wrong. The person who would know, though, is Mary McKenna, but you're not likely to get her to tell you, grandmother, or no grandmother."
Laura smiled. "Your right there, Abigail," she replied.

* * *

For the next few hours Laura and Abigail worked in near silence, punctuated by the odd telephone call and perpetual mugs of coffee being made and delivered by Abigail.
Laura was just starting to think about going back to the Crow's Nest to see Kieran when her mobile phone rang. Laura looked at the screen to see the name Saskia appear. Her initial thought was to leave it, but curiosity took over and she took the call.
"Laura Eastwood," she said as if she didn't know who was calling her.
"It's me, Sas," came the bubbly reply. "How are you?"
Laura took a deep breath. "I'm fine Saskia," she replied. "What brings you to call me?"
"Well, to see how you are getting along mainly," Saskia replied. "But also, to see if there's any way I can help resolve the issue between you and Vic."
"What issue?" Laura replied, not wishing to make Saskia's life any easier.

"The breach of contract issue," Saskia remarked. "Vic's told me about it, and I've volunteered to try and act as intermediary."
"That's part of an account manager's role now, is it?" Laura asked sarcastically.
"Oh, haven't you heard," Saskia replied. "I'm now Vic's right-hand woman, I'm Office Manager now, so this dispute does fall under my area of responsibility."
Laura rolled her eyes. "Well congratulations," she replied.
"Thanks, Laura," Saskia said as if she'd genuinely felt Laura meant it. "It's been an absolute whirlwind here since you left. Business is going great and Vic and I have been working flat out day and night looking at ways to restructure and align the team to meet the new challenges."
"So, lots of evenings together in the gym, I expect?" Laura remarked spitefully.
"Oh, we've had no time for any leisure activities, Laura," replied Saskia, again seemingly unmoved by Laura's sarcastic comments.
"What are you proposing regarding my situation?" Laura asked.
"Well, I was hoping you'd be able to come in one day next week so we could all talk it through," Saskia replied. "I was thinking maybe on Monday."
Laura puffed out her cheeks. She desperately wanted to get it all resolved but the prospect of sitting across the table from Vic and Saskia wasn't something she relished. "I'll have to check my diary, but Tuesday may be better for me," Laura replied, although she knew full well that she could make pretty much any day next week.
"Oh, that's fine," Saskia replied. "When you've had a chance to check out your availability, why don't you call

Brenda and tie everything up. She's doubling as my PA, too, now, so she'll have mine and Vic's availability."
"Fine," replied Laura, who was in no mood to allow the conversation to continue any further.
"Are you back with Kieran now?" Saskia enquired. "It's just that when I called you last night, he answered your phone."
Laura could feel her blood boiling, "Look, Saskia, I'm going to have to go," she replied in as calm a voice as she could. "I've got a client waiting for me in reception."
"Okay," replied Saskia. "Hopefully, we'll see you on Tuesday."
"I'll talk with Brenda," replied Laura. "But Tuesday's probably going to suit me better."
Exasperated and tense, Laura ended the call and decided to take an early lunch.

Chapter 58

On her way home Laura decided to pick up a couple of filled rolls from the Tea Shop on the high street. She'd done this a few times before, but in the light of what Abigail had told her that morning, she thought she'd try and discover who Miriam was.
When she arrived, there was a small queue waiting to be served and just two people sat drinking tea on separate small round tables.
Laura waited her turn.
When eventually the waitress came to take Laura's order, she deliberately paused as if she was finding it difficult to make up her mind. With there being nobody behind her, Laura felt comfortable striking up conversation.
"It's so hard to choose," she remarked.
The middle-aged waitress behind the counter smiled.
"It's hard," she replied in a thick eastern European accent. "I run the place and I can't choose myself sometimes."
"It's your shop," replied Laura. "So, you must be Miriam?"
The woman behind the counter looked shocked. "Yes, I'm Miriam," she replied.
"I'm Laura, by the way," Laura remarked. "I was told you used to work in the circus."
Miriam smiled. "Yes, but that was long, long ago. I've been here now for over twenty years."

"What did you do in the circus?" Laura asked, keeping her eyes fixed on the sandwiches and rolls to give the impression she was still trying to choose.
"It was a small circus," replied Miriam, "so I did many things."
"Was your circus Donnelly's, the one that comes here each year?" Laura asked.
"Yes," said Miriam, who was starting to look anxious about being asked so many questions. "Do you know what you want yet?"
Laura looked up at Miriam. "Yes, I'll have a ham salad baguette, an all-day breakfast sandwich on white and two Chelsea buns, please."
Miriam quickly selected the items for Laura, placed the baguette and sandwich in two separate bags, put the Chelsea buns in another and placed them all on the counter, then rang the amounts into her till.
"That will be nine pounds, forty-seven," she said.
Laura opened her purse and handed Miriam a ten-pound note.
"I work at the events business around the corner," Laura remarked. "It was Billy McKenna's; did you know him?"
Miriam stared back at Laura. "Everyone knows everyone here," she replied. "I knew him, but not well."
"What about his mother, Mary and his brother, Stephen?" Laura asked.
"I know Mary," Miriam replied. "But I don't know Stephen."
As she listened to Miriam's reply Laura watched her closely. Laura wasn't sure, but she sensed that Miriam was lying about Stephen. Given that there was still nobody behind her and, as yet, she hadn't been given her change, Laura just carried on with her questioning.

"I'm Billy's daughter," Laura replied. "I only found out that Stephen existed a few weeks ago, so I'm trying to find out more about him. I was told that he died about thirty years ago, but that he'd had a relationship with someone at the circus. I was wondering if you knew anything about it?"
Miriam's face seemed to harden. "I know nothing about Stephen. I told you already," her words firm and final. "Here is your change."
Miriam slammed the coins onto the top of the glass cabinet that separated her from her customers. "Now leave me, please, I have work to do."
Laura picked up the bags and her change, smiled, and made her way out of the shop. As she left, Laura glanced at the hygiene certificate fixed to the door, which gave the premises five stars and was made out to the proprietor, Ms Miriam Anchova.

* * *

"Honey, I'm home," Laura said playfully, in her best American accent, as she burst into the apartment.
Kieran was sat at the kitchen table transfixed by his laptop screen.
"Hi," he replied, clearly surprised to see her. "You're early."
Laura placed the bags on the table and planted a kiss on his forehead. "I spoke to that cow, Saskia," she replied with venom in her voice. "After that I just had to get away."
Kieran looked up from his screen. "I thought you weren't going to call her," he remarked, his eyes still fixed to the computer screen.
"I didn't," Laura remarked. "She called me again. Anyway, what have you been doing?"

"I've had a fairly unsuccessful morning," Kieran replied. "I tried to see if I could find Stephen McKenna online. I checked on LinkedIn, and I did find three people with that name in New Zealand. One is about the age your uncle would be if he's still alive."
"Really," replied Laura. "And where abouts is he in New Zealand?"
"A place called Taranaki," said Kieran. "Look, here's his profile."
"I guess it could be him," Laura replied, "but he'd be mad to keep his name, wouldn't he?"
Kieran nodded. "I agree," he replied. "But I thought I'd check it out anyway."
Laura opened the bags from the Tea Shop and passed over the all-day breakfast sandwich to Kieran. "I bought you this," she said.
Kieran grabbed it off her and took a hefty bite.
"Anyway, what have you been up to?" he enquired; his mouth still unattractively full of sandwich.
"Well," she replied, "I've discovered that Abigail's grandfather was a lifeboat man when Stephen disappeared. And, according to Abigail, he doesn't think it's likely Stephen drowned. He thinks he faked his death."
Kieran nodded, with his mouth still full of sandwich.
"Also," added Laura, "Abigail told me that the woman who runs the Tea Shop used to work at that travelling circus where Stephen is supposed to have attacked someone."
"Really," replied Kieran, who was clearly impressed with this piece of news.
"When I was buying these, I spoke to her," Laura continued. "She denies knowing Stephen, but I'm sure she's lying."
Kieran smiled. "What's her name," he asked.

"It's Miriam Anchova," Laura replied.
"And you spoke to Saskia, too," Kieran added. "What did she want?"
"Well, according to Saskia, she's now second in command at Meridian," said Laura, her tone clearly indicating her displeasure at that news. "She's making out she's trying to be some sort of mediator between me and Vic and has suggested that I go to see them next week."
"And will you?" Kieran asked.
"I don't want to, but I need to get this resolved," Laura replied. "So, I'm going to call Brenda, the PA there, and try and set something up for Tuesday."
"I'll come with you," Kieran remarked. "I need to do a few things, so I'll join you, assuming you want some company?"
"That would work," Laura replied. "I'll get on and sort that out later."
Kieran demolished the last morsel of sandwich and peeked into the other bag Laura had brought in with her.
"Ah, Chelsea buns," he exclaimed. "My favourites."
Laura shook her head in disbelief. "I've never met anyone who can eat as quickly as you," she remarked.
"Thanks," replied Kieran.
"It's not a compliment," Laura added, with a look of displeasure.
"Anyway, what are you going to do this afternoon," Laura enquired.
"I thought I may go and have a chat to my drinking chum, Father Mallory," Kieran replied. "I figure that if Billy confided in anyone it would be him. I know he's not going to share any confessional secrets with me, but he may be able to help us understand more about what is going on here."
Laura nodded. "Good idea."

"And what about you?" Kieran asked.
"I'm just going to get back to the office," Laura replied. "I've got loads to do. I'll also give Brenda at Meridian a call, too."

*　　　*　　　*

Laura arrived back at the office at twelve thirty to find Abigail working tirelessly, head down at her desk. "You can go for your lunch now," she remarked.
"Thanks," replied Abigail, who didn't bother to look up. "I'll go in a minute; I'm just trying to organise setting up the account for the Charity Trek in May."
Laura wandered over to Abigail's desk. "Can't you just use the account Billy always used?" she asked.
"That was all handled by Mary," Abigail replied. "I'm not sure she'll be that helpful, so I thought I'd open a new account."
Laura looked surprised. "So, all the money that Billy raised over all those years was collected and managed by Mary?"
Abigail nodded. "With the help of Billy and Mr Diplock. I didn't get involved."
Laura frowned. "It would appear that Mary McKenna and Nigel Diplock are involved in just about every aspect of activity in Blythwold," she replied.
Abigail nodded. "Oh yes," she concurred. "They've got fingers in everything."
Laura smiled. "Why don't you get off for lunch now," she said. "That can wait until this afternoon."
Abigail looked up. "You're right," she said. "I need some fresh air."
On that note, Abigail grabbed her coat and bag and headed out of the door.

Once she was alone, Laura decided to call Brenda. She picked up the phone on Abigail's desk and dialled the eleven digits that she knew by heart as the switch board number to Meridian.
"Can I speak with Brenda, please?" Laura asked.
Within seconds Laura was put through.
"Hello, Brenda," she said. "It's Laura Eastwood here."
"Good afternoon, Laura," Brenda replied, her voice sounding genuinely pleased to hear from her. "How's life by the sea?"
"It's good," Laura replied. "I hear there have been a lot of changes since I left."
Brenda chuckled. "Oh yes," she replied. "Not all for the good though."
Laura smiled, she didn't know Brenda that well, but liked her just the same. "I've been commanded by Saskia to arrange a meeting at Meridian with her and Vic next week," Laura added. "I was asked to sort it out with you."
Brenda laughed. "Yes, Saskia told me you'd be calling."
"I was thinking Tuesday," Laura suggested. "Is that going to work for them both?"
Brenda replied almost instantly. "Yes, Tuesday would be fine," she replied. "How does a late morning meeting fit with you?"
"Great," Laura remarked. "Shall we say eleven thirty?"
"Perfect," replied Brenda. "I look forward to seeing you, Laura."
"Me too," Laura replied. "Have a nice weekend."
As Laura replaced the handset, she suddenly sensed that she wasn't alone. Turning quickly, she noticed the familiar figure of Nigel Diplock standing a matter of yards away from her.
"I didn't hear you come in," Laura remarked.

"You were on the phone, so I thought I'd wait for you to finish your call," he replied.
"To what do I owe this honour?" Laura added.
"I just wanted to apologise for my behaviour yesterday," Nigel Diplock replied. "My comments and attitude towards you were totally inexcusable. I just wanted to say sorry."
Although Nigel did seem sincere, Laura remained suspicious. However, Laura didn't want to create any unnecessary friction. "That's fine," she replied calmly. "Apology accepted."
Nigel Diplock took a few steps towards Laura, which unnerved her a little. She was about to ask him what he was doing when Abigail burst in through the door.
"I'd forget my bloody head if it was..." she exclaimed but stopped when she saw Laura with Nigel Diplock.
"I'll leave you to it then," he remarked and headed quickly out of the door.
As soon as the solicitor had left, Laura let out a massive sigh of relief.
"What did he want?" Abigail asked.
"I'm not sure," replied Laura. "But I'm glad you came back when you did."

Part Eleven

Vivien's Revenge

Chapter 59

Vivien Chakraborty hadn't any idea about her husband's proclivity for frequenting seedy strip clubs and lap dancing bars until they had been married a good few years. Although she was livid when she first made the discovery, she desperately wanted to save her marriage, particularly as they had two beautiful girls who adored their father.

She tried to reason with Vic and at first even believed his promises to stop chasing other women.

But the truth was that despite his numerous assurances, Vic did nothing to curb his passions. He was certainly careful to ensure his favourite pastime remained tightly concealed from his business associates and work colleagues, but his wife knew exactly what he was up to, and although, as time passed, she appeared to tolerate his behaviour, she hated him for it and was determined he would not get away with it.

Once the marriage was beyond any chance of repair, Vic tried hard to persuade Vivien to give him a divorce. But Vivien remained consistent in her stubbornness. She refused point blank to allow her errant husband to exit their marriage. This was partly on religious grounds and to make her unfaithful husband as miserable as she could, but mainly to allow herself time to build a cast iron case to ensure that when she made her move it would be swift and as painful for Vic as she could make it.

With the bulk of the capital invested to set up Meridian coming from Vivien's family, and the remainder from city investors introduced to Meridian by Vivien's father, Vic legally owned no part of the company; a position Vivien had no intention of allowing him to alter in any way. In short, she wasn't going to allow Vic to get his hands on any shares in the company, however small. Vivien was patient, too. She had quietly bided her time while she built up enough ammunition to nail him good and proper!
She had, for several months, engaged a private detective to help her gather evidence of his activities, and Vic being Vic had given the detective more than enough material to convince the courts of his infidelity.
Vivien knew all about Svetlana and his weekly visits to her apartment. She also knew that Vic was paying her rent, and as far as his mistress was concerned, his name was Rex; a fact that annoyed Vivien as it was her father's nickname. Yet, Vivien didn't want a divorce at any price. What she needed was to be able to prove that Vic's behaviour was adversely impacting the business at Meridian. She wanted to make sure that the family and other investors, when presented with the evidence, would sack her errant husband. At which point, and only then, would she file for divorce.
Despite having more than enough evidence of Vic's unacceptable behaviour in his private life, the detective had struggled to uncover anything substantial enough for Vivien to present to the family and board regarding malpractices that negatively impacted on the business. Without such evidence Vivien feared that Vic could end up being paid a substantial severance settlement from Meridian, which she was determined to avoid at all costs.

Based upon their lack of progress in this respect, her private detective came up with the idea of putting a plant in the office to keep closer tabs on Vic's behaviour. Although Vivien had initially been sceptical about how successful this would be, the idea proved to be a triumph. Having been in place for almost six months, Vivien was delighted when she learned that, in the view of her private detective, the secret agent had accumulated enough hard evidence for them to make their move.

Chapter 60

Friday 18th September

After years of humiliation by the behaviour of her husband and after months of waiting for firm evidence of all Vic's transgressions, Vivien was eager to meet with Andrew Ramsey, her private detective, to see what he and his company mole had unearthed.
As always, Vic was staying in the flat, so Vivien had no need to create an excuse for the meeting she'd arranged with Ramsey, who had specifically requested that they meet at his small office in Clapham.
Vivien wanted to make sure she was back by the time her twins came out of school, so she organised to meet Ramsey at ten thirty am which, even with the travel time being over an hour, would allow her plenty of time to see what he'd discovered and get home to collect the girls at three thirty pm.
"So, what have you got for me?" Vivien enquired eagerly as she sat down in Ramsey's small office.
Vivien had been put in touch with Ramsey by a friend who'd engaged his services to help her build a case against her own badly behaved husband. On the three or four occasions they'd met, Vivien had not been overly impressed by the slightly built detective. However, she'd been assured by her friend that he was thorough, discrete and, above all, honest.

The private detective remained impassive. "I think we've now got more than enough to build a compelling case for you, not only in the divorce courts, but also with the investors at Meridian. Once they see our dossier and listen to the recordings, they will be horrified at what we've managed to uncover."
Vivien smiled broadly. "Tell me more, Mr Ramsey," she urged.
Ramsey passed a file across the table which recorded, in chronological order, a series of events involving Vic over the last six months. Vivien slowly turned the pages which recorded Vic's visits to strip clubs and bars, punctuated with copious photographs of her husband with young women, some of whom were performing private dances for him in his favourite haunts.
"Good God," Vivien remarked with her eyes fixed on the pages. "It's actually worse than I'd thought."
Ramsey nodded in agreement. "To be honest, Mrs Chakraborty, your husband's behaviour is as bad as I've come across in over twenty years in this job. The only good news is that we have so much evidence that it's impossible for him to argue against us."
Vivien nodded. "What about the girl he's put up in the apartment?"
Ramsey gestured with his forefinger to get her to keep turning the pages. "Her working name as you know, is Svetlana," he remarked. "She's a Czech national but has been living in London for five years.
Her real name is Jolana Burnas, she's twenty-seven and a known escort. She still has quite a few admirers other than your husband, but she's careful to entertain her other clients in expensive hotels in the West End. As far as I can see it's just Vic, or rather, Rex, as she knows him, that ever uses the flat."

"I'm not surprised," replied Vivien. "If he's paying for it there's no way she'd risk being caught by Rex at her flat. You'd have to be completely dumb to jeopardize that little perk, and she may be many things, but I suspect she's not stupid."

Ramsey looked shocked to hear Vivien being so unemotional about what she was seeing, given the sheer amount of explicit material he had put in front of her. "Yes," he agreed. "Not many escorts can boast about being treated to an expensive flat in London. Svetlana must think it's Christmas every day."

Vivien looked up from the folder. "It won't be for too much longer," she replied with a steely assurance. "When I've finished with him, her generous benefactor won't have a penny left, so poor Svetlana will have to look for a new patron."

Ramsey allowed Vivien the next twenty minutes to read and digest the contents of the file, which she did without the need to ask any questions.

Once she'd seen enough, Vivien closed the folder and placed it on the table. "You've done a comprehensive job, Mr Ramsey," she remarked. "It's more than enough to guarantee I get a huge settlement when we divorce. But we had plenty of evidence of his infidelity already. What about the rest of it? What about the evidence I can share with the investors at Meridian?"

Ramsey grinned. "I have that here," he replied as he extracted a Jiffy bag from his desk drawer.

* * *

Vivien Chakraborty had successfully concluded her business with Mr Ramsey by twelve forty-five, which allowed her plenty of time to drop in on her family solicitor, Ted Crowther, before heading back to Surrey.

She was keen for Crowther to join her at the house that evening when Vivien planned to announce to her husband the extent of her intentions.
For the first time in years, she couldn't wait for Vic to return home.

.

Part Twelve

Searching For The Truth.

Chapter 61

Friday afternoon, 18th September

Kieran arrived at St Steven's Church at around three pm. He located Father Mallory in the vestry.
"Do you have a moment, Father?" Kieran enquired.
"Oh, it's you, Kieran," cried the cleric enthusiastically. "I've not seen you in the Admiral since Tuesday evening."
Kieran grimaced and placed his right hand to his forehead. "No," he replied, "I think I need to be careful of that local brew."
Father Mallory laughed. "It's strong, that's for sure," he replied. "Anyway, what can I do for you? I'm sure you've not come to ask me about the local ales."
Kieran smiled. "I'm after some help," he said. "Laura and I are trying to understand a little more about her birth father and her family. And it's proving quite difficult."
"Well wouldn't it be better if you both spoke with Mary McKenna?" replied Mallory. "After all she's Billy's mother."
Kieran's facial expression was enough to answer the Priest's question.
"I take it Laura and Mary are not seeing eye to eye," Mallory added.
"That would be an understatement," Kieran replied. "In fact, the impression we're getting is that Mary is trying everything she can to get Laura to leave Blythwold."

Mallory nodded. "Look, I'm due to be at the primary school at the other end of the town in thirty minutes," he said, "but if you care to walk with me along the way, I'll help you as much as I can. You must realise though that I've only been in Blythwold a few years myself so I may not be able to answer many of your questions."
Kieran smiled. "I'd appreciate that," he replied.
The priest took down his coat from the hook behind the door, put it on and headed down the aisle towards the grand, large wooden door. "What do you want to know?" he asked.
"Firstly, what sort of man was Billy?" Kieran asked.
The priest considered the question for a few moments before he answered.
"I found Billy to be essentially a good man," replied the priest. "He was only human, like all of us, but I'd say that he was a good man."
"Did he ever talk about his time in prison and the reasons he was put there?" Kieran asked as they strode down the church path.
"Several times," Mallory replied. "Much of which was in the confessional, so outside anything I can discuss with you. But I think it's fair to say that he accepted full responsibility for his actions back then and that he regretted what he did."
"And what about Laura," continued Kieran. "Did he ever mention her?"
"Did he ever," replied Mallory. "He regretted causing the separation from her deeply. It was why I tried so hard to persuade her to come to his funeral. He would have been so relieved that she attended. He'd also be very proud of her, as she appears to be a fine young woman."
Kieran smiled, "She's certainly that," he replied. "But what about his brother?"

"Stephen," remarked Mallory in a way that initially suggested to Kieran there may be more than one brother.
"Yes, Stephen," Kieran confirmed.
"No," replied the priest. "To be honest I was only made aware that there was a brother after Billy died, when I was putting together his eulogy."
"I see," Kieran replied. "And did you ever benefit from Billy's fund-raising exploits?"
"Not me personally," retorted Mallory with a smile. "But the church received a fair amount of money over the years. To be honest, I was wanting to talk with Laura myself about that."
"In what way?" Kieran asked.
"Well to see if she was going to carry on the good work." Mallory replied.
Kieran laughed. "It would appear so," he replied. "Certainly, the round East Anglia Trek is going ahead, with me being dragged into it, too."
"Ah, that's wonderful news," remarked Mallory, his face beaming as he spoke.
"And what about Billy's relationship with Abigail," Kieran enquired. "Were you aware that they were …"
"Romantically involved," interrupted Mallory.
"Yes," replied Kieran.
The priest stopped in his tracks. "That's the big regret I have about Billy's death," Mallory said, his face serious and his eyes moistening. "I should have been more insistent with Mary. That poor girl should have been allowed to his funeral. That was a bad thing that was done there."
"So, you knew about him and Abigail before he died?" Kieran asked. "Of course, I did," the priest replied. "Billy told me months ago."
"Did he also mention about making Abigail a partner in the business?" Kieran asked.

"I thought she was already," Mallory replied. "She owns a third, doesn't she?"
Kieran shrugged his shoulders. "No," he remarked. "It's all been left to Laura."
"I must have got it wrong," replied Mallory. "I thought that had all been sorted. Maybe I was mistaken. However, I do know for sure that Billy intended to give her a third of the business, he told me so. Maybe he just didn't get around to making it legal."
As Mallory finished his sentence, they arrived outside the small primary school gates.
"I'm going to have to get on in," Mallory added.
"Of course," Kieran replied with a smile. "Many thanks for your help."
Kieran remained stationary as he watched the priest walk slowly down the path that led to the school door.
"Bloody Diplock," he muttered under his breath before scurrying away in the direction of the high street.

*　　　*　　　*

It was just before five o'clock when Laura received the call from Blythwold police station.
"You've what!" Laura exclaimed. "You idiot, what were you thinking? I'll be over in ten minutes."
"What's the matter?" Abigail enquired.
"It's Kieran," Laura replied angrily as she grabbed her coat and handbag. "He's got himself arrested for assaulting Nigel Diplock, he's at the police station. Can you lock up for me?"
Abigail, shocked by what she'd just learned, nodded. "Yeah, no bother," she remarked.
As soon as Laura had departed, Abigail allowed herself a huge smile. "Go, Kieran!" she shouted out loud.

Chapter 62

On the short walk back from the police station, Laura didn't say a word to Kieran. It was nine thirty pm and she was tired, hungry, and furious after sitting in the reception at Blythwold police station for over four hours.
"What were you thinking!" Laura shouted at him as soon as they were safely behind closed doors inside the Crow's Nest.
"I didn't intend to hit him," Kieran protested. "He just irritated me so much with his smarmy attempts to squirm his way out of all this and belittle me."
"So, you belted him!" Laura yelled.
Kieran flopped down on the sofa. "Yep," he confirmed with little remorse. "I smacked him one. Just one punch, but it was a beauty."
Laura shook her head. "Well, that beauty of a punch will probably cost you a tidy sum when it goes to court, and you'll now have a criminal record."
"It won't come to court," Kieran replied. "He won't dare press charges because if he does, I'll be able to tell the court why I went round and, if I'm correct, there's no way he'll want what I've got to say coming out."
"And what have you got to say?" Laura asked sarcastically. "That you hate his guts because he was interested in me?"

Kieran smiled. "Well, of course that's true," he conceded. "But I spoke to my drinking mate, Father Mallory, this afternoon and I think I know what's going on, and that bastard Diplock is right in the middle of it all."
Laura sat down next to Kieran. "Go on, Hercule," she urged. "What have you deduced?"
"On one condition," Kieran remarked, mimicking his fiancés well used phrase.
"Which is?" Laura replied.
"That we order a Chinese takeaway first," he continued. "I'm bloody starving."
Laura smiled, stood up and shook her head. "I'll get the menu," she remarked as she strode over to the sideboard drawer.
Five minutes later, after their order of vegetarian spring rolls, sesame prawn toast, lemon chicken, beef and cashew nuts in a black bean sauce and a portion of special fried rice had been phoned through, Laura sat down again next to Kieran. "Go on then, tell me your theory."
Kieran swallowed hard. "Well, I may be way off the mark here ..."
"For your sake I hope you're not," Laura interrupted.
"As I was saying before I was so rudely interrupted," Kieran continued, "I may be off the mark, but I think Diplock did know about Billy's desire to give Abigail a share of the business. In fact, I would not be surprised if Billy hadn't instructed Diplock to get the wheels in motion before he died."
"Why do you say that?" Laura asked.
"Well, Billy told Father Mallory that he wanted to give Abigail a third of the business, so I find it totally inconceivable that he didn't also tell Diplock," replied

Kieran. "And when Mallory was telling me this earlier today, I think he was thinking that, too."
"Okay," Laura remarked, "I get that, but I don't know how we prove it."
Kieran nodded, "Proving any of this will be the challenge," he conceded. "However, if we take as read that Diplock knew Billy's true wishes regarding the business, we then have to ask ourselves why he's trying to suppress that information and why he's willing to allow it all to come to you."
Laura thought hard about what Kieran was saying. "Well, I guess he has to let it come to me because that's what's in Billy's will."
"Assuming the will you saw was legitimate and also assuming it was Billy's most recent will," said Kieran, his excitement palpable in his voice. "My guess is that the reason Diplock is so keen to get everyone to believe the will he showed you is the real one is because of the clause in it which states that if you don't last a year, the whole of Billy's estate goes to Billy's charity. I've not worked out how that benefits Diplock yet, but I'm sure it will, somehow."
Laura nodded. "Actually, that makes total sense," she replied. "Abigail told me today that the charity was administered by Mary and Diplock, so if Billy's estate went to the charity, it's not beyond the wit of those two to make sure funds were syphoned off to them."
"There you go!" exclaimed Kieran. "That's the piece I'd been struggling with."
"So, why was Mary paying two grand into the business account every month?" Laura asked.
Kieran shrugged his shoulders. "I'm not sure, but it looks like they are trying to keep the business afloat. My guess, after what you've just told me, is that the money almost certainly came from the charity account."

Laura nodded. “But if that’s true, then it’s highly likely Billy must have known.”
“Possibly,” replied Kieran. “But maybe he didn’t, maybe he just thought his Mum was doing him a favour.”
“Two grand a month is a massive favour,” Laura remarked, her eyes wide and her brow furrowed with suspicion.
“I suppose so,” Kieran replied.
“But we can’t prove any of this,” Laura added. “Unless we find a different will, or unless Nigel Diplock comes clean.”
Kieran nodded, “To be honest that was what I was trying to achieve when I went to see him,” Kieran remarked. “But he was having none of it. He just laughed at me and told me I was fantasising.”
“So, you hit him,” Laura added.
“Well, to be fair, I only lost it with him after he’d indicated that you only agreed to marry me when he’d lost interest in you,” replied Kieran.
“So, you were protecting my honour, in a way,” Laura remarked, in a tone that suggested she wasn’t totally buying Kieran’s excuse.
“You know, I suppose I was,” Kieran replied with a smile, seeing an opportunity for a few brownie points.
Laura shook her head slowly before kissing his forehead. “So, how do we prove any of this?”
Kieran looked perplexed. “I’ve no idea,” he replied. “But once that bloody Chinese arrives, I’m sure it will come to me.”

Chapter 63

Saturday 20th September

Whether it was the events of the day, or whether it was having eaten so late, Laura once more found it hard to get to sleep. She tossed and turned while her head spun as she tried to make sense of everything that was going on around her. Kieran, as usual, went out like a light and, to make matters worse, aggravated Laura even further by stealing most of the duvet which he held in his vice like grip, and worse still, snorting and snoring like an old man with a forty-year smoking habit.

After more than two hours of misery, Laura gave up and grumpily decamped to the living room for some peace and quiet.

With a cup of cocoa by her side, Laura decided to make a summary of everything that was going around in her head.

By the time the clock on the wall read four am, Laura had finally dropped off, albeit still sitting in her chair with her head slumped awkwardly onto the armrest. By her side, however, she'd constructed a comprehensive list of points that she intended to discuss with Kieran when eventually, they both emerged from their slumbers.

*   *   *

Kieran woke up at seven and was shocked to find himself alone. When, after a further fifteen minutes in bed, he decided to venture out into the lounge, he was surprised and slightly amused to see Laura fast asleep with the side of her face flat against the armrest.
Kieran filled the kettle, plugged it in, and then went over to where Laura remained motionless.
After a few seconds, he noticed the scrap of paper that Laura had been scribbling on and picked it up to read her notes.
In typical Laura fashion her jottings were written in a highly organised style, which made him smile.

- *Why would Nigel and Mary try to exclude Abigail?*
- *Why did Mary pay £2K into Billy's business account each month?*
- *Why did Mary offer Mum £50K to get Laura to leave?*
- *Why is Mary so close with Nigel - seems closer than she was with Billy?*
- *Where is Stephen?*
- *Why did Mary try to warn me off dating Nigel?*

It was while he was reading through her notes that Laura started to wake.
"What time is it?" she enquired, wiping her eyes as she spoke.
Kieran bent down and kissed her. "It's nearly seven thirty," he replied.

"You found my notes," Laura observed as she started to shake off her tiredness.
"Yes," replied Kieran. "What time did you do this?"
"God knows," Laura replied. "I couldn't sleep so I thought I'd try and jot down what was in my head."
"Interesting," Kieran replied. "Especially number six."
Laura stood up and peered over Kieran's shoulder at her note number six. "Yes," she remarked after realising what Kieran was talking about. "She let me know in no uncertain terms that I was not to start dating Nigel," Laura continued. "Her exact words as I recall were, ***I want it to stop forthwith***."
"Really," Kieran replied. "And your reply was?"
"I'm not exactly sure how I worded it," Laura remarked as she wrapped her arms around Kieran and pulled him close to her. "It was something like – ***if I want to have sex with him on the pier that's my…."***
"I see," interrupted Kieran, who wasn't happy to hear Laura mention sex and Diplock in the same sentence but, nevertheless, admired her forcefulness.
"But it is a weird thing for her to mention, don't you think?" Laura added. "At the time I just thought she was, in her own clumsy way, trying to warn me about him, but now I think about it, maybe it was the other way around. Maybe she didn't think I was good enough for Nigel."
"You're right," Kieran confirmed. "Mary and Diplock seem to be like partners. It's almost like he's her son, not Billy."

*　　　*　　　*

Having showered and had some breakfast, Laura sat down at the kitchen table and started to scribble some more. By the time Kieran emerged from the bathroom, all preened and smelling of his favourite fragrance, Laura had written two more sentences.

- *What if Billy's death was no accident?*
- *What if Mary or Nigel had him killed?*

Kieran looked at the two additional sentences on Laura's list, the perplexed look on his face suggesting he wasn't convinced by either of them.
"I know this may be crazy," she added after clocking his expression, "but what if Billy's death wasn't an accident. What if Mary or Nigel had him killed?"
"Why would they do that?" Kieran asked.
"Maybe it was because he was going to give Abigail a third of the business," replied Laura, her explanation lacking any real conviction.
"That's not a very strong reason to kill someone," Kieran remarked. "I can certainly see them committing murder. But I can't see her killing her own son, and anyway, I thought Billy was driving the car when it crashed. I'm not sure how they could have planned that."
Laura nodded. "There's something we're missing here," she said, her frustration evident in her voice.
"Yes," replied Kieran. "What's missing is that we've no motive. Until we know what that is, we're going to struggle. I guess we could always pay a visit to Mary?"
Laura shook her head. "I'm not sure that would get us anywhere," she remarked. "And of course, now you've assaulted Nigel Diplock, we're unlikely to get him to open up."
"So, who else does that leave us with?" Kieran asked.
Laura smiled, as if a giant bulb of inspiration had been lit up in her head. "What about the passenger in the

car," she exclaimed. "He'd be able to tell us if he thought there was anything amiss with the accident."
"Who was that?" Kieran required.
"I can't remember," Laura replied. "But it was in the article I read a few weeks ago about the accident. Let me get my laptop, I saved it on my hard drive. Let me see if I can find it."
Within a few minutes, Laura had fired up her laptop and had located the article from the East Suffolk Gazette she'd read back in August when she was trying to do some research on Billy McKenna.

"Here you go," she said triumphantly as she found the piece. "Alan Langham, of 5, Thorn Heights, Blythwold, who was also in the car, suffered only minor cuts and bruises. He said of his childhood friend, Billy had the biggest heart of anyone I have ever met."

"Google that address," said Kieran. "Let's see where that is and then let's pay a visit and have a chat with Mr Langham."

*　　　*　　　*

Thorn Heights was a block of six flats on the outskirts of Blythwold, but no more than ten minutes' walk from Laura's apartment.
When Laura and Kieran arrived, the front door to the block was open, so they made their way up the two sets of steep steps to the second floor. The large wooden door to flat five was located to the right at the top of the stairs.
Kieran knocked loudly on the door.
After two further knocks, each one louder than the one before, Kieran turned to Laura. "I don't think Mr Langham is home."

At that moment they heard footsteps coming up the staircase. "Maybe that's him," Laura remarked.
The couple waited while the footsteps grew ever closer.
"Morning," remarked the short stocky man who eventually joined them on the top landing. "Are you looking for me?"
"Mr Langham?" Kieran enquired.
The stocky man shook his head. "No, mate," he replied. "I'm Jeff Morgan, I live at number six."
"We're looking for a Mr Alan Langham," Laura remarked. "Do you know if he's at home."
The stocky man frowned. "There's nobody living there," he remarked when he realised they'd been knocking at number five. "Apart from a guy who was there for about three weeks, a month or so ago, the flat's been empty for about six months."
"Are you sure?" Kieran replied. "We thought Alan Langham lived here."
The stocky guy shook his head. "Never heard of anyone of that name," he replied as he took out his front door key. "The last couple in here were a Nigerian couple with a small kid. Noisy buggers actually, I wasn't sad when they moved out. I can't recall his surname, but it wasn't Langham."
The man was just about to enter his flat when Laura said, "If you don't mind me asking, who owns these flats? It's just so we can contact them to see if they can help us."
The man turned back to face them. "They're let out by Lockwood's in the high street," he replied. "But they're bloody useless. I'd just get in touch with Mrs McKenna," he replied. "She owns the whole block as far as I know. She's a funny old bird, but to be honest, she's always been approachable when I've needed to speak with her. She lives down ..."

"We know Mrs McKenna," Laura interrupted. "Thanks."
The man nodded and disappeared into his flat, closing the door behind him.
Laura and Kieran looked quizzically at each other before quickly making their way down the two flights of stairs and out into the street.
"Now, that is interesting," Kieran remarked as they walked briskly back towards Laura's apartment. "Yet another avenue leading straight back to Mary McKenna."

.

Chapter 64

"What do we do now?" Kieran asked as they continued their walk along the windswept sea front.
"I'm not sure," Laura replied. "I'm tempted to suggest we go and talk with the police, but to be honest I'm not sure they'd take us seriously."
Kieran laughed. "Yes, they'd be totally unimpressed if we wander in and say we think your hoary old granny and the local solicitor murdered your father then fraudulently allowed you to inherit everything at the expense of the young woman he was having an affair with."
Laura nodded. "I know," she conceded. "Without any proof our theories don't have any legs. We desperately need to find a motive. And we could really do with finding this Alan Langham guy, even if all it does is confirm that Billy's death was just an accident."
"In that article you found it said that Langham was a childhood friend of Billy's," Kieran remarked.
"Yes, that's right," confirmed Laura.
"If he was, then surely Bev or Mike would know him, too," Kieran added. "When we get back to the flat why don't you call them and ask if they remember him?"
Laura seemed to like the idea. "Yes," she replied. "But first we could try our luck on LinkedIn and Facebook. You never know, Alan Langham may be on there."

*   *   *

As soon as the pair arrived back in the apartment, they grabbed their respective laptops and started to scour the internet for any mention of Alan Langham.

In a matter of moments Laura shook her head with dismay. "Surprisingly, there are only about a dozen people of that name on Facebook," she remarked. "But none look like they fit our man."

Kieran kept his eyes fixed on his computer screen. "Never mind," he mumbled.

"What about on LinkedIn?" Laura asked.

"Well," replied Kieran. "There are five people on LinkedIn. Three of them are based in the US, so I doubt they'll be our man, and one in the Midlands, but he only looks like he's in his thirties. However, there's this chap here that might be our man. He's in his fifties and he's down as being based in Auckland, New Zealand."

"New Zealand!" exclaimed Laura. "Then surely that rules him out, too."

Kieran shook his head. "No, not necessarily," he replied. "Remember last night in the restaurant your dad said he thought Stephen's dad might have fled to Australia and New Zealand. Well, what if Stephen did the same thing and then changed his name to Alan Langham?"

Laura shook her head. "That's a real long shot," she remarked with an air of dismay in her voice, "but, come on, let me see his picture."

Kieran turned his laptop around so that Laura could see the face of Alan Langham from Auckland.

"Oh my God," she replied, "I know that man."

"Really," said Kieran with surprise. "How come?"

Laura looked closely at the photograph. “Remember the evening when I came down here the first time? It was when you were in Germany.”
“Yes,” Kieran replied. “It was the evening before Billy’s funeral.”
“Well, that was the taxi driver who picked me up from Darsham station,” she remarked. “I’d remember him anywhere. He made me feel quite uneasy, yeah, he was quite creepy.”
“Are you sure?” Kieran asked, eager to make sure Laura wasn’t mistaken. “You could only have seen the back of his head.”
“Yes,” replied Laura. “I got a good look at him when I got out and paid the fare. Anyway, I’d remember those sinister eyes peering back at me through the rear-view mirror. It was definitely him.”
“And did he have a New Zealand accent?” Kieran asked.
“Not a bit of it,” replied Laura. “He sounded like he was from around here.”
“Let’s print off a copy of his picture and email it over to Mike and your mum,” Kieran suggested with excitement in his voice. “I know it’s over thirty years, but maybe they will be able to see some resemblance between our Mr Langham and the Stephen McKenna they remember from when he was a teenager.”
Laura nodded, “This could be the breakthrough we’ve been looking for,” she remarked with glee.

* * *

“It’s not easy to be certain,” Mike Eastwood remarked as he and Laura’s mum studied the photograph which Laura had emailed to them. “But it could well be Stephen.”
“What does Mum think?” Laura asked.

"She's not sure either," her dad replied. "But if it is, he'd be taking a massive risk coming back to Blythwold, in case he was recognised, so I'd be tempted to say that it's probably not."
Laura felt deflated as she listened to her dad. "I guess you're right," she agreed. "Maybe we were just letting our imaginations get the better of us."
Her dad laughed. "But if you're certain he was the guy who picked you up from the train station, surely you can just go and speak to the taxi company," he added. "There can't be many taxi companies in that part of Suffolk with yellow cabs."
"Good suggestion, "Laura replied. "I'll get on to that right away."
"Sorry we couldn't be of more help," remarked her dad. "Is there anything else?"
"Actually, there is," Laura remarked. "When they were young, did Mary have a favourite, between Stephen and Billy?"
"God, yes," her dad replied without any hesitation. "The sun shone out of Stephen's proverbial, in Mary's eyes. It didn't matter what he did she never could see any bad in him. But poor Billy couldn't do a thing right. It was apparent even to us kids."
"Really," Laura replied. "Why was that?"
"I've no idea," remarked her dad. "But it was so obvious. Anyway, why do you ask?"
"It's just a sense I had," Laura replied. "I've only talked to her a few times, but I never once got the impression that Mary was that distraught about Billy's death. And Kieran and I both seem to feel that she's got a stronger bond with Nigel Diplock than she had with Billy."
"I can't help you there, sweetie," her dad replied. "I know Mary has been a close friend of Nigel's parents

for years. In fact, I think she and Nigel's mum were at school together, but I don't know the son at all."
"That's fine, Dad," replied Laura. "You've been a great help. I'll let you go, and I'll get off and try to locate the taxi company."
"Whatever you do, take care," was her dad's final comment. "There may be absolutely nothing amiss, but don't underestimate Mary, she may be an ancient old bird, but she's a nasty piece of work and I wouldn't put anything past her."

* * *

It took Kieran and Laura less than ten minutes to locate the taxi company, given that there was only one taxi firm between Lowestoft in the north and Saxmundham to the south that appeared to have a fleet of yellow taxis. 5Star Cabs were located a few miles south of Blythwold, in a small village called Sawtry Heath.
"Let's get over there," Kieran remarked grabbing his car keys. "We could get some lunch, too, while we're out; I'm starving."
Laura smiled and followed him as he made a dash for the door.
Although the summer was well and truly behind them, the skies around Blythwold remained clear and blue, and the temperature remained reasonably warm.
"Shall we have the top down?" Kieran asked as he started up the engine of his precious BMW Z4 Roadster.
"Go on then," replied Laura, who would have preferred not to be blown about as they sped down the winding Suffolk roads, but she knew it made Kieran's day to have the top down and, after all, this was probably the last real chance he'd have until at least next May.

"If Langham is Stephen, what do we do?" Kieran shouted over to Laura as they started their journey.
"If he is, we definitely have to tell the police," Laura yelled back, holding her hair with one hand to stop it blowing all over the place. "There may well be nothing else going on that's illegal, but fabricating your own death is certainly a matter for the authorities, even if it did happen thirty-odd years ago."
Kieran nodded back to signify he agreed. "How about some sounds," he shouted, before turning on his expensive sound system.
With the sound of the Foo Fighters blasting from its speakers, Kieran's car roared its way south towards Sawtry Heath.

Chapter 65

The main office of 5Star Cabs was located in a shabby little hut situated behind a small service station about a mile north of Darsham train station.
As Kieran's car pulled up, there were two yellow cabs parked beside the hut.
"Yep," remarked Laura. "That was what the taxi looked like that picked me up that evening."
"Okay," replied Kieran as he clambered out of the car. "Let's see if they know our Mr Langham."
Laura and Kieran walked over to the hut and opened the rickety wooden door.
"Afternoon," remarked the jolly, ruddy-faced man sat behind the desk. "Do you need a taxi?"
"No," replied Laura as she walked over to where the man was sitting. "We're looking for a man called Alan Langham," she said pulling out the picture Kieran had downloaded from LinkedIn. "We understand he works here."
The man behind the desk took the photocopy from Laura. "We've nobody here called Alan Langham," he replied with a shake of his head. "And I've never seen this man before. Who told you he worked here?"
"We know someone who he picked up from the station about a month ago in one of your cars," Kieran added.
"Well, my names Andy Burnham and I'm the manager here. I do all the hiring and firing, and I can assure you

he's not one of ours and never has been. In fact, I've never clapped eyes on him before."
Laura and Kieran exchanged a glance before Laura turned back to the man behind the desk. "I know it sounds weird but could anyone else have got access to one of your cars at any time?"
Burnham's brow furrowed and he shook his head. "No chance," he replied. "I think you've been given a bum steer; this guy couldn't possibly have driven any of my cars without me knowing about it. I'm certain."
"Okay," Kieran remarked. "Thanks, sorry to have bothered you."
Despondently the young couple turned and headed for the door.
"Anyway, what has this man done?" Burnham asked.
"Nothing," replied Laura. "I think he may be a distant relative of mine," she added. "I'm just trying to trace him."
When Laura and Kieran were safely back in Kieran's car and well out of earshot, Kieran turned to face Laura. "Why did you say that?" he asked.
Laura smiled. "Maybe it's about time to shake the tree a little," she replied. "I'm getting a bit tired of chasing shadows, let's start taking the initiative."
Kieran shook his head. "I only hope you know what you're doing, Laura," he replied as he fired up the BMW.
Laura grinned even wider. "It's one thirty and I'm getting hungry now, too," she remarked. "Come on, let's find a pub and you can buy me that lunch."

* * *

The Friar's Rest was as isolated a pub as any that Laura and Kieran had ever visited. Except for a couple of small

flint houses some half a mile down the lane, the pub was about as far removed from civilisation as Laura could imagine.
"How on earth do they make a living out here?" Laura remarked as she studied the paper menu located on the long mahogany-coloured bar.
Kieran shrugged his shoulders. "Beats me," he replied, looking around at the empty tables.
"What would you like to drink?" the smiling barmaid asked as she emerged through a narrow doorway behind the bar.
"We'd like to order some food please," said Laura, looking up from the menu.
"We only do cold sandwiches during the week," replied the barmaid. "Not much call for hot food here until the weekend."
Laura's first inclination was to leave, but before she could say anything, Kieran firmly declared his order.
"I'll have a ham and cheese sandwich, on wholemeal bread," he announced. "And a pint of Patterson's bitter shandy, please, with lots of lemonade."
"I'll have a glass of Chardonnay, please," Laura added. "And I'll have a cheese and ham sandwich, too."
"Is that a large glass of wine?" the barmaid enquired.
"Yes, please," Laura replied, with a smile.
"And do you want your sandwich on wholemeal, too?" asked the now smiling barmaid.
"Yes, please," Laura replied again.
"Then take a seat," the barmaid instructed them. "I'll bring your drinks over to you."
Ten minutes later the sole customers of the Friar's Rest, nibbled at their sandwiches in the corner of the lounge.
"So, where do we go from here?" Kieran remarked. "It doesn't look like we're going to locate this Alan Langham character."

Laura thought for a few seconds before responding. "Yeah," she said despondently. "Unless we find him, I can't think what else we can do. We've no good reason to talk with the police, they'll just laugh at us. And after your little adventure yesterday, it's clear that Nigel Diplock isn't going to admit to anything."
"What about Mary McKenna?" Kieran enquired. "Is it worth talking to her?"
Laura shook her head. "No chance," she replied. "Whatever is going on here, she's in the middle of it orchestrating everything, so there's no chance of her telling us anything. I'm certain of that."
"Well maybe not you," Kieran replied. "But she doesn't know me. Perhaps she would tell me something."
Laura screwed up her face. "Like what?" she asked with incredulity.
"I don't know," responded Kieran. "I could pretend to be a reporter wanting to get some information on Billy,"
Laura shook her head slowly but with conviction. "Absolutely not!" she said firmly. "You're already in trouble with the local plod, please don't make matters worse by harassing Mary."
Kieran shrugged his shoulders and took a sip of his shandy.
"No," Laura announced with cheerless resignation, "we just need to face it; we've hit a brick wall. I hate to say it, but whatever Mary and possibly Nigel have been doing or are planning to do, we have nothing tangible on them. As for Alan Langham, if he is Stephen then my guess is that he's long gone now, anyway."
Kieran nodded. "Yep," he concurred gloomily. "Guess that's it. It does seem really unfair on Abigail, though," he added. "As it's clear Billy had intended to make her a partner in the business."

"Well at least that bit is in my power," Laura replied with a small self-righteous smile. "Once the year's up I'll certainly give her a third of the business, as Billy had intended. But I can't do that until I've done my year and fulfilled that stupid will he left."
"But no doubt those two schemers will be doing all they can to make sure you don't last a year," Kieran observed.
"I know," replied Laura, "but Mary and Nigel can think again. There's no way I'm letting anyone deprive me of my inheritance."

Chapter 66

Sunday 21st September

Laura snuggled up to Kieran's bare chest, which faintly rose and fell again as her fiancé inhaled through his open mouth. She was now so thankful he'd turned up unannounced a few days earlier and was even more thrilled and relieved that he was planning to remain with her for a further two more weeks. Kieran being there had made such a big difference and although she'd never tell him, she was starting to wonder how she was going to cope when he eventually jetted off to America.

Once again, the weather outside was warm for the time of year. The sun, now much lower in the sky, streamed through the window making Laura blink.

"Morning," Kieran mumbled as he started to stir from his slumbers. "Where's that sex-crazed woman I went to bed with last night?" he muttered in Laura's ear.

Laura smirked and jabbed him hard in the ribs with her elbow.

"Ouch," he yelled, his left arm clamping her naked body tightly to his side. "That really hurt," he continued, although his laughter tended to contradict his attempt to protest.

"Good!" Laura shouted as she tried in vain to pull herself clear.

"You know," added Kieran, "we've been engaged for three days, and I've not had as much as a bacon sandwich brought to me so far."
"Dream on!" Laura replied as she managed to wriggle free from his grip and in one swift movement, exit the bed taking the duvet with her as she departed, leaving Kieran languishing on the large double bed in his tartan, checked boxer shorts.
"What time is it?" Kieran enquired as he covered his eyes from the sun's piercing rays.
"It's time you got your lazy carcass out of bed and got ready for our early morning run!" Laura shouted back at him.
Through his squinting eyes he managed to see the time on Laura's small alarm clock on the bedside table. "It's Sunday and it's only eight thirty!" he replied.
"We agreed!" Laura replied in her best reprimanding voice. "Run, then breakfast on the pier."
Kieran rolled his eyes as he remembered the conversation, they'd had the evening before. "This bloody trek is ridiculous," he replied. "I'm not sure why we're doing it and anyway, it's not for months."
Laura laughed. "It's a commitment Billy made before he died which we have to honour. And you're so out of condition, you'll never manage it unless you get into training pretty damn soon."
"You're no Mo Farah yourself," Kieran replied spikily.
"That's why I'm going for a run," Laura remarked before closing the bathroom door behind her. "And remember, we agreed last night, the last one to the pier pays for breakfast."
"This is ridiculous," Kieran mumbled as he rolled to the edge of the bed and threw his legs over the side so he could sit upright, scratching first his head then his private parts.

* * *

"You bloody knew the cafe on the pier was closed until ten on a Sunday," Kieran moaned as the two exhausted and sweat drenched runners reached the door of Laura's apartment. "How far do you reckon we ran?"

Laura shrugged her shoulders. "A couple of miles I'd guess."

"God it's got to be more than that," Kieran exclaimed. "It must be at least five!"

Laura glanced back at his pained face as she turned the key in the door. "We were only out there for about forty minutes, and we walked about half of the time," she replied. "If we did more than three miles at the very most, I'd be amazed."

"And this run, next May," Kieran added. "Remind me, how many miles is that?"

Laura laughed as the door opened. "A hundred and twenty miles in three days," she replied.

"No flaming chance," Kieran muttered as he followed Laura into the flat. "If you're right, and we only did do about three miles, that's just four we will be doing an hour. We'll have to be out for ten hours a day for the three days to do that distance!"

"What's this!" exclaimed Laura as she bent down to pick up a large brown envelope which had been pushed under the door while they were out.

Kieran heard her but his immediate need was to sit down. He walked past Laura and slumped down onto the sofa.

Laura opened the envelope and extracted an A4 sheet of paper. As she read the contents of the letter, Kieran watched Laura's facial expression change from one of curiousness to outrage, then glee.

"Read this!" Laura exclaimed as she handed Kieran the letter. "I think we've now got something to show the police."
Kieran grabbed the letter from Laura's hand and read the ten simple words printed on the paper, a couple of times.

Leave now you nosey cow!
Otherwise, you'll both be sorry.

"Yep!" Kieran remarked. "The Suffolk plod has to take this seriously."

*   *   *

It was almost three pm by the time DC Risby arrived at Laura's apartment and, after listening for twenty minutes to Laura and Kieran's concerns and theories, decided to summarise matters.
"So, your grandmother, in her eighties," Risby stated, "and Nigel Diplock, in your opinion, have deliberately denied Abigail Adams a third share in your late father's business, which you have now inherited."
DC Risby looked up from his notes, to ensure that neither Laura nor Kieran were dissenting so far. When he could see they were happy with his synopsis, he continued. "You believe, for reasons not yet clear to you, that the pair are keen for you to fail to meet the condition in your father's will, namely that you should remain in Blythwold for a year, and you say your mother was offered fifty thousand pounds by your grandmother to persuade you to leave the town."
Again, DC Risby gazed up from his notes.

"So far that's correct," Laura remarked, although she could feel that DC Risby wasn't totally convinced that much of what he was repeating held any credence.
"I will of course need to talk with your mother to verify this claim about the fifty thousand pounds," remarked Risby.
"I'll write down her number," Laura replied.
"In addition," DC Risby added, his voice precise and emotionless, "you believe that Alan Langham, the passenger in the car when your father died, is actually your uncle, Stephen McKenna, who was reported drowned over thirty years ago. You also believe that he was the taxi driver that picked you up from Darsham train station on the evening of Wednesday 19th August, but yesterday, Mr Burnham, the taxi company proprietor, denied Mr Langham had ever been in his employ."
Laura shrugged her shoulders. "I know it all sounds incredible," she admitted. "But there really are some unexplained things going on here."
DC Risby offered no opinion. "So, based upon all you've said so far, your feeling is that this note is the work of either Mary McKenna, Nigel Diplock or Alan Langham, the man you believe to be your uncle?"
Laura nodded, "In my view it can't be anyone else," she remarked. "Nobody other than one of them has any need to try and drive us away." As she spoke, Laura slid over to DC Risby the scrap of paper on which she'd scribbled her mum's telephone number in Spain.
"Is there anything I've missed?" DC Risby enquired.
Laura and Kieran exchanged a glance. "No," Laura replied.
The young detective smiled and carefully picked up the threatening note from the table, placed it into its

envelope and, clutching the envelope in his left hand, stood up.
"I'll let you know how my investigations progress," he remarked before walking towards the door. "If you get any more threatening notes, please call me."
Laura quickly got up and walked briskly towards the door. "Thanks for coming," she remarked as she opened the door to allow DC Risby to depart. The policeman smiled and made his exit.
Closing the door behind him, Laura turned to face Kieran, her expression enough to indicate what was on her mind.
"I know what you're thinking," said Kieran with an air of disenchantment in his voice. "He doesn't fill me with much confidence, either."
Laura nodded gently. "And, worse still, he clearly doesn't believe that much of what we said is true."

Chapter 67

Monday 22nd September

When Kieran awoke, he glanced drowsily at the clock on the bedside table which indicated it was nine o'clock. He did not need to check, Kieran instinctively knew that Laura would have already left for the office, so he just lay still for a few moments to give himself time to wake up properly.

As he slowly came round, he realised that, unlike the last few days, the sun wasn't streaming through the window; in fact, the sky outside looked grey, angry and unwelcoming.

Eventually, Kieran clambered out of bed and wandered over to the window. The new morning looked far from inviting, with strong winds from the east howling around the roof tops making eerie whistles and shrill wails. Fine rain had stippled the outside of the window, blurring the view of the seafront below, but he could see the tide was in, breaking high over the groynes that segmented the beach into one-hundred-metre sections. He stared outwards mesmerised by the powerful brown waves which crashed relentlessly onto the beach, throwing up small pebbles, some of which had been tossed high up onto the concrete walkway.

The few people who were bold or foolish enough to brave the wild weather did not linger, instead they

rushed along as they went about their business. Only the seagulls seemed to enjoy the conditions, as they first soared high in the air at impossible speeds, then, in an instant, fell rapidly, flying low over the cars and houses, before rising again like rockets to the heavens.
Kieran remained at the window for several minutes as he observed the scene from the comfort of Laura's warm third-floor bedroom.
Indeed, it's likely he'd have remained there even longer had his hunger not ultimately caused him to amble away from his cosy vantage point in the direction of the kettle and the toaster.
True to form, Laura had left him a note, which as he could have predicted, contained a mild rebuke for being so lazy. It also suggested that he meet her at noon for lunch.
Kieran smiled as he read her sarcastic words, a smile which widened when he saw three large crosses, the kisses she'd left at the bottom.
"Toast," he muttered to himself. "I need toast and coffee."

*　　　*　　　*

Laura was astonished when at eleven am DC Risby and a colleague arrived at the office.
"Hi," she remarked, a surprised and puzzled look on her face. "Have there been any developments?"
Risby smiled. "Is there anywhere we can go to talk privately?" he asked having glanced briefly in Abigail's direction.
"Actually, I was just about to go for an early lunch," Abigail tactfully lied. "I'll see you in an hour, Laura."
Laura smiled back at Abigail as her assistant quickly grabbed her bag and made her exit.

As soon as they were alone DC Risby looked in his colleague's direction. "This is DCI Doyle," he said. "He'd like to ask you a few more questions following our conversation last night."
"Of course," Laura replied. "Please take a seat."
Laura pointed to the area in the corner of the office where there were a couple of bright-red leather, low-level settees; not the most comfortable pieces of furniture, but the only area in the office suitable for more than two people to have a meeting.
The two officers walked over to the seats and made themselves as comfortable as they could. As soon as Laura sat opposite them DCI Doyle spoke. "DC Risby has briefed me on your conversation last night and I'd like to ask you a few questions, if I may?" he asked. "I can't divulge too much to you at this moment, but I'm working on another case, and I think you may be able to help me."
Laura felt excited, but at the same time a little uneasy. "Of course," she replied. "I'll help as much as I can."
DCI Doyle nodded gently. "Thank you," he remarked with a kindly smile. "I'm investigating some allegations about the use of the donations given to your late father for his charitable activities. I was wondering if you knew much about them?"
Laura shook her head. "No sorry," she replied. "I didn't know Billy McKenna and to be honest, until he died, I had no idea he was so active as a charity fundraiser."
DCI Doyle nodded. "But since you've inherited the business, surely you've had an opportunity to review his activities?" the DCI asked. "Have you discovered anything unusual?"
Laura shook her head. "The charity funds are nothing to do with the business," Laura replied. "Neither Abigail nor I have any involvement in that side of things at all. I

believe that was all managed by Mary McKenna and Nigel Diplock."
"So, to your knowledge, none of the funds could ever have been mixed up with this business?" DCI Doyle enquired.
"No," replied Laura without hesitation. However, as soon as she heard the word leaving her mouth, Laura remembered the two-thousand-pound monthly payments she'd discovered being paid into the business. "Well, I'm not sure," she added rather guardedly. "Having said that, there are some payments that were made in the past that I cannot account for."
"Really!" Doyle remarked with genuine interest. "Can you elaborate a little more?"
Laura walked over to her desk and retrieved the folder containing the company bank statements. When she returned to where the two officers were sitting, she opened the file and pointed out the two-thousand-pound cash payments that were being made each month into the business account. "It's these," she remarked. "They stopped when Billy died, but they seem to have been a regular payment as far back as I have statements and so far, I have not been able to discover why they were made."
DCI Doyle looked closely at the records of each two-thousand-pound transaction. "So, who made these cash payments?" he asked.
Laura shrugged her shoulders. "I told Nigel Diplock about them," Laura remarked. "He told me the bank had advised him that they were made by Billy. However, Abigail's sister works in the bank and according to her, the payments were made by Nigel Diplock, and he made them each month after himself receiving two thousand pounds as a transfer from Mary McKenna."

"So, what did Nigel Diplock say when you discussed this other claim?" DCI Doyle enquired.
"Well, to be honest," Laura replied. "We've not had that conversation. Abigail was keen for me not to implicate her sister and being totally honest with you, my relationship with Mr Diplock is not that good."
"And I assume from what you told DC Risby yesterday, your relationship with Mary McKenna isn't that good, either," Doyle observed.
Laura smiled. "That's correct," she replied.
"Can we take these statements?" DCI Doyle asked.
Laura nodded. "Of course," she replied.
The two officers stood up in unison.
"We'll get on and leave you alone," DCI Doyle remarked. "You've been really helpful."
Laura wasn't about to let the officers go before finding out what progress had been made with the threat, she'd received the day before.
As the policemen reached the door she asked, "Have you had a chance to speak to my Mum yet or to either Mary McKenna or Nigel Diplock about the threat I received?"
DC Risby smiled. "Not as yet," he replied. "I aim to speak with them both later today."
As the officer's words left his mouth, Kieran appeared at the door, his face full of rage. "You can add criminal damage to the list," he shouted angrily. "All four of my car tyres have been slashed and there's a massive scratch right down the side of the car. I can't prove it but I'm certain it will be one of those two evil buggers that did it."

* * *

"In fairness to DC Risby, he seems to be taking this seriously," Laura remarked as she and Kieran sat in Miriam's coffee shop waiting for their sandwiches. "He did go with you to the car, and he took a fair few photos of the damage on his phone."
Kieran shook his head. "I admire your optimism," he replied irritably. "We reported that note at about ten in the morning yesterday, it's now over twenty-four hours later and he's done bugger all!"
"Shh," Laura whispered. "Miriam might hear us."
Kieran shook his head. "What are we doing in here anyway?" he asked in a hushed but still angry voice. "For all we know she may be in on whatever's going on around here."
"I doubt that," replied Laura, her eyebrows raised to confirm her view.
"Actually, they all might be," continued Kieran. "It's a weird bloody town if you ask me. Nothing would surprise me."
Laura shook her head. "You're starting to sound like Dad!"
Kieran puffed out his cheeks. "So, plod thinks that some of Billy's charity money was being filched, do they?"
Laura nodded. "Yes," she replied excitedly. "I bet the two grand Nigel Diplock was paying into Billy's account came from the charity money. If that's true, then maybe that's our motive."
Kieran shook his head. "Motive for what?" he remarked disparagingly. "If Mary and Diplock are dipping into the charity money, they could still do that without paying anything into Billy's business, so that has no bearing on them trying to force us out or from excluding Abigail. No, there must be another reason."
Miriam arrived with the couple's order. It was clear from her frosty demeanour that she remembered Laura

from their meeting three days earlier. Without uttering a word, Miriam plonked the sandwiches onto the table in much the same way she'd dumped their coffees a few minutes earlier.

As soon as Miriam was out of earshot, Laura leaned over towards Kieran. "What if she is the woman who Stephen attacked all those years ago from Donnelly's circus," she whispered.

Kieran turned his head to look at Miriam before returning his attention to Laura. "But why would she settle here if she'd had such an awful experience in Blythwold? Wouldn't that be the very last place you'd want to be if that had happened to you?"

Laura nodded. "I guess so," she replied. "But it seems such a coincidence that someone from the circus has decided to settle here and she was clearly uncomfortable when I asked her questions about Stephen."

Kieran shrugged his shoulders. "I'm really not sure what to think," he replied frankly. "But you're right, she's not the friendliest waitress I've ever met."

For the next few minutes Laura and Kieran said very little, as they both tried to work out what was happening.

"So, what are you going to do with your car?" Laura enquired.

"I've already spoken with the nearest tyre fitters," Kieran replied. "They're based in Lowestoft, but they say they can get a van out here tomorrow and replace the four tyres."

"I thought you wanted to come to London with me tomorrow?" Laura replied.

"Oh bugger!" Kieran exclaimed. "I clean forgot about that. Do you mind if I give that a miss?"

Laura smiled. "It's no problem for me," she replied. "I'm just going to have my meeting with Vic and Saskia

and get back home as soon as it's finished. I can easily get the train."
Kieran nodded. "You'll have to get a taxi to Darsham," he added. "But hopefully I'll have the car sorted by the time you come home so I can pick you up when your train gets in."
Laura nodded. "That's no problem," she remarked. "But I won't be using 5 Star taxis, that's for sure!"

Chapter 68

Tuesday 23rd September

Laura's journey to London was largely uneventful. Her taxi had picked her up from the flat at seven twenty am and the seven minutes past eight train from Darsham had, thankfully, left the station on time. The ten minutes Laura had at Ipswich was plenty of time for her to catch her connecting train, which arrived in Liverpool Street leaving her almost an hour and a half to get her circle line train to Victoria for her meeting.

Despite all that was going on back in Blythwold, Laura had spent almost the entire journey thinking about her meeting with Saskia and Vic at eleven thirty. The numerous letters she'd received so far had been consistent in demanding she pay the company what amounted to almost a quarter of her salary with Meridian; as they put it, 'in consideration of her not working her notice'. Laura figured that the fact they wanted to talk with her suggested Vic was now softening his stance. Laura had no desire to pay anything, especially now that her so-called friend, Saskia, was to be involved, but she was keen to resolve matters and during the journey she came to the conclusion that if she were able to secure a compromise of a figure half what they were suggesting, she'd settle and be done with it.

As Laura walked down Vauxhall Bridge Road, she reflected on how much her life had changed in just five short weeks. In almost no time at all she'd been offered a new job by McCauley and Bernstein's, then resigned her position at Meridian, in acrimonious circumstances, only to be told later that the offer had been rescinded. She'd fallen out with her best friend, who'd callously stabbed her in the back. She'd broken up with Kieran, but now found herself reunited with him and delighted to be engaged. She'd learned that her birth father was a criminal convicted of fraud, but that he'd made her his sole beneficiary; albeit his will was strange, to say the least. She'd also discovered, to her amazement, that she, a city girl, liked the quiet life on the Suffolk coast. To her surprise, she had also learnt that the people in sleepy Blythwold were perhaps not as they first appeared, and that her mum and dad were not above deceit themselves, even if their lies were well intentioned.
Laura wondered what other revelations lay in store for her. She had no idea what they'd be but was certain there would be more coming her way; and, in a strangely masochistic way, she was looking forward to it!
As she arrived outside the Meridian offices, Laura felt the throb of a text coming through on her mobile. It was from Kieran. She paused to read it.

HI SEXY, IT'S ONLY ME! HOPE ALL GOES WELL AT THE MEETING. TYRES ALL REPLACED, SO THE GOOD NEWS IS I'LL BE ABLE TO MEET YOU AT DARSHAM LATER. BAD NEWS IS IT COST ME NEARLY £1000. ☹ XXXXXX

*　　　*　　　*

Laura was not surprised at all to be left waiting in the reception area for over twenty minutes. She could imagine Vic saying to Saskia, 'just let her stew for a bit,' and she could picture Saskia's smug face as she willingly complied with Vic's instructions.
However, Laura was determined to remain calm and business-like. Even if things did not go her way, the last thing she wanted was for either Vic, or, worse still, Saskia, feeling that they had her rattled. "Stay powerful, confident and in full control," was the mantra she kept saying over and over in her head.
"I'm so sorry to keep you waiting," Brenda remarked contritely, when she eventually arrived in the reception area. "As you'll find out shortly, the last few days have been quite hectic."
Laura smiled. "It's no problem, Brenda," she replied with sincerity. "I know how things can be here."
Laura followed Brenda through the double doors and up the three flights of stairs that led to the board room. It seemed weird to be in the building without being an employee of the company, but it had been her choice, so Laura was determined not to let this or anything else intimidate her. "Powerful, confident and in control," Laura kept repeating in her head.
When the door opened and Laura was ushered in, she was not surprised to see two people already sat at the long boardroom table. She was, however, shocked to see that neither of them was Vic or Saskia.
It took Laura a few seconds to recognise Vivien Chakraborty. They'd only met a couple of times and on each occasion, it was at functions with a large group of people. It was only when Vivien started to talk that Laura realised it was Vic's wife.

"I can see you're a bit shocked to see me," was the first thing Vivien said as Laura entered the boardroom. "If you'd care to take a seat I'll explain."
Still perplexed, Laura did as she was told and sat down.
"Brenda, please stay," Vivien added as she saw the PA make a move to the door. "It's important you are here, too, to hear what I have to say to Laura."
Brenda duly obliged and sat herself down a few seats away from Laura.
"First of all, Laura, I'd just like to thank you for coming in today," Vivien continued, her words clear, but it was evident she was nervous. "I know you were expecting to see my husband and Saskia today, but both are currently unavailable, as I'll explain in due course."
Laura nodded but said nothing.
"This is Mr Crowther," Vivien added, gesturing to the middle-aged man sat next to her. "Mr Crowther is my legal advisor."
"Right," Laura replied, although she had no idea what on earth was going on.
"I'm not at liberty to tell you all the details, Laura," Vivien added, "but as of yesterday morning, Vic resigned from his position as MD of Meridian."
"Resigned!" Laura exclaimed.
Vivien nodded. "As I say, I cannot reveal the full background, but he is no longer an employee of Meridian. As you probably know, the capital behind the business is largely from my family, so the board have asked Mr Crowther and me to take charge on a temporary basis until a permanent replacement can be put in place."
"I see," replied Laura, who was still very much in shock. "So, what about Saskia?"
"At this juncture Saskia Skinner and all the other Meridian staff are unaffected by Mr Chakraborty's

resignation," Mr Crowther added, "however, there are still some ongoing activities that may warrant further action with other employees."
The astonished look on Laura's face was probably a prompt for Vivien to decide to share a little more information than she'd intended.
"Without going into too many details, the situation is this, Laura," Vivien continued. "Vic's behaviour here at Meridian has been a concern to some members of the board for some time. As a result, the board decided to investigate. This has been an ongoing investigation and one that has involved various means. Brenda here was specifically hired to report back to the board if she saw any instances of practices or behaviours that were against company policies or were morally or ethically wrong."
Laura glanced at Brenda who smiled back in Laura's direction.
"I see," Laura replied. "But I'm not sure why you're telling me this. I'm no longer a Meridian employee and I certainly was unaware of any wrongdoings when I was here."
Vivien smiled. "Oh, your honesty is not in question, Laura," she reassured her. "In fact, it's precisely the opposite. In the course of Brenda's very thorough investigations we have, to our horror, discovered that you've been an unsuspecting casualty of the actions of my soon to be ex-husband."
"I'm sorry, Vivien," Laura remarked, "I've absolutely no idea what you're talking about."
Vivien looked sideways at her lawyer, who looked uneasy as if he was nervous about what Vivien was about to say.
"It's your job offer at McCauley and Bernstein's," Vivien said in a calm voice.

"How on earth do you know about that?" Laura remarked.
Vivien exchanged a second look with Mr Crowther. "Well, during Brenda's very meticulous investigations we have discovered that the offer, or rather the withdrawal of that offer, was instigated by Vic. Without going into the full sordid details, it would appear that he called in a favour from one of the McCauley family."
"That would be Ben McCauley," Laura interrupted, as he was the only member of the family I talked with."
"It would be inappropriate for us to comment too much further," Mr Crowther added. "However, as Mrs Chakraborty has said, we are one hundred per cent sure that the offer was withdrawn as a result of unethical intervention by Vic Chakraborty."
"I don't believe it," Laura remarked, her voice shrill and angry. "That's outrageous! Are you sure?"
Brenda nodded gently as if to provide her confirmation but said nothing.
"As we've indicated before," Vivien added. "It's totally at odds with the ethos and values of Meridian and for that reason, I wanted to apologise to you in person."
"And as a means of compensation for the damages caused to you," added Mr Crowther. "We will provide you with a one-off settlement equal to three months' salary at McCauley and Bernsteins." As he finished his sentence Mr Crowther pushed an open envelope across the desk.
"The letter inside outlines our compensation offer," he continued. "We recommend that you talk to a solicitor about the offer, but I think it's a fair offer given the circumstances."
"And Meridian will obviously pick up any solicitor costs you incur relating to this unfortunate incident," Vivien added.

Laura opened the letter and spent the next few minutes reading its contents, which were clear and in line with what Mr Crowther had outlined to her.
"What about the action against me for leaving without working my notice?" Laura asked.
Vivien shook her head. "We'll drop that ridiculous claim," she replied. "God only knows what Vic was thinking there."
Stunned by everything she'd just heard Laura couldn't think of anything more to say.
"Well, once again thank you for coming, Laura," Vivien remarked, indicating that, in her view, the meeting was over. "Unless there's anything more you want to know; I'll await your formal response to our offer."
Laura stood up and smiled at Vivien and Mr Crowther before making her exit.
It was only when Laura and Brenda were descending the stairs that the PA spoke. "I'm sorry I couldn't let you know what I was doing when you worked here, Laura," she remarked, "but it was essential I remained under the radar."
Laura laughed. "Well, you certainly fooled me," she replied. "So, what else was Vic up to?"
Brenda shook her head. "I can't tell you I'm afraid, but put it this way, Vivien has enough ammunition to secure a thousand divorces for adultery."
As they reached reception and Laura went to shake Brenda's hand, she suddenly wondered about Saskia. She was about to ask if her ex-friend was implicated, when the double doors opened and through walked the women herself.
"Hi Laura," she piped up in a cheery tone suggesting that their relationship was sweetness and light.
"I'll leave you both," Brenda remarked before shaking Laura's hand and making a quick exit.

Laura, aghast at the cheek of her old friend, couldn't believe how friendly she was sounding and how pleased she appeared to be to see her.
"I know I've been a cow," Saskia said as if there'd only been a minor falling out between them. "Let's go to Borini's and I'll explain."
"You are unbelievable," Laura exclaimed. "How you can have the front ..."
"I'm paying," interrupted Saskia.

Chapter 69

After the mobile tyre fitter had finished, Kieran moved his car to a parking space directly outside Laura's apartment. He knew that wouldn't necessarily prevent a reoccurrence of the vandalism, but at least if it was there, he figured, he'd be able to keep a bit of an eye on it.

With the time getting close to twelve and having had only a few slices of toast to eat, Kieran decided to stroll into town and buy himself some fish and chips. He'd seen a chip shop at the far end of the High Street, which was only about ten minutes' walk, so decided to give it a try.

As he wandered down the High Street, Kieran could see up ahead passers by being accosted by a middle-aged woman handing out leaflets. His initial inclination was to decline, but as he got closer to her, he figured his best course of action would be to take her leaflet and just bin it when he got home.

"I hope we can count on your support!" the lady remarked as he took her flier and stuffed it in his jacket pocket.

Kieran smiled, said nothing, and marched on; his stomach's needs were much more important than any discussion he was likely to have with the middle aged leafleteer.

Fifteen minutes later, back at the Crow's Nest, Kieran opened the chip paper and started to eat his lunch. Picking up a huge lump of battered fish, Kieran gazed at the handwritten list Laura had written over the weekend. Despite having a fair few theories, in truth they had yet to produce an accurate answer to any of the questions Laura had so meticulously documented. Kieran looked at Laura's extended list of eight questions. Although they all needed answers, the main thing that troubled him the most was a lack of motive. He reached into his jacket pocket to find a pen. After pulling out the leaflet that had been thrust upon him earlier, Kieran found a small blue pen and scribbled a ninth item at the bottom of Laura's list.

No motive for Mary & Nigel to disinherit Abigail or try to drive Laura out!

As he did, Kieran's attention was drawn to the headline on the leaflet, which he started to read.
"Bloody hell!" he exclaimed as he realised, he may well have just found their motive.

* * *

Laura didn't fully understand why it was she'd agreed to go to Borini's with Saskia, but for some bizarre reason she found herself sitting opposite her estranged friend.
"So, come on then," Laura remarked. "Just tell me why you lied to me and deliberately connived to ingratiate yourself with Vic at my expense?"
Saskia tilted her head slightly to one side and lifted her shoulders a few inches, held them in that position for a three of four seconds before bringing them back down

again. “It wasn’t like that, Laura,” she tried to argue. “I admit I was a bit out of order, but you were leaving anyway, and I was only doing what anyone else would have done in my situation.”
“No!” retorted Laura angrily. “No, Saskia. Only a scheming cow like you would think of doing that. It was unforgivable.”
“Well, Vic’s gone now,” Saskia remarked glibly. “So, I’ve not gained anything have I?”
Laura could not believe what she was hearing. “Saskia, that’s not the point and you know it. You were prepared to do anything to climb Vic’s greasy pole and that included stabbing me in the back. I thought we were friends!”
“I didn’t do that,” Saskia replied. “I wasn’t one of Vic’s conquests, I can assure you. Anyway, I’m probably going to leave Meridian. Martin has asked me to move in with him and as he’s loaded, I probably won’t need to work.”
“What are you talking about?” Laura asked.
“I told you about Martin,” Saskia added. “He’s the guy I met a month ago at the gym. Well, he’s a merchant banker in the city with a flat at Canary Wharf. He’s mad about me and has asked me to move in with him.”
“I wasn’t talking about Martin, whoever the hell he is,” snapped Laura, who by now was regretting her decision to meet up with Saskia. “I was talking about your comment about Vic’s conquests. Did you know he was having affairs?”
“Not until yesterday,” Saskia replied. “And I certainly wasn’t one of his paid escorts.”
“What!” Laura exclaimed. “I was told earlier that Vivien has strong grounds for divorce, but are you saying that Vic was involved with prostitutes?”

"Was he ever," Saskia added, her eyes positively gleaming with the excitement. "It's all over the office. Apparently, he was a frequent visitor to several lap dancing bars in London and he was paying the rent for an eastern European escort somewhere in London. They're also saying he had a private mobile phone in his desk drawer which he used to call her and his other female friends. It's the truth, I'm telling you."
Although Laura was shocked and deep down was keen to learn more, she wasn't prepared to allow Saskia to believe that she'd either forgiven or forgotten how badly she'd behaved. And although Saskia had yet to deliver on her promise and buy her lunch, Laura decided that she'd had enough.
"Sorry," she announced as she stood up from the table. "I've got a train to catch. Have a good life, Saskia, but please don't try to include me as I don't want to know you anymore."
Before Saskia had a chance to answer, Laura marched out of Borini's and headed off down the road in the direction of Victoria underground station.
Saskia remained in her seat for a few minutes, until she suddenly noticed Laura's mobile phone, which she'd left on the chair next to them.
"Silly cow," she muttered before picking up the phone and dashing out of the cafe to catch up with Laura.

* * *

Excited by his discovery Kieran decided to call Laura. The mobile rang four times before it kicked into Laura's messaging service.
"Hi Laura," Kieran said as soon as Laura's recorded voice had suggested he leave a message. "I've worked

out their motive. Call me and I'll tell you. Hope the meeting went well ... talk to you later."
Saskia realised that a call was coming through, and she could see on the screen that it was Kieran, but she just let it ring. She could see Laura about thirty yards ahead of her entering Victoria tube station so she knew she couldn't lose any time taking her call.

*　　　*　　　*

Laura was still in a state of shock as she entered the tube station and pushed her ticket through the barriers. She wasn't sure what had shocked her the most; the revelation that Vic was some sort of sex addict and that he'd deliberately scuppered her appointment at McCauley and Bernstein's, the generous settlement being offered to her by Vivien, or the fact that Saskia still couldn't see what she'd done wrong.
The eastbound side of the circle line was surprisingly quiet as she reached the platform. Laura looked up at the electronic screen which indicated there was just one minute until the next train arrived. As she walked along the platform Laura could feel someone very close behind her but thought nothing of it. Then she heard that unmistakeable sound of the train approaching and the whoosh of warm air hitting her as the train started to emerge from the tunnel.
"Laura!" bellowed Saskia, who could see what was about to happen.
Laura half turned as the figure behind lurched towards her, now just inches away.
The train came rumbling towards Laura just as the man's arm went to grab her shoulder. It was then that Laura recognised who he was.

Laura ducked down to avoid any contact and the man's arm narrowly missed her head. Her attacker, now totally off balance, swivelled round with the force of the lunge and overbalanced, falling onto his back, his momentum making him roll on his side and over the end of the platform.
Laura looked in horror as her attacker disappeared onto the track just as the circle line train came thundering into the station, her pained expression matched only by the haunted look on the train driver's face as he realised the inevitability of what was just about to happen.

Chapter 70

Saskia and Laura sat in silence on the small bench on the platform at Victoria station while the station staff, paramedics and police rushed frantically around them after the accident.
"Who was he?" Saskia eventually asked.
"I think it was my birth father's brother," replied Laura. "He called himself Alan Langham."
"So why would he want to kill you?" Saskia asked.
"I've no idea," Laura replied.
They remained in their seats for several more minutes without talking.
"How come you followed me down here?" Laura asked.
"You forgot your phone," Saskia replied as she handed her friend the mobile.
"You saved my life, Saskia," Laura announced.
Saskia smiled and put her arm around Laura's shoulders. "Yes, I did, didn't I," she replied. "Does that make us friends again?"
Laura kept her eyes fixed to the platform floor. "I guess it does," she replied.

* * *

It was almost four pm by the time Laura was allowed to leave Victoria Police Station. Having made her

statement and having provided answers to the scores of questions being asked by the detectives investigating the case, Laura was free to make her way home.
She had no desire to travel by underground to Liverpool Street, so she hailed a black cab. Along the way the driver tried in vain to engage Laura in conversation, but his banter fell on deaf ears. After parting with thirty pounds to cover the cost of the taxi journey, Laura walked slowly down the stairs that led to the train terminal, through the barrier at platform eleven and onto the four fifty-five train to Ipswich.
Although the train was busy, with some commuters already heading home, Laura did manage to find a seat and messaged Kieran.

Will be at Darsham at 7pm. Can you pick me up please? Love you xxx

Within a matter of minutes Laura received a reply.

No problem. Spoke with DCI Doyle earlier. They've arrested Mary and Nigel Diplock. See you soon xxx ☺

*   *   *

The two-hour journey to Darsham seemed to race by as Laura considered everything that had happened to her that day.
It was only when the train reached Saxmundham, just a short distance away from her point of departure, that Laura realised there was a voice message for her on the mobile.
As she listened to Kieran's excited voice telling her that he'd worked out their motive, Laura smiled. It was not

for the first time in the last few days that she'd had reason to thank her lucky stars that Kieran had come back and asked her to marry him.
As expected, Kieran was waiting for her on the platform when her train pulled in.
"You've had an eventful day then," he remarked, making light of her trauma.
Laura hugged him tightly. "Take me home, Kieran," she remarked. "I'm absolutely shattered."
Kieran dutifully walked arm in arm with Laura down the platform to where he'd parked the car.
"A car with new tyres!" Laura announced as they reached his BMW.
"Bloody expensive ones, too!" replied Kieran, who was relieved that Laura seemed relatively okay.
"So, what was their motive?" Laura asked as the car sped off in the direction of Blythwold.
"Greed," replied Kieran. "Pure greed."
"Come on I need a bit more than that," Laura retorted, her curiosity quite evident in her voice.
"There are plans to build a block of luxury apartments and houses in Blythwold," Kieran remarked. "It's been a contentious issue for about a year or so."
"So," replied Laura who was becoming impatient at the deliberate way Kieran was sharing the information. "How does that impact on us?"
"Well, the planning permission has been granted," Kieran added. "And Billy's office, or rather your office, is part of the proposed site."
"How did you find that out?" Laura enquired.
"I was handed a leaflet earlier today by a protester," Kieran replied. "It had a map showing exactly where the flats and houses are to be built."

"But isn't that a bit strange," Laura remarked. "Why would someone get planning permission if they didn't own the land?"
"I thought that, too," replied Kieran. "So, I checked out who owns the rest of the land and guess who it is?"
"Don't tell me," Laura replied. "Either Mary McKenna or Nigel Diplock."
"It's owned by a consortium of three people," Kieran replied. "Namely, Mary McKenna, Nigel Diplock, and guess who?"
Laura shook her head. "I've no idea," she replied.
"Andrew Burnham," Kieran announced with delight and more than a hint of smugness in his voice.
"Really!" Laura replied.
"Apparently Burnham's the owner of a few businesses here and about," Kieran added. "Not just 5 Star taxis. He's also on the town
council responsible for planning, so it doesn't take Einstein to work out his role in all this."
"Has he been arrested, too?" Laura enquired.
"Yes, according to DCI Doyle, they've nicked him, too," Kieran confirmed.
"So, you think Mary and Nigel were trying to get me to default on the terms of Billy's will so the property would revert to the charity they controlled," Laura suggested.
"Yes," replied Kieran eagerly. "And I think that's why they made sure Abigail was excluded."
"So, what about Billy?" Laura enquired. "Do you think he was in on it?"
"I guess only Mary, Nigel and Burnham know that," Kieran replied. "But I wouldn't be surprised if he did. And, if Billy did know, and if he objected, that would certainly be a reason for someone wanting to kill him."

Chapter 71

That evening Laura and Kieran took a gentle walk down the sea front and onto the pier. The sun was starting to go down behind them in the west as they looked eastward out to sea.
"So, besides narrowly escaping being pushed under a tube train and forgiving Saskia, you've also gone and got yourself a few grand compensation," Kieran remarked. "I bet you never predicted any of those things when you boarded the train this morning in Darsham."
Laura snuggled close to Kieran who acted as a good wind break against the cold southerly wind. "No," she admitted. "That's true."
"What I don't understand though," Kieran added. "Is how Alan Langham, or rather Stephen McKenna, knew you'd be in London let alone on that platform. If he'd followed you on the train, you'd have seen him at Darsham, surely!"
Laura nodded. "Yes, the police asked me that when they questioned me this afternoon," Laura replied. "The only thing I can think of is that he took another train, maybe an earlier one and waited for me to come out of the Meridian offices."
"But how did he know you'd be there today?" Kieran added.
Laura remained impassive and thoughtful, her eyes staring out towards the glimmering lights of a passing

ship several miles out at sea. "I think Nigel Diplock told him," she said. "He was in my office when I called Brenda last week. I bet he overheard the conversation. If he did, he'd know what day and time the meeting was due to be held, so all Stephen had to do was get there a few minutes after the meeting started and wait outside for me to emerge."

"And if you hadn't gone for a coffee with Saskia and left your phone he'd have succeeded," Kieran added.

"Yes," replied Laura with a wry smile. "At long last that self-centred cow has done something useful."

Kieran pulled Laura close to him. "I'm glad you two have made up," he remarked. "I know she is a selfish cow, but you've got to admit she's an endearing selfish cow!"

Laura glanced up into Kieran's eyes. "If you say so," she replied.

Kieran took in a deep breath. "Do you know I asked someone to marry me here once," he remarked.

"Really," replied Laura sarcastically. "I bet she turned you down!"

"Initially maybe," he continued, "but she saw the error of her ways, eventually."

Laura stood on her tiptoes and placed a warm lingering kiss on Kieran's lips. "Let's go home," she suggested.

Chapter 72

Friday 26th September

Laura and Kieran heard nothing from the police for a few days, however, on Thursday evening DCI Doyle called Laura and asked them both to come into the police station the following morning.
They were greeted in reception by DC Risby, who ushered them through to a small interview room at the rear of the station, where DCI Doyle was already waiting for them.
"Good morning," DCI Doyle remarked as they entered. "Thanks for coming."
Laura and Kieran sat down across the small desk.
"I just wanted to update you on where we are with the case," Doyle continued. "We've now formally brought charges against Mary McKenna, Nigel Diplock and Andrew Burnham. These charges range from crimes such as fraud, embezzlement and attempting to pervert the course of justice to accessory to murder." As he spoke, he looked directly at Laura and Kieran.
"We have a long way to go before this will all come to trial, but in my opinion, they are all looking at long prison sentences if they are found guilty, and I'm certain they will be found guilty."

"So, what happens to them in the meantime?" Laura asked.
DCI Doyle looked pensive. "We managed to convince the court that Nigel Diplock and Andrew Burnham should be remanded in custody," he replied. "However, the court did not feel that Mary McKenna, being eighty-two and never ever having held a passport, was either a threat to the public or at risk of absconding, so she's been bailed pending the hearing."
"Seems a bit unfair," Kieran remarked. "But I guess she's now reasonably harmless without the others being around to carry out her wishes."
DCI Doyle nodded, "I think that's the way the court saw it," he replied.
"So, have they admitted anything?" Laura asked.
"Well, Nigel Diplock is refusing to cooperate at all," DCI Doyle replied. "Mary McKenna has been a little more forthcoming. She's confirmed that Alan Langham was her son Stephen. She's also admitted that she and Diplock were paying two thousand pounds into Billy's business account, but she says this came from her own account and was to make sure his business stayed afloat."
"I'm surprised she's admitted that Alan Langham was Stephen," Laura remarked.
DCI Doyle nodded. "Yes, that surprised me, too, at first, but I now understand she did that so he can be buried under his real name here in Blythwold. But like Diplock, she's flatly refusing to accept any involvement in the fraudulent activities with the charity or any part in Stephen McKenna's attempt to kill you, Laura."
"So, not too much then," Laura remarked.
"Well, that's not quite everything," replied DCI Doyle. "When we searched Nigel Diplock's office we found

this." As he spoke DCI Doyle produced a document which he passed over to Laura.
"What is it?" Kieran asked.
"It's Billy McKenna's last will," replied DCI Doyle. "It's dated just a week before he died."
Laura opened the will and read it carefully.
Once she'd finished, she passed it to Kieran.
"Abigail gets a third of Billy's business," Laura said. "And there's no clause about me having to remain in Blythwold for a year."
DCI Doyle nodded. "Yes, apart from a third of the business, which goes to Abigail, you own everything else."
Laura smiled. "Well, that is going to please both of us," she said. "I'll tell Abigail as soon as we're finished here."
"That's not all," DCI Doyle added. "We also found a whole series of emails on Diplock's computer and letters in his file regarding the planning application for houses and flats where your offices are located."
"Oh yes," Laura replied, eager to understand more.
"It looks like Mr Diplock had put himself forward as, initially Billy's, then your spokesperson, and he is clearly indicating a willingness to sell should planning permission be granted."
"So, do you think Billy knew about the potential offer for the land where the business is located?" Laura asked
"It's not clear from the correspondence, but Andrew Burnham is saying Billy did know and wasn't interested," DCI Doyle replied. "Burnham maintains he doesn't know for sure, but he thinks Stephen McKenna caused the accident."
Kieran and Laura exchanged a quick glance. "You were right, Sherlock," Laura muttered, much to Kieran's delight.

"Why is Andrew Burnham being so accommodating?" Kieran asked, his tone clearly perplexed.
"Well, he's a completely different kettle of fish," replied DCI Doyle. "He's being very helpful. But don't think he's doing it out of any remorse. He's just trying to get himself a reduced sentence."
"So, what else is he saying?" Laura asked.
"I can't go into too much detail, but I'm confident that through his evidence we will have a very strong case. As I said, he's saying Stephen probably did cause the crash which killed Billy. He's also told us that it was Stephen who picked you up from Darsham station the evening before your father's funeral and he's admitted putting Stephen up in his house after Billy died."
Kieran glanced again in Laura's direction. "You had a lucky escape there," he remarked.
"What I can't understand is why Stephen came back?" Laura asked. "He presumably had a new life in New Zealand, so why did he risk that to come back to Blythwold?"
DCI Doyle looked sideways at DC Risby and smiled. "Well according to Burnham," he said, "when Stephen learnt about the opportunity to make a huge profit from the sale of Billy's business, he decided to come over. Burnham thinks he was running out of cash in New Zealand."
"And I bet Mary was keen to see him again, as from what I've been told, Stephen was always her blue-eyed boy," Laura added.
"That may well be true, too," DCI Doyle remarked.
"And," added DC Risby, "if Burnham continues to cooperate as he has done so far, we'll be able to add considerable weight to charging Nigel Diplock and Mary McKenna with a whole host of crimes, including their part in the attempt on your life."

"Has he also admitted pushing the note under Laura's door and the criminal damage to my car?" Kieran asked. DC Risby shook his head. "Strangely, he is adamant they did neither of them," he remarked. "Which, to be honest, did shock me."
"Well, if they didn't, who did?" Kieran asked.
DC Risby shook his head again. "I'm not sure," he replied honestly. "It may be that he's lying or maybe Diplock did it unbeknown to Burnham, but it is weird he's not holding his hands up for it if he has done it, as he's admitted far worse already."
Kieran glanced at Laura. "Well, I hope it was one of them otherwise we may still get more of the same."
Laura put a comforting hand on Kieran's leg. "I doubt we'll be troubled anymore," she assured him.
"Well, that's about all I can share with you at the moment," DCI Doyle continued. "However, I'll try and keep you up to speed as much as I am able."
Laura and Kieran stood up and, after shaking hands with DCI Doyle, followed DC Risby back once more to the reception area.

* * *

"What do you think?" Kieran asked as they walked away from the police station.
Laura smiled, "It does look like they've got enough to lock up Mary, Diplock and that other bloke for a long time," Laura replied. "And I'm pleased they've established that Stephen was the guy in the car with Billy."
Kieran nodded. "Yeah," he replied. "But we still don't know who sent us that note or why Mary and Nigel were in cahoots. They seem such an unlikely pairing."

Laura stopped in her tracks as she pondered Kieran's words. "I think I know someone who will be able to help us with those answers," she replied. "And it's about time we knew the whole truth."

*   *   *

Miriam Anchova spotted Laura and Kieran as they crossed the road and headed towards her front door. The shop was empty when the pair entered, the tiny bell attached to the door tinkling as they opened then closed the door behind them.

Miriam gave out a forced smile, but Laura could see the coffee shop owner was apprehensive, which reassured Laura that her hunch was going to be proved right.

"Can we have a quick word with you please?" Laura asked, although from her tone it was absolutely crystal clear that Miriam didn't have a choice at all.

Miriam nodded slowly; her earlier look of apprehension now replaced by a look of guilt.

"Can we sit down?" Laura asked pointing at one of the small tables.

Miriam nodded again before coming out from behind the counter and walking over to the door, which she locked with a quick flick of the lever on the brass yale lock. After turning the open sign over to indicate the shop was closed, Miriam joined Laura and Kieran who had sat themselves down at a table out of sight of the large shop window.

"I need to talk to you about Nigel Diplock," Laura began as soon as Miriam had sat herself down. "I'm not sure if you know but he has been arrested."

Miriam nodded, her eyes unable to look Laura in the face. "Yes, I heard," she replied rather meekly.

Laura didn't want to upset Miriam but was determined to get the truth out of her.
"Why did you settle in Blythwold?" she asked. "It seems a very unlikely place for you to want to live."
Miriam shrugged her shoulders. "I like it here," she replied. "It's a nice place."
Laura shook her head. "I don't believe you, Miriam," she replied calmly. "I think this place has very bad memories for you. I think this place is the very last place most people having gone through what you went through would want to live."
Miriam's eyes at last made contact with Laura's. "I don't know what you mean," she replied although her words carried little conviction. "I'm happy here."
Kieran remained silent. He could sense that Laura was on to something and saw no need to intervene.
"Tell me about Stephen McKenna," said Laura her tone quiet, calm, and sympathetic. "Tell me what he did all those years ago."
Miriam shook her head. "I told you before I don't know Stephen McKenna."
Laura could see Miriam was becoming distressed, but she had no intention of relenting with her questions.
"Let me tell you what I think," Laura remarked.
"Yes, you do that please," Miriam replied in her thick eastern European accent. "Then you can get on your way and leave me in peace."
Laura glanced briefly at Kieran and took a deep breath before starting to relay her theory.
"I think," Laura stated, "that many years ago Stephen McKenna brutally attacked one of the female artists at Donnelly's circus where you worked. And I think, that to prevent the attack being reported to the police, Mary McKenna paid the woman for her silence. How am I doing so far?"

Miriam shrugged her shoulders.
"Were you that woman?" Laura asked.
Miriam's face cracked and a small smile appeared.
"You're not so clever," she replied. "The woman wasn't me."
"Then who was it?" Laura asked.
Miriam paused for a few seconds as she considered the question.
"She was my sister," Miriam replied, her words delivered slowly and calmly, although as she spoke, her eyes started to moisten. "It was Maria."
Laura sent a quick look in Kieran's direction, her eyes indicating her excitement at making some progress.
"Tell us what happened, Miriam," Laura asked. "I know it's hard for you, but we need to know." As Laura spoke, a couple of regular customers tried the handle of the door. After a few tries they clearly realised the coffee shop was closed and ambled away, confused at why it was shut at that time of day.
As soon as it was silent again Miriam cleared her throat and took a deep breath.
"Maria and I were born into a circus family," she started. "And from as early as I can remember, we helped out with the shows. It was a hard life but a happy one." As Miriam recollected the story her eyes started to stare ahead, and a smile appeared on her face.
"My father did many things at the circus. He was the ringmaster sometimes, when old Mr Andretti was too drunk to perform, he was the knife thrower and was also one of the clowns. My mother was a bareback horse rider and did the trapeze. They were such happy times."
Miriam's face then returned to portray a grey sadness.
"Maria was five years older than me," she added. "So, she did more than I. When she was no more than fourteen or fifteen she performed with mother on the

trapeze – and she was so good, too, even better than our mother."
"So, what happened to her?" Laura asked.
"When I was about eleven," Miriam said, her voice trembling, "my mother told me that Maria had gone away to stay with friends. She did not say why or for how long. I was heartbroken and for months and months I kept asking my mother and father where she was, but they would not tell me. Then one day when I was about thirteen my father told me that she had brought shame on the family, and we would never see her again."
Laura could see Miriam becoming distressed but wanted to know the full story. "Did you ever see her again?" she asked.
Miriam nodded. "Only once," she replied. "When I was about eighteen, I received a letter from her telling me that she was in London and wanted to see me." As she spoke, Miriam's eyes lit up. "I was so excited, but of course I knew my parents would not allow me to visit her so I did not tell them. Over the next few months Maria and I secretly exchanged letters and I waited until the circus moved close to London. After about six months the circus was in Slough, and I took my chance and went to the address in London to see Maria."
Laura could see by Miriam's face that her story was not a happy one. "What happened when you met her?" Laura enquired.
"I could not believe what I saw," Miriam replied. "My beautiful big sister was living in a horrible dirty house, with such awful people. She was thin, she was pale, and she looked like she was a woman of sixty rather than a young woman in her twenties. I couldn't believe it."
"What did you do?" Laura asked.

Miriam shrugged her shoulders. "I asked her to come back with me, but she refused. She said that she could never go back but would not tell me why."
Miriam looked straight into Laura's eyes. "And that was the last time I saw her."
"What happened to your sister?" Kieran asked.
Miriam moved her head and looked Kieran in the eyes.
"She died," Miriam replied. "About six months after our meeting I received a letter saying she'd died of pneumonia. I went to her funeral; I was the only person there from the family as my parents refused to go. Then a few months later, I received a letter from a solicitor saying that I'd inherited over twenty thousand pounds from my sister's estate and that she'd left a letter for me to read after her death."
"Twenty thousand pounds," Laura exclaimed, "but I thought you said she was living in squalor?"
Miriam nodded. "She was," she replied. "That was the crazy thing."
"So where did the money come from and what was in the letter?" Laura asked.
"The letter explained what had happened and why she'd been sent away," Miriam replied. "I still have it."
"Why was she sent away?" Kieran asked.
"Because when she was here in Blythwold when she was just sixteen, she'd become friendly with a young man," Miriam replied. "She said it was just a little romance to her, but that after a short time the young man wanted more. And when she refused, he attacked her, and he raped her."
Laura and Kieran remained silent as Miriam recounted the story.
"She was so scared and ashamed that she decided not to tell anyone," Miriam continued. "But after a few weeks

she realised she was pregnant and, frightened about what she should do, she told the boy's mother."
"Why?" Laura remarked, bewilderment in her voice. "Surely she was the last person she should have been telling."
Miriam shrugged her shoulders. "In her letter she says that the mother had always been kind to her and had always seemed nice. Maria was scared to tell our mother as she knew she would tell our father. We always feared our father, so I guess she felt trapped."
"And I assume the woman Maria went to was Mary McKenna, and the man who raped her was Stephen?" Laura added.
Miriam nodded. "Yes, that is correct," she replied.
"What did she expect Mary to do?" Laura asked.
Miriam shook her head. "I don't know," she replied.
"But what did Mary do?" Kieran asked. "Did she say in her letter?"
Miriam nodded. "Mary told Maria that she would help her while she was pregnant and help her financially, but there were conditions to this help."
"Which were," Kieran asked.
"That she was to leave Blythwold and live with a friend of Mary's somewhere in London until the baby was born, that she was not to tell the police about what had happened, that she was to tell my parents that she had run away with a man and would not be coming back, that she would have nothing to do with Stephen and that she would give up the baby to Mary's friends after it had been born."
"And she agreed," Laura added.
"Yes," replied Miriam. "That's what the letter says."
"And the money?" Kieran asked. "Where did that come from?"

"The money was exactly what Mary McKenna paid Maria," replied Miriam. "She never spent a penny."
"Why?" Kieran asked. "When she was obviously so poor when you met her."
Miriam shook her head gently. "I can only think she regretted what she did and felt guilty spending money she'd been given for giving away her baby."
"That's terrible," Laura remarked. "How awful."
Miriam nodded. "Yes, it must have been dreadful for her."
"What happened to the baby?" Kieran asked.
"She didn't say in the letter," replied Miriam. "But my first thought when I read it was to find the child. I wanted to make sure it was being looked after and when it was old enough, to let it know who its mother was and how brave she had been. I decided to use the money Maria had left me to help in that goal."
"Did you have any clues as to where the child was?" Laura enquired.
Miriam nodded again. "Maria shared three pieces of information in the letter," Miriam announced. "The first was that the child was a boy, the second the date of the child's birth and the third was the Christian name of the lady who she stayed with when the child was born. With that information and knowing the woman was a friend of Mary McKenna it was very easy to find him."
"And that child is Nigel Diplock," Laura interrupted.
"Yes," replied Miriam. "Nigel Diplock is my sister's boy, my nephew..."
"And my cousin," Laura added.
"Yes," replied Miriam with a smile. "We are related through him."
"Does he know?" Kieran asked.
"Oh yes," replied Miriam. "When I found him, he was already a teenager. I waited until he was twenty-one. By

then he was already a trainee at his adopted father's solicitor's practice. But one day I told him who I was and where he came from."
"And what did he say?" Laura enquired.
"He told me he didn't want anything to do with me and that he had no interest in a birth mother who had sold him," Miriam replied.
"So why have you stayed?" Laura added.
Miriam smiled. "Because I felt that he may change his mind one day and I did not want anyone else from the family to let him down."
"Did you know what he was involved in?" Kieran asked.
Miriam shook her head once more. "I didn't know any details, but I knew he was no angel. Although I hoped he would have inherited his mother's kind nature, I fear that he appears to have more of his father in him than my beautiful sister."
"What about Mary McKenna?" Laura enquired. "Does she know who you are?"
"Oh yes," replied Miriam, "but she does not worry me. She came to see me shortly after I told Nigel the truth and tried to threaten me. However, when I showed her a copy of the letter and told her that I'd make it public if she caused any trouble, she soon backed off. She also knows that my solicitor has a copy and is instructed to make it public when I die, so I knew she wouldn't try and harm me."
"Smart lady!" Kieran remarked.
"Oh yes," replied Miriam. "I may seem a pathetic woman, but I can look after myself."
"Why did you send me the note?" Laura asked. "It was you, wasn't it?"
Miriam nodded. "Yes, I'm sorry about that and about the tyres, but I did not want you stirring things up here.

Mary is an evil woman, and I was concerned that they may hurt you as they did poor Billy."
"You think they killed Billy?" Laura asked.
"I don't know for sure," replied Miriam. "But I think so."
"Why?" Kieran asked.
"Because," replied Miriam slowly, "he only got to know the truth about his brother and who Nigel was just a few days before he died."
"How did he find out?" Laura asked.
"Because I told him," Miriam replied. "And when I told him he was so angry with Mary and his dead brother."
As soon as Miriam said dead brother, Laura swivelled her head and exchanged a puzzled look with Kieran.
"What's wrong," Miriam asked.
Laura ignored Miriam's question. "Why did you tell him?" she enquired.
Miriam's expression changed to one of embarrassed gloom. "He and I became good friends over the years," she remarked. "So much so, that he did sometimes talk to me about his troubles. Before his death he was quite frustrated with his mother about the housing project. He said she wanted him to sell his office, but he didn't want to. It was when he was bitching about her, I thought I'd tell him about what his dead brother had done to Maria and that Nigel was in fact his nephew. To be honest as soon as I'd told him I wished I hadn't. He went crazy and said he'd have it out with her. He died a few days later."
Laura and Kieran looked at each other, their thoughts clearly the same.
"Stephen didn't die at sea," Laura remarked. "He faked his death."
"So, where is he?" Miriam enquired; the anger etched across her face. "If he's alive he has to pay for what he

did," she said through gritted teeth. "If he had not raped my sister none of this would have happened."
"He didn't die all those years ago, Miriam," Laura replied. "But he's dead now."

Chapter 73

Laura and Kieran sat together in the dimmed light of Le Rayon de Miel.
"This was a great idea," Laura remarked, before sarcastically adding, "I'm assuming this time it will be just you and me?"
Kieran smiled. "That was the plan," he remarked, "but I can easily call your mum and dad again if you want. I'm sure they'll get the next flight over if we ask them nicely."
"No thanks," Laura replied. "And anyway, there's no chance of us ever seeing them back here again."
"Your starters," the grinning French waiter announced as he appeared from nowhere.
Laura and Kieran eased back in their chairs to allow the waiter to place a bowl of tomato soup in front of Laura and a terrine de sanglier in front of Kieran.
"What is that again?" Laura enquired.
"Wild boar pate to you," Kieran replied. "I had it once on a business trip to Paris."
"How cosmopolitan," remarked Laura cynically. "I'll stick with my tomato soup."
"What made you think Miriam was the person who'd sent you that note and slashed my tyres?" Kieran asked, as he spread a thick layer of the potted meat on his toast.

"I don't know really," replied Laura. "I knew she was here for a reason, but to be honest, as I'd suggested to you on Monday, I expected her to tell us that it was she who Stephen had attacked."
Kieran nodded gently as he nibbled on his toast.
"I'd also been wondering why Nigel was so close to Mary," continued Laura. "The only conclusion I could come to was that he was related. And, if that was the case, he had to be Stephen's."
"But how did you twig that Nigel was adopted?" Kieran enquired before taking a bigger bite of his toast.
"It was when we were here before," replied Laura, "and Dad told us that Mrs Diplock was a school friend of Mary McKenna. That's what got me thinking he may be adopted. Nigel's in his early thirties which would make Mrs Diplock in her late forties or even in her fifties when he was born. So, she's unlikely to be his real mother."
"I'm impressed," Kieran replied.
"You shouldn't go too overboard," Laura remarked. "I only got it partly right."
"Well, you weren't to know about Miriam's sister," Kieran replied. "You got everything else spot on."
Laura smiled and took a sip of her soup.
"It does explain why Mary was so close to him," Kieran added.
"Yes," replied Laura. "And why she tried to warn me off him. She clearly didn't want her precious grandson getting hooked up with the likes of me."
Kieran smiled. "Another one of her grandchildren," he remarked sarcastically.
"Yes, but clearly not one of her favourites," Laura added.

"Well, I may not like her very much but that was good advice she gave you," Kieran said. "I'm glad you decided to stick with me."

"Me too," Laura agreed.

The couple remained silent for a few minutes while they tucked into their starters.

"Do you think Stephen killed Billy in the car," Kieran asked as soon as he'd cleared his plate.

Laura thought for a few seconds before answering. "With him now dead, I guess we'll never know," she replied. "But my hunch would be that he did. Maybe he grabbed the wheel and deliberately steered his car into the other vehicle. There's no way of knowing for sure now, but yes, my guess would be that he did."

Kieran nodded. "I tend to agree, and it's what Miriam thinks and Andrew Burnham, too, by all accounts," he remarked. "And if I was to hazard a guess, I'd say it was as a result of either Billy challenging Stephen about Maria, or maybe it was so that the sale of the office went ahead."

Laura nodded. "There are only two people alive that could help with those questions," she added, "and I don't see either Nigel or Mary being forthcoming, do you?"

Kieran shook his head. "No chance," he replied.

"If Stephen did kill Billy," Laura added, "he might not have told Mary, Nigel or Burnham."

Kieran nodded again. "You may be right," he said reluctantly. "I'm not totally sure about Nigel, as far as I'm concerned, he could have been in on it, but I find it hard to accept that Mary would have been involved in Billy's death. Even if she did favour Stephen over Billy, as it appears, surely even Mary can't be that evil."

"We'll just have to see what comes out at their trial," Laura added as the waiter appeared to collect their plates.

"Anyway, what did Abigail say when you spoke to her this afternoon?" Kieran asked.

Laura beamed widely, "She was over the moon. I'm so pleased we sorted that out, and I'm even more pleased I don't have to work a year before I get my inheritance."

"So, there's no reason for you to stay here," Kieran added. "If you wanted, you could always come with me to America."

Laura raised her eyebrows, "I could," she conceded, "but I want to help Abigail with the business for a while. Let's just keep to the plan, shall we?"

Kieran raised his hands in mock surrender. "No problem," he replied hastily. "It was just a suggestion not a condition."

Laura smiled. "As long as we've got that clear," she added resolutely, but with a wry smile.

Chapter 74

Four Months Later

Kieran flew out to America in early October, leaving Laura in Blythwold to focus her attention on the business and on getting herself fit enough to complete the Coastal Trek in May.
Despite having little experience or much love of exercise, Laura pushed herself hard in order to complete the five-mile run she did each morning before going to work. Initially she found it exceptionally difficult, even though the route she took along the sea front was flat and level. But, after about three weeks, she started to find the going much easier, and increased the distance to eight miles each morning. However, the misery and hardship returned once again when winter started to bite in the sleepy Suffolk seaside town. Laura discovered that running and cold winter mornings were not her favourite mixture.
Over the Christmas and New Year period Laura flew to New York where she spent ten wonderful days with Kieran. It had been nice to see him again and enjoy Christmas and welcome in the New Year in a style unique to that vibrant, exciting, if indisputably over the top, city.
The one major issue Laura encountered, though, during her stay in the Big Apple, was the realisation of just how little training Kieran appeared to be doing. She was

amazed and a little disappointed to discover how difficult he found keeping up with her on their morning run, which had become non-negotiable during her stay. "You're going to have to really get down to some hard training to stand any chance of completing this trek in May," Laura had remarked one morning, when for the second time they'd had to stop in Central Park for Kieran to recover from a stitch, which he found so painful that he tried to convince Laura that he was having a heart attack.
"I'll be ready," Kieran had insisted, but none too convincingly for Laura's liking.

* * *

The business in Blythwold was flourishing. Abigail had always been a hard worker, but she seemed to have found an extra gear since she'd become a partner and was constantly astonishing Laura with her bright ideas and endless energy for work. The only area the two disagreed upon was whether to relocate the office to another part of town to reap the benefit of the highly attractive offer which had been put on the table by the developers. Laura wasn't keen as she knew selling up hadn't been what Billy had wanted, but Abigail had no such qualms. She saw this as a no-brainer. "We could find a much better office," she kept saying, "and we'd pocket a fortune from the sale."
Deep down Laura knew Abigail was right, but owning the majority share in the business, she had the casting vote.

* * *

Laura had no desire to see, let alone talk with, Mary McKenna. It was true she had numerous questions she wanted to ask the old lady, but she figured her paternal grandmother was unlikely to be too forthcoming and she doubted the old woman would want to see her anyway.
It was, therefore, an immense surprise to Laura when, one Thursday morning towards the end of January, Father Mallory paid a visit to Laura just as she was about to set off for the office.
"Good morning," Mallory remarked as Laura opened her front door. "Can I have a quick word with you?"
Laura smiled and ushered the aging cleric into the apartment. "Sorry about the mess," said Laura, who had not yet managed to iron or put away the huge pile of clothes she'd extracted from the drier a few days earlier and dumped unceremoniously on the settee. "Let me move these."
As she spoke, Laura grabbed the offending items, took them through to her bedroom and plonked them on the bed.
"Don't worry," replied the priest with a warm smile. "It's okay with me."
Laura appreciated him appearing fine with the state of the flat but felt there was something not quite right about her various garments being in full view of the local priest, especially her underwear. So, Laura was glad she'd moved her creased clothes from out of his sight.
"I assume you're wondering why I'm here," remarked Mallory.
"Well, yes I am," Laura replied.
"It's Mary," Mallory continued. "She's asked to see you."
"Really," replied Laura with a tinge of hostility in her voice. "I don't think so."

Mallory nodded. "I can understand your position, Laura," he continued with a smile, "but she's now quite poorly," he added. "So, it may be your last opportunity to talk to her and her last chance to explain things to you."
Laura paused. "I'm not sure I've anything to say to her," she replied frostily. "And to be honest, I'm not sure whether it's right for us to talk. Not before the court case."
Mallory smiled. "I understand the trial is set for June," he remarked.
Laura nodded. "Yes," she replied. "Although I don't understand why it takes so long."
"Well, it's highly unlikely Mary will be still around by then," he remarked, with some surety in his voice.
"Typical," snapped Laura. "I should have known she'd find a way to cheat justice."
To her surprise, Mallory didn't appear to be shocked or disturbed by Laura's comment. "She may avoid her punishment in the secular world," he remarked, "but she'll have to account for her actions to a higher judge. She won't be able to shirk that, I can assure you."
Being a confirmed nonbeliever, Laura could not bring herself to agree, but was not going to openly argue with Father Mallory, who she liked and, after all, was just the messenger. "I still don't think so," she replied. "I really have nothing to say to her and can't think of anything she could possibly say to me that would be of any use."
Mallory was clearly not prepared to take no for an answer. He remained rooted to the sofa. "I can't force you," he added, "but I think you should go. It will not take that long and if, as you think, it is just a waste of time then what have you lost, other than an hour of your life? However, if you don't see Mary and she dies, then

you may forever wonder whether you made the right decision."
Despite not wanting to, Laura found herself agreeing with the priest's logic. "Okay, I'll come," she replied reluctantly. "But if she tries to fob me off with lies and denials, I'll be out of there like a shot."
"And you'd be well within your right to," agreed Mallory.
"So, when does she want to see me?" Laura asked.
"I think now is as good a time as any, don't you," remarked Mallory with a grin and a sparkle in his tiny blue eyes.

* * *

Whether it was to provide moral support or whether it was to make sure that Laura didn't change her mind, Father Mallory remained no more than two feet away from Laura from the moment they left the flat until they walked through into Mary's small bedroom.
As she made her way to the house, Laura, whilst exchanging small talk with the cleric, had been racking her brains to try and remember how many times in total she'd spoken to Mary. Granted it was still less than a year since she even knew of the existence of the elderly lady who'd evoked such a feeling of detestation within Laura, but Laura could only recall them having spoken on four occasions. The first time in church after Billy's funeral, in the Black Swan on the same day, then when she came to Laura's flat unannounced, and the last time, when Mary had summoned Laura to her house to request a meeting with Laura's Mum. They were all very short conversations, too, which put together would have probably added up to little more than an hour in total. Not much time to have spent with a blood relative,

Laura concluded, but enough time for Laura to decide she loathed Mary.
Mary's bedroom in Dove Cottage, the tiny house where Laura's grandmother lived was small and dark, just as Laura expected. The ceiling was low and in between the exposed oak beams the plaster bowed and bulged indicating it had been years since any significant alterations had been made. The room had just one small double window which was split into around forty small diamond shaped panes of glass, held in place by a crisscross of leading. Each of the two windows were dominated at the centre by a beautiful green and red floral motif. Laura was no expert, but these looked original.
Around the room were just three old oak pieces of furniture; a double wardrobe, a small chest of drawers and, at the side of Mary's large metal bedstead, a small bedside cabinet with a brass lamp perched on top.
Mary, looking very frail and tired, was situated in the centre of her bed, the top of her back and head had been raised up a foot or so by two or three massive stuffed pillows which had partially moulded around her head.
"I've got Laura here, Mary," Mallory said in a loud voice.
"I'm not deaf," remarked the old lady rudely, as if the way Mallory had delivered those five short words had been an insult to her. "I can see her too."
Seeing Mary looking so weak surprised Laura and initially did give her a slight twinge of sympathy, but she quickly regained her resolve.
Laura was determined not to allow her grandmother an ounce of compassion, even if she was at death's door.
"It would appear you've summoned me again, dear Granny," Laura remarked curtly. "What is it this time?"

Laura could see that her words had shocked Mallory, who remained steadfast by Mary's bed but said nothing. For the first time ever, Laura noticed a slight smile appear on her grandmother's face. "You sound like a McKenna," she remarked in a croaky voice.
"If that's supposed to be a compliment, don't waste your breath," Laura snapped back impatiently. "So, what is it you want to tell me? I need to get to work."
Unlike the sensitive priest in the room, Mary seemed unphased by Laura's harsh words. "I wanted you to understand that I didn't know Stephen was going to try and hurt you," she said. "That was not something I'd have approved of. He acted on his own in that regard."
Laura shrugged her shoulders. "Maybe that's true," she replied. "But his son Nigel must have known because he's the only one that knew I was going to London that day. So, your precious grandson knew."
Mary rolled her eyes upwards. "So, you worked out that Nigel is your cousin," Mary remarked as if she'd been impressed by Laura's revelation.
"It wasn't hard," replied Laura. "Your affection for him was quite clear to me when you tried to warn me off him. And once I knew his mother was a school chum of yours, it didn't take a Harley Street gynaecologist to work out she was unlikely to be his birth mother. It was confirmed, too, by Miriam, who as you may know has given a letter to the police from Maria. Remember her Granny? She's the young circus girl who your son Stephen raped and who you paid off to guarantee her silence and a child for your friend, Mrs Diplock."
Mary again remained unmoved by Laura's frank and pitiless outbursts. "A proper little detective aren't you," she muttered. "Well let me tell you," she continued, her voice a little louder but still weak and faltering. "There was never any proof that Stephen raped Maria. They

were in a relationship, and she got pregnant. Stephen to the end denied it was rape."
"And you believed him?" retorted Laura.
"Yes, I do," replied Mary. "He was my son; of course, I believed him."
"But not enough to prevent you from faking his death so he could make a fresh start on the other side of the world, or to stop you buying Maria's silence and her child," Laura added angrily.
Mary nodded. "Of course, I helped him," she replied. "What mother wouldn't? But that doesn't mean I believed he raped that girl. That's unproven and now that Maria and Stephen are both dead, we'll never know for sure, will we?" Mary added with a defiant look on her frail grey face.
"The letter Maria sent to her sister indicates it was rape," Laura continued, determined not to allow her grandmother any satisfaction. "What sort of person would make that up?"
Mary remained impassive. "That's just one side of the story."
"Anyway," continued Mary after a short pause. "You can believe what you wish about what happened back then, I'm telling you I did not know about Stephen following you to London and trying to harm you."
"And what about the evening before Billy's funeral?" Laura asked. "Did you know Stephen picked me up from Darsham train station posing as a taxi driver?"
Mary nodded gently. "Yes, I did," she replied. "We just wanted to make sure we knew who you were. Stephen did you no harm; he merely wanted to identify you. Remember we'd not clapped eyes on you for over twenty years."
"But I don't recall seeing him at his brother's funeral," Laura added.

"No," replied Mary. "We decided it wasn't wise for him to attend in case he was recognised. But he was able to describe you to me after he'd picked you up. A skinny, plain-looking slip of a girl was how he put it as I recall. I recognised you straight away in the church."
Laura decided to move the conversation on, even though her blood was boiling inside. "So, what about Billy?" Laura enquired. "Did you know Stephen was going to kill him?"
"What are you talking about?" Mary replied angrily. "They were brothers and Billy died in a car accident."
"Are you sure?" Laura asked. "I think that Stephen deliberately grabbed the steering wheel and crashed the car, killing Billy."
On hearing this latest accusation, Father Mallory's face turned pale, and he looked angrily at Laura. "That's a cruel thing to say," he remarked firmly. "There's no evidence of that, Laura."
"There may not be," snapped Laura in reply. "But I know that Billy only found out about Nigel being Stephen's son a few days before the crash and he was very upset by the news. I also know Billy had no intention of selling the office to the developers, which was a problem to Stephen, Nigel, and Mary here, so I wouldn't put it past precious Stephen to kill his brother."
Then turning to face Mary, Laura continued. "And deep down, dear Granny, I think you have your suspicions, too."
By the pained look on the old lady's face Laura could see she'd hit a nerve.
"Anyway, dear Granny, is that everything?" Laura added calmly but coldly. "Can I go now?"
Mary shuffled uncomfortably in her bed. "No," she replied. "There's one more thing, although after your impertinence I don't know why I'm doing this. I want

you to know that I've made my will and left everything between you and Nigel."
"What!" exclaimed Laura. "I don't want anything from you."
"Well, you're getting half whether you like it or not," replied Mary. "If you can't stomach spending your half then give it to the church. I'm sure Father Mallory would be more than pleased to receive the money, as it will be quite a tidy sum, I expect. But that's for you to decide when I'm gone."
"I don't get it!" Laura announced. "It's not that long ago you thought I wasn't good enough for your precious Nigel, but now you're leaving me money in your will."
Mary smiled. "It was never anything to do with you not being good enough for him," replied the old woman. "It was simply that you were related. I don't care what the law says, I don't believe it's right for blood relations to become ..." Mary stopped, appearing to struggle to find the right words.
"Anyway, I suspect most of the money you leave me will need to go back to Billy's charity," Laura remarked, not wishing to wait for Mary to think of the right way to end her last sentence. "Let's face it, you nicked thousands from it, didn't you?"
A smile returned to Mary's face. "I suspect you'll have to forfeit some," she conceded, "but, even after those minor deductions, you'll be a wealthy young woman when I go."
Laura shook her head in disbelief. "You're priceless," she remarked, the irritation clear in her voice. "As long as I live, I'll never understand you."
Mary smiled. "Whether you do or do not doesn't concern me," she replied. "I had a duty to protect my family when I was alive and to provide for them when I die. I've always done the former no matter what they've

done, and I've now put in place the mechanism to discharge the latter, too. I'm at peace now knowing I can look my maker in the face when the time comes, with a clear conscious."
Laura stood aghast; her mouth open with shock at what she'd just heard.
"Now you can go my dear," Mary announced. "I'll not ask you to call on me again."

*   *   *

Father Mallory accompanied Laura as they made their way out of Dove Cottage and walked slowly down the narrow road away from Mary's house.
"Are you glad you saw Mary?" Mallory asked.
Laura stopped walking and looked back into Mallory's blue eyes. "Strangely, I am," she replied with a smile. "I can't say I'll ever
understand or even approve of what Mary has done, but I'm pleased I had an opportunity to have it out with her. I'm not sure what good it has done, but at least I've been able to tell her how I feel."
Mallory smiled. "And in a strange way," he replied, "I'm sure Mary will be contented, too."
Laura shook her head and started to walk on.
"Will you accept her money after she's gone?" the priest enquired.
"Oh yes," replied Laura without any hesitation. "But unlike poor Maria or my dad, I'll not worry about spending it. For me the money won't be tainted like it was when she tried to pay them off."
Mallory stopped walking and allowed Laura to continue her journey away from her grandmother's house alone.
"That's a shame," he muttered quietly to himself. "St Steven's church could have done with a large bequest."

Epilogue

Mary McKenna died peacefully in bed on 30th March, ten weeks before her trial was due to commence. She had a simple funeral at St Steven's church a week later, which was attended by many people from the town, including her grandson Nigel Diplock - who appeared in handcuffs and was accompanied by three prison guards. Laura didn't go.
At Laura's request, Mary's will was put on hold pending the outcome of the court case and any subsequent actions that the court chose to pronounce relating to her estate.

The East Anglian Trek was completed by Laura and Kieran in May. They raised over twenty-five thousand pounds and despite swearing beforehand never to attempt anything like this ever again, Laura agreed to have a stab at an equally ambitious fund-raising event for the following year.
It took two weeks before Kieran was able to walk pain-free after the trek and as a result of the experience, he refused point blank to be drawn into making a similar commitment for the next year.
The trial of Nigel Diplock and Andrew Burnham took place at Norwich Crown Court on 8th June. It lasted for six weeks, after which the jury found both defendants guilty of a range of offences, including fraud and attempting to pervert the course of justice. The crown prosecution service decided not to press charges for

manslaughter, due to their belief that there was insufficient evidence to gain a conviction.
Nigel Diplock was sentenced to eight years imprisonment. Andrew Burnham received just three years, due to his involvement being relatively minor and due to him cooperating fully with the police.
In sentencing, Justice Wellbrook instructed the court to ensure that all monies fraudulently siphoned from the charity set up by Billy McKenna should be reclaimed from Nigel Diplock and from the estate of Mary McKenna.
Laura attended court every day to listen to the proceedings and, as a major benefactor of Mary McKenna's will, committed to the waiting media that she would ensure every penny taken from Billy's charity would be returned and that she would add an additional ten thousand pounds from her inheritance.

Abigail Adams eventually persuaded Laura to sell the office to the developers and relocate to a smaller office above Miriam's Tea Shop, in the High Street. Then, with her share of the proceeds, Abigail successfully bought Laura out and now runs McKenna Events, employing three young people. The business continues to go from strength to strength. Laura made it a condition of the sale that Abigail also took over the running of Billy's charity; the books of which are, for probably the first time ever, scrupulously managed and available for proper scrutiny.

Miriam Anchova remained in Blythwold and continues to run the Tea Shop. She visits her nephew, Nigel Diplock, in Her Majesty's Prison, Hollesley Bay near Woodbridge, every other week. Their relationship remains distant, but Nigel welcomes her visits to get news about life in Blythwold, and a regular supply of cream cakes.

The whereabouts of Vic Chacroborty remain a mystery. He was divorced by Vivien and has since disappeared. Rumours had indicated he'd moved to Thailand and was involved in running nightclubs specialising in catering for Western European tourists, but those reports remain unsubstantiated.

After her divorce, Vivien Chacroborty reverted to her maiden name of Bartlett and remains closely involved in the running of Meridian. She tried, unsuccessfully, to persuade Laura to become CEO at the company; but eventually accepted that Laura wasn't going to change her mind and appointed a high-flying American to take the helm. Ironically, the American was poached from McCauley and Bernstein, who offered no objection to the move.

Brenda remains at the company as HR Director, reporting straight to Vivien Bartlett, with a specific brief to ensure the company's ethics and integrity procedures and policies were observed and upheld at all times.

Saskia Skinner moved in with, then married, Martin. They have three homes: a flat at Canary Wharf overlooking the Thames, a six-bedroomed house near the south coast of Devon and a villa in Tuscany. While in London, Saskia spends her time shopping, socialising, and relaxing at home or at her gym. During the summer she and Martin typically spend a month in Italy and always ensure they are in Devon over the Christmas period. As yet they've not found time to have a family. Saskia occasionally messages Laura, but, apart from their respective weddings, the two have struggled to find time to meet up; largely due to Saskia's rammed social calendar.

Laura and her mum are back on good terms, and rarely discuss the McKennas. Mike and Bev still live in Spain and have no intention of returning to the UK. Despite several invitations, the pair steadfastly refuse to come to Blythwold, so much so that Laura no longer even asks them.

Father Mallory continued to be Priest at St Steven's Church for a further four years, however ill health then caused him to take a less strenuous position in a smaller village, thirty miles inland. He visits Blythwold regularly and is still found on occasions, at the bar in the Admiral sampling the local brew.

Kieran's career in New York skyrocketed. He became head of department within three years and is now vice president for international business development. He's based back in London but travels all over the world. Kieran and Laura have two young boys.

Laura, financially secure after selling the business to Abigail, and having received a significant seven-figure legacy from Mary McKenna's will, decided to temporarily relinquish any thoughts of a career and concentrate on bringing up her children, despite several attractive offers. She invested a large proportion of her inheritance in properties in Blythwold, which she rents out as holiday lets, and which are doing very nicely. She retained the house in SW 18, which is her main family residence, and The Crow's Nest in Blythwold, where

she, the children and Kieran (when he's not travelling) spend most of the school holidays.
Every year Laura makes sure she's available and ready for the annual fund-raising charity event organised by Abigail, in whatever guise that takes.
She's fulfilled and supremely happy – or so she says!